The Twilight Time

Bereft of week-day workers, this part of town had a desolate air. Very quickly, Anna became aware of shadows in doorways, the odd car cruising by. A lone man walking rapidly through, hands in pockets, head firmly down. You could smell it. Sex and fear and loathing. Two young girls outside a sauna, gulping nicotine like milk. Their faces gaunt in twilight, hair pulled angry-back from hard angles and dark kohl. The smaller one held what looked like a pile of banknotes, which she stuffed in her pocket as they approached. Streetlight caught her on the diagonal, striking off a little silver horseshoe pinned to her lapel, and shading her face in two. Clad in short Lycra and boots, the other, taller girl was obviously pregnant. She stared dully past Anna and Derek to somewhere else.

KAREN CAMPBELL

THE TWILIGHT TIME

HODDER

First published in Great Britain in 2008 by Hodder & Stoughton
An Hachette Livre UK company

First published in paperback in 2009

5

A CIP catalogue record for this title is available from the British
Library

ISBN 978 0 340 93560 6

Printed and bound in the UK by CPI Mackays, Chatham ME5 8TD

Hodder & Stoughton policy is to use papers that are natural,
renewable and recyclable products and made from wood
grown in sustainable forests. The logging and manufacturing
processes are expected to conform to the environmental
regulations of the country of origin.

Hodder & Stoughton Ltd
338 Euston Road
London NW1 3BH

www.hodder.co.uk

I'd like to thank the following for all their help and support:

Garry, for his beefy technical advice; Alexis, for some cracking stories; Agnes, Kenneth Rybarczyk & everyone at the Polish Club; Stefan Pikulicki for the Polish words; Richard Winetrobe & Rodge for the Hebrew words; Gordon for some fine phrases; Dorothy J for her early reading efforts; Willy for his wise counsel; Tanya, for New York; Ian, for snaps and talking sense; Nathalie, for picking me out of the pile; the wonderful Lisa for keeping the faith; Suzie (not Breadknife!) for her incisive editing; everyone at Hodder and, most of all, Dougie, Eidann and Ciorstan – without whom I couldn't write.

The writer acknowledges support from the Scottish Arts Council towards the writing of this title.

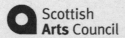 Scottish
Arts Council

For Dougie:
Best mate, soulmate.

Preface

'Put your arm back through.'

'No, darlin', no. I got to breathe.'

Thin-haired arm, persistent in its defiance.

'You have to do what I say.' You have to obey me.

'I don' want it shut, man.'

You draw out your stick, bang it hard against the door. 'I'm in charge. Put your arm back through.'

'But baby, I got to breathe.'

And it won't go back, this wizened spider limb that can't reach you. So you hit it and you hit it to protect yourself.

1 Drag

It was the right kind of day for it. Skies blown inside out, a brisk shower wiping the morning clean. It was going to be a fine day.

Bring it on. Anna could see her teeth, bared and shining in her shoes that were skirting puddles. She was pleased with the gloss – so chuffed, she never saw it coming: the sharp parping of a comedy hooter that forced her back on the kerb. A man, near prone in a Sinclair C5, shook his head as he glided past.

She waited until he slid round the corner, then crossed and shoved the plate-glass door. Instantly, that familiar kick of Dettol, shoe polish and pee, slicking the back of her throat. She didn't know the code for the inner door, so stood like a chooky, hands full of kit. Cops were buzzing through the glass partition. The Controller sat hunched at her console, droning for a station to attend a shoplifting, the Duty Officer chewing a sandwich over her shoulder, dropping crumbs on the screen. Radio 2 tinkled quietly, and there were no Old Firm games that weekend to mess up the cells. A picture of the perfect backshift.

An ancient sergeant turned his head in Anna's direction as he stretched to answer the phone. 'Stewart Street. Naw. Try a plumber. Aye, you and all.' He looked like a coconut ice, spider-veined face frilled by white hair. The hair tufted over his collar, dandruff reaching his crumpled trousers. He raised one eyebrow at her. 'Aye?'

'Hi,' Anna called over. 'I'm Sergeant Cameron. I'm starting in the Flexi Unit today?'

He lumbered to the public counter and slid the glass a little wider. 'The what?'

'Flexible Policing Unit. Mix of plain clothes and uniform?'

No reaction.

'It's *your* division's initiative – street offences, disorder and that? You must have heard of it.'

This time he picked his ear.

'I've come from headquarters.'

'Is that right?' The buzzer clicked. 'Away through the foyer and take the lift up tae one. Someone'll show you.' He stooped to take a file from a shelf.

'What was that?' asked Anna.

The man kept his head down, white flakes dropping as his stubby hand stroked the grey.

'You say something?' she asked.

'Naw.'

'Could've sworn I heard you say "split-arse"?'

Viscous eyes looked up at her, a slight flush on the hollows below. 'What's that supposed tae mean?'

'You tell me.'

'Naw, your hearing must be away tae buggery, hen.'

'Just like your good looks, you mean?'

'First floor, like I said. Then turn left.' His eyes slumped back to his paperwork.

When she got punted to Community Safety, a few years into her service, Anna used to do safety talks for women – button up, hide your jewellery, always hold hands with a grown-up. As time passed, she deviated more from the script. Don't be a victim, she'd tell them. Some guy eyeing you in an empty train carriage? You're at that point when you *know* you can feel his stare? Then he smiles, enjoying your discomfort – and you wonder if it would be 'rude' to move? Bugger that, she'd say, enjoying her audience's surprise. Belch. Fart. Pick your nose. Anything unexpected. Throws them off balance, buys you some time.

So, why tell folk some tosser groping their bum's an indecent assault, if they met an old git like that when they came to report it? Mind, it was better than getting a bloody civvy. *Good morning, welcome to Police Inc. plc. How can I help you? Oh, you'd like to see a* police officer. *I'm sorry, have you made an appointment?*

The lift creaked, yawned. Anna turned through a set of swing doors, and on to her new home. In a brightly lit office, a six-foot penguin was packing stickers in a poly bag. The door opposite was open, and Anna could hear voices.

'No joking. Ended up in the bogs together. Pissed as a fart. He was saying to Jamie, "Help me save my career. She's wild."'

'And what did Jamie say?'

'What *did* Jamie say?' asked Anna, pushing the door. Three heads swivelled. She dumped her gear on a nearby desk, and scanned the room, searching for a friendly face. One smiled back – a handsome young boy with a jet-black crew-cut.

'Hi.' She held out her hand. 'I'm Anna Cameron, your new sergeant. Pleased to meet you.'

The boy's grin curved deeper. 'All right, Sergeant? I'm Alex Patterson. This is Jenny Heath and Derek Waugh.'

Alex motioned to a guy in his early forties, tan bomber jacket and rumped hair screaming 'polis in plainers'.

Derek shook her hand, grinned. 'Welcome to rent-a-mob.'

The girl, Jenny, hung back, blonde hair swinging round her pointed face. Made up with a trowel, thought Anna, as they smiled their hellos.

'So, now you know who's who,' said Derek.

Anna leaned on the desk behind her, checking with her fingers before she rested her weight against it. 'Well, folks. Good to meet you. I'm not going to make some big speech just now. I'd rather have a chat with each of you before I set out any action plans.'

'Fair enough.' Derek seemed to be the senior man on the squad. 'Fancy a quick shuftie round the now, or will I give you the lowdown on what's what?'

He was a sturdy brown barrel of a man: ruddy, pock-marked cheeks, brown wiry hair, brown moustache, brown jacket stretched round his stocky frame – and everything with a sweaty, slightly slimy sheen. Like a wee turd on legs. Anna liked him straight off.

'Well, I've to see the boss in half an hour, Derek, so I wouldn't mind a wee look round first – and get rid of this stuff too.' She nodded at her assorted bags.

'Your office is through-by, gaffer. Come and I'll show you, then you can get the guided tour.'

They carried her kit to her new cubby-hole, then Derek took her back downstairs. The uniform bar, she'd already encountered. *Star Trek* modern, with four computer consoles and a special big seat for the inspector who was Duty Officer – conversely called the OD. In all her service, she'd never worked out why. The OD issued her with a locker key. He ran a tight ship, he said, folding his *Glasgow Herald*. Reminded her that CCTV had been installed at the back bar. But not in the yard where the vehicles came in. The back bar, where you charged, searched and locked up your neds. It was good to see one again – she'd been in headquarters too long, shuffling paper when she should have been hoovering shite.

'This is us, gaffer,' said Derek, stopping outside a plywood door. 'Mr Rankin's office.' He knocked twice.

'Come in.'

'Ah, sir, this is Sergeant Cameron.'

The super shoved something in a drawer. 'The new girl, eh? Well, in you come, dear. I won't bite.'

It was the man with the Sinclair C5. Bushy black brows and hair too long on his collar. Anna shut the door on Derek, held out her hand. 'Pleased to meet you, sir.'

'Sit down then. Smoke?'

'Eh, no, I don't.'

The super lit a cigar. On the wall behind him was a series of maps studded with blue and red pins, some framed diplomas and a signed photo of him grinning, one arm round Seve Ballesteros.

'Anna, isn't it? I'm Mr Rankin. I'll be brief, dear. As you know, you weren't the first choice for the job. Granted, we need some females to deal with the hoors, but it's your *service*, dear, your service. I'm concerned about your background. You've not got much operational experience, have you?'

Quality, not quantity. Would he smile if she said it? Unlikely. When she and Community Safety parted company, Anna had applied for the Support Unit. Two years later, she was an Authorised Firearms Officer; had searched, sealed and escorted scores of VIPs, bagged up body parts from various explosions, and written a dissertation on 'The Role of Multi-disciplinary Units in Modern Policing' (though she wished she'd stuck with the 'Multi-layered Cop-Shops' title). It had got her some of the highest marks ever recorded in a Master's, hence the promotion to Policy Support. It was also, presumably, the reason they'd sent her here.

Rankin's wet lips puffed blue rings. She talked a good game, that's what he was thinking. Anna could read it in his damp sneer. That was the way of the polis. You could have grafted on the street for years; soon as you got a cushy number writing reports at headquarters you were an office-wallah. The guys at the sharp end were quick to forget, and slow to forgive. And the slower they were at the sharp end, the more they disliked her.

She coughed. 'Not in years, sir, no. But I *have* done considerable research into mixed-purpose units, which is what's being trialled here. I'm sure my experience'll help with your plans for the Flexi Unit.'

Just this side of humble. Oh, but the demon was nipping at her arse. She glanced towards the certificates. 'I see you've won the Force Golf Tournament twice, sir. That must have taken a lot of commitment.'

'Don't piss me about, Sergeant Cameron.' The smoke curled from Rankin's nostrils, in the fashion of a B-movie baddie, she thought – but with a twist of Kenneth Williams in the flaring. 'I'll be watching your progress very closely. You'll report directly to me. Your remit is everything I tell you. Plain clothes mostly, but

uniform if required. Street offences, housebreakings, OLPs . . .'
He took another puff. 'That's Theft by Opening Lockfast Places,
in case you don't remember. Cars and stuff . . . hmm? Ring any
bells?'

She kept her face blank. *Blink twice for 'Fuck off and die.'*

'I'll leave it to you to prioritise, but I want weekly reports. And
I want results.' He flicked the cigar, smiled. 'Old school, me.'

'Me too, sir.'

'Oh, one other thing. Don't let your hoors run the show. The
Drag is *not* a no-go area – understand?'

'Yes, sir.'

Derek was waiting for her outside. 'How'd you get on?'

'Fine.'

'What did you think of him?'

'Seems all right.'

'He's shagging the cleaner.' Derek smirked. 'Aye, likes things
squeaky-clean, does the Tank.'

She thought he'd said wank. 'The what?'

'Aye. Rank the Tank. Brand-new, he is. Pure hates neds,
junkies, hoors. His idea, this scouring out the Drag, Sergeant.'

'So – he doesn't like folk paying hoors, but he'll coup the
cleaner?'

'Aye, but – naw, Sergeant. It's a pure meeting of minds with
they two . . .'

'Derek, I *really* don't want to know. Anyway, call me Anna if
we're not on the street. Where does the Drag run from exactly?'

Derek shifted the gut above his belt, easing it into a more comfortable droop. 'Basically from the saunas down the bottom, past
where the bus station used to be, up to Blythswood Square. Used
to be a pecking order depending on your position on the hill, but
it's all junkies now. The decent hoors tend to work earlier in the
evening, or from rooms and phone box cards and that. Then of
course you've your saunas. Lot of foreign lassies too now – from
the Balkans and that. City of *Culture*, us. City of Shite more like.'

He laughed at his own joke. 'Will we head down there after piece break, then?'

They went into the refreshment room for a cup of tea. Derek making it, Anna watching. Thinking she should help, thinking she should not. No canteen this, just a collection of rusty pots and a microwave with stalactite spatters. No way was she cooking in that. She asked him about the rest of the squad.

'Two others: Davie Brown – annual leave the now – and Jumbo. James Worth. Great guy, so he is.'

Crack-shot cheek slap.

'Jamie Worth?' A bite across her memory. Licking tongues of leather, stubble at her neck, scratching, there, at the nape. She rubbed it, pretending she was yawning. Trying not to feel the kick in her gut. 'Black hair? Used to work in the Gorbals?'

Derek nodded. 'Aye, that's him.'

'Yeah, I joined with him actually.'

'That right? Well, he's off this weekend. It's his wee one's christening the morrow.'

'He's married?' *How did that come out?* Anna looked in the fridge for milk, cooling cheeks, concealing confusion.

'Aye, his wife used to be in the job too.' Derek stirred the tea. 'You might know her. Nice lassie – Catherine. Worked here a while, then ended up at London Road.'

Her hand held fast to the milk carton. Cool and pliant, sharp squares boxing liquid. If she squeezed it, it would burst. Burst like eggs, spilling life in puddles.

So he married her.

Catherine Forbes. They'd not been on the same course – she'd been the year behind Anna and Jamie. Tall girl, won some award at the college. All dimples and curly mad hair. Jamie said he'd never even kissed her, but she *knew*. That night, when she saw them in the car park – she wasn't fucking stupid.

And so he married her. Babies too.

'Aye, I think so. Vaguely. Jeez – what's that stink in here?'

'Och, that'll be the eggs,' said Derek. 'Ronnie on Two Group's aye bringing them in – lives near a farm. Tries to punt them. Here – gie's them out and I'll chuck them.'

Anna slid out the cardboard tray. 'Much does he charge?'

Derek shrugged. 'I'm no sure. But he only sells them in bulk, that's the problem.'

'No, that would be fine. A tray this size would be ideal.'

Derek squinted at her. 'All that cholesterol's not good for you, Sergeant.'

'Och, I'm not going to *eat* them,' she said, dropping the tray in the bin.

'Ri-ight.'

She smiled, said nothing.

'Eh – will we move on then?' said Derek.

Tour over, they returned to the Flexi office. Jenny was perched on a desk, one hand on Alex's shoulder. She eyeballed Anna, raised her coffee cup to her lips.

'Jenny, could you show me where the female locker room is?'

'Through the wardens' room, follow the smell of hairspray. Canny miss it.' She put down her cup, lit a fag.

So. Let the games begin. Jenny wore too much blusher as well. Anna never managed to get blusher right: too high on the cheekbones and you looked like a Red Indian, too low and you were a china doll.

'Tell me, what are you guys working on at the moment?'

Jenny sucked smoke from mouth to nostrils. 'You're the sergeant. Your wish is our command.'

'Jenny, you don't seem very busy.'

Jenny burped, circled her fag in the ashtray.

'Maybe you'd like to bring me up to speed on everything the unit's been involved in? I mean, I assume from your outfit you've been dealing mostly with vice? Come and see me when you've finished your coffee, eh? And,' Anna turned to Derek and Alex, 'can I suggest you two take a wander down the town? Judging from the Sub Divisional Officer's map there's been a load of cars screwed in the multi-storeys. Check it out and get back here for five, right? Oh, and by the way, Jenny, this is a non-smoking office.' Anna said it all in one breath; left before her lungs combusted. Her office was just next door – no more than a cupboard, with a partition wall – but it was somewhere she could close herself in. Not before she heard Jenny's voice float down the corridor though.

'Who rattled her cage? And what was that dig about vice for? Just cos she's a face like a hen's arse.'

Some sniggers.

'Aye, and I like her style – she think we've all been sitting here with our fingers up our arses till *she* came along? I'm away to the bog. Her Majesty can bloody well wait.'

As Anna closed the door she saw Jenny exhale one last clouded breath into the corridor.

'All sisters together.' Derek's voice came, muffled, through the wall. 'C'mon then, gorgeous. Let's hit the shops and you can try out your charm on the salesgirls. I'm wanting a polis discount at Slessingers, and you're the boy to get it.'

'Piss off.' That must be Alex. 'That's an old man's shop. We'll hit the Italian Centre.'

'That's a bloody pedestrian precinct. Nae chance of getting a turn there.'

'So, we'll tell her we went on shoplifting patrol instead. She'll not be here long anyway.'

Fucksake – did they not know she could hear them?

'Och, she's all right. Reckons she knows Jumbo – says they joined together.'

Anna moved closer to the wall.

'Oh, that'll piss him right off. Someone else he joined with getting promoted before him. And how do you mean *knows* exactly? In the biblical sense, like?'

'Can you no get your mind above your dick? Right, move it. We're going to Slessingers – via the multi-storey if you *don't* mind, young man.'

Anna leaned her forehead against the partition. Why had she not checked the shift list? So keen to jump up and bite at the big carrot that she'd never even thought to see who she'd be working with.

'Sergeant?'

Jenny's fist was poised in mid-air at the open door. Anna had shut it – she knew she had.

'Will I come back later?'

'No, that's fine.' Anna straightened up. 'Come in.'

'I mean, you look a bit preoccupied. Can I get you a glass?'

'Pardon?'

'Of water, I mean.'

'Just come in, Jenny. And shut the door, eh?'

The girl was all hair and nails. Hard nails. A hard wee ticket, and her hair too long. No need to wear such a tight T-shirt either. But it was her eyes that got Anna most: darting amber ferret eyes that would never miss a trick. Best just to go for it with this one. 'Look, Jenny. I don't want us to get off on the wrong foot, but've you got a problem taking instructions from me?'

'How do you mean?' Jenny crossed her legs and sat back, extending her toes.

'I mean, because I'm new, because I'm female, because you don't like my hair?' Anna shrugged. 'I don't know, and I really don't care. Bottom line is, Jenny, I'm your sergeant, I'll be doing your appraisal and, yes, you're right, I will decide where our resources are deployed. However, I'd appreciate a wee bit of co-operation from you guys. I don't intend to come in here and tell you how to do your jobs. You're a police officer, for God's sake. I expect you to work with minimum direction. I presume you do actually make decisions when you're on the street?'

'With respect, Sergeant, I worked for five years on the street and three in the Female and Child Unit before coming here. I think getting chibbed with a crowbar and dealing with pre-school rape victims will have knocked a wee bit sense into me by now.' Jenny moved forward in her seat. 'Of course, *I* don't have the experience of the Policy Unit in headquarters behind me, which I'm sure is much more vital for the job, *Sergeant*.'

Anna cleared her throat. Whatever she said now would just inflame this – she'd tried her best to be reasonable, given the girl a chance and that was what she got. On the street, they called it the attitude test: if someone's polite, gives you your place, you let them off with a warning. Smart-arsed or argumentative, and they get the works. Jenny had failed the attitude test on both counts, and Anna hadn't even hung her jacket up yet. 'Constable Heath, take this as a wee bit of advice. I don't like your attitude, and I don't think it'll get you very far. Maybe you should consider broadening your horizons. If you do nothing *but* deal with neds and whores, it starts to affect your judgement. Maybe you should start honing your people skills a bit.'

Anna stood, gestured to the door. Too dramatic? Too late. She let her arm wave about a bit, just to show she meant it. 'Now just leave those files there. I'll read them later. I see you're down for report-writing this afternoon, so off you go and get on with it. Oh, and tomorrow I want you in uniform, so lose the warpaint, yeah?'

She waited till she heard the door shut, then sat back down. Unclenched her hands and opened the wad of reports and briefing entries before her. Her job was to lead, not be liked. Anna had to keep reminding herself. She thought of ringing Martin. But folk would wonder if she kept phoning the boss at Policy Support. Nothing was anonymous in the police. They could read your e-mails, check your calls, vet your partner, endorse where you lived. She couldn't phone Martin at the house, and his wife had answered his mobile more than once. Empty unease filled her, drifting loosely when she wanted to be fixed. It felt like the day she joined all over again, or the first day of school.

Stuff it. Anna dialled Martin's work number. She would hang up if . . . Not in. Of course; it was a Saturday. No one normal was in. She had to get used to these shifts again. Only tossers like Rankin would come to work on a Saturday if they didn't have to.

Something – she should be doing something. Back through to the main office, where Jenny was dictating a case. Anna's neck ached with the weight of the atmosphere. Picked a law manual from the bookshelf, walked back out, both women breathing a sigh of relief. Anna pressed her door fast against its frame, busied herself going through old cases until teatime. She hadn't been sure what they did for food, so she'd brought two cheese sandwiches and an apple in a Tupperware box. Should she eat it in her room, or go through to the main office? Or the kitchen? Maybe someone would come and tell her?

It was past six. She picked up her pieces, went to the refreshment room. All her squad were there, had been a while, judging by the amount of curry they'd consumed.

'Oh, hiya, Sarge.' Derek's mouth was full. 'Grab a seat.'

Anna sat beside him, still clutching her Tupperware.

Derek waved a piece of naan over the tinfoil dishes. 'Nobody tell you we get a Ruby on the backshift?'

'No problem,' said Anna. 'I'm not very hungry anyway.'

'Watching our weight, Sergeant?' asked Jenny.

She was saved from making a pithy retort by Alex, thrusting some pakora on her. 'Here, Sarge – paneer they call it. Some sort of cheese. S'magic.'

Anna dipped a piece in the day-glo sauce. 'Guys,' she said. 'Please call me Anna. It's only Sergeant if we're in uniform – or,' with a keek in Jenny's direction, 'if I'm giving you a bollocking.'

Even Jenny smiled. Kind of.

'Bollocking? Not us, *Anna.*' Derek laughed. 'Best bloody unit in the whole division, so we are.'

'So, how many car thieves did you lift this afternoon?' It was only a question, one she had every right to ask.

Alex shifted the weight on his bum. 'Em, none, actually. Took plenty of observations, but nae action.'

'Funny, that.' Anna clipped the plastic lid tight on the piece box. 'Thought I heard a shout on the radio just before I came through here. OLPs in Cambridge Street car park?'

She waited for a reaction.

'Maybe in future we'd be better splitting our piece breaks, so there's always cover on the streets. What do you think, guys?'

'Aye, sure, Sergeant,' came the mumbles.

'Okay, let's finish up here, then, Derek, and you can show me the sights of the salubrious Drag. And you two' – she nodded at Alex and Jenny – 'can hit the car parks.'

Grey daylight was filtering to dusk when Anna and Derek left the office; the bitter scent of buttered yeast wafted from a brewery into the night-time air. Derek offered to take a car out, but Anna preferred to stretch her legs, breathe the place in a bit. Best way to get your bearings. They passed the high flats crowding the police station, then through a littered underpass, coming out on the other side of a busy dual carriageway. Stretching downhill before them was the city centre. Glasgow was not a pretty town, but it was gallus. It sprawled and lolled, taking up more than its fair share of the west of Scotland, like a fat woman on the bus. Ringed with post-war schemes, built over stately homes and green fields, the city was a sink with a grey rim. A livid motorway ripped through the douce Victorian tenements at its heart; shiny hotels and office blocks exclaimed skywards over empty factories and decaying docks. Continental bistros sat next to fern-clad, piss-stink closes; and nearly every boutique had its own *Big Issue* seller outside. Enough boutiques to make Glasgow the shopping capital of Scotland too.

The town was jumping. Glaswegians liked to party, and throngs of white-legged, white-shod girls joined hard men in T-shirts and shivers, prowling gridded streets enclosing square upon square of bodies and buses. Anna and Derek went west, away from the bars and restaurants and down towards the quieter streets, sixties office blocks, underground car parks. Bereft of weekday workers, this part of town had a desolate air. Very quickly, Anna became aware of shadows in doorways, the odd car cruising by. A lone man walking rapidly through, hands in pockets, head firmly down. You could smell it. Sex and fear and loathing. Two young girls outside a sauna, gulping nicotine like milk. Their faces gaunt in twilight, hair pulled angry-back from hard angles and dark kohl. The smaller one held what looked like a pile of banknotes, which she stuffed in her pocket as they approached. Streetlight caught her on the diagonal, striking off a little silver horseshoe pinned to her lapel, and shading her face in two. Clad in short Lycra and boots, the other, taller girl was obviously pregnant. She stared dully past Anna and Derek to somewhere else.

Derek went over, spoke to the pregnant one. 'Howzitgaun, Angela?'

The woman turned, eyes dilated, in the direction of the noise. Took a few seconds to register that someone was speaking to her. 'Oh, hullo, Mr Waugh,' she slurred. 'How you doing?'

'No bad, no bad. Just showing my new gaffer round. Angela, this is Anna Cameron.'

Slowly, Angela refocused her gaze. 'All right?'

'Yes, how are . . . Aye, fine, no bother.'

Angela wasn't fooled. 'She aye look like she's stood in shit, Mr Waugh?'

'Don't you believe it, hen,' said Derek. 'Pure ball-breaker this one. So, who's this then?' he asked, nodding at the younger female.

'My wee sister Francine, so it is,' she drawled. 'Just breaking her in, like.'

'And how old are you, Francine?' Anna's voice was soft.

The younger girl's eyes widened, and she looked towards her sister.

'Aw, c'mon tae fuck, Mr Waugh,' protested Angela. 'It's no our turn the night.'

'I only asked what age she was,' said Anna.

Francine was defiant. 'I'm eighteen, by the way.'

'Of course you are,' soothed Derek. 'Well, we'll be off, girls. Watch yourselves, eh?'

He took Anna by the arm, ushered her away. Actually led her, like a dog.

She shook him off round the corner. 'Derek, what the hell do you think you're doing? That girl's never eighteen.'

'Look, Sergeant, that Angela's a good tout of mine – when she's no away with the fairies. Sorry if I pissed you off, but it's taken me months to get her to even speak to me. And believe me, she's actually twenty-three, though she looks about twelve. I'm sure it runs in the family. Genetic, like.'

Anna could put him on paper for this, insubordination or something. Derek was starting to pant trying to keep up with her. A good cop learned the balance of charm and harm; always weighing up the options at her disposal. Anna, then, was not a good cop. Lash out first, before the bastards got you – that's what she always did. But if she lost Derek, she lost them all. Maybe she had been too quick to fire in. No way she was apologising though.

'Fine.' The tiny word was painful. 'I'll take your word for it. But, Derek, don't *ever* call me a ball-breaker again. Understand?'

'Sorry, gaffer.'

'Anyway, what did she mean about it not being her turn?'

Derek explained that because there were so many prostitutes working the area, they couldn't jail them all. No room and not enough hours in the day. If the girl was a first-timer, she'd get a warning. If she did a repeat performance, it would be a caution in the police station. After that, she was a known prostitute, fair game. The worst the punter would get was being asked to be a witness to the offence – an offer that was invariably declined.

'So,' he continued, 'we've a kind of rota system going in terms of who gets arrested when. Saves time and effort and means everyone knows where they stand.'

Anna slowed down. No way. Not while she was in charge. Break the law and wait your turn for a turn?

'It also means the girls've a decent chance to earn the money to pay off their fines. Plus, we canny just jail them all – there's no room for a start, and no enough of us. We're talking nearly a thousand lassies down here, you know.'

She was still unconvinced. 'Rankin said something about the Drag not being a no-go area though—'

'Naw, he knows the score all right, gaffer. Fucksake – he'd go ballistic if we huckled two hundred a night into the station. Can you imagine!' Derek shook his head. 'Naw, he probably means in terms of laying down the law. The lassies are awful bad for keeping schtum about stuff. Like, a couple of the girls have been cut up recently, but we only get to hear about it on the grapevine.'

'What grapevine's that?'

'Jenny mostly. She's well in there with the lassies. Firm, but fair – they know where they stand with her.'

Probably swap make-up tips, thought Anna.

They wandered in silence for a while, up and down, across and over the square-set streets, knots of fragile women embroidering the corners. As they finished their circuit, Anna saw Francine clamber out of a car parked up an alley. The girl tottered back to her sister, still outside the sauna. Obviously, pervert trade for pregnant shags was slow. Angela took the proffered cigarette from Francine, straightened her wee sister's collar. Francine grinning too bright, like she'd won a medal. Her sister took a sheaf of notes from the girl's outstretched hand, stuffed them in her handbag as the car's engine revved up, reverse lights on. A tartan baby seat jiggled in the back as the car chugged off.

There were few girls out so early in the evening, and even fewer punters. Once more round the block and they'd head back to the office – Derek's guts were playing him up. 'I'll just away into these bogs first, Sarge. Touching cloth, you know? Bloody curry.'

Anna leaned against the wall, eyes skimming her new domain. Over the road a wee runt in purple shoes was tracing his hand down the cheek of a skinny blonde. The girl was leaning back, away from him, barely able to mask her disgust. You could see it in the widening of her eyes, in the way her tongue flicked her crusty lips. She would have been a pretty girl once – there was a china line peeking beneath the sickly circle she'd painted on her face. It ran out just at her chin, like a mask, the starkness of her throat quivering under wakening streetlamps. Toulouse-Lautrec would have had a ball here. As Anna watched the couple, another man rolled round the corner. A stunted shell-suit caricature, baseball cap clamped over Neanderthal brow. Anna could feel him sweep her, take in her fitted jeans and shiny hair.

'Ho, doll. No seen *you* here before. Need someone to look after you?'

She ignored him.

'Ho, bitch. I'm talking to you. I own this pitch, see. So you canny just waltz in and start working it without my say-so – understand?'

She folded her arms.

'Don't you fucking ignore me, ya cow.'

Anna turned her neck slightly, levelled her eyes with his. 'Away and take a flying fuck to yourself.'

'Who the fuck do you think you're talking to?' The nasal hit screech-tone as the man lunged at her hair, yanking it towards the ground.

Swiftly, Anna fell to her knees, lessening the pressure on her head. As his fist propelled towards her face, she pulled her baton from inside her jacket, slamming it up full force between his legs. Buckling in pain, he fell on top of her, smashing her nose into the pavement, her face all squashed to one side. From beneath the sweating weight of the ned she could see Derek emerging, doing up his flies. He stopped, gawping like a fish until she yelled, 'Derek, get this arsehole off me, and radio for transport. One male for breach and police assault.'

The man groaned as Derek yanked him to his feet. 'I didny know she was a fucking polis, man, I swear.'

'Course you did,' lisped Anna. Her mouth was inflating. Out of the corner of her eye she could see her top lip pumped up and glossy, purple flesh straining under segmented skin – a look some women pay for. 'I ID-ed myself soon as I told you to stop swear-ing – didn't I, Derek?' She looked around, to see if the girl was still there, but she and her companion had disappeared.

'That's right, Sergeant. Just before he swung a punch at you.'

Derek wrenched the man's arms up his back to cuff him, spun him round. 'Why, it's Lenny McVeigh, stickman of this parish. And wanted on warrant too, I do believe.'

'Excellent,' said Anna, dusting herself down. 'Right, let's get you back to the office, you wee shit.' She shoved Lenny towards the approaching van.

'I'm sorry, Anna,' said Derek, 'but I have to say it. Lenny, my man, congratulations. You've just met our new ball-breaker.'

Anna smiled as enigmatically as she could, what with the blood trickling out her nose.

2 Virtuti

Cath Worth sat on the mat. By the door, on the floor. The clatty kitchen floor, which she was going to clean, as soon as she'd finished the baking, hung out the washing and had a pee. Her scones had topped themselves, and here was she, on all fours, trying to salvage what she could. At least the crash hadn't wakened Eilidh – no, shit, of course it had. Frozen by a whimper. The whimper grew louder, turned to an indignant cry, triumphed in a full-blown bellow.

Cath got to her feet, palm smarting scarlet from the baking tray singe. Automatically unbuttoning her shirt as she walked to the front room, she plucked the child from the pram. Twisted her fingers through blanket mesh as Eilidh latched on to a solid, bruised apple of breast. Cath prised apart the chomping lips, which hung, pouting, until they could latch back on, jaws working against the bursting flesh, cramming in the entire nipple, easing down the milk as Cath eased into the chair. Surrendering to the inevitable, knowing it could be hours she was hostage there. The kneading at her breast relaxed her, dripping tickles pulling down her eyelids.

Eilidh's christening was in two hours and Jamie was at a football match. To be fair, it was a schools' tournament, and he was refereeing. Most weekends, and every Wednesday, unless he was on a backshift, he'd be down at St Patrick's Primary, training a bunch of ten-year-olds. He'd taken it on when the Townhead community cop retired. *C'mon Cath*, he'd wheedled. *If I don't do it, the weans don't get to play. The thing'll just fold.* But even so – he didn't need to do it today.

Cath hated football. Stupid little dancing men, watched by stupid little shouty men. They'd pissed down her back, first time she was on duty at a football match. Warm spattering on her raincoat, salting the tip of her ponytail. Cath's mind dipped further and further inwards, vortexing to nothing but shapeless, fluid echo. Finally, with a little, milky sigh, the vacuum broke, and Eilidh lay back, replete. Asleep. If she got up, Cath would wake her. Conscious of the clock, and the churning mess churning her churning stomach backing up the bile in her panicked throat, knowing he'd be home biting back the buts – *but you're not even washed; but you've been up for hours; but what have you done all morning* – she decided to risk it. Pointy-prancing across the room, she laid her daughter in the pram, contorting her arm to cradle the sleeping head right to the last, slipping out deftly as the mattress touched.

Back to the kitchen, the floor sticking to Cath's feet. She'd have to get a cloth and scrub, digging ragged nails through a layer of fabric to pick away at whatever it was. Then pick it from her nails and rinse. Everything was rinse. Change and rinse, feed and rinse, clean and rinse. Chaps, her granddad called them, these weals on her hands that she would wipe in handcream, chip fat, anything moist. Like Jamie said, what was there left to be done? Run round with the hoover and stick some sausages on sticks. Stick you on a stick. Splintered wood cleaving deep between your pink buttocks. Not sore enough? Not a slim, rigid stick, then. Try ten pounds of flesh that writhes and kicks as you push it, then. Shove that up your arse. Jamie's major life change had been no sex for two months – a few weeks before, when even doing it on their sides made Cath need a pee, then a few weeks after, until her stitches dissolved.

Now Cath's life was here, in these dirty, confused rooms, and his life carried on as before. Unhindered and unmoved. Sometimes, she hated him nearly as much as she loved him. Yet, as she glanced through at her sleep-breathing baby, lips hinting at a smile, she pitied him too. Pitied this passing through their lives.

Ach, this house was humming. Disinfectant, scouring bins. Rinsing, rinsing, her hands were raw. She went to bake batch number two. Even Cath could make scones. If she calmed down, took it slowly, even she could. Reaching for the flour, knocking the remaining box of eggs off the worktop, knowing it and seeing them as they spun and somersaulted through trembly, too-late fingers. Holding on with every last hangnail, crouching to retrieve the leaking shells. Cracking her head on a Formica edge.

Cath heard herself scream, a scream to be proud of, and even as she was screaming it she was thinking, This is stupid, but it kept on coming in a solid slice of noise until her throat was cracked into her head. She unclenched the grip round her aching skull, moved from squatting, sliding in jerks to kneel on the floor, her cheek wiping on the laminate cupboard door as she went down. And all the time, she held herself hard. Held on tight as she fell and fell and fell. She twisted from her knees, leaned back against the cupboard. Bitter venom scalded her cheeks. Slime and shells oozing beneath her flaccid calves, the dead eggs' viscosity clinging and minging.

'Cath – hey, Cath, you okay?' It was Jamie crouching over her, his face tripping him. He was clutching a huge brown envelope.

'Of course I'm okay,' she snapped. 'I'm just having a wee lie down.'

'On the *floor?*'

'Well – I'm knacked – I *was* in the middle of humping the eggboy.'

Soon as she'd said it, she wished it away. Arm half towards her, he hesitated. For a long, deep second his eyes were on hers. She could hear his leather jacket creaking, taste his breath. Then he got to his feet and left the kitchen. Cath lay on her back in among the broken eggs. 'Please, God, help me,' she whispered to the cobwebs up above. She would go through, say she was sorry.

Jamie was flopped on the couch, pretending to read the paper.

She waited for him to say something. Same page, eyes not moving, his shoulders tensed for the next blow. Cath wiped the hair from her forehead, opening fingers to avoid the egg-stuck tugs. He looked so sad.

'What's this then?' She picked up the envelope. 'That my P45?'

He sighed.

It was a *joke. Jamie, it was a joke.*

'Ted Morris asked me to give it to you.'

'Who?'

'Community cop, down at Woodlands. One with the big 'tache.'

'Oh, him. Magnum PI.' Cath opened the envelope. Reams of coloured paper, folded inside. She shook the contents on to the floor. 'Is this a wind-up?' Papery lace, like handfuls of doilies, all joined in a circle. 'Has the guy been on *Blue Peter* or something? I don't need bits of origami cluttering up the place.' She straightened the frondy edges with the back of her hand. It was actually quite beautiful, like the snowflakes kids made from tissue paper.

'It's not from him,' said Jamie. 'He said there's a note with it – some old punter gave him it to give to you.'

Stuffed at the bottom of the envelope was a little parchment scroll. Cath unwrapped it.

Dear Catherine
For your dziecina. May it bring her luck

The Lord bless you and keep you
The Lord make his face to shine upon you, and be gracious
unto you.
The Lord lift up his countenance upon you, and give you
peace.

She turned the paper over, in case there was something else on the back. Saw only egg-white fingerprints, smudged like grease.

'I do not have a clue who that's from – did Ted say anything else?'

'Nope.' Jamie kicked off his shoes.

A piece of eggshell had worked its way beneath her fingernail. She pressed it further with her thumb, waiting for it to hurt. Nothing. The numbness was everywhere, and the only thing that seemed to shake it was rage. She wouldn't let him ignore her.

'D'you think it's from the women's shelter in West Princes Street then? The Asian one – remember I used it as a doss when I worked there? The woman that ran it did a lot of arts and crafts. Did Ted say it was from a man or a lady?'

'Dunno.'

'James, would you move your shoes? I've just hoovered in here.' Cath shook the envelope again. 'But the blessing's not exactly Muslim, is it? Or maybe they use it too – d'you think?'

'Maybe.'

Cath folded the paper cut-outs back into the envelope, and stowed it in a drawer. 'Well, will you ask him?'

'Who?'

'Bloody Ted! Ask him who it was.'

'Hmm.' Jamie moved one hand to settle comfortably in the waistband of his boxers.

'I suppose I'd better get on then,' she said.

'What d'you want me to do?' He had that dopey look.

'Oh, good of you to offer. Where do I begin? I've still to clean the bathroom, get the glasses out of the loft, move all the chairs into the front room. It won't get done itself, you know.'

Jamie stood up. 'Right. Where do you want me to start then?'

Cath rubbed her forehead. It was going to bruise. 'For God's sake, James. It's your house too. I'm not your mother. *You* decide.'

'But . . . I don't know what bits you've done yet.'

'I've worked my bloody arse off all morning, and you can't even see where I've cleaned.'

'Cath – honey, I'm sorry. You *said* I could—'

The noises started overhead. Little animal grunts awakening. They both stood still, willing silence. But the vibes sparking through the house were jaggy, and the whimpering turned to a wail. Violent, exhausted anger coursed through Cath. 'Now look what you've bloody done.'

She ran out, leaving Jamie standing in the middle of the room.

At last, the baby was calmed, washed, fed and clad in silk, and they were ready to leave. A damp autumn day had turned to gold, fat leaves mellowing crisp and loose. They walked the couple of streets to the old kirk. Warmed by love and the pale sun, Cath slipped her hand inside her husband's. He felt a sneeze coming on, took a hanky out his pocket. Blew his nose loudly, then let his arm swing by his side. She waited for him to take her hand again, but he didn't, and she bloody well wasn't going to make all the running. One seething silent, the other wondering if he'd enough beer in, they made their way to the baptism of their firstborn.

Anna Cameron's phone rang. It was the Controller, a right nippy sweetie. 'You no got your radio on? I've been shouting you and shouting you.'

Anna checked her PR. 'Sorry, eh, Lynsey. It was switched off.'

'Aye, well, I need a sergeant to go to Ashley Street. I've two thick as shit probationers who don't know if they're dealing with a racist incident or not. Can you go and advise?'

'Eh – where is it?'

The Controller's voice rose. 'Look, I know it's your second day and it's no your remit, but I've no one else. I've three men on the shift, the gaffer's fucked off and—'

'Lynsey. Calm down. I'll go. I just don't know where it is.'

'Oh, right. Sorry. Number 12. Just off Woodlands Road. Flat 2/2.'

There was an unmarked car Derek had pointed out, shared between Anna's squad, the shoplifters and Community Safety.

Anna grabbed the keys from behind the bar and went into the yard. The chill breeze slapped her still-sore face. She'd have preferred to hide away indoors. A careful application of concealer had dulled the redness of her nose but it was still more bulbous than yesterday, shining resplendent above one cracked and puffy Elvis-lip. She checked the mileage, signed the log book. No bloody diesel. There was a pump at the far wall, so she drove the car over and filled it up, scooping fag packets and crisp pokes from the back seat into the bin. Drove back to the gate, got out and opened it. Sooner they went electric the better. The exit to the yard was narrow, and she prayed she'd never to drive a Transit through it. Got through, got back out, shut the gate behind her. Got back in, adjusted the seat and drove to Woodlands Road. Too bad if the call was urgent.

Woodlands Road used to be the posh end of town, one of four wide streets converging on Charing Cross, on the sumptuous Grand Hotel with its fountain, the twinkling lights of Daley's, cake shops and hat shops, the verdigris dome of the Mitchell Library, Charing Cross Mansions, majestic Sauchiehall Street. Then the motorway came, in typical Glasgow fashion, marching straight where it wanted and bugger the consequences. Tenements tumbled, communities halved and now Woodlands Road ended in a concrete slash.

Anna turned into Ashley Street, double-parked like everyone else. They were building new flats over the way, on the red dust left by sandstone, but there were still tenements on this side. Dirt-streaked, with broken doors, sheets hung like curtains at whistling windows. Two wee Asian girls sat on a step, playing with a doll in a cardigan. Youths further down the street tinkered with a car. A gable wall glistening with silver paint.

FUCK OFF PAKI'S

Bubbly, futuristic letters; the apostrophe denoting only an absence of education. What were they teaching them at school?

And what were they teaching them at Tulliallan? A five-year-old could tell that was racist graffiti. Anna went to the door of number 12, one of the few that was locked. She took her PR from inside her denim jacket. 'Alpha 51 to Control. Would you tell your sprogs that's me here? I'm assuming they may need glasses.'

She heard a snib click, then the door opened. A young Chinese boy stood there, dressed up in a checky hat. He looked about twelve.

'Sergeant Cameron?' he asked.

She nodded, went into the lobby. 'And you are?'

'Wong. Constable Billy Wong.'

The boy was staring at her swollen lip, watching it flap out of time with her words.

'Well, Constable Billy Wong. What exactly is the problem?'

'Up here, please.'

They skirted a bike, some bins, climbed two flights of stone stairs. An old man waited on the landing. He wore a threadbare raincoat and a soft tweed hat, which he raised on seeing Anna. 'Good afternoon, madame. I am sorry for your trouble.' His accent was stilted, guttural.

She smiled at him. 'Hello, sir. My name is Anna Cameron. I'm a sergeant from Stewart Street. Now, what seems to be the trouble?'

'Ach, it is only this.' He waved at his front door. 'I would wipe it, but the boy insisted. Keep, he said, to show you.'

The old man moved aside. A Star of David, overlaid with two black, interlocking swastikas, shone across the cornflower-blue panels.

Anna took out her notebook. 'May I come in, sir?'

'Wajerski, please. Ezra Wajerski.'

A single room, with a single bulb. One mattress in the corner, one chair by the window. A gateleg table covered in packets: Porage Oats, coffee, lentils, dried milk, the packages spilling on to a little cupboard alongside. A small cooker and a broken sink, tap dripping metronome torture. The other probationer jumping up from the chair.

'Do you know what time this happened, Mr Wajerski?'

'Like I say to your officers, madame, only since breakfast. I am out one hour, maybe two.'

Anna turned to Billy. 'Have you spoken to any of the neighbours? There's some boys in the street.'

The probationers looked blank. It wasn't their fault. They shouldn't be out on their own. Not yet finished training and they were expected to know every crime, every offence, each power of arrest, how long a detention could be and on what grounds, where New City Road was, if a metal comb was an offensive weapon, how to label a drugs wrap and, always, that perennial favourite, *Excuse me, officer, do you know the time?* They should be neighboured with tutor constables – experienced eyes and sensible shoulders – but the calls were too many and the cops too few.

She sighed. 'Go and ask them if they saw anything.'

The old man smiled. 'They are very young. Please. Take a seat.'

'No, I must—'

'Would you take coffee with me?'

His face too thin, soft white stubble on whiter skin. An elegant nose and a scrawny neck, tucked like a turkey above collar and tie. Her grandpa had always dressed like that too: bowling club blazer and regimental tie, even as he'd sat waiting for the nurse to change his catheter. *Dignity*, he'd said. *You can always keep your dignity, Annie-kins.*

Anna stood by the only chair. 'Where are you from, Mr Wajerski?'

'I come from Poland. The wartime, you know. I help with the planes.'

'A pilot?'

'Not at first, madame, no. A technician. I was a goldsmith, used to um . . .' he played his fingers like scales through the close air. 'My hands were good with, you know, the tiny things.'

'Intricate things?'

'Intricate, yes. But then, as time went on, they needed more of us in the sky. So, I learned. And I flew.' A shrug. 'Please. Please sit.' He handed her black coffee in a glass mug.

'Why did you not go back?'

'After the war? Ah,' he shrugged. 'Many reasons. My country, for one, no longer mine. A lady . . . yes, once I was handsome, madame.' He chucked his chin, laughing. 'And, as you see' – he widened his hands in benediction – 'I am a Jew.'

Anna sipped her coffee. It was good. Soft spores of fur climbed the wall opposite, where a childish cut-out pattern had been pinned. Round, rustic symmetries of birds gaping from folded newsprint. 'I like your picture.'

'You think?' He laughed. 'I try my hand at *wycinanki*, but it is difficult with old fingers.'

'Vichanky?'

'It is an art in Poland, Miss Cameron – when done well. However' – his eye twitched, like a wink – 'There were some things I did well. Please, would you look?' He bent at the cupboard, pulled it open. Inside were clothes, some tins. He took out a leather case, eyes bright as he placed it in her lap. 'You see?'

Anna pushed against the clasp with finger and thumb. Four medals on watered silk; metal flowers with ribbon stalks. Mr Wajerski took the smallest from the case, draped it across her finger. It was a gold, six-point star, a crest of coloured enamel at the centre, suspended on blue ribbon with a thin yellow and black stripe.

'They're lovely.'

'They're mine. This one,' he lifted a medal that looked like an Iron Cross, 'is carved, not cast. You see the workmanship?'

'What are they for?' asked Anna.

He pointed to the two remaining in the case. 'This silver one is my Air Medal. See here – it says *Polska Swemu Obroncy*. And this, with the crowned eagle, is *ratowanie* – em, to make rescue, you know?' He fingered the red and white ribbon rising from the silver disc. 'Ach, I was just a boy then.'

Anna wanted to ask him about the rescue, but he hurried on.

'This, she is the Order *Virtuti Militari*.' He showed her the cross he held. Not iron but dull silver, on a blue and black striped ribbon. At its heart, another proud eagle, its wings more elegant than those of the first. 'Each one unique – made by the finest jewellers in Poland and France. You can see the craftsmanship. Beautiful.' He dropped it back in the case. 'And this,' taking the little star from Anna's hand and straightening up, 'this baby one is my Air Crew Europe Star. Is quite rare, you know.' He dangled it at eye-level, diminutive facets against the light, shining on his gentle, eager face.

'Thank you for showing them to me. They're beautiful.'

'Here is not so bad. We have the Polish Club – you know it?'

Anna shook her head.

'Some of your colleagues, they drink there.'

'I've not been here long.'

'You should get to know your beat, no? That is what they tell me, these men. Perhaps I may show you? One other time? Fine place. You can buy Polish sausage and bread. And ladies, you know, they can drink there also. One of your friends – she was even engaged there, I think. We had—'

Anna put the mug on the table. 'Yes, that would be nice, Mr Wajerski. Now, about this mess outside.'

'Ach, it is little.' He closed the leather jewel case, put it on the table.

'It is vile. Do you know of anyone who would do this to you?' He frowned.

'Have people called you names before? In the street, I mean?'

'Many times, yes. But Mrs Jarmal, she has' – he clacked his tongue, like a bad taste was there – 'please forgive me, she has had the dog mess in her letterbox.' His face reddened, hand at his lips. '*That* is vile.'

'It could be the same people who did this to you.'

The old man walked stiffly to the open door. His finger traced one line of the swastika. 'You think they know when they scratch this? That it was scratched into flesh and bone?' He shook his head. 'If they knew they would not do it.'

'Mr Wajerski.'

'Ezra, please.'

'Ezra. I'm going to give you my card. It has my phone number on it. If you think of anything that could help us, will you call me?'

He inclined his head. 'Indeed.'

Anna stood. 'Thank you for the coffee. I'd better go and see what haud-it and daud-it are up to.'

'Hold it?' He frowned.

'My very young colleagues.'

'Ah.' He smiled. 'You too are very young, madame.' He took her hand and kissed it, his face open, like a child's. His grip was firm, dry, with a vigour that felt stronger than it should.

The tiny, damp room began to concertina inwards. How could people live like this? 'You'd better put your medals away.'

'Ah, yes.' He dropped her hand, pulled the cupboard door. A roll of notes fell out. The old man stooped to reach them, but they were already in Anna's grasp. The paper crackled between her fingers: folded brown tenners, fifteen at least.

'This is a lot of money to have lying about, Ezra.'

'Yesterday, I go to the bank.'

'D'you not think the bank's the best place to keep it? Why take out all that?'

'Tomorrow, I will buy present. For my nephew. George is being married.' He held out his hand.

'Oh, I see.' Anna handed him the money. 'Well, please be careful, Ezra. Put it in your wallet before you go outside, and don't take it out till you're paying for the stuff.'

'Of course.'

He stood at the doorway as she left.

'What will you do now?' It suddenly became important that he was going somewhere, with someone.

'I? I may read. Perhaps dine at the Polish Club. And you?'

'I will find out who did this. Goodbye, Mr Wajerski.'

He dipped his neck, the slow swoop of a swan. 'Good afternoon, Sergeant Cameron.'

Anna snapped downstairs like gunfire. She'd need to take the segs out her Docs now she was in plain clothes. She'd worn moccasins at headquarters, and no way was she wearing her own boots to skulk about the Drag. You never knew what you were standing in. From the street, she looked up at Ezra's flat, his silhouette dark in the empty window. She reached up her hand to wave, then thought better of it. Flicked the hair from her collar instead.

In among all the noise and eating after the christening Jamie stood with a bottle of beer, beaming round the assembled group. His mum and Cath's mum were playing tug-of-war with Eilidh while Aunt Betty showed them snaps of the new caravan. Cath's friend Helen was spooning jelly in her toddler's mouth, talking to a neighbour. 'Well, I suppose you could say it's like your life just ends. I mean, we, or rather, *I*, never get out. And, as for sleep – well, you can forget all about that . . .'

'And sex,' muttered her husband Paul.

Jamie winked at his mum as he took Eilidh for a wee nap. The old dear had done well, considering. He'd watched her in the church, stooping to kneel, then checking herself. Heard her say *trespassers* instead of *debtors*. Nearly did it himself. He'd wanted a mass too – not for himself, more for luck. Passing the kitchen, he saw Cath – cream cake in one hand, large glass of wine in the other, and his smile died away. She was moaning that she never got out any more. Always bloody moaning about something. When did he get out either, apart to go to work? Jamie carried his daughter up to her cot, then remembered he should have taken the robe off first. Fear of a wifely doing overcame fear of disturbing the baby. As the white satin slipped over her hair, Eilidh beamed at her daddy. The dimples were just Cath. Jamie's heart danced at the recognition, and the memory of Cath when she smiled.

First time he'd ever clocked her, she was covered in pondweed, laughing her head off. He'd been on his second stage of training – a whole year on the street under his belt, while Cath was a baby basic probationer, fresh out the wrapper. The baby basics had returned from the legendary bench run – teams of probationers shouldering wooden benches, running for two or three miles. The finale was always the order to run into a foul-smelling loch, still with bench aloft. They never made you go any deeper than the waist though, in case of dysentery.

Someone had dropped their end of the bench on Cath's toe, and she'd screamed. A passing sergeant made a comment about 'having no character'. Bruised and soaking, slimy spatters on her face, she'd looked away, and caught Jamie's gaze. Beautiful green eyes, thickly lashed and damp. Jamie had grinned, said something stupid about her being the funniest-looking character *he'd* ever seen, and she'd started to giggle. Laughter like crystal. All day he'd thought about this beautiful girl, black seal-hair glistening. Well, the burning image had been her soaking T-shirt clinging to her breasts, but he'd thought about her nonetheless. Evenings flirting in the bar led to a furtive weekend date. She'd been seeing a guy back home, and he'd been with another girl on his own course. Total opposite of Cath – cool, blonde and destined to go far. Kind of girl that swallowed guys up, then spat them out, maybe keeping a couple in cages for when she was bored. She'd reminded him of his favourite sweetie – a long pale twirl of barley sugar. Rippling curves of rock-hard sweetness; a gorgeous, brittle, independent woman, who would never need someone the way Cath did. No, Jamie doubted she'd even noticed when he was gone.

And, ever since then, it had been Cath and Jamie. Soft, fiery, huffy, funny, impatient Cath, who used to laugh up at him like the world was in his eyes. Who gave him this – his daughter. Eilidh's hair was tickling his lip. He hummed to her, something about a mockingbird. Birdies were her best thing; throwing them bread, pointing to them out the window, flapping floppy arms. Eilidh's eyelids fluttered, skin like opal and the eyeballs still moving underneath. Same as her mother, fidgety. Jamie couldn't make Cath happy any more, and he didn't know why. Just living underwater, gulping air through a tiny gap, sometimes glimpsing a ripple of what they'd been. Gently, he placed his daughter in her cot. When he came back downstairs, Cath was waiting.

'Where's Eilidh? I'm going to feed her.'

'Sorry, love, I just put her to bed. She was knacked.'

He might have said he'd murdered their child.

'Oh, for God's sake, Jamie. You know it's time for her feed. She'll never sleep tonight now. That's her routine completely buggered up. Thanks. Thanks a bloody lot.'

'She never sleeps at night anyway.' Jamie desperately didn't want a fight.

'Don't I fucking know it.'

Jamie pushed past, took another beer from the kitchen. Cath's sister's boyfriend cornered him. 'Haw, Jamesie-boy. You a poof or what? Take a dram for God's sake.'

Cath watched him, laughing and joking. Didn't have a bloody clue. No point in waking Eilidh now, so that would be Cath up through the night again. Every bloody night, three and four times, till it was easier just to lie the baby beside her, one breast permanently exposed, like a sow with her litter. Breast was best though. No one could accuse her of bottling out.

The phone rang. A female voice asking if Jamie was there.

'Who's speaking?'

'Oh, this is Sergeant Cameron, from Jamie's work. I wondered if I could have a word with him.'

'Jamie's a bit busy just now.' Cath could hear him in the kitchen, belting out 'Flower of Scotland'. 'Can I take a message?'

'Yeah, I wonder if he could come in a bit early tomorrow. I'm hoping to have a team meeting with the whole unit, and it's the only chance I'll get to have them all together.'

Female gaffer, team meeting *and* an early start. Jamie and his hangover were going to love that. 'Fine. I'll tell him.'

'Thanks. Eh . . . is that Cath? Cath Forbes. It's Anna Cameron here. I . . . I was on Jim – Jamie's course at Tulliallan. I think I remember you from there.'

Anna. Was that not the girl he'd been all wrapped up in, or under, when they first met? Strange how he'd never thought to mention who his new boss was. 'Oh right. Yes, I think I remember your name. Anyway, I'll tell him. Bye.'

Cath hung up. She took a bottle of wine from the sideboard, climbed upstairs. No one would notice that mother and child were missing. She'd only made all the sodding food, cleaned the house and given birth to the reason for today's shindig. Stuff the lot of them. She swigged deeply, curling up beside her daughter. But especially, stuff him. The ache in her throat that she thought was pride hadn't dissolved since they left the church. When she was with other people, it masked itself. Lying alone, sounds of a party milling below, it clotted like curds across her airway. She stared at the ceiling, hating its bumps and cobwebs because they were there. Didn't respond to the gentle tap. They'd think she was asleep, go away. Go away. The door opened and Helen let herself in.

'All right, pal?' said Helen. 'That's us away now.'

'Cheers. Thanks for coming.'

'Catherine, are you all right?'

'I'm fine, Helen, really. See, to be honest, I'm tired, I've a splitting headache and it's taken me all this time to get Eilidh to sleep. I just want a bit of peace, if it's all the same to you.'

Helen turned away. 'Suit yourself. See you later then.'

'Yeah. See you later.'

The door closed and Cath willed her friend to come back. She moved her hand to rub her hair from her eyes, unclenching a fist that was sticky. Red on her fingernails, red on her palm; little teeth marks of sharp clenched nails. She pulled her hair back, tight behind her ears, and held the bottle close. Anna Cameron had beautiful hair.

3 A Policeman's Lot

Stewart Street Police Office was corralled at the top of the town, a post-war 'So?' pebbledashed in several greys, and quite rightly hidden out of sight. Slices of blue patched under windows provided some jarring colour, and there was a single crisping fig tree in the foyer. Behind the scenes was even less attractive. Jamie ambled down the corridor, looking better than he felt. A struggle to get up, not helped by the fact that Cath was in a foul mood – again. He'd not heard the baby crying through the night, and she'd had to do it all – again. The office was deserted. Shit. He knew he was a *wee* bit late, but this new boss must be the type to sweep his broom eagerly from day one.

He made his way to the sergeant's office, knocked on the door. 'Sorry I'm late, Sergeant, but—' He stopped mid-sentence. 'Bloody hell, what are *you* doing here?'

His accusing stutter made her familiar, like a neighbour spied on a foreign beach – nodded to at home, hailed as the prodigal when out of context. He knew her, knew he was pleased. Shocked and pleased and groping. The folds of his mind birred over, fumbling to register this recognition.

Anna yawned. 'Afternoon, Constable Worth. Nice of you to pop in. Not quite when I asked, mind, but you made it all the same.'

'What do you mean? I'm only fifteen minutes late. Anyway, what are you doing here?'

'I phoned yesterday, left a message with your wife, asking you to come in early.'

'Och, we were both pished . . . I mean, it was the wean's christening . . . anyway. You're not Archie Clough.'

'Ever thought of the CID, Jamie? You're very observant.'

Anna stood up, came round her desk. She'd tucked her hair
back in a ponytail, and put on a wee bit of lip-gloss. It didn't hide
the swelling, but he'd always said her lips were her best feature, and
so what – they were dry. 'Archie'd to go in for an operation. All
very last minute. So they sent me instead. How, do you no think
I'm up to the job?' Hands on her hips, pulse throb in her neck.

'No . . . no, I just wasn't expecting to see you. God, it's been
years. You're looking really well, Anna. Really well.' He peered a
little closer, patted his own mouth. 'Apart from the trout pout,
mind.'

If he was a flash git like Alex, he'd have reached out and
hugged her, kissed her on the cheek, something. He just stood
there, flummoxed, trying to remember the last time they'd
spoken . . . Shit, he didn't think they had. Did he stand her up,
had he phoned her?

'Cheers. A wee welcome-to-the-neighbourhood, from one of
your local neds.' Anna folded her arms. 'Anyway, Jamie, you
know me. Straight to the point. I'm really looking forward to
working here, and I hope we can both be professional, put any
personal issues behind us.'

His hairstyle hadn't changed. Not even that wee V at the back
of his neck. Number two razor – she used to shave it in the bath
for him.

'Right, sure. No problem.' God, he must have stood her up
right enough.

'I hear you're married?'

'Yeah, that's right. Seven years. We've a wee girl – Eilidh. And
you?'

'Married to the job, me.'

'What, good-looking girl like you?'

No, no. This was wrong. She was supposed to be the one leading this conversation. She'd had a chance to rehearse, she was the

wronged woman – she was his boss, for God's sake. Anna tried again. 'This isn't what I mean by being professional. It's great to see you and all that, but, see, as far as anyone here's concerned, we joined together, and that's it. I don't plan to shoot my mouth off about your prowess or otherwise, and I'd appreciate it if you did the same. Understand?'

'Sure thing, *Sergeant,*' he saluted. 'Anyway, you'll no be seeing much of me this morning. I'm off to court. But maybe we can catch up later, yeah?' He smiled as he closed the door. *That* smile: the one where his lips parted and his eyes made promises, and he looked about sixteen.

Anna scored the skin of her tangerine with her thumbnail, stripping it in one continuous loop. She threw the peel towards the bin; missed. Another shitty day. *Move on, move on.*

Stop.

Hurting.

Me.

Think work, think trivia. Okay – what about Jenny? At the morning meeting, Jenny Heath sat sullen, as the others discussed priorities for the weeks ahead. Anna had noticed the long red nails clashing with Jenny's uniform, and wondered if she was being paranoid, or if Jenny had genuinely forgotten. Either way, the girl clearly didn't give a toss, and Anna wasn't going to carry someone like that in her unit. Give her a month or so, then she'd get her put back in uniform permanently – preferably somewhere far away.

She flicked through some reports, seeking comfort in the mundane. Orange juice dripping as she turned the pages. Put a piece of tangerine in her mouth, pressing with her tongue till the fruit burst open. Slowly, squeezing each segment, sucking it dry then swallowing the papery remains. Still, her heart was pummelling her chest. Stop. Stop beating so hard. Stop beating.

And it had for a while. Only ticking; marking time and years.

Jamie was it, had been it. Black hair, dark eyes and long pale limbs, which she'd have kept wrapped round her for a lifetime.

She was never given that option. And now, she was glad. Time taught her she had no need of it, the cloying ever-presence of another half. People were made whole – with amorphous edges certainly, that could overlap and blend like eggs in a frying pan. Only for a while though, then you could cut those edges neatly with a spatula. But what a frigging mess when you burst the yolk.

It was Martin's suggestion that she come here. Keep things from going stale, he suggested. As well as being an excellent development opportunity. And it was, it would be; but Anna missed the thrill of workplace flirting. Knowing there was a reason to put on perfume; knowing there might be a comment on how nice you were looking. Knowing someone was a wee bit yours.

Anna lived alone. She liked it. She was thirty-three. Liked that too. Good age – not too old, not too young. Just right, like porridge. Hoped she might have been an inspector by now, mind. One guy she'd joined with, a graduate, had gone into headquarters a sergeant and come out a chief inspector. Still, there was plenty time yet. She was good at her job, dedicated. If you were a woman, you could never say no. Unpaid overtime? Great. Extra studying, more exams? No problem. Anna would baton a ned, jump in a fight, challenge a knifeman, when prudence would dictate holding back. There was nothing worse than being the one who held the hats while the guys got stuck in. She would embrace dark places, volunteer for dirty jobs. Yes, she'd feel the fear, but she'd do it anyway. Equal pay for equal work – that feminist equation was what she joined for. Late-night drinking sessions with the CID, double shifts, triple workload. Which made a part-time relationship ideal.

The last of the tangerine slithered thickly past her tongue. She was new, female, how many more crosses did she need? There was nothing between her and Jamie bar the ghosts of youth. She remembered when Jeff, a black cop, had started on her shift in Easterhouse. One of the old boys shouted by way of welcome,

'Ho! Son, you a Proddy or a Tim?' To which Jeff had replied, 'D'you no think I've enough problems already?'

Which reminded her: she needed to speak to Billy Wong. Stirring the mix for her omelette that morning, strands dripping from the fork in glossy strings, she'd seen the old man's neck folded in the mixture. It shocked her. You never knew the time when one would reach through the bubble and touch your flesh. With Anna, it was rare.

Billy arrived ten minutes after she shouted him on the PR.

'Right, Billy, d'you get anywhere with the neighbours? Mr Wajerski, remember?'

He took out his notebook. 'No reply at 1/1. Lady at 2/1 – Mrs Jarmal – didn't speak much English. I said I'd go back today, around four. Her son'll be home from school then, he can translate. Bottom two boarded up, and 1/2 looks empty. The flats on the top are just doss-houses – you know, mattresses on the floor, old beer cans.'

Closed the book, looked up. The boy had a very direct stare.

'Thanks, Billy. Good idea to go back when the wee boy's home.'

'I used to do it for my grandmother.' He placed his notebook in his pocket. 'So, ma'am—'

'Not ma'am, Billy – that's inspectors and above. Though if you've got a wire at all, do drop my name in, eh?'

'Sorry. *Sergeant*,' he stressed. 'A wire?'

'Joke. They talk about someone being "wired" – meaning they've a champion somewhere – you know, an uncle who's an ACC or a mate in Personnel.'

'I see. Then no, I most definitely do not have a wire. No champion here or at home.' He scratched his ear. 'This is not my family's choice of occupation. Anyway, I wanted to check: is this a racist incident?'

Anna thought he was smarter than that. 'What do you think, Billy?'

'It's graffiti.'

'It's neo-Nazi filth. Of course it's racist. Offence under the Public Order Act 1986. *To incite racial hatred by means of abusive words, behaviour or written material.*'

Billy was impassive. 'When this happens to our home, we don't report it.'

'Well, you should.' She sounded peevish.

Again, the stare. 'Too many times, and nothing is done. It's quicker for my grandmother to clean it. So with this I should . . .?'

Anna outlined the procedure. 'Have you raised a CR – a crime report? Good. Well, you'll also need to complete a racial incident form. That goes to the SDO, Mr Rankin, who'll monitor the inquiry's progress. We have to prioritise these sorts of incidents, and the boss'll send Mr Wajerski a letter telling him this. We can even do the letter in different languages.'

Billy was noting it all down on a scrap of paper.

'Billy, that won't be necessary for Mr Wajerski. He speaks perfect English.'

A scrape of pencil-score across his notes.

Anna continued. 'A copy of the racial incident form'll be kept on file, so we can see if there's a repeat pattern . . . In fact, have you checked to see if anything previous's been recorded at that address?'

'No, Sergeant. Not yet.'

'Well, why don't you do that before you go back to Ashley Street. Get some background info on the area, eh?'

'Thank you, Sergeant.'

A thought came to her. 'Billy, did your own sergeant not tell you this yesterday?'

The boy's eyes did not meet hers this time. 'I think he was too busy.'

'What shift are you? Two Group?'

'Yes, Sergeant.'

'Keep me informed, eh? I'd like to know what happens. And while you're about it, get on to the council to clear up that gable wall too. I think they've got some special graffiti team.'

'Yes, Sergeant.'

Billy turned with drill precision and left the room.

Anna tore off the page she'd been writing, started another clean sheet. She'd her first weekly meeting with Rankin that afternoon and very little to report. Her men kept getting dragged off to make up shortfalls on the shifts. And she'd just been told that Davie Brown – the cop she'd never met – wouldn't be back to the Flexi Unit – he was now on secondment to Training. How was she meant to run productive initiatives with four staff who were never there?

A rap on the door.

'Come in.'

It was Derek. 'Gaffer, I thought you should know – another one of the lassies got a doing last night.'

'How come I didn't see the CR?'

'There isn't one. It was Amy at the Den telt Jenny when she went round for her breakfast.'

A kind of safe house for prostitutes, the Den was a one-stop shop where the girls could come for some tea and a blether, get free condoms or arrange a blood test. Some used it to keep warm between jobs, or get mopped down and patched up.

'So we've no complainer?'

'Naw. And that's the third now in a couple of months.'

'Blade again?'

'Aye. Rips the face off them, then grabs the night's takings.'

'Derek, have we got a note of the other two attacks you mentioned?'

Derek went to a file on the windowsill, passed it to Anna. It was labelled FAI.

'What's this – Fatal Accident Inquiries?'

'Naw – Fuck-All Information. It's where we keep all the useless wee snippets we hear on the street. If they don't want to talk, there's not a lot we can do. But you never know when you might need it.' He opened the file for her. 'Of course, we pass it all to the Divisional Intelligence Officer too, but it's handy to keep tabs here.' He tapped a thin metal chest of drawers behind her. 'Cross-reference it with the cards and all.'

'The cards?'

Index cards were last century. Everything should be held centrally and updated on computer. Not bloody Biro.

'C'mon now, Sergeant – keep up. We keep our own cards on every known prostitute: how many weans they've got, who their stickman is, their HIV status. What they like for breakfast. Canny beat local knowledge.'

'You're a dinosaur, Derek.' Anna started reading the pages he'd indicated. Hoors getting a doing was nothing new, but these two were horrible, vicious muggings. Six weeks ago: Pamela Macklin, aged twenty-eight. Address: Salvation Army Hostel, Clyde Street. Her attacker had taken a chunk from her cheek and stolen one pink vinyl bag containing approximately £200. Then, two weeks later, Simone Carruthers. Only eighteen, she lived in Dennistoun, but her previous address was Bearsden, where the coal came in *secks* and ladies lunched between manicures and golf. Again, she'd been grabbed from behind, slashed on the cheek. The notes said it was a five-centimetre tear, possibly with a serrated blade. Simone's bag was leather, but had held just £50.

There was no doubt both girls had their faces targeted deliberately. Some kind of a punishment maybe? Punters didn't mind about suppurating ulcers crusting on a girl's thighs – too busy getting their dicks out by that stage – but they didn't like bruised, bloody cheeks. Julia Roberts never had bruised, bloody cheeks in *Pretty Woman*.

'What's the third girl called?' she asked.

'Wee blonde one – Carole Guthrie. Hell of a nice girl. Here's the notes on her.'

'And none of them will speak to us?'

'No chance. Claim they didny see a thing, but I reckon they're all too feart.'

'Okay, Derek, thanks. Leave it with me.'

Three girls slashed, all grabbed from behind, all with their bags stolen. And all seeing nothing at all. Anna put Carole's notes beside the other two. Attack occurred between 3 and 4 a.m. Stolen: yellow purse, containing house keys, lipstick and £240. Discharged from hospital this morning. Jenny's scribbles said that the blade had opened up her left cheekbone. Left? Anna checked back. The other two didn't say what side. She thought a minute, mimed the action of slashing someone from behind. If you hit their left cheek, that would make you right-handed. So, if all three were on the left there would be a clear connection.

She began to scribble her report – the MO, the loci, the times. Surely Rankin would give her more men now? The solution was obvious: two teams of three, working alternate shifts for a whole week to saturate the area. Shite – no Davie Brown. So, now she only had five and one of them was her and she should be leading, shouldn't she, not part of the team, and she'd just been told to provide another man to cover Four Group's night shift and Martin *still* hadn't called her.

Last time she'd seen him, last weekend, he'd been lying in her bed, stroking her left breast, a sheen of sweat above his half-shut eyes. One raw wrist where the scarf had cut in. She'd rolled on top of him, kissing his neck. Wiggling down towards his chest.

Martin had raised himself up on the pillows. 'Look, Anna. Do you mind if we don't? I really need to get back. It's just, well, I promised Harriet I'd take her to the golf club for lunch. She, um . . . she thinks I'm playing squash.'

Anna sat up. 'You knew I was off today, Martin. This is bloody ridiculous.' She tugged the covers across her breasts. 'When'll we see each other then?'

Already pulling on his T-shirt, bum peeking out like a toilet-training toddler. 'Look, I've a lot on my plate, Anna. It's non-stop at work just now.' He hopped into his sports socks. 'And Beth's got her finals coming up, so she's locked in her room studying day and night. And Simon's never home.' He turned to face her, tucking himself into his pristine Y-fronts. 'Harriet wants us all to make more of an effort. Happy families, that sort of thing. So we're having a family lunch – I couldn't get out of it.'

He had turned beseeching eyes on Anna as he hoisted up his tracksuit bottoms. 'And I have to go to the vet's. The dog's been passing blood.'

'Oh, for God's sake, Martin, just go. I've a lot to do myself anyway.'

'Right then, my sweet. See you soon.' And he was off, clattering down the stairs and out the door before he'd even tied his laces.

See you soon. Precisely what you say when you've no intention of doing so.

Glasgow Sheriff Court stood on the south side of the river. A sleek and solid marble square, it glowered censoriously over the Clyde to the city centre beyond, sombre and no-nonsense, like the judgements delivered within. With fortress slits for windows, the interior was a surprise. Bright and airy, pale marble soaring to an atrium dome. Broad balconies coiled upward from the central reception hall, tiers of courtrooms to serve the Dear Green Place. And that was where the minimalist design scheme fell down. Ranged round the reception, spoiling the building's splendid restraint, were the clients. The dodgy dealers, shifty neds in shiny suits, sniffing, twitching serial shoplifters, joyless joyriders and sober drunks. The last had an air of superior contrition. Of course they were sorry, but they *weren't exactly criminals.*

Years of hanging about half the morning had made Jamie wise. He slipped in at 10.30 a.m., half an hour after the time on his citation, but not so late they'd be looking for him. He'd walked there, a civvy jacket hiding his uniform. Giving him some time to think.

Anna Cameron. Walking in on her, unexpected like that, had chilled him like ice cream on a sore tooth. A delicious sweet shiver that was very bad for you. He *had* stood her up, he remembered now. Or rather, he'd slunk away without explanation, like the tosser he was; dizzy on the newness and joy of Cath. Of course he'd thought about Anna over the years, but as a safe memory to be stashed away, along with photos of him in a wedge haircut, and jeans that were too tight. Not as a live, ticking reality that might reach into his life at any moment. And truly, genuinely, she'd hardly changed a bit. If anything, time had honed her features even finer, pulling skin translucent over her bones. Seeing Anna flashed Jamie back to the start, when his future rolled bright and bouncy as a red plush carpet, and life was a laugh. Anna and he had been good together, sparking off one another. Amazing how quickly they'd slipped back to their banter. Within a few minutes of meeting again; that shorthand closeness that never goes away. A sign of true friendship, according to the *Red*s and *Cosmopolitan*s Cath insisted on leaving by the loo. Which he only read if he'd forgotten the newspaper.

Alex was at the entrance to the police waiting room. 'How you doing, Jumbo my man? Think we'll get a quick turnaround the day? I'm meant to be days off.'

This was Jamie's third time lucky in the case against Walters. A nasty wee bastard who'd pulled a Stanley knife on a girl as he was grabbing at her tits. She got away before he did any damage, but that wasn't the point. Both times previously, a warrant had been issued for his arrest. Both times previously, he'd been rearrested on warrant, cited to attend court and then released. Both times previously, he then failed to appear. A senseless circle, particularly for the girl Walters had indecently assaulted, who now lived in Aberdeen and had to travel to Glasgow each time they had another go.

'Does it matter? They just swap your days so you're working anyway. My overtime is virtually non-existent.'

'Aye, but I'm still hoping for a flyer. Have you met our new sergeant by the way? She's a wee doll – told me no to bother coming back in.'

Jamie shook his head, laughing. 'Aye, I've met her. What it is to be young and good-looking, eh? Did you bat those long eyelashes at her?'

Alex puffed out his chest. 'If you've got it, flaunt it, pal. I've had no complaints. Anyway, a wee bird tells me you and her go back a long way – is that right?'

They were interrupted by the Tannoy: *Would all witnesses in the case against Walters please go to Desk Four.*

'Yuss!' Alex clenched his fist and bounced out into the first-floor reception. Over by the exit, Jamie could see their complainer being hugged by her boyfriend.

'Hang on a minute, Alex, I'm going to speak to her.' Jamie hurried to catch them as they waited for the lift. 'Excuse me, Sarah? Hi.'

Pink pillows beneath her eyes. When she recognised Jamie, fresh tears welled up. 'How can this happen? How can you let this happen? That's three times I've gone through this. Every time, I get more and more het up about seeing him, then I get here, and I sit around and nobody tells us anything. And now I've to go away and come back again. What kind of place is this?'

Her boyfriend tried to calm her. 'Ssh, pet. Try and not upset yourself.'

'Upset? I'm bloody furious. You know, I wish I'd never bothered reporting it. Because, see going through this . . . it's like he's done it four times now.'

'I know,' said Jamie. 'Believe me, I hate this as much as you do. Just hold on a minute and I'll try to find out what's happened.'

He went over to Desk Four. 'Case against Walters? What's the story?'

The clerk was monotone. 'No show. You'll be issued with another citation in due course.'

Jamie wanted the bastard jailed, not a tree's worth of citations. 'He was supposed to be in custody this time. How the hell did they let him go again? This is the third time he's not turned up.'

'Nothing to do with me, pal. You wanting a stamp or no?'

Jamie handed his citation to the clerk, who initialled it and stamped it with the time of release. As he turned from the desk, he saw Sarah and her boyfriend get into the lift. He checked his watch. He'd better get back up the road too. Anna had said nothing to him about a flyer, and he didn't want her to think he was taking the pish. But first, a wee detour. Still parched from yesterday, what he needed was a roll and egg and potato scone, and a can of Irn Bru.

Anna scrunched up another sheet of A4, lobbed it in the bin. She'd be as well trying to solve a Rubik's Cube. Any permutation of officers she tried buggered up the one before. If she moved Alex to there, then there'd be no cover for Tuesday night.

'Knock, knock.'

Jamie.

'Oh, hiya.' She straightened up, ran her fingers through her hair.

'Thought you might be hungry.' He dropped a white poke on her desk. Glorious, gorgeous bacon smells oozing through the paper. A greasy godsend.

'Thanks. I am actually. Starving.' She bit in carefully, trying not to slever down her chin. 'What do I owe you?'

'Don't be daft.' He sat on the edge of her desk. 'You okay?'

'Hmm, fine.'

'Really? Away, I know that face. C'mon, tell your Uncle Jamie.'

His bum cheek curved towards her. Tight and pert, smooth cradled in his jeans. Right size to cup gently in your hand and bite.

'Man trouble, is it?'

She picked up her pen. 'That's none of your bloody business.'

'This,' he said, tapping the rosters in front of her. 'Manning.'

'What? Oh, yes. Aye. I need someone to cover Seven Section next week for Four Group.'

'Well, why not ask Jenny? She used to work that area when she was in uniform.'

'Yeah, suppose . . .' She wrote a big *J* on the blotter. 'And they're looking for two spares to do the last half of Three Group's backshift. Spares. That's a bloody joke.' She tore off another leaf of paper.

Jamie took her hand. 'C'mon, you.'

'Pardon?'

'I'm taking you on a wee trip.'

'Jamie, I've got far too much to do . . .'

He tugged her fingers. 'Up. That's a girl. You still like cats, by the way?'

Anna let herself be led. 'Uh-huh.'

'Good.'

They used the wee runaround. She noticed he never signed the log-book, never filled the car up though it was nearly on the red. Her feet rested on top of a McDonald's carton.

'This car's a shite-heap.'

'How?'

'Look at it.' She kicked the litter in the footwell.

'Aye, but it's a great wee runner. Been round the clock once and still starts first time. Even after we took it down the Sixty Steps.'

'You did what?'

The Sixty Steps was the name the beatmen gave to a steep range of stairs near to Kelvingrove, linking Park Terrace with Park Gardens below. For pedestrians.

'Aye, we thought someone was screwing the old mortuary there – it was the quickest way to get to it. Though my arse was killing me for weeks.'

Jamie took her back towards Woodlands Road. Anna thought about going up to Ashley Street while she was there, see if Mr Wajerski was okay, but she'd nothing more to tell him.

'You like fish?' Jamie asked.

'Jamie, where are you taking me?'

He tapped the side of his nose. 'It's a secret, but I need your help. I need you to do me a favour.'

'What?'

'You'll see. Cheer you up, too.'

'And how do you know I need cheered up?'

He swung the car round a corner, sharper than he needed to. 'Believe me, I can see the signs.'

'How d'you mean?'

'Cath.' One short syllable. 'You know that Bluebells song about her? "It takes a lot to make me laugh." Well, that's us at the moment. She's finding it really tough, with the baby and everything. You know . . . well, you probably don't but—'

'Oh yes, *Mrs Worth*. When did you two get together, exactly?' Anna tried to keep her tone light, like it didn't matter. Which it didn't.

At Tulliallan, Jamie had been the class clown, asking stupid questions, imitating the instructors, slipping off for a fag during cross-country runs. Anna was quiet, studious, and the only asset she had to buy attention was her brains. People saw her excel in all the practical exercises, spout forth definitions and cases, argue points of law in the class, and soon her fellow probationers started coming to her for help with their revision, or asking her opinion on how she'd handle this situation or that – trading her knowledge for their skill in bulling shoes or practising drill. It felt wonderful, like she was part of a gang. Velma maybe, not Daphne. At first, Anna had seen Jamie as one of her projects, helping him learn the intricacies between common law and statute, encouraging him to study instead of downing beers every night. Then, one night, he touched her; idly playing with her hair as they pored over the Road Traffic Act. Each stroke opening out inside her belly, burning down between her legs until all she could see, every day, everywhere, were dark brown eyes and a smile as wide as summer. They became lovers after a few weeks, taking every chance to disappear in his car, to her room or once, in the night, down to the silent gymnasium. First love, worst love, fuelled by loneliness and lust – and spoiling you for all the rest.

Then it was over before she knew. And worse, before he knew. Anna wrapped her arms across her belly.

During the last few weeks of their training, Jamie grew more and more offhand. He'd still meet her late at night in the car park, but in the evenings he studied in his dorm, or went on boys' nights out to nearby Kincardine. She was too clingy, he said. But she'd seen him, chatting up the baby basics as they arrived, all shiny and new. She wasn't fucking stupid. Smiling down at that frizzy cow like he'd smiled at her. And once, when she couldn't sleep and she knew he was still out, she'd waited for his car to come back. Hidden in the hedge surrounding the car park, she'd seen his hands entwined in curly hair.

Even then, she'd said nothing, willing him just to see her face and *know*. After their passing-out parade, he'd pecked her cheek, whispered, *Stay cool.* Said that he'd give her a ring, and left arm-in-arm with his mother. She had his phone number, he had hers. But he never called, and she never would, not for a decade. And here they were now, like it had never happened.

Jamie gave her that grin. 'All water under the bridge now, isn't it?' He stopped the car outside a row of shops. 'Out you get, madam.'

The sign said TROPICS YA DANCER. Sticky purple hand-prints spanned the window, each joined to the next by a silver cord fishing line. In the centre was a three-foot lamé goldfish model, tail twisted as if it were kicking the stack of boxes beside it. Findus boxes, all promising 100 per cent fresh cod. The giant goldfish was holding a banner between its fins: *Fishy fingers – Goldie strikes back.*

Jamie held the door for her. It was a fish shop, right enough. Not food fish. Living fish, tiny jewel fish flicking through tepid tanks. Accessories too – goldfish bowls, grit for the bottom, wee nets, big aquariums. Strings of fake green seaweed drooping from the ceiling, which was swathed in old net. A small, curly-haired man in a pink overall came out the back. Jamie greeted him. 'Michael, my man.'

'Jamie. Good to see you, pal. And it's no Michael, it's Michelle now – or Shelly to my pals.'

'Fair enough. This here's my lovely friend Anna.'

'Howzitgaun?' Michelle held out his hand. The cuffs of his overall had sequins round the edge. 'Love your hair by the way, doll.'

Anna looked at him closely. Those curls could be a wig.

Michelle clasped his hands together. 'Yous wanting a wee cuppa?'

'Och, that would be grand,' said Jamie.

'So, what's up?'

'Nothing much. A wee bird told me you'd had a special delivery.'

Michelle stopped, one hand part-way through the beaded curtain to the back. 'And what would that be exactly?'

Jamie leaned his arm on the counter. 'Och, you know, Shelly. *Pussy.*'

Michelle let out a shriek. 'See you, ya bastard. Had me shitting myself there, so you did. Aye, well, you heard right.'

'Let's see the merchandise then.'

Michelle disappeared through the curtain. A sinuous, glittering mermaid was embroidered on the back of his overall, underwritten with the legend, *Do you smell fish?* Anna glared at Jamie. He stuck out his tongue. What kind of wind-up was this? He'd brought her to a transsexual tropical fish shop. Any minute now Michelle was going to wheech up his overall and show them his fanny.

'Is he a friend of yours?' she whispered.

'My sister-in-law lives in one of the flats upstairs. Michael's all right, you know.'

Michelle's head popped back through the beads. 'Are yous wanting tea or pussy first?'

'Och, hang the foreplay and gie's the pussy, man.'

Anna noticed how Jamie's accent had slipped to rich Glaswegian. A good skill to have, the ability to talk with, instead of up to or down. One that Anna hadn't perfected. She blamed it on her nose. High-arched eyebrows and one of those noses that looked permanently aggrieved. Kind of face to inspire folk. They'd wax lyrical with original gems such as, *Cheer up, hen – it might never happen.* She could be planning her holidays, reliving last night's shag or singing a song in her head and some complete stranger would feel the urge to comment. One day she'd scream, *All my family have been burned in a fire!* just to see the looks on their faces.

Michelle reappeared, clutching a perspex fish tank. He put it on the counter. '*Et voilà!*'

Anna peered into the tank. No water in it. A strew of grit on the base, some plastic greenery and one of those castle-arches fish enjoyed so much. The grit looked lumpy, as if it had been disturbed. All of a sudden, a wee furry face keeked through the archway, teeth bared in a silent growl. Anna jumped back.

'Jesus Christ.'

'Naw, doll. Gallus Alice.' Michelle put his hand in and lifted out the tiny kitten. Its stripy head was ten sizes too big for its body, its eyes still blue. The stumpy tail flailed wildly in the air as it spat and spat and spat.

'Ssh now, darling. There's my baby.' Michelle rubbed the kitten up against his cheek. 'Soft as bum fluff, so she is.' He sighed. 'Here.' He offered it to Anna. 'You wanting a shot?'

The kitten was thrust into her hands, on its back, legs kicking in indignant freefall.

'Give her some of this. Pure loves it, so she does.' Michelle sprinkled some sawdust stuff on Anna's hand. 'It's all right,' he said. 'It's fish food.'

The kitten rasped the food from her fingers, purring as it licked.

'So?' said Jamie. 'Do you like her?'

Anna's nose was on the kitten's belly. 'Look at you, precious. Look at you . . .' She looked up, blew a stray hair from her nose. 'She's gorgeous.'

'Yours if you want her, doll,' said Michelle. 'You'd be doing me a favour. Her maw Julie Andrews is a big hoor. Got humped by God knows what – pure wildcat, I reckon. Anyway, I've homes for most of them, but wee Alice here's the runt.'

It sat on her palm, licking between its pipe-cleaner legs. 'You're on.'

Michelle clapped his hands like an excited schoolgirl. 'Brilliant. My brother wanted tae drown her. Can you imagine? Wee soul. Now, she canny leave her maw for another week or two, but yous can come and visit her any time you want.' He went to boil the kettle for a celebratory cuppa.

'What on earth made you think I'd want a kitten?' Anna asked Jamie.

He took the cat from her. 'Hello, pussy cat.'

The kitten rubbed its face along the side of Jamie's finger, pink tongue lolling, eyes lidded with membrane. Anna watched it, stretching and dribbling to oblivion, focused on the feel of hand on fur, sensations of back and forward, then it flicked its head to the other side, pushing down with its face and Anna wanted to do it too. Wipe her cheek slowly across his hand, till the smell of his fingers passed her mouth.

'Well, you did want one, didn't you? Spur of the moment – you know me. I remembered you loved cats. Mind you'd that stupid sweatshirt with the ears on?'

Anna hit his arm. 'Shut up.'

Jamie leaned towards her. He made the cat wave a paw. 'Hello, Mummy,' he squeaked. 'You should have a cat. Cats suit you.'

4 Bedtime

On a West End street, Jenny Heath picked her way over dog-
dirt and chip papers. A fine drizzle was falling, softening the
grey and pink angles of the tenements. From a distance, all the
terraces had the same grandeur. Up close, they were faded and
gappy – like a genteel widow's teeth. Doors blocked up,
destroying the symmetry, and basement stairways locked in
rust. Beyond the grasses growing in cracked walls, and the
office nameplates shining where bellpulls once hung, there was
still a uniform splendour. Houses three or four storeys high,
flanked by elegant columns, with brittle prim ironwork bor-
dering communal gardens. Where rich merchants once lived,
students now squatted. Those elegant edifices not dissected
into bedsits had their guts ripped out anyway, forming bright
open-plan offices. With the office came the car. Hundreds of
them, double-, triple-parked, in streets built for clip-clop car-
riages.

Jenny was issuing parking tickets. In lieu of jailing someone, it
was a good enough way to vent her frustrations. Thoughts of
Anna kept her warm. Sergeant Anna obviously had problems
with women in the job. Well, stuff her – and the stupid wee calendar she'd stuck above her desk. Cats, for God's sake. Jenny
could see Sergeant Cameron twenty years from now: retired,
sucking Werther's Originals and reading the *People's Friend*. Only
her pussy for company. See the way she looked down that witch's
nose, like an old film star – Bette Davis or Greta Garbo – one of
those haughty cold bitches. All beige and aloof. Looked like a

frigging primary teacher too, with her jeans and her blouse and her stupid bob.

Slap. Gotcha, Mr Mercedes. Double yellow, don't you know? As Jenny was tucking the ticket under the wiper, an elderly woman hirpled up, her face distorted, like she'd just stood on glass. Surely she didn't drive a Merc? She was that wee – how could she see over the steering wheel?

'It's my husband. Oh, help me, dear – he's fallen over.'

'Okay, Madam, where exactly is he?' Jenny took the old lady's arm.

'Just round here. Oh, quick, quick, he was moaning all funny. He's no been keeping well.'

Turning the corner, Jenny saw the usual assembly of gawkers round the poor soul on the pavement. His skin the pallor of slabs. As she radioed for an ambulance, she searched for his pulse. Either dead faint or dead. She moved the old guy's head back, raising his neck, and began to give mouth to mouth, aided by the ever watchful crowd, and a now hysterical old dear, who was vigorously shaking her husband between puffs. *Jeezo, he hasn't got his teeth in. Lovely. Please come, ambulance, please come and take him away before I have to tell her he's dead.*

If she hadn't been in uniform, none of this would be happening. Not to her, anyway. She could be as anonymous as anyone in her T-shirt and jeans. But stick on this stupid uniform and you stood out like a big blue bruise. Made you as proud as fuck when you put it on all right – as long as you didn't have to go out in the stupid thing. Cause then everyone saw you, and knew you. You must vote Tory, you're probably a dyke, you know how to get to Auchenshuggle when the motorway's closed, and you are a lying, officious bully who can rescue cats from trees and pick weans from canals. Feared, reviled and relied upon in equal measure. *I pay your wages – ya fascist pig.*

Please come, please come. Please don't be dead. Jenny's prayer was answered with a splutter and a groan, just as the siren wailed down the street.

'Oh, thank you, dear, thank you,' the old lady sobbed as she was helped in beside her stretchered husband.

'What's your name, madam?' Jenny shouted.

'Iannucci. Mrs Iannucci.'

Off they sped, and Jenny turned to disperse the crowd. But they'd gone and done it themselves, moving back into their own lives.

Cup of tea. She may not have been in uniform for a while, but that didn't stop Jenny remembering all the good dosses. She deserved a treat. Il Pescatore it was. Over the hill to the wee bistro, where Toni welcomed her into the kitchen like a long-lost relative. One plate of pasta later, she jumped off the catering-sized drum of vegetable oil she was sitting on, and went to face the world. It was then she noticed she'd chipped a nail. Looked so cheap.

After her geriatric snog the rest of the evening was uneventful, which was just as well – Jenny wanted to conserve her energy. Since Sergeant Shitface had stuck her down for a night shift anyway, her evening was buggered. So Jenny had seized the chance for a bit of overtime by coming out early. She'd started at 6 p.m. and would be on now until 6 a.m. Twelve-hour shifts were thankfully rare, but the money was very welcome. Plus, it got her away from the Flexi, and Anna Cameron breathing down her neck.

Jenny wondered how Mr Iannucci was doing. There was a bus passing that would take her right along Cathedral Street and up to the Royal Infirmary. The old pump who was Four Group's gaffer didn't know who half his own shift were, so he'd never miss Jenny if she skipped off her beat for a bit. All those gumsy ministrations – it'd be crap if the old boy pegged it now.

The hospital was a Gothic pile, standing startled in front of a snake's nest of roads. Jenny passed through the familiar doors of Casualty, made her way to reception. She was directed to the ward sister at Intensive Care. No one at the nurses' station, but Jenny recognised a purple crocheted hat through the window. Someone else was there too. He was a big porker – looked a bit like Robbie Coltrane, but with close-cropped hair. Too much Italian cooking, probably. The big guy stood just behind the old woman, who had cricked her neck round to listen to him.

'I'm telling you, granny. I'm no gonny go away.'

Then the man caught Jenny's eye, and faltered. He swayed for a moment, caught between moving forward and back. The woman turned back to her husband. The old man was attached to drips, and she clutched his claw-hand in her own, two porcelain birds nesting. He'd had a heart attack, they'd said. Comfortable. Well, he didny bloody look it. The fat man came outside, and made to walk past her.

Jenny blocked his way. 'Hi there. Is he – is your grandad okay?'

'What?'

'It was me that – well, I called the ambulance. How's he doing?'

'Eh, oh – he's fine. Cheers. I – eh – I'm just going for – tea.'

'All right, pal.' Jenny patted his arm. 'Well, you take care – and tell your gran I was asking for her. All the best.'

She slipped away, back through Casualty to go outside. Passed a mother, growling at her whining child. 'Now, see if you don't behave, that polis'll come and take you away! You and your bloody moaning.'

Jenny turned back. Very polite – made a point of it. 'Look, madam, I'd really appreciate it if you didn't say things like that to the wee one. We want kids to think they can come to us if they're lost or frightened, and making the police into the bogey man really doesn't help.'

The woman's face flushed pasty to puce. 'What did you say? What a fucking cheek! Who d'you think you are, telling me what I can and canny say to my wean?'

Oh, God, I've wound up a time bomb here. 'Look, madam, I didn't mean to offend you. It's just that—'

'It's just that yous lot are all the same, that's what it is. I want your number. I'm gonny complain. Fucking polis bastards!' shouted the woman.

Everyone in the world was in that waiting room. Watching. Jenny's head fizzing. She should rent her own crowd to follow her round. She bent down low, spoke through her teeth. 'Right, that is *enough*. One, you don't use language like that to me. Two, you're in a public place, and you're bawling like a fishwife. Three—'

'Three is I'm gonny fucking gub you, ya stuck-up bitch. I've been sat here three hour waiting, and the last thing I need is some wee polis bint giving me a lecture.'

The child began to cry, provoking sympathetic tuts.

'Are you threatening me, madam?'

'No, hen, no, I'm no threatening you. I bloody mean it.'

The woman plonked her infant on the chair beside her and stood up. Always a bad sign.

'Right you, sit down now,' shouted Jenny, pushing her back in the chair.

'Did yous see that! That polis woman assaulted me. Fucking cow!' she bawled, launching herself at Jenny. One sharp heel scraped down Jenny's shin, while a hand tugged at her radio wire. The clip broke off, as they were designed to do, sending the woman flying backwards. Wrestling on the floor now, the woman's knickers flashing, Jenny managed to grab her PR. 'Treble 5 to Alpha. Officer in need of urgent assistance. Casualty at the GRI.'

The child, seeing his mother being attacked by the demon polis, was screeching louder than them all.

It was a fair bet Jenny's little homily hadn't worked.

By the time the cavalry arrived, Jenny had handcuffed her prisoner and dragged her to her feet. Although her flailing arms were no longer a threat, the woman's legs had doubled their efforts. Whether Jenny stood beside or behind her, the woman's scuffed heels pierced her shins. Like a bizarre Irish dance, watched by the whole of Casualty, Jenny balanced, dignified as she could, on her left leg, trying to hold her right leg over the front of the woman's knees. But the cow kept wriggling her legs out, flipping her heels back sideways to score down Jenny's legs. A nurse was holding the inconsolable wee boy, drawing Jenny daggers.

But you're supposed to be on *my* side, thought Jenny.

The scene became perfect when Sergeant Cameron waltzed in. 'You all right, Jenny? What happened? She a junkie?'

'No,' said the nurse shortly, depositing the boy in Anna's arms. 'I think you'll find she's just a tired, frustrated mother. I presume you'll be dealing with the child now? We've still to treat him. And obviously, with his mother being carted off to jail, you'll have to find his dad.'

'Hope you're more bloody lucky than I was. He's a bastard and all,' yelled the woman, as she was huckled outside by the van crew.

'Perhaps it's a Social Work matter then,' said the nurse, disappearing towards the treatment rooms.

Anna handed the child to a passing constable, told him to wait until she could contact a relative or Social Work. 'Eh, Alpha 51 to Control. Cancel assistance at the GRI. Under control. One female custody.'

Then she turned to Jenny. 'Right, Constable Heath, what the hell's going on here? In fact what are you doing here? This isn't even your beat. You were supposed to be covering Seven Section.'

Jenny's cheeks were carmine, her hair damp worms across her eyes. 'The woman became abusive to me. I'd no option, Sergeant.'

'Yes, but *why* did she become abusive to you, Constable Heath?'

Somehow, it didn't sound like it had happened when Jenny tried to explain, and Anna couldn't be bothered to listen.

'Look, put it all in your notebook, Jenny, because I reckon there'll be a complaint – don't you? And I think the chances of you finding a witness round here to corroborate your account are pretty slim, so I don't think this one will be going to court. Well, not with that woman in the dock.'

Anna moved towards the exit. Then, just in case Jenny was in any doubt, she called back over her shoulder. 'Make sure *all* your paperwork is completed before I go off duty. Which is in just under an hour.'

'Em – any chance of a lift then, Sergeant?' said Jenny, looking at her watch.

Anna drove them both to the office, mouth clamped in a bitter line, and one hand anchored to her PR. Social Work were coming to deal with the boy, but she'd just been told the mother had assaulted two cops and the Duty Officer back at the station. They'd have to charge her now. The radio zizzed into life: 'Alpha to Alpha 51. Apparently the wee boy's just wet his pants. The OD asks if you could go via the twenty-four-hour Asda's and pick up some shorts or something.'

'Any particular colour?'

'What?'

'Aye, roger Control.'

'Alpha to Alpha 51. The OD says, when you're finished, can you bring him in a fish supper?'

Frigging Anna Cameron. That cow had made her buy the shorts out her own pocket. Jenny's head ached. Frigging night shift. Frigging Murder Lane. She didn't know why she called it that. All she knew was she'd always hated checking it at night. It stank and loomed, tenement backs menacing either side, windows black shut. The worst bit was the end – leading no-where. Slamming abruptly, like clamping jaws. The lane was cobbled and sloped upwards from the street, twisting once, so from the road you couldn't see where it went. The years she'd spent checking it. Tiny yards and high stone walls offering no light. Just grim, crowding stone, built for access and servants. No mews here, not like behind the grand houses, higher up the hill.

Jenny was drawn by a fear that if she didn't poke her torch into the lane's dark fissures, in the morning they'd find a body, a dosser or something. They'd know his time of death, that he'd been there since midnight, and that she hadn't checked the lane. It could happen. One of the prostitutes had her face stoved in here, just last week. Claimed she'd been walking by, and the man had pulled her into the lane, but that was a load of bollocks. The girls didn't come all the way down to the West End unless a punter had driven them in a car. Anyway, if it happened again tonight, it would be one more thing that could be blamed on Jenny.

So, fear of humiliation conquered her fear of the lane. Or muffled it sufficiently to allow her in. Three years away from the street, three years without night shifts, and it was burning bitter as ever. That witch Cameron knew. That's why she chose Jenny for night shift.

On the way up the lane, she clutched her torch, striking shadows with blows of light – even though a *real* cop would check with his torch off – Doc Martens crunching deliberately loud on God knows what under her feet. The street could see her at the moment, neon lights and students spilling. Closer to the end she got, the lane narrowed in, buildings leering, closing out the stars. If she looked up, her head spun like standing at the bottom of a stairwell, craning to the skylight above. Once she turned the snaking bend, no one could see her. Not from the street anyway. Thick air of decades cloying, waiting for a fresh breeze that never came. Quick flash into either corner, then about-turn. This was the bit, each time, where her heart slid. On the way up, light and life behind, an opening she could run to. It was when she turned round, to return to where the light was, that the shadow became intense. Watch your back. Watch your back. Watching your back. Blood echoed sighing and she quickened her pace, not running, just slurring her steps slightly so they would elide and not pause and keep going and, then, it was over. Out under sodium skies, wide breadths of streets stretching vistas to black-green parks and the world gasping out again.

'Fuck me,' she exhaled. No extra payment for doing a night

shift. She'd forgotten the misery of rising at three, dinner for your breakfast. Setting out for work when others were off to bed and your body was in a different place from your head. Forgotten the night-filled boredom of pulling padlocks, spiced with an over-active mind drawing up every last horror film you ever saw till you shat yourself when a rat ran past. Forgotten the loneliness. In the Flexi Unit there were always two of you, because they were elite, the squads. No longer were you some poor bastard of a uni-form carrier. Get into a squad and it was like going on your holidays.

She crossed over Woodlands, past Charing Cross and into St George's Road. The road near empty, cool grey concrete brushed occasionally by a long-distance lorry or a Black Hack with a decent fare. There was a car showroom in St George's. Since the old night watchman was beaten up a few years back, he always welcomed a visit. With its comfy armchairs, discreetly placed television, and free coffee machine, it was the nearest to night-time Nirvana you could get. The gaffers tolerated it, so long as you'd the decency to pretend to be somewhere else when they shouted for you on the radio.

One final sweep and that would be her for the night. Check the Carnarvon Bar – door locked, lights out. It had been known for vigorous checking to set off alarms – public houses were partic-ularly sensitive for some reason. Then the keyholder would be called. Would sigh, smile, open up. Offer a wee nip to keep the chill out. Jenny needed coffee, not whisky. Her legs throbbed where the woman had kicked her. She'd not slept in the day and was getting that shaky way, aching tiredness crawling up her spine, softening her neck so the circulation fuzzed thicker than the pelt on her tongue. Up Carnarvon Street and into Ashley. Some scabby wee closes and a patch of waste ground. Squats and doss-houses and DSS dumps. A cursory peek and she was done. She passed the door because she'd expected what she saw. Splintered wood and staggered gait, half-on hinges pinging with the strain of taking up the slack. These people lived like animals.

Passed it before the nagging started, told her to go back. Told her to look again. The wood was dark, then pale bright yellow where it gashed and gnashed against itself. A single hinge-pin rattling tinny-time with the breeze. One clear, muddy bootmark mid-way up the broken door, that slippery chill up her back.

It had been raining till an hour ago, and rain would have washed that boot mark clean away. She should call for assistance. They might still be in there.

Jenny pulled back into an adjacent doorway. 'Treble 5 to Alpha,' she whispered. 'Possible housebreaking in progress at 12 Ashley Street. Stations to assist.'

'Ah, stand by, Treble 5.'

A creak from inside. Turned her PR off, pushed the door. The bottom corner grated squint against the wall. She held it steady, squeezing through the smallest opening she could make. A slice of streetlight followed, and she switched off her torch. The ground-floor doors were boarded up. She waited, listening to the not-breathing welling inside her eardrums. Nothing. Took the stairs carefully, keeping to the edge nearest the banister, where footsteps rarely went. First-floor doors were open, empty. On to the second floor. Each step a step further from escape. Jenny felt the darkness at her back, soft as an air-pumped cushion, filling up the space. Could feel it touching her neck, pushing upwards, over, like a caul. Someone was watching her. Two doors facing. One with a cardboard nameplate, something Arabic. The other dark, smelling of paint. She took a glove from her pocket and wrapped it round the handle of the first door. Turned quickly to catch out whoever was behind. Locked.

Went to the second door, turned the handle. It opened; Yale on the snib. Jenny stopped, listening again. No sound from inside. They could be behind the door, holding their breath. Holding a jemmy. She put on both her gloves, shoved the door, primed to strike at any movement with all the weight of her Maglite torch. Nothing.

An uncovered window, stark with the outside streetlight

coming in, made her blink rapidly. She pointed her torch towards the shadows, saw they were a table and a bed. Cupboard, cooker, and a body on the floor. She screamed, dropping her torch, which rolled towards the shape.

'Treble 5 to Alpha. Treble Fucking 5 to Alpha.' Her hands were jittering, pressing on the call button. Shite, she'd never seen a dead body before. Not like this, fresh-dead . . . maybe he wasn't – protect the locus; preserve life. Life came first, fucking breathe you stupid cow check his pulse check his airway. Jenny stretched out her hand, keeping as far away from the corpse as she could. His eyes were wide, eyebrows in his sticky hair. Blood not yet congealed around his ear.

'Treble 5 to Control . . . Treble . . . work, you fucker.' She'd turned it off, hadn't she? Cleared her throat, tried again. 'Alpha Treble 5 to Alpha.'

'Go ahead. What's your position, Treble 5?'

'Within the locus. Urgently require CID and Scenes of Crime.'

'Is it housebreakers, Treble 5?'

'That's a negative. Believe it's a Code . . .' The airwaves went static, and she'd to repeat the code for murder. A phrase flashed into her head. *Homicide is committed when a human being is killed by another human being.* Those were the words they taught you. This warm lump was reality.

She lifted the old man's wrist, going through the motions so she could say she did it. He looked so frail, he wouldn't have stood a chance. Skin very dry, no warm blood flow she could detect. A handspan bruise had started to bloom across his cheek, three, maybe four stripes fluttering. On his back, one arm thrown above his head, the other loose by his side. She left the sticking-up one, in case it was important. Legs were slightly splayed and his trousers undone, a darker patch spread across the crotch.

'Poor old bastard.'

He must have lain there, dying, knowing he needed to pee, trying to do something about it. Not mess himself. She looked round the room. The bedclothes had been ripped off, the mattress slashed. A small cupboard was open, old clothes pulled out. Shards of crockery glinted on the floorboards. Did he lie here, listening, as they smashed up his house?

'Jenny. *Jenny.*' It was Alex, hissing at her from the hallway.

'What the fuck are you doing here?'

'Pleased to see you and all. Me and Jumbo were doing a backshift, mind? We got asked to stay on – there was some rammy up the Bar-L and they needed to send a team up. Money, money, money.' He sang it. 'Heard you struck lucky, but. Gie's a shuftie then.'

'You don't set foot in this bloody room. Contaminating a crime scene, remember?'

'Aye, I know, but gie's a butcher's.'

Jenny stood up. 'There you go. Exciting enough for you?'

'That it?' Alex stared at the old man staring at the ceiling.

'Aye, that's it. Now bugger off and stop shedding skin on . . . Shit, Alex – don't touch that.'

He was fingering a tin cup.

'Sorry.' He rubbed at the cup with his jumper.

'Just put it down. Where's Jumbo anyway? How come he's let you off the lead?'

'He's upstairs checking the top floor.'

'Good. Least he's doing something useful.'

'Jenny. You all right?'

Jamie pushed Alex away from the door.

'Aye.' She nodded. 'Well, bit spooked actually, but I'm okay.'

'You don't need to wait with him,' Jamie said.

'Do I not? I thought I'd to preserve the locus?'

'You have. Just come out and leave the place as you found it. Upstairs is clear.'

They waited at the front door to the close. Alex went via a lane to look at the back court. The gate was locked, the wall low enough to vault. Within a few minutes electric-blue strobing signalled a polis car. Then another and another, blue disco-beams bopping. *Danger – these flashing lights could induce a migraine.*

Jenny folded her arms. 'Crawling out the woodwork, so they are. All desperate for a speaky.'

'Too right,' said Jamie. 'Five and a half hours overtime at court if you can say you were there. Each one a material witness.' A fourth car drew up. 'Jesus, would you look at them all?'

A beefy DC bounced out of his saloon like Tigger. 'All right, troops? What we got, then? Oh, Jeez, it's the car-park and wanking squad. That your hoors plying their trade down here now?'

'Piss off, Graeme,' said Jenny. 'It's an old man. Looks like he disturbed a housebreaker – the place has been trashed.'

The DC winked at Jamie and Alex. 'Cheerie then, boyos. I think me and the lady can manage from here, know what I mean?'

As they walked to the mouth of the close, the Controller shouted Jamie's number. 'Alpha to Alpha 523.'

'Two three. Go ahead.'

'Aye, Jumbo, sorry about this. The place is going like a fair and I've nobody in Six Section at all. You've got wheels, haven't you?'

'Aye.'

'Well, can you attend a report of an RTA at Charing Cross – believed one fatality. Traffic are en route.'

'Jeezo,' said the DC. 'It's like buses, this place. Nae action for yonks, then two deid buggers all at once. Okay, doll' – he winked at Jenny, then shoogled his groin – 'I'm coming.'

Jenny looked him up and down. 'If you're coming, Graeme, then I'm going.'

5 Pay-off

Anna had been at the gym. Workout, sauna, facial, swim. Two blissful days off in a row, and she was determined to use them productively. Working odd hours gave you excuses for no exercise and extra eating.

The answerphone was flashing. She knew before pressing play it would be Martin.

'Anna, darling. *Sorry* I've not been in touch. It's just been hectic, you know? And we don't want the gossips to . . . Anna.' He was plaintive now. She could picture him pouting. 'Are you there, darling? Pick up, please. No? Look, I'll be round this evening – some time after eight. Harriet's got her . . . bzzz.'

Well, I'll be out then, you complete and utter tosser. But where? Out-of-hours plans were made with Martin in mind. Martin consumed the spare bits of her life. She had friends, yeah. Few of them polis. Once, at headquarters, she'd overheard a policewoman describe her as a 'hard-faced bitch'. After the initial shock, Anna decided she quite liked this description. Forthright. Expecting the same high standards of others she demanded of herself. But it didn't make you many friends. The pals she had were from uni, the gym. A couple of stalwarts from school. People to go with to the cinema, to catch up with over meals. Always catch up. There was a pattern. Change of shift, call-off, catch up. Half the time, it wasn't true – she just couldn't be arsed going out. Anna's mother and stepfather lived abroad, and she never missed them either. Was there something wrong with her?

Anna wore the police like skin. She loved the power and the privilege. Like most cops she knew, she joined because she wanted to 'do some good'. The cynicism and smart-arsed swagger come later. If enough people fear and despise you, you feed on that, digesting the hard bits to form a shell. But Anna still believed protecting the weak made you strong. Made you *good*. Work was her life, and she was proud of that. It was Martin that filled a gap. But probably anyone would do.

Her belly groaned, that familiar dragging ache. She looked for some Anadin, still wondering what she could do with herself. Not double up in bed with her womb withering in cramps, that was for sure. There was a pay-off for old Jimmy the CID clerk, somewhere in town. Most likely the Station Bar – a pub serving the police, fire and ambulance stations, all of which were located companionably round the same two streets. Pity the poor folk who lived in the surrounding flats. Their days and nights were shattered by a choice of three different sirens. No danger of Martin turning up at the Station Bar. Mixing with the lower ranks was a privilege he reserved for Anna.

She found painkillers in the kitchen, rinsed them down with a glass of water. A cardboard egg box sat on her window ledge. Six smooth orbs, which she lifted out one by one. Two of them cracked, the others perfect. She peeled the dissecting strips of sellotape from tiny holes top and bottom. Light as helium, she felt they would fly away if she loosened her grip. Some people preferred to paint them first, but Anna always slipped the silver wires through, soon as they were clean and dry. Jewellery wire, gossamer-thin, so she could suspend the shells on her mug tree and decorate them in one fluid movement, holding the wire right down at where it disappeared inside the shell. More difficult than painting them on a flat surface, but more perfect too. They would cease to be brittle deposits at the first caress of colour. Blowing the contents was disgusting. Mucous clear globules, then the gentle forcing of embryonic yellow. Always, always a thread of red which she pretended not to see.

Anna put the cracked eggshells in a bag and hit them with a milk bottle, crumping with the base until round was flat. These would become mosaics. Some she painted before crushing, some would be left in their natural state. Natural was in, and went with everything. The police didn't allow second jobs, so she gave them to Oxfam to sell. Coming up to Christmas, jewelled baubles were all they wanted, garish Fabergé and rosy red robins. And she was going to try her hand at that *wycinanki* stuff too, that old Ezra had shown her. It looked easy enough – she could do tiny cut-outs and make them into cards.

It was early yet, she had time to run herself a bath. When she was lathering her hair, the phone rang twice. Loudly. Her house was always quiet. Anna didn't like radio drone corroding her space, TVs talking to air. Their intrusion offended her, like telephone salesmen at teatime. Her big toe hooked round the plug chain, water sliding and gurgling from her flesh. When there was no water left, she heaved herself out, long cream bathrobe over pale yellow towel, then wandered into the kitchen and peered in the fridge. Some pasta sauce, more eggs and a lemon chicken meal for one. Her tummy still hurt, but hot food always made it feel better. Anna stabbed a fork into the film lid, chucked the container in the microwave. Then she checked the phone. First message was from Jamie Worth.

'Hi, Anna. Listen, em . . . I don't know if you know, but Jimmy Black's having his pay-off tonight in the Station. Most of us lot are going. It starts about seven, so, if you're there, I'll see you – buy you a pint – or a gin, if that's what you're still into. Right. Cheers.'

Almost an invitation. Being an afterthought was fine – showed a healthy reserve between officer class and the rabble. She made a Martin face and pressed for the next message. Speak of the devil.

'Anna,' it whispered. 'Change of plan. Harriet's not going out now. Try and pop round later on. Sorry to let you down, sweet-pea, but can't be helped. Ciao.'

Later on. Did that mean tonight, tomorrow, next week? There was no bloody point having a gap plugged if the Polyfilla was wet and old.

Ping. Microwave for 'dinner is served'. She tore off the plastic and dumped the paste on a plate. It tasted better than it looked, helped by a couple of glasses of Soave. Anna rinsed and dried her plates soon as she'd finished, putting them back in the blond wood kitchen cabinet. After a pudding of chocolate digestives, she took more wine into the bedroom and looked in her wardrobe. A desert of beige and taupe. She went to take down a pair of loose cream trousers, then thought of the beer stains and worse that were likely at a police night out. Plus any other stains . . . God, could you imagine recovering from that one? *Ah, here's Sergeant Fanny-Pad comin.* Reaching into the back, she found a pair of black jeans and some old black boots. Carefully, she blowdried her hair into its usual sleek curtain – some things you just don't mess with – and inserted a pair of silver hoop earrings. Checked herself in the hall mirror. Black trousers and cream shirt, with a short fawn trenchcoat, freshly washed pale hair. Neat. Scoosh of Lou Lou, and that was her.

She picked up her keys, set the house alarm. Noticed one of the curtain tie-backs was undone. Alarm off, into the living room to sort it. Setting the bleeping buttons once more, she slammed the door and headed for the train.

It wasn't traditional to take anything to a pay-off. Often, it would be a free bar, at least for the first few drinks. But Anna hadn't contributed to Jimmy's leaving sheet, and she knew the old boy from previous encounters. On her way out of Glasgow Central, she bought a bottle of single malt. The man twisted the neck of the paper bag, passed it through the grille.

'Cheer up, hen. It might never happen.'

Anna kept to the centre of the pavement as she walked up bustling Hope Street. Basic common sense – too many buses on her left, too many dark lanes on her right. Plus, people didn't push you out of the road so much if you met them head-on. She dodged a bunny-eared crowd on a hen-night, rattling a chamberpot and collecting money for kisses. Two of the women flashed perma-tanned breasts at a passing taxi, as a young family scuttled by. A team of drunk boys tumbled from Caesar's Showbar over the road, shouting obscenities at the doorman. Anna fixed her gaze on the slope unrolling before her, and began the long walk to the top. She never made eye contact in this city, unless she was on duty. It was too much of a challenge, an opening for someone to say, *What the fuck are you looking at?*

'Evening, miss.'

Anna looked round. One of Derek's touts, the younger one, Francine, stood in the doorway of a shuttered sandwich shop.

She nodded at Anna. 'Off somewhere nice?'

It felt wrong, a reversal of protocol, to respond. Anna asked the questions, not this skinny waif.

'Just out for a drink. You?'

'Och, nothing much.' Francine tied the belt of her jacket tighter.

'You're not working, are you?'

Francine shrugged. 'No yet.'

'Not here you're not, Francine. Away back over to the Drag.'

'But, miss,' she whined, 'I'm too feart. Have you no heard about the Ripper? Some of the lassies are sayin he's gonny kill someone.'

'The Ripper?'

'Aye – the one that's carving up they lassies. It's like he's come back fae the dead, tae get his revenge.'

'Is that right? Well, maybe if you lot started telling us a bit more about him, we could get him locked up and off the streets.'

'He's dead big, with pure starey eyes. Like a fuckin zombie, man. Ma pal Donna says he licks the blood aff their faces. Miss, she says he's a fuckin nutter. Like he isny human, know?'

'Have you actually seen this man, Francine?'

'Naw. Naebody has. He comes up behind folk, wi a big devil mask on.'

'Is that right?'

The girl's pupils were wild and distended, her body juddering. 'Aye.'

'So, d'you know of anybody who could give us a statement then? Maybe look at some pictures for us?' Anna opened her bag to get a pen. 'What about this Donna?'

'Fucksake, miss. No way. She says that's who he's gonny kill.'

'Who?'

'First person what grasses him up.'

'Okay, Francine. I think it's time you were heading up the road, eh?'

Francine staggered out of the doorway. 'Gonnae tap us a tenner, miss?'

'Tell you what, Francine – we'll make a deal.' From her open bag, Anna drew out her mobile phone. 'You get yourself hunted, so I don't see you again tonight, and I'll not phone Stewart Street to give you the jail. How's that?'

'Thanks a fuckin bundle, miss.' Francine held on to the edge of the building, steadying herself. 'You got a fag then?'

Anna began to punch in numbers. 'Two rings, three tops, and they'll answer.'

'Ach, away yi go tae fuck,' Francine muttered, as she began to weave her way round the corner.

'You have a good night too,' Anna called after her.

Anna reached the pub about nine. The hot, sweet air swelled when she opened the door. Music booming, dark. At first, she saw only unfamiliar faces, felt a nip of panic. She couldn't prop up the bar on her own, or sail up to a complete stranger and start chatting. Then, through the crowd, she saw Jamie waving to her, moved gratefully towards him.

'What you having?' he shouted over the din.

'Is there a kitty going?' she shouted back.

'Yes, but I'll get this one. As a thank you for saving Gallus Alice's life,' he added.

'Okay. Gin and tonic then, please.'

'So, I was right.' He grinned.

'Yeah, creature of habit, me.' She laughed back. 'He wouldn't really have killed Alice, would he? The brother?'

Jamie didn't hear her. 'Guys are over there.'

He fought his way to the bar, and Anna went to where Alex and Derek were sitting. Derek had his head slumped on the table.

'Hi there, troops.'

'Oh, hullo, Sergeant,' said Alex, jumping to his feet. 'Can I get you a drink?'

'No, thanks, I'm getting one,' she shouted. 'Gonny call me Anna off duty?'

'Right you are, Sar— Anna.' He nodded, sitting back down.

'I'm just going to give this to Jimmy,' said Anna, holding up the whisky. 'Back in a minute.'

Jimmy was holding court in the far corner of the pub. The old detective, who'd been in the pub since two that afternoon, hugged her close and kissed the whisky she offered. Insisted she share it. The taste reminded her of moustachioed uncles, and she gulped it so the fire slid past her tonsils before her tastebuds noticed.

'Take another, hen,' the old boys cheered. She obliged. Just like drinking oysters really – or egg yolks, which she'd also done. Not for a hangover or to build up muscles, but as a *Jackie* magazine potion for finding your own true love.

'You're a wee darling, darling. Are you still on the lookout for a big strong man, cos I'm here if you want me?'

'Now, Jimmy.' She laughed. 'You know you're my fantasy man. But I don't know if I could handle the reality. And I don't think you could either.'

His pals started pissing themselves as Jimmy reached for her, overbalanced, and slid down the wall. She left him singing 'I'll Take You Home Again, Kathleen' and went back to her colleagues. Jamie had returned with her drink. Jenny Heath had also appeared. 'Wouldny have thought this was your scene, Sergeant.'

'Well, Jimmy's done me a few good turns in the past, so I thought I'd slum it with the rest of you. And it's Anna off duty.'

'Oh no, ma'am, I know my place.' Jenny raised her glass at her boss, and bowed her head.

'Jenny, don't.' Alex nudged her.

Jenny, who had also been in the pub since two, flung her arm over Alex's shoulders. 'C'mon, gorgeous, you don't like her any more than I do. Let's go where there's *nice* people to talk to. Anyway, I'm sure ma'am and Mr Worth want to be alone – you've a lot of unfinished business to discuss, don't you, folks? C'mon, Alex,' she urged, dragging at him.

Jamie touched Anna's back. 'Anna, just ignore her, she's pished . . .'

Anna darted at him like a cobra. 'What did she mean – unfinished business? What have you said to her? For God's sake, Jamie, my job's hard enough without the rest of the squad laughing at me behind my back. I mean, did you tell them how easy I was? Did you tell them what I was like in bed? Did you tell them how you strung me along for weeks, then dumped me for a scrawny wee cow with Brillo Pad hair? Don't hold back, now.'

'Anna.' He pushed her towards a quiet anteroom, where a forgotten buffet was congealing. 'Calm down to a frenzy. I didn't say a word to them. I promise you. You think it's in my interests to have them all knowing? Jenny must've heard it from someone else. Or maybe it's just a lucky guess, and you're playing right into her hands if you make a scene.'

'How could it be a guess?' retorted Anna. 'What on earth would give her the idea?'

'Oh, I don't know. Body language maybe. Way we look at each other?' He seemed to move a little closer. 'Who knows?'

Anna stared back at him. Her body, flushed with whisky, wine and gin, felt languid, as if it would be the easiest thing just to drip into his arms.

'I'll tell you this much – Cath would be delighted to hear

anyone call her scrawny nowadays, believe me. Anyway,' he continued, tucking her arm into his and leading her back to the crowded bar, 'let's not give them anything else to get their teeth into.'

The noise was worse when they rejoined the throng. Someone had cranked up the karaoke and two traffic wardens were belting out 'I Got You Babe'. Jamie started talking to a couple of guys, and Anna stood alone, unsure if she was meant to hang about till he'd finished. The nervous rumbles started again, and she downed another gin. There was no one else here she wanted to talk to.

'That was quick, eh Sarge,' leered Jenny. 'Must be losing your touch.'

'Jenny, you're drunk, and you're making a complete arse of yourself. Otherwise I'd try to work out what on earth you're talking about. Still, I'm back at work tomorrow, so we can have a little chat then.'

'Ooh. Quaking in my boots. Fact'm bricking it, Sergeant, really.' Jenny came closer, beery fumes wafting into Anna's face. 'You're pished and all, aren't you? Good. Listen.' She hiccuped. 'I don't like you and I don't respect you. But, I doubt we'll be putting up with you long anyway. We all know you've friends in high places, and that's the only reason you're here.'

Anna moved to walk away, but Jenny grabbed her arm with her bony fingers.

'See me, I'm a grafter and I hate people like you. But s'long as I do my work, then there's fuck all you can do. We've a good team in the Flexi Unit – so don't start buggering about with it. Or with any one of the team in particular.' She swayed off to take her turn at the karaoke.

Anna tried to catch Jamie's eye, tell him she was going, but he was engrossed in describing some goal he'd scored. She emptied another glass – possibly vodka, certainly not hers.

Someone spoke beside her. 'These parties are not very sociable, are they, Sergeant?'

That boy from the vandalism. Benny – Billy. He looked older in civvies, like a man. 'Hi, Billy – didn't see you.'

A leather jacket draped from his finger. 'I was just leaving. I was sorry to hear about the old man.'

'What old man?' Anna was still watching Jamie.

'Mr Wajerski.'

A slow droop of swan neck, kissing her hand. She smiled. 'What about him?'

'He was killed. Just the other night.'

Anna put one hand against her ear. It was impossible to hear in all this noise. 'What? What d'you mean?'

A ripple on Billy's brow. 'In his house – intruders, I think. Smashed in his head, wrecked his room. I thought you would know.'

She shook her head, placed the glass on a table. 'Come outside.'

They went into the street. The air was thin there, smoke-free. Anna shut the door on noise and bodies. 'I thought you said killed for a minute, Billy. Is he ill?'

'I did say killed, Sergeant. Mr Wajerski has been murdered.'

Anna pulled in breath. Pulled it through her nostrils, through her mouth, till it filled her head and ratcheted her ribcage. Chill wisps made her cough.

Billy's hand upon her arm. 'You okay, Sergeant?'

She pulled away. 'I'm fine. Change in temperature. So, when – who was there?'

'Some time in the early morning. I think. One of your guys – Jenny, is it?'

Jenny. It would be Jenny. Stomping round his house like a carthorse, making jokes, blowing smoke rings. Miserable rage swam the channels of Anna's veins. 'Was he – was it quick?'

'Let me get someone, Sergeant. You don't look well.' Billy sat her on a low wall, went back inside. He came out with Jamie, pointed at Anna. 'I'm sorry, I have to go or I'll miss my bus.'

She didn't understand why Jamie was on his knees before her.

'Hey, c'mon, Anna, ssh.' Her face must be all twisted, she could feel the muscles wobbling. Arms across her spine, bending her forward. Soft moistness on her cheek. Familiar smell, and a V of hair to wipe her face on. She wormed her nose into the roughness of his collar. No one could see her there.

'He was just an old man.' She was snivelling like a bloody girl. 'On his own. And I did nothing to help. Jamie . . . I said I would help him, and I didn't.'

'It's shite. This job's shite, Anna.' Jamie pushed her shoulders away from him. 'Look at me. You just do the best you can, then go home and forget about it.'

She scrubbed at her eyes, edged further back on the wall. 'I know that. But sometimes . . . you can't.'

'I know.' Jamie sat up beside her, pulling her into his side. One arm loose across her shoulder. 'I was there too, with Jenny. He didn't look too bad.'

'How bad?'

'Just the back of his head stoved in.' He was stroking her hair absently, like you would a child. 'And a wee bruise on his face – but you know how easy old folk bruise.'

'Yes, but . . .'

'Try not to think about it. Keep your life in box files, that's what I do.'

'How d'you mean?'

'One for work, one for home. One for fun, one for hobbies. Whatever.'

She sniffed catarrh back down her throat. Was that what was wrong with her – that she couldn't see the joins? Life was just life; work, home, shopping, gym, one big knobbly chunk, that was what she was. How could your essence be unpleated into several strands? Jamie was still stroking her, round the back of her neck now, kneading sweeps. It was out before she . . . *no*. She knew when she said it.

'Shouldn't home be fun for you?'

'You'd think so, wouldn't you?'

They stayed drooped on the wall, rhythmic stroking making Anna sleepy. God, that pain in her belly, firing up until she could hardly bear it. His smell was lemons and something powdery. He smelled softer than Martin, kinder. Jamie's other arm lay across his lap, almost touching her. Sallow, muscular, with a punctuation of black hairs. He turned his forearm over, and Anna glimpsed a paler underside, thin greenish veins. She could see the workings of his body, could see his blood. More than naked, until the veins disappeared beneath his palm. Slim hands, fingers slightly curved and she remembered them spanning out across her breasts, rubbing up to her face. Across her cheeks with a hammer or a brick, Jesus, it could have been a tin of beans from the wee stack in his cupboard they'd used to smash him, smash his head, bruise his old, tired face. Hands that could hold and make. Ease and tease and tear and take.

Curious drunks tottered from the bar to waiting taxis, and Jamie's fingers were still in her hair, twining and tugging, till she knew nothing but the pressure of flesh on scalp. That and her fringe framing stars, growing colder as the day aged. Someone walked by eating from a paper poke, acrid vinegar stinging like an alarm call.

'I'm Hank Marvin. Fancy a chippie?'

His fingers moved, whispering down her nape, her shoulder. A brusque squeeze, then they were gone, back in their own place. Anna's tummy was hurting again. She stretched to relieve the ache. 'No, you're all right. Think I'll just head up the road.'

'Sure?'

'Yup. Thanks for the pep talk.'

'Any time. You sure you'll be okay?'

'Yes.' She pretended to be exasperated with him. 'Now bugger off and stop cramping my style.'

He waved, went back inside the pub.

Anna didn't want to go home. What if Martin did come, and she was sitting waiting for him? There was a late-night café on the main road. She could go in there, pass some time. Now would be as good a time as any to tell Martin to bugger off. All the way home, she rehearsed what she was going to say. If she kept her brain busy then she didn't have to think. Didn't have to picture an old man being beaten to death in a country far from home, no one listening to his cries for help. His last words would have been in Polish and shut up, shut up, this time it was final. Final. Enough of Martin's wife, his dog, his moods. She would be clear and direct, so he was left in no doubt.

By midnight, Martin still hadn't arrived. Anna locked up and went to bed.

Cath was awake when Jamie came in, waiting up to tell him about their day. Heard unsteady footfalls on the stairs and closed her eyes instead. He stumbled to the loo, no doubt spattering everywhere but the pan, then lurched into bed with his shirt on. Stinking of fags and perfume.

Was the perfume stronger than the fags? If she let it, Cath could feel the tears well up inside her. It didn't take much – a dropped tray of scones, a dress that didn't fit. A child breathing, a husband out without her, mixing with folk that were thin and had jobs, who talked in a jargon that was almost foreign to her now. Young, giggly probationers, out of uniform and on display.

Trust was all she had. If she banned nights out, what would that make her? Made no difference anyway. Cath knew the proximity of dark lanes on the night shift, quiet car confessionals. Adrenaline rushes and back-slapping celebrations – and that was without any history for kindling. God, don't go there. Please let Anna Cameron have got all haggard and old. Not that Anna would go to shift nights out. First nights at the opera were more her thing, surely. Cath had deliberately not asked Jamie anything about his new boss. Of course, he'd mentioned her – couldn't miss another excuse for a fight, like when she'd forgotten to pass that stupid message on. It was her daughter's christening, for God's sake, but Jamie seemed to think she should have been writing down every last telephone call that came in too. Apart from that time, and a few bits and pieces when he was in a chatty mood, he'd not really talked about Anna Cameron at all, and Cath was too frightened to ask. Everything she said to him nowadays was misconstrued as a whine or an accusation. Christ, everything she said to everyone was. Even Helen hadn't been in touch since the christening.

She wondered if he'd try to shag her tonight. Jamie's perfunctory access visits were now always approached from behind – biggest bit to grab on to, and most remote from her face. Cath lived in perpetual exhaustion anyway, so would lie there, compliant, while he wapped it in and out. Or sometimes sobbing softly into the pillow that was clenched across her chest, as she watched the digits flick on the alarm clock.

Not tonight, it seemed. He farted, sniffed, and humphed on to his side, their buttocks grazing briefly. Was her best friend still in there, somewhere in the mire? They'd made a pact when they first got married, born from both being at shift dos where the wife would be sitting across from the girlfriend, oblivious to the whispers and nods. To be the last to know would be the ultimate humiliation, worse even than the knowledge of your husband inside another woman. Jamie wouldn't do that to her. He'd said he wouldn't. And who was Anna Cameron anyway? Just the girl he'd left for Cath. Fat, dull-as-death Cath who'd fled from the village shop that morning when Mrs Lees introduced her as 'the policeman's wife, dear, aren't you?'

'Yes, that's me. And Eilidh's mummy. I'm the policeman's wife and Eilidh's mummy. I don't actually have a name myself, you know.'

She'd grabbed her change and run, propelling the pram before her like a battering ram. Safe inside, she'd dumped Eilidh in her playpen and shut herself in the loo. Pants at her ankles, Cath sobbed and sobbed until there was nothing left, like bile after vomit. For a long time, she'd sat there, head on knees, her mouth pressed for comfort on the dimpled flesh.

Plenty of girls went back to the police now, juggling shifts and kids. Cath made out it wasn't an option. Her stock excuse: what with Jamie and her both on shifts, all their money would have gone on childcare, and they'd never see each other. It was easy to get held on a backshift till way past midnight, forced to fetch your sleeping infant from a childminder's cot in the dead of night. *I'm sorry. You've just been raped? Well, could you give yourself a wee clean up then pop back along tomorrow some time after nine?* Still, folk managed all the same. Dedicated folk.

If Cath was being honest, it suited her fine to leave the police. Less of a failure if she did it with great reluctance. In fact, people could view it as an admirable sacrifice, instead of a lucky escape. Ever since she set foot on the beat, Cath had been crapping herself someone would reveal her as a fraud. Oh, she could learn all the laws and regulations quickly enough, but ask her to wrap up a drugs production. Or investigate a car theft. Or spot a ned at ten paces. She was useless.

Most cops got a buzz from unravelling a case. Anna Cameron for instance. She was what they called a *good cop*. Cath heard the admiration in Jamie's voice when he spoke about *the gaffer* – as if Anna was a man – the ultimate, sexless accolade. So, well then – he couldn't fancy her still, could he? She'd never thought of that. Good.

It was with relief as much as regret that Cath handed in her notice. Like dying young made you a hero, so quitting while ahead left your dignity intact. Life was so much easier if you had no staying power. She'd done it at school, and she'd done it at college. Shine for a brief while, then move on, ostensibly to better things, leaving ahead of the posse.

Eilidh, though, was not something she could move on from. Cath had fully embraced her mothering task. She'd gone to aquanatal classes. She'd gone to National Childbirth Trust classes. She'd given birth drug- and stitch-free, squatting upright as Sheila Kitzinger advised. She had, however, passed on eating the placenta. She'd been breastfeeding for nine long, life-draining months. Cath had proved herself not just capable, but textbook. Except nobody else saw her screaming at a terrified child in a baby walker, locking herself in the loo so she couldn't be followed by the ominous squeaking of tiny wheels.

Of course she loved her daughter. She loved her with intensity and pride. But nobody told her life would never wholly be hers again. She should have guessed when the thrill of pregnancy changed to claustrophobic panic. It hadn't just been fear of the unknown. It had been the sense that life was leeching from her to her child, dominating her belly, filling her breasts. Before the child fed from her, it fed on her, and that was the way it would always be. Only a void left for Jamie – and fuck-all for herself.

He said she had to *make an effort. Get out more.* If she turned over, she could tell him that they'd ventured to Mums and Toddlers. How pathetic was that? Full of Mamazons and bovine goodness. Weans rampaging everywhere, Eilidh just screaming. All she'd wanted to do was feed, so once more Cath had got her tits out for a bunch of strangers. For free, too.

How did Cath Forbes end up at Mums and Toddlers? Constable Catherine Forbes with shiny buttons and bulled-up shoes. People would see her, feel guilty; be good. Look up to. Avoid. All they saw were the shiny buttons, and it made you feel so safe. Hidden in a blue serge shell, aloof, unknown. People did what you said. Choose your words carefully, for they will be hung on, repeated sagely, may be used in evidence, have been hanged on. No, really. A cop. Me, yes. They let women out on their own nowadays. Night shift too. A real cop, yes. She even missed that – the party talk. So, what do you do? *Really?* God, she missed that more than anything.

Through the darkness came a bleating like sheep. On and on Cath let it rumble, until Jamie spluttered awake. 'Shit, Catherine. Gonny get her?'

'She's fine.'

'She need fed?'

'Christ, I'm not a bloody cow.'

He rolled out of bed, feeling for his dressing gown. 'Is that right?

6 Postcards from the Edge

DI Cruikshanks leaned back in his chair. Pale dawn was filtering through the high frosted windows of the office, patterns forming shadow snowflakes on the wall. A limpid light, neither night nor day, and Cruikshanks savoured the little pool of stillness he found himself in. It wouldn't last.

The aftermath of a murder was weird. That initial clamour and faff, everyone charging round to get their piece of the action for a corpse that's not going anywhere. The panic was over for them, that body that was somebody. The time they wanted rushing and helping and all hands on deck was over; yet, too late, the eager hordes dashed to their aid, sirens screeching in pointless urgency.

Of course you want it solved quick, he thought. Want the disparate sum of all these parts sewn together, thread bitten with a flourish. There. It is done. An enigma unpicked, reworked and explained. But you had to be thorough – and the overtime was good too. Cops used to survive on ovvies, moonlighting and free gifts. In the beginning they were bailiffs and beadles, calling the rabble to order and minding the peace. Modern policing was a profession, bristling with diplomas and degrees, technology and initiatives, benchmarks and targets – but the reason remained. To guard, watch and patrol, to preserve life, protect property and investigate crime.

And so the investigators of murder sifted through lives, leaving only the detritus of final days, final connections with the outside world to be held up to the light and examined for what they are worth. Invisible fingerprints raised from dead skin, silent footfalls lifted from bare boards. Photos taken, streets taped off. Men and women shuffle by, logged in, logged out, mindful of Locard's Theory – that whatever is taken into a crime scene can also be taken back out. An incident room is set up, doors are knocked, statements taken. Hundreds of clueless words, each one a potential key. Sometimes, they all shake down like arrows, jabbing towards the one, the only. Sometimes witnesses see and hear, corroborate your suspicions, back each other up. Other cases linger like ghosts. Reluctant, pointless deaths where you widen your circles and widen them again, eddying in a vacuum.

Detective Inspector Thomas Cruikshanks was Incident Room Manager in Ezra Wajerski's murder. He knew already that this case would be one of the latter. One to get your teeth into. Second day and he had nothing. The old boy's tenement was empty, they'd need an interpreter for half the street, and the other half had been pulled down. Very little was coming back in the way of dabs. What he did know was that the old man had died of a blunt trauma to the back of the skull. Probably a relief after what they'd done to him, poor bastard. Christ, shitting in folk's houses was bad enough, but to do *that*.

Cruikshanks put his feet up on the desk. He'd torn his hamstring doing the garden and it was still niggling. They were going to have to start using HOLMES. Folk thought it was some kind of super-computer that could play chess and tell your fortune. He liked that line. It's what he always used in his spiel to probationers up at Tulliallan. *The Home Office Large Major Enquiry System does not solve murders*. It was just a fancy bit of hardware, only as good as the intelligence going into it. And the intelligence interrogating it. He was going to have a Big Softee from Greggs, then another bloody briefing. See what gen had come back on Wajerski.

Cruikshanks was just lifting his coffee to his lips when Anna Cameron waltzed in. She aye looked like she'd trodden in something, that superior pained face that meant to be somewhere better. Shagging some gaffer up Pitt Street. And it was rumoured she was doing a line with big Jamie Worth – apparently they'd got off with each other at Sadie's do. Ach, God love him, he'd be a hard act to follow, Sadie – so dubbed when a geriatric sergeant who should've been put out to grass years ago, kept cutting off a punter with the words, *Sorry, we've nae Sadie Clark here.* When the caller finally got through to someone else, they discovered he'd been phoning for the CID Clerk all along. And so Jimmy was reborn as Sadie.

Cruikshanks put down his mug, rearranged his expression. She wasn't a bad cop, Cameron. Had a good wee team working for her. That Tonka one, the girl that found Wajerski, she'd done it all by the book, minimal interference with the locus, no cross-contamination. And she was a wee cracker – Tonka that is, not Cameron. Nah, Cameron would bite your cock off if you let her. Tonka – cracking name too. He guessed they never let on to her face. *Big toys for little boys*, that was how the advert went. He wiped his mouth.

'Good morning, Ms Cameron. And what can we do for you?'

'It's about Mr Wajerski, sir. I saw him a few days before.'

'I know you did, Sergeant.' That put her gas at a peep.

'Right, well, I thought you'd maybe want to speak to me.'

'All in good time, Sergeant.' He took a bite of his Softee, egg mayonnaise erupting like pus from either side.

'It's just – he was the victim of a racial incident, sir.'

'I'm well aware of that. No leads, though, were there?'

'No, but – did you know he was Polish, sir?'

He burped slightly. 'Wajerski – Ezra – nah. Away? Seriously?'

'Ha bloody ha.' The cheeky besom took the Softee out his mouth. 'You can get this back when I've finished. Are you aware he had a collection of war medals?'

Cruikshanks shook his head, still chewing.

'And he had a roll of notes in his possession on the day I saw him – couple of ton maybe – to buy a present for a nephew.'

'No, *ma'am*. I was not aware of that. Anything else I've been remiss in finding out?'

'Well, shouldn't you be writing all this down then? I take it the money wasn't there?'

Cruikshanks snatched back his roll. 'What do you think?'

'And the medals?'

He shrugged. 'Were they valuable?'

She tried to remember her conversation with Mr Wajerski. 'I don't know – he said one was. Called it virtuosity or something like that. It was a metal cross.'

'Can you put all this in a statement?'

The Softee was dripping down his wrist.

Anna handed him two sheets of A4. 'Like this?'

'Now, that's why I like you.'

'Liar. Oh, there's a Polish Club, somewhere nearby. He used to go there sometimes.'

'Fucksake – were you in a long-term relationship with this man?'

'Just a woman's touch; works every time.'

Where other lassies would've winked at him, she stuck out her tongue. Bit skinny, but quite a looker when she smiled. Cruikshanks took his feet off the desk, tossed the remainder of his roll in the bin.

'Listen, Anna, this isn't common knowledge yet, but the old guy wasn't just belted.'

'Did they hurt him?'

'Aye. Well, he was – they found traces of spunk. Round his crotch and buttocks.'

Anna nodded, sucking her lips in a concave. Picked up the cup on his desk and swigged the lukewarm dregs round her mouth.

Cruikshanks leaned back in his chair. 'Help yourself, why don't you.'

'Sorry. Dry throat.'

'You reckon he was straight?'

Anna was emphatic. 'Absolutely. He mentioned a woman. He was a war hero, you know. Jewish.'

'Think he went back home much?'

'No. Settled here after the war, in a shitty wee bedsit with no curtains.'

Cruikshanks was writing on the pad in front of him. 'It couldny of been that shitty, if he'd that kind of cash rolling about. Old soldier or no, you've got to ask what he was up to.'

'Could have been his life savings for all you know. Whatever it was, he didn't deserve that.' Anna handed him back the cup. 'Look – I . . .'

'Anna, I'll keep you up to speed, I promise. Likewise, if you hear anything from anywhere, give me a shout, eh? We've not got much to go on.'

Anna stood up. 'Have you spoken to the neighbour yet?'

'Cannae find any.'

'There's one on his landing – Mrs Jarmal. I mention her in the statement. She's had trouble too.'

'No trace so far. I'll get someone to try again, okay?'

'Okay.' She opened the door. 'He was a nice old man, you know?'

'Aye. I know.'

Anna washed her face in cold water, letting it soak her fringe and collar, clammy against her neck. Lifted her hair, shook it out. Avoided the mirror. How could one person do that to another? Ezra Wajerski had died with little fuss, it seemed, even when they defiled his body. No signs of a struggle. Gentle, mannered to the end, he'd lain waiting to catch up with his memories. Vigour and power and courage were in his history; a story of other men and other days. Did he know that his present humiliation was his last taste of earth? Did he see the murderer yank out his penis, did he shut his eyes and pray? Dear God, thank God you don't exist. Anna wanted to go home. Go to bed, and wake in another place and not think about fragile old bones, quietly stooped and festering, which should have been wrapped in wool, kept safe by bigger, stronger folk.

She should have done more: gone back to see him, asked the shifts for extra attention to his flat. Ach, what difference would it have made? Jamie was right. The world was not her fault. Cold coffee taste still dripped like snotters, coating Anna's gums. God, how must that have looked – taking a swig out of Cruikshanks's mug? Trying to wash sweet caffeine against the metal bile, someone else's slevers tasting better than her own. All the time Cruikshanks was talking, she'd been watching him through the two sockets that burrowed back into her head, trying to think of attributes to prove what Ezra wasn't. He wasn't some sad old renter of boys, who died in a lover's tiff. He was a gentleman.

He'd kissed her hand.

It took seconds to find the document she was looking for – her notebook, stuffed inside the top shelf of her locker. Write everything down, an ingrained trait. She even wrote lists on her days off now: shopping lists, things to do, things to remember. If it wasn't captured on paper somewhere, then it had never been.

The habit was annoying. Anna had a friend who worked in television. Loved it at first, but now he could never stop analysing. Every programme he watched for pleasure, he would look at how it was lit, what camera angles were used, the cuts, the sound – anything but the bigger picture. Anna's notes were like that – even a trip somewhere, a museum, say, she'd not enjoy the exhibits, not soak up the history. She'd be too busy collating, or reading someone else's notes about what she was supposed to be seeing to see the bloody thing herself.

The last entry was marked with an elastic band. Anna thumbed back a few pages. Before she'd entered Mr Wajerski's house, she'd noted the markings on his door. She'd also copied down the swirly lettering across the landing, on Mrs Jarmal's door. Strangely, she'd never written anything about the medals he'd shown her. She put the notebook in her bag, and resecured her locker. Police stations were renowned for light-fingered borrowers. Like the little people who lived behind the skirting board, unseen hands would carry off handcuffs, batons, cravats and waterproofs. You could leave a tenner lying on the floor, and it would be there at the end of your shift, but leave an item of police gear on the loose and you were asking for it. First winter of her service, someone had knocked her raincoat, left just the epaulettes with her numerals on the radiator.

Anna shoved her shoulder against the locker door. It was buckled where it had been forced by a previous occupant, but would still lock with a good dunt. Sergeant's stripes shining through the latticed fretwork – her tunic hanging pristine. She missed wearing it. Strathclyde was one of the last forces to retain them, for ceremonial duties. Like haircuts and body piercings, Anna thought it a sad decline in standards. You could hardly stand proud in a woolly pully.

The rest of the Flexi Squad were out – hopefully doing warrants as instructed. She went to the pinboard where the detail was, saw Derek and Alex had put themselves down for 'observations on shoplifters'. How was she supposed to get her returns done if they persisted in disobeying orders? Warrants and citations: quick, simple, tick the box, increase the numbers. Waste of time watching shoplifters – too much effort for little result. Rankin liked ticks and percentages, and he didn't seem to bother his backside what they were for. Devolved responsibilities meant budgets and balancing books.

That Jenny had asked if she could get away early. No reason, no apology, just a straight demand. First time they'd spoken since the pay-off; a subject Anna had decided to avoid. She'd been late for a meeting, said she would get back to Jenny, but it had completely slipped her mind. She wanted to ask her about Mr Wajerski too. Better try and find her now. She went through to the main office. Jenny was heading the other way. In her coat.

'Off somewhere nice?'

Jenny looked tired. 'Look, Sergeant, I'm sorry, but I did ask this morning if I could leave early.'

'Yes, Jenny. And I did say this morning that I would get back to you.'

'With respect, Sergeant, it's now half an hour before finishing time.'

Anna was also tired. 'Just go, Jenny. Perhaps tomorrow we can look at rearranging the entire force's shift pattern to fit in with your social life.'

Good opener for a bit of jousting, but Jenny wasn't wanting to play. Just walked out of the door, running as she reached the stairs. Anna went back to her office, closed the door. Tomorrow. She would deal with Jenny tomorrow. Definitely. Shuffled some folders on her desk. Multiplying like germs – she could almost see them divide and grow. If she'd wanted to sit behind a desk all day, ticking boxes, she'd have been a bloody teacher.

Anna needed a good walk and some fresh air. Ashley Street would be cordoned off, but she could still maybe sneak a look at the locus. Not that she wanted to tramp on CID's baby. No way. Everyone thought CID was some kind of promotion, an elite of egg-headed experts. Glory hunters, that's all they were. No, she just wanted to go there. Stand at the foot of Ezra's stairs and say she was sorry. It pissed her off that Jenny had been the one to find him. Made her jealous actually, and how sick was that?

She wanted to look at the door again too. Cruikshanks thought this was a housebreaking gone pear-shaped. Was he even considering that whoever painted the swastika had returned with a more pointed message? She put her phone through to the main office, pulled on her gloves and jacket.

White smoke-breath puffed in time with her paces, growing denser as she climbed the hill at Buccleuch Street. One of Glasgow's plum-duff drumlins, this was not the most direct route to the West End, but it avoided passing the noise of the motorway. She loved it too, being high above the city. Here, as she was labouring upwards, peching like a bellows, Anna could imagine Glasgow growing, bleeding over hills and glens. Could feel the swell of triumphant earth beneath her feet, rising up from the flat and forcing pavements to curve and tenements to stack down an extra layer at the back. One of her favourite pictures was an etching in the Mitchell Library. It showed a bucolic view of eighteenth-century Glasgow, from the west of Blythswood Square, with reams of cropping fields stretched way past Gilmorehill, where the uni was now. Seeds that were there still, cased in concrete, feeding the soil.

Over Charing Cross she went, past a gun shop and a Mediterranean Café offering falafel and couscous, and into Woodlands, with its ethnic grocers and second-hand furniture shops on one side and its spread of parkland on the other. She stopped near the top, outside Michelle's place. If it had been the other kind of fish shop, he could've called it that – Michelle's Plaice.

A woman with a buggy was struggling out of the close next to the shop. Anna held the door for her.

'Oh, cheers.' The woman manoeuvred out backwards, tipping the pram on its back two wheels. 'These things are a bugger . . . oh, shit.' A bunch of orange chrysanthemums slithered off the hood and dropped to the ground.

Anna picked them up. 'Here you go.'

'Thanks.' The woman's mouth curled up in the semblance of a smile, but her eyelids were puffy, and scarlet-rimmed. Anna knew her face from somewhere.

'Doddy,' gurgled the baby, pointing at Anna.

'No, Eilidh, that's a lady. Sorry.' The woman shook her head. 'She thinks everything's a doggy at the moment.'

It was the baby's name that clicked. 'Sorry, it's Cath, isn't it? Cath Forbes?'

The woman frowned. 'Yes . . . Well . . . Worth actually.'

She held out her hand. 'Anna Cameron. We spoke on the phone? I was the year ahead of you at Tulliallan.'

'So you were. You're working with Jamie at the moment, aren't you? My husband.' Cath shook Anna's hand. Damn near crushed it with her grip.

'Yeah, for my sins.'

She waited for Cath to say something.

'Keeping him in line, are you?'

'More like the other way round. He's been really good – they all have. Helping me settle in and that.'

Cath said nothing, one hand gently shoogling the pram. Then her lip began to quiver.

'Hey – are you okay?'

'Hmm, fine. Bit of a cold, that's all.'

'So, what you up to?' said Anna.

'Oh, this and that, you know. Up visiting my sister.' Cath nodded back to the close. 'She's become a West End trendy.'

'Och, that's right.'

'You know her?' Cath asked sharply.

'No, Jamie told me. We were up here, on patrol.'

'Right.'

'Still, West End, eh? Always say you can't beat the South Side.'

'Yeah? We're out that way too. Well, the outskirts. Wee village near East Kilbride. Though you probably know that.'

'No, no. Sounds nice. I'm Shawlands, me. Well, Battlefield actually. Just at the bottom of the hill?'

There was a pause.

'Well, I'd better be getting on.'

'Yeah, this one'll be needing fed.'

Anna bent to look at the baby for the first time. 'Oh, she's . . . lovely,' she said, the way women are supposed to. The child stared back, dark, deep eyes like her father, but with her mother's unkempt hair. 'Lots of curls.'

'Well – I . . . I really need to go,' said Cath, swallowing hard. 'Nice meeting you.'

'You too – we should go for coffee some time, catch up.'

Why the hell had she said that? Anna's head was mince – too

much going on to take this all in. This frizzy lump with Cath Forbes' face. Wheeling her triumph before her.

'Yeah, that'd be great.'

'Okay. Great. Bye, Ally.' Anna flapped her hand in a baby wave.

'*Ae-lee.*'

'Sorry, yeah. Bye.'

Tropics Ya Dancer had changed its window display. A papier-mâché whale jaw gaped across the window, while scuba-diving Action Men pirouetted on fish hooks from the fake teeth. Apart from their face masks and strapped-on knife belts, the dolls were naked. Anna went inside, her hand still tingling as she pushed the door. God, Cath'd got so fat, Anna had hardly known her. A large, thickset man stood behind the till, his hair shorn into the wood. He wore a khaki T-shirt. Daddy Action Man – he had to be the giver.

'Aye?' Two massive arms shuddered on the counter. Anna was expecting a lisping mince; this guy sounded like a klaxon.

'Oh, hi. Is Michelle in?'

He shouted through the back. 'Haw, Michael. Get your arse out here. Some *wumman* tae see you.'

'I've telt you no tae call Colin that,' came a reedy voice. 'It's no his fault . . . oh, hiya, Maddie.' Michelle swept in, the curtain jingling like earrings.

'Maddie?'

'Aye. I've decided you look like Madonna. In her Eva Peron *oeuvre*. D'you no think so, Choo-Choo?'

'I've fucking telt you – call me that again and I'll have you.'

'Andrew, meet my new pal Anna. She's a polis wumman, so she is.' As he said this, Michelle reached up to tap his hand against the man's cheek.

The man's demeanour altered. Head down, shrinking in his girth like he was letting out air. 'Right, well, if that's you, I'll away then. Eh. Cheerio.' He edged past Anna and went outside.

'Grrr. Ya big mongrel!' Michelle screwed his face up at the window. 'All bark and nae bite, that yin. You can see why I'm all for the runts of the litter, can't you?'

'What d'you mean?'

Michelle smoothed the collar on his overall. Its tiny crystal droplets were twisted together on the left-hand lapel, and he rubbed them gently to separate them. 'Him – that's my big brother. One that wanted tae kill your cat.'

Mismatch of the gene pool there. Too bad if the mum had wanted a boy and a girl, 'cause she'd ended up with neither.

'Talking of killing,' said Anna, casual as you like, 'did you hear about the old man in Ashley Street?'

He gave a dramatic shimmy. 'Aye, pure terrible, so it is. Hope you guys get the bastard that done it.'

'Did you know him at all, Michelle?'

'Naw. Seen him about a few times, feeding the pigeons and that.'

'What about his neighbour – Mrs Jarmal?'

'Mrs Who?'

'An Asian lady, lived across the close.'

'Och, a Paki? There's hundreds of them round here. My brother reckons—'

Anna wasn't sure if he was winding her up. 'That's not very PC of you, Michelle. I thought you'd be a "live and let live" kind of guy.'

'Ooh, hark at thee. You're just narrow-minded, that's what you are.'

'How?'

'Presuming poofs havny got prejudices. Typical polis bigotty bastard.' He winked at her.

'But I am kind to animals,' said Anna. 'How's my pussy then?'

'Hold on and you can ask her yourself. Oh, Alice. Alicey Wallisey Long-legs. Mammy's here.' Michelle fetched the fish tank Alice lived in. Alice was cleaning her bum.

'Does she ever get out?'

'*Aye.*' Michelle sounded shocked. 'There's nae lid on it. She *likes* it. Watch this. Hoopla. Hup now, girl.' He took some fish food in his fingers, wafted it under the kitten's nose. Then he moved his hand away so she followed it. Rapped the outside of the tank with his other hand. The kitten crouched on her haunches, trembling, eyes bugging black. Then she leapt, higher than the length of herself, flying up the side of the tank and scrabbling on the rim. For a second she balanced there, head out, tail in. Wobbled, pushed with her back legs and launched herself at Michelle's hand.

'Oohya – you wee bitch. Look at that – drew blood so she did. Bad Alice. Bad.' He put her on the counter, wagging a finger reproachfully. 'You've hurt your finger? Puir wee man! Your pinkie? Dearie me!'

Anna finished the rhyme for him. 'Noo, juist you haud it that way till I get my specs and see!'

Michelle whooped. 'A lady of hidden talents, that's what you are. Beneath that cool exterior . . .' He drew his hand across his brow, then blew on it, as if it was burning.

Anna ignored him. She was running fingers like demented ants in front of Alice. The kitten's eyes whirled wildly in their sockets trying to keep up. Then Alice jumped again, landed on Anna's hand. The back legs dug their claws in, while the front paws grabbed tight. Anna tensed herself for the bite, but instead Alice started purring, licking fingers with minute pink flicks.

'When can I take her home?'

'Another week, doll. She canny leave her mammy till she's six weeks. You can have visiting rights though – if you're good.'

'You know, Michelle –'

'Gonny call me Shelly, doll.'

'Okay. Shelly, I'm sure your window display contravenes some indecency law.'

'Indecency? Indecency? What are you like? Now, if you want indecency, there's this pal of mine's—'

Anna raised a hand. 'Don't want to know. Anyway, that's me

had my Alice fix. And, if you hear anything about Mr Wajerski, let me know, will you?'

'Oh, you fag-hag – you'll be wanting tae take down my particulars next.'

'You just keep your particulars all tucked away, and we'll get along fine.' Anna blew the kitten a kiss. 'Mummy'll see you soon, gorgeous girl.'

'Oooh. If they could see you now.'

'Piss off.'

Cath carved the buggy through pedestrians and parked cars, down to Charing Cross. She could get the bus at Sauchiehall Street. Jamie always took the car to work, where it sat all day in a car park. He could've got the bus the odd day, surely, leaving her and Eilidh some means of transport that didn't involve apologising to folk every time you ran over their feet or hit their head with the changing bag.

So. That was serendipity then. *Just* the person she wanted to meet. And so tired, and lined and careworn. Not. In Anna Cameron's case, it was bloody true – she hadn't changed a bit. Tall and slim, confident that she and the world were ever at one. Hair skimming her neck in a butterscotch cuff. Nah, make that beige. Bad enough bumping into her any time, let alone today, when Cath felt even worse than usual. Her reflection blinked at her from a plate-glass window. Actually, it looked embarrassed to be seen out with her. Leggings: puckered. T-shirt: stained. Hair: horrific. Bags: five, two under each eye and one polythene, which had held the flowers and now had a dirty nappy wrapped inside. Cath chucked it in the mock Victorian bin nearby, and started to cry.

That poor old soul. Poor, lovely old Ezra. When Jamie mentioned this morning that he'd died, *how* he'd died, Cath wept till it hurt, moving Jamie to turn up the telly and mutter, 'For God's sake, Cath, you hardly knew him.' But she *did* know him – knew him more than all those nutters sobbing for

Princess Di knew *her*. After Tulliallan, Cath was sent to Cranstonhill. Now, that really was serendipity. Same division as Jamie, but different office. This whole area had been her beat – Ashley Street and Great Western Road and Park Circus – all of Seven Section sometimes, if they were really busy. One night she'd been getting hassle off a bunch of students intent on taking a set of temporary traffic lights home with them. Then one of them decided it might be a right laugh to knock her hat too. All of a sudden this majestic, dapper old man strode out from the shadows, brandishing a trilby in one hand and a walking stick in the other, razoring Elvish words down on them like Gandalf on acid. Once he'd got them to leg it, he'd offered her coffee. Too late, she'd realised there was a generous swig of voddie in there too. After that, Ezra's place had been a regular doss, offering a wee respite from plodding the streets. She'd nagged him to get Social Services in, or meals on wheels at least. She'd even spoken to the local council about some kind of grant to do the place up. But Ezra would have none of it. He had all he needed, he'd say, with a gracious wave of his long, thin hands. Judging by his flat, he needed very little – even when it came to the company of others.

Ezra was all alone – no family, on that he was firm – and he rarely spoke of friends, though he ate often at the Polish Club. In fact, it was his idea Cath and Jamie should hold their engagement party there. Once the gaffers found out she and Jamie were 'in a relationship', they moved Cath to E Division instead. Cath hadn't minded; one of her best pals worked there, and anyway it was better than the olden days, when policewomen got bumped off the street soon as they were engaged, and were required to resign if they got married. When Cath left the division, though, she and Ezra lost touch, his elegant face replaced by many other old souls ekeing out an existence off the London Road instead. But that didn't mean she wasn't allowed to feel sorrow at his death.

She felt something else too: a wistfulness for the past, when all things were simple and just within reach. So she'd gone to lay flowers, thinking there would be a cluster of them. There always was, nowadays – cellophane cones, with crinkly ribbon, littering pavements and roadsides. Then Anna Cameron had shimmied into view, and near given her a heart attack.

Of course, Cath had known her right away; she'd just kept her head down and hoped Anna wouldn't recognise her – not in this state, with soggy eyes and Lycra leggings on an arse the size of a bus. But no, SuperAnna had to come to the rescue of a damsel in distress. Why could she not have just let the door crash into the buggy like every other bugger would? Cath couldn't have changed that much either, mind, if Anna recognised her. That thought cheered her up. A little. They'd chatted a couple of times in the college canteen, just after Cath started her course. As Cath and Jamie got more involved, he'd explained Anna was being difficult about them splitting up. He didn't want Cath to get a hard time, so he'd insisted they kept their relationship quiet. Cath wondered if Anna was still difficult. Her hair was lovely though. Like polished caramel. Cath had been dragging her hair back in a ponytail since Eilidh was born. Thick, black and frizzy, it was a big hairy hassle, and some days, she got the urge to shave it all off – she did, after all, have an Alien baby devouring her.

At the bottom of Sauchiehall Street, just before the turn for the Art School, was one of Cath's favourite buildings: an Egyptian warehouse designed by Greek Thomson. Thomson's churches and houses were dotted across the city, but few tourists came to view them. What they came to Glasgow for was Mackintosh, and the Art School was the genuine Rennie, its elegant lines rising up behind shops and offices, hinting at the splendid whole. It was worth the climb just to reach its Nouveau portals. Meanwhile, rather than being lauded as another, more sedate part of *smart, successful Scotland*'s architectural heritage, the older Thomson building at its feet was given over to a hairdresser's and an ice-cream shop.

'Doddy,' said Eilidh, pointing at the giant plastic cone in front
of her.

'You want a strawberry doddy or a vanilla doddy?'

'Doddy.'

'If Mummy gets you a doddy will you be a good girl? Mummy
wants to get a doddy too. A hair-doddy.'

Cath never spent anything on herself. She deserved a treat.
Jamie would love it. She'd feel great. He'd just done a load of
overtime because they were skint. Nearly a week's shopping.
They agreed she should stop work. She could've been a sergeant – she got her tickets, before Jamie did too. Could be Anna
Cameron – sharp, sussed oracle who wore nothing but neutrals
and would never smell of milk.

'C'mon, Eilidh, let's both get a doddy.'

Blue and white tape strung like gala ribbons at Ashley Street, a
uniform on the door. Anna thought they'd all have been away by
now. It was the young Chinese boy, on his own again.

'Hi, Billy. Sentry duty, is it?' said Anna.

'Yes, Sergeant. I think they're just clearing up now.'

'Is it okay to go up?'

'Sure. Need to put you on the log, though.'

The tenement had been scraped and scarified. A guy in white
overalls was rolling some matting down the close stairs. Anna
skirted the edge.

'Okay to walk here?'

'Aye, you're fine, hen. We're just heading.'

The door to Mr Wajerski's flat was boarded shut, two taped
crosses for emphasis. Anna didn't want to see inside; it had been
desolate enough the first time. Beneath the fresh paint a darker
cross was still visible, with flicks like feet or razors. She had come
to check the Jarmals' place. It too was locked and silent, though
she listened through the letterbox just to be sure. As she straightened, she realised the card with the ornate curlicues had gone.
The door belonged to no one.

What did they used to talk about, these neighbours? The old Polish airman and the young Asian mum. Anna ran her hands along the cold plaster wall. What had this building seen and heard, in the hundred years it had stood there? The advent of inside toilets, the chatter of children playing ring bang skoosh. The gabble of foreign voices – Gaelic and Italian and Urdu; the dinging of trams; the courting of lovers. The blood of an old man, quietly trickling away. All he'd wanted was a room and a table and Polish bread once in a while. White dust spilled from her fingers – shit – she'd gouged a line with her nails. Fucking shit. Fucking fucking shit. How dare they come and kick his head in. How dare they mock his dying body. How dare they feel the urge that rose within her now – to kick fucking fuck out their fucking heads, until the bone was shrapnel that pierced their brains. Why did people want to do that?

On her way out, Anna spoke to Billy. 'Mind you were going back to the Jarmals' when the wee boy got home. What happened?'

'There was nobody in. I went back several times, Sergeant, honestly, but it was always empty.'

'No, I'm not suggesting you didn't. It's just odd, that's all. The lady – what age was she? Who else was in the house?'

'Em – early thirties maybe? And there was an old lady, and a baby and a wee tiny boy.'

'So what age was the other one?'

'Don't know. She just held her hand up, about this high,' he pointed to his chest, 'and said "Boy will speak, boy will speak." Then she pointed at the clock, to four o'clock, you know. I guessed what she meant.'

'Okay. Thanks, Billy. How long you stuck here for?'

He shrugged.

'Have you'd a break yet? It's nearly the end of early shift.'

'We are very short.'

'Yeah, but even so.'

'Please, Sergeant. I'm fine.' He looked embarrassed. So he

should. Last time he'd seen her, she was half-cut and had bubbles coming out of her nose.

Definitely home time. She'd just pop into Cranstonhill office first; she thought there was an Asian ethnic liaison officer there. When she'd been at headquarters, there were two guys who specialised in the Chinese – more from the Triad point of view than community relations, she reckoned. They'd taken her for a 'proper' Chinese meal one night, and terrorised her with battered chickens' feet that moved when you pulled a tendon.

'Right, Billy, I'll see you later . . .' Anna paused, catching a flash of orange, bristling from the gutter. Propped against a nearby lamppost was a bunch of chrysanthemums.

'Billy, who brought these? They weren't here when I came in.'

He shook his head. 'I don't know, Sergeant – I was only watching the door. I'm sorry, should I have—'

'No, no, it's fine, Billy.' She bent to see if there was a card attached. Nothing but a 50 per cent extra free sticker on the cellophane. 'Doesn't matter.'

It was time to go back. Anna walked up Lynedoch Street, along the beautiful terraces at Claremont and Woodside, and down towards Anderston. Along Kent Road, she passed an old brick building. It was closed up, two big doors like a warehouse, with a smaller one set into it. Soon as she passed, Anna remembered someone telling her there was a temple in Kent Road. She didn't know what culture or religion the temple served, but the writing above the door of this building was the same style as the stuff on Mrs Jarmal's door. She went back, knocked on the door for several minutes, then took a postcard from inside her notebook. She scribbled her name and phone number, to 'whom it may concern', asking the occupants of the building to phone her, or to get a Mrs Jarmal of Ashley Street to call. Anna hesitated before adding her personal mobile number. There was no letterbox, so she slipped the card underneath the door. Twanged the elastic band back round her notebook and put it in her bag.

The action caused her to think again. If Mrs Jarmal didn't

speak any English, it was a fair bet she wouldn't read any either. There was something else she could write. Anna once more took out her notebook, pulled another postcard from it, and carefully copied out the markings that had been on the Jarmals' door. Slid it under to join the first card.

7 Heroine

Chill, late autumn in the city. No russet hedges and sepia-tinged trees; simply varying bands of grey upon grey. The weather suited her mood. Anna was working late. All this week, day and night would merge in a twilight of sleep eat work eat sleep. Rankin had found a meagre amount for overtime, in the cheap little biscuit tin he kept under his desk, and he was now insisting the Flexi Squad use it. At the same time Anna was brushing her teeth for bed last night, the same day she'd visited Ashley Street, another prostitute was being attacked. This time, the man had used a broken bottle, jagging it viciously into the girl's cheek. Two night-shift cops had found it lying by her. Not a whole bottle. Just the base, shattered in such a way that one scalpel point could be used as a pencil, leaving not the usual ragged gouge, but a single, fine stroke from eye socket to the square of her jaw. No prints on the bottle, no witnesses to the assault. No comment from the girl, who reckoned she'd tripped and fallen. Rankin seemed to think it was Anna's fault. Why were the Flexi Squad not providing a reassuring presence – as well as jailing the girls, of course? Dual-purpose policing: protecting and prosecuting. Talk about Best Value. Anna had tried to explain about needing extra men.

'Show me some results, dear,' puffed Rankin, 'then I'll look at extra resources. In the meantime, two of your mob can do twelve-hour backshifts for the next five nights. I *think* my budget will stretch to that.'

So, Anna and Jamie were on patrol till midnight. They'd

already processed a young redhead caught *in flagrante* with a sailor. There was a Royal Navy frigate visiting Glasgow that weekend, so they were expecting a few turns. Sure enough, there was a woman in her forties emerging from a back court, hugging a shell-shocked boy. His mates waiting for him, giving him a cheer. Oblivious to Jamie and Anna, the woman shouted, 'Right, lads. Who's next for shaving?'

'All right, Lily?' interrupted Jamie.

'Oh, for the love of God. No yous lot.'

'Afraid there'll be no more sailors plundering you the night, Lily.'

Anna pretended to walk towards the group of boys, who swiftly disappeared.

'Now, look, son,' remonstrated Lily. 'If yous can just give me half an hour, I'll have enough to pay my fine and get my messages the morrow. I mean, it's a bloody goldmine here the night.'

'No can do, Lily. You know the rules. Should've seen us coming instead of advertising your wares.'

'Bastards.' She stood compliant, waiting for the van to arrive. Then she tried a different tack. 'You know, times are hard for girls like me, son. It's no the same any more, all they junkies coming in and mucking the place up.'

Nobody made these women do it. Anna clocked the woman's greying perm, her big, square glasses. Looked like somebody's mum.

'Well, maybe it's about time you hung up your garter, Lily.'

'Aye, well, that'll no feed the weans, will it?'

'Neither will a dead mother. Have you not heard there's some bunkernut out there? One lassie got a doing just last night.'

'Aye. Only those and such as those, dear.'

'What d'you mean?'

'Och, I mind my own business, hen. But, I'm telling you – it's just no the same here any more.'

Anna nudged the woman's arm, all pals together. 'C'mon, Lily, what are you telling us?'

'I'm telling yous lot fuck all.' She moved away from Anna, linked her arm through Jamie's as the van trundled up. 'C'mon then, son, that's the bus here.'

There was a queue at the back bar when they brought Lily in: couple of breaches, a housebreaker, then it was their turn.

'Anna, glad you're back,' said the OD. 'See that hoor you brought in—'

''Scuse me – d'you mind?' interjected Lily.

'Sorry, madam. See thon erotic creature of the night – the ginger one – she's causing Betty no end of grief. You're going to have to strip search her.'

The female cells were on the top floor. Betty, the female turnkey, had her kitchen just outside the cell passageway. She clipped out at the clank of the lift. Poker-straight black hair and hand-crafted eyebrows in permanent shock. Straight lines across her brow, straight lines across her mouth. Three gold Creoles in each ear, arranged in order of size, mirroring the bags beneath her eyes. If you turned her upside down, her expression would stay the same. Grimy purple talons opened the first gate.

'Och, Sergeant, see that wee redhead – she's a pure bind. Keeps setting off the smoke alarm, so she does.'

'Right, Betty. Let's get this one away and I'll sort it out.'

Lily waved from behind Anna.

'Oh, it's yourself, Lily. How you doing?'

Lily took off her shoes and jacket, handed them to Betty. 'No bad. Where d'you want me?'

'Number four's free.'

'Is Jean Wilson still here?'

'Aye.'

'Can I no go in with her then?'

'No, hen, you know the rules: either one or three tae a cell. Maybe later if we get busy. Away up and get yourself a blanket and mattress, you know where they are. Mind, don't touch the pile in the corner. That last alky had fleas on her, I'm sure. Bloody clawing myself for hours.'

Betty led Lily into the cell and locked the door behind. 'If you need any bog roll, just gie's a shout. Right, Sergeant,' walking briskly down the passageway, 'she's a pure wick, this one. Haw, you' – Betty banged on the green studded iron – 'that's the boss in tae see you now.'

'Big fucking wows,' slurred the occupant.

Betty dropped down the hatch, checked where the female was, then unlocked the door. The girl was spread-eagled on her mattress, staring at the ceiling.

'Twice, Sergeant. Twice I've tae come in here and find her smoking dowts.' Betty folded her arms.

'What's your name again?' asked Anna.

'Nooch.'

'Nooch – no, what's your right name?'

'Antonia Iannucci, so she is,' said Betty, handing Anna some surgical gloves.

'Should've been a film star, eh?' The girl pointed her filthy toes, smudges of black and blue indenting where the muscle tautened.

'So, where you from, Antonia? Have I not seen you someplace before?'

'Nah. I'm based in London, me.'

Anna checked her notebook. 'You gave us an address in Barrington Drive.'

'Aye. Just up on business, like. And tae see the folks.'

'Okay, Antonia. Stand up.'

Anna snapped on the gloves, her hands shades behind the creamy thin rubber, bulging on the knuckle bend. The insides of the gloves were powdery, little clouds puffing hints of clinic up her sleeves. 'We're going to have to strip search you. Take it you've been searched before?'

'Aw, no way, man. Look, I'm sorry. I've nae more smokes left – Brownie's honour.'

'You've been pissing off my turnkey. Get up.'

The girl screwed up her eyes. 'Gonny no, miss, please.' She lowered her voice. 'It's my bad week.'

'Doesny stop you hooring it though, does it? Now stand up.'

'Fuck off.' The girl lay back.

Some of the bruises on her legs and arms were inflamed and weeping. Anna walked to where Iannucci lay and brought her foot down on one of the abscesses, grinding her heel in the soft livid sponge. The girl's scream tore through her, and immediately Anna regretted doing it. She'd thought the girl was drifting further from feeling than that.

'Right, Antonia. All right, we heard you. Now – up.' Anna offered her a hand.

The girl got to her knees, rose unsteadily.

'We'll do it in stages, okay? Preserve your dignity.'

She didn't mean it to sound so snidey. 'Top first.' She handed the T-shirt to Betty. 'Check the seams for matches, Betty.' Anna took the lilac bra, ran thumb and finger across the frill. 'You any sharps?' she asked.

'Naw – don't think so.'

'I'm not fucking joking. If I jag myself on anything – you'll be fucking praying it was just your abscesses I was bursting.'

'Naw, honest. I'm clean, man.'

Antonia lifted up her breasts, to show nothing was taped to the underside. Anna checked through her hair, behind her ears. She gave the girl back her bra and top, waited until she'd put them on.

'Between your toes – hold them open. Fine. Right. Bottom half now. Take off your skirt.'

The girl unzipped her skirt, shook it out. 'See?'

'Betty, check that, would you? Right, Antonia, scants off.'

Anna's stomach lurched. The girl was wearing children's pants, decked with flowers and Winnie the Pooh. 'No, right down. That's it.'

Antonia bent forward, lowering her pants past her knees. Lining the gusset was a wad of screwed-up toilet paper, black with old blood. Anna recoiled. 'Jeezo – Betty, got any Tampax?'

'Aye. Hold on.' Betty scampered towards the kitchen. 'What d'you prefer, hen? Tampax or towels?'

'Doesny matter.'

This was always the worst bit, even with crotches that were clean. Anna went round the back of the prisoner. She turned her head to the side, took a deep breath. 'Now, Antonia, I'm not going to touch you . . .'

Antonia spoke more rapidly and lucidly than Anna had heard from her all night. 'Fucking right you're no – I know my rights. Yous've got tae get a doctor before anything goes up my crack.'

'. . . but I need you to open your legs a bit more. Bend further forwards, that's it.'

The girl's arse was nearly in her face. Track marks right up to her groin, and there was something hanging out. A small white string.

'You got a tampon in already?'

'Naw, I . . .' Antonia's voice was muffled.

Anna stood up. 'Right, Antonia, pull it out.'

'It's stitches, miss. I canny,' she whined.

'Fucking pull it out. Now.' Anna walked round so she was standing in front of Antonia.

The girl straightened her back and thrust her hips forward, one hand holding her labia apart, whilst the other hooked inside. The stink was rank: menstrual blood, a smorgasbord of semen and rotting, rotting – tobacco. Antonia drew out a small polythene bag. She untied the string with jittering fingers, and dropped the contents into her own hand. Two nipped fags and half a dozen matches.

'Fucking great job you dykes've got.' Antonia was crying. 'Own private peep show – turn you on, did it?'

Betty returned with tissues. 'Here, you'll just have tae scrunch a wad of these up, hen. I've nae Tampax left.'

Anna carefully peeled off one of the gloves, held it by a single finger and thumb of her other, covered hand. Then she rummaged through her pocket, handed Antonia a tampon. 'Here you go. Fair exchange. Betty, get me a bin bag, will you? Well, it was nice meeting you, Antonia.' She left Betty to clear up.

Jamie was waiting downstairs. 'There's an old lady out the front. Claims she's the redhead's granny. She's in some state.'

'Did you speak to her?' Anna asked.

'No.' He grinned. 'Woman to woman, you know. Thought you could handle it better.'

'Cheers.' Anna opened the door from the bar to the public foyer. An old woman in a duffel coat, with what looked like a nightie underneath, was scrunched on a plastic chair.

'Excuse me, you here about Antonia?' Anna called.

The woman leapt from her seat, spilling the contents of the plastic mesh shopper lying on her knees. Anna helped her scoop up coins and coupons, handing her a brolly that had rolled beneath the seat.

The woman gripped Anna's wrist. 'Is my Antonia here? Is she? Two big polis came to the house, asking if she stayed with us. But I don't understand – they said she was a solicitor. My Antonia's no a lawyer, she works in a big shop in London . . .'

Anna helped her up to the seat. 'Mrs – Iannucci?'

The woman nodded.

'Mrs Iannucci, we do have an Antonia Iannucci here at the moment. She'll be getting out later on.'

'Well, I'll wait then.' Mrs Iannucci gripped her bag with a firmness her lips couldn't match.

'Might be a good few hours yet.'

'Oh, I can't leave Poppa that long – he's no well. What's she here for anyway?'

'I'd better let Antonia tell you that herself.'

'Look, dear, can I not just see her? Just for a wee minute.'

'Sorry, it's not allowed.'

'But I haven't seen her in months. Please,' she begged.

'You mean she's not staying with you? We can't release her if she doesn't have an address.'

Anna's brusque tones made the woman flustered. Another example of her inability to be all things to all people. Sometimes she said things as a joke, and nobody got it. Other times, like now, she would switch from kindly to harridan in an instant, and scare the shite out of someone who thought she was a nice wee lassie. 'Skinny Malinky Long Legs, wi big banana feet' – they'd even written a song about her.

Mrs Iannucci was teetering on tears. 'No, well, aye, of course she is. Any time she's here, of course she stays with me and Poppa. But she's no been in touch for ages – we were getting that worried about her. I didn't know she was back. Och, please let me see her, hen.'

'I can't.'

'Can you give her a wee note, then? From me?'

Anna relented. 'Okay.'

'Eh – have you a pen and paper, dear?'

Anna leaned against the wall while Mrs Iannucci scribbled.

'Is there any envelopes, pet?'

'Just fold it over. I'll not read it, I promise.'

'Tell her, mind. Tell her Poppa's not well, will you?'

'I'll make sure she gets the note,' said Anna. The paper was creased, once, twice, several times, screwed up in a childish package. Anna put it in her pocket. She would give it to Antonia later. They'd spent enough time farting about in the office. She opened the door to the street. Barren windows flat against the orange streetlamps, and Mrs Iannucci pulled her coat tight across her pigeon chest.

Anna checked her watch. It was 3 a.m. 'How did you get up here, Mrs Iannucci?'

'I got a taxi.'

'D'you want me to phone you one back then? It's a long way to Barrington Drive.'

'Eh, no, it's fine, dear.'

'It's no problem. And it's awful dark out there.'

'I . . . I came out without my purse.'

Old broken bodies smashed up by youth. Anna had had her fill of them. She couldn't cushion every delicate sinew against a fucked-up world, but she could get this old lady a lift.

'Wait there and I'll get one of the boys to run you.'

'Och, no, I'm fine.'

'Please. Take a seat.'

Jamie tapped his watch as Anna came through from the public foyer to the bar. 'C'mon, you. It'll soon be home time and we're missing all the action. It's like shooting fish in a barrel the night.'

Anna leaned towards the young policewoman behind the counter. 'Hi, could you possibly arrange a lift for . . .' She stopped. The girl had tears spilling from four corners. 'Hey, what's up?

'I've killed it,' the girl whispered.

'Killed what?'

'The police dog.'

'What police dog?'

'No one told me I was meant to feed it. I've been here four nights and I was meant to feed it. But the sergeant only told me to tonight. And when I went to check it – it was dead. At least, I think it's dead. I'm feart to go back and look.'

Anna felt a twinge of sympathy for the girl. Face starch white, the creases on her trousers ruler precise. Brand-new out the box, hair even bound in a hairnet. Just the shiny bawface to give her away. 'Show me.'

The policewoman led her out to the yard.

'This your first week?' asked Anna.

The girl nodded.

'Is it what you thought it would be?'

'Kind of – my dad's a cop.'

There was a small, fenced-off pen at the back of the yard, where they stored traffic cones, lost bikes and stray dogs. The policewoman took out a key and undid the padlock.

'In here?'

'Uh-huh.'

Part of the pen was covered over, and it was impossible to see anything inside. Anna flicked on her mini-Maglite. Lying on its back, all four legs pointing accusingly at its Maker, was a very stiff mongrel showing the whites of its eyes.

'It is dead, isn't it?' asked the girl.

Anna tried not to laugh. 'Few days now, by the looks of it.'

'Oh God.'

Anna switched off her torch. 'Tell me, did your dad never tell you about polis wind-ups?'

'Oh, yeah,' said the girl. 'There was this one time, he said, they got the probationer to go and count all the ducks in the park – said there'd been a theft. And another daftie they convinced was his job to get up a ladder and clean the traffic ligh— shit, I'm an idiot, amn't I?'

'Mmm-hmm. You ever seen a Heinz 57 varieties jumping out a dog handler's van?'

'Suppose not.' A bitter laugh. 'Bastards.'

'What's your name?'

'Sylvia.'

'Well, Sylvia. Up to you how you deal with this. You can stomp in there and complain to the gaffer . . .'

'It was him that told me I'd to feed it.'

'Or you can go out and round up the fiercest, slavering mutt you can lay your hands on.'

'Why?'

God, the girl was slow. They'd pick the meat from the bones with this one. 'So you can chuck our ex-dog in the incinerator, throw the angry live one in here, and tell them you think there's been a resurrection,' Anna explained. 'First one in to check gets his arse bitten off.'

Sylvia beamed at her. 'Cool.'

Back inside, Jamie was lying on the row of chairs in the public foyer, feet drooping over the end one. Mrs Iannucci wasn't there.

'Did anyone get her a lift?'

'Who?'

'The old lady.'

He sat up. 'Dunno. We heading or what?'

Ach well, she'd made the effort. Couldn't babysit every hoor's granny that came along.

Soon, they were back on the street, concealed in a yard behind some giant wheelie bins. A favourite place for the girls to bring clients, even though there had been an attack nearby. Last night's made it four now. Usually, the lassies looked out for one another, noted reggie numbers and passed them on if there was trouble, but this time nobody was telling the polis anything.

'What d'you think about these slashings then?' Anna asked. 'Rankin's doing my nut in to get a result, but they all seem so random. Different places, different times. Did you and Jenny go through their indexes like I asked – see if there's any links?'

A relic from days gone by, the files Derek had shown her when she started were now essential reading. The ten shoebox-sized metal drawers that sat one on top of the other in her office were each filled with a hundred or so handwritten index cards. Each card had a name, description, date of birth, details of arrests, home lives, children, associates, special warnings and anything that might be relevant. Some that weren't. Anna had noticed Elaine McGovern's card with *Looks like Jordan, but with bigger tits* scrawled on it in Alex's hand. She'd need to speak to him about that. Each year would see a new card clipped to the old. Some girls had sheaves of cards, others only one. All moved to the back of the drawer when the date of death was added.

'Of course we did. Jenny left a report on your desk. How, d'you think we dyke stuff you ask us to do?'

'No . . . I must have missed it. Give me a synopsis then.'

'Couple in their teens, couple in their twenties. Two of them are from Govanhill, but they're not listed as associates, one West Princes Street, one from Dennistoun. All junkies – no surprise there – all claim not to know each other. Jenny spoke to them individually—'

'I never told her to do that.'

'So? It's her job, Anna – she's a good cop, you know. Anyway, she reckons they're shit-scared.'

'Well, duh, they've all been chibbed.'

'No, like they're hiding something. Or protecting someone.'

'Stickman?'

'Doubt it. Two are self-employed and the other two work for separate guys.'

Anna sighed. 'Well, we're going to have to dredge up something quick – or Rankin'll burst a blood vessel.'

Jamie kicked at something on the ground. 'See wee Francine's been busy.'

'How?'

'Purple johnnies – getting to be her trademark.'

'Ach, that's disgusting.' Anna's torch beam illuminated the spent condom, oozing like a slug.

'I dunno – safe, fun and colourful. Just like a ride at the circus. Aye, purple sheaths and daft wee brooches – she's developing her own unique wee brand, is Francine. Had a big jewelled spider on her tits last time I jailed her.'

Francine. That girl Angela's wee sister, who was convinced Jack the Ripper was haunting the Drag. 'What's the script with her – she really not a juvey?'

Jamie snorted like a pig. 'Francine? Nah. Old as the hills, her. Sister, too – the lovely Angela.'

'We've met.'

Jamie laughed. 'Doll, isn't she? Still, Uncle Derek looks after her.'

'What do you mean?'

'Christ, chill, woman. Nothing untoward. She's been in care most of her life, has Angela. Guess Francine has too. I think they see him as a father figure. He's been looking out for them, that's all.'

Anna was getting cramp. She wriggled her foot, thigh brushing against Jamie. Decided not to adjust her position further. There wasn't much room, and it was getting chilly. Jamie's haunch was pressed against her, his profile – neat. Straight, clean lines, just like her kitchen. Black instead of Martin's strawberry blond, but she could live with that. Except she couldn't. Of course not. Black beside her blonde. What colour would that have made?

'So, how's life? How's Cath getting on?' she asked.

'Yeah, great. Doing great.' A tang of bitterness in his tone.

'She tell you I met her?'

'No. When?'

'Other day. I was at Michelle's to check out his pussy. The wee one's the spitting image of you.'

Black hair, brown eyes – they were always dominant. No, sometimes you got black hair, blue eyes. Or blond hair, brown eyes. Palomino children. Ghost babies.

'You think? Aye, well she's got my eyes maybe.' His voice grew softer in the dark. 'She *is* a wee doll though, isn't she? All those curls – I think she's more like her mum.' There was a pause. 'Greets all the time like her mum does too.'

'*Jamie.*'

'Och, I know, that's not fair. But it's true. I haven't heard Cath laugh in months, Anna. She just sits and cries and eats biscuits all day. Never wants to do anything, never goes out – then she goes and spends a fortune on a stupid haircut no bugger's going to see. Jesus. Explain women to me, Anna, will you?'

'Can't help you there, pal. I think you're asking me to explain wives.'

'Tell you, you had the right idea. Look after number one.' She could hear breath through his teeth.

'You okay? Got that out your system now?'

'Aye.'

She couldn't see his expression with the torch off.

'So, how you doing? Any news on the Polish guy?'

Anna moved her leg to get the blood flowing. 'Mr Wajerski? Apparently not. CID are convinced it's housebreakers, but I'm not so sure. Why would anyone break into a mouldy old close like that? There's an Asian family opposite gone to ground too. So scared they've left their house. I'm sure it's got something to do with the swastika – you know, National Front or something like that.'

'Oh aye, the West End's a hotbed for skinheads, so it is.'

'Nah, I'm not saying that, it's just – well, he had nothing to steal, for one thing. Unless someone else knew he had that money.'

'What money?'

'Oh, just some dosh for a wedding present he was going to buy.'

'That doesn't sound like Ezra nae-pals,' said Jamie.

'You knew him?'

'Not really – it was Cath knew him. She kind of adopted him when she used to work Seven Section. Bit of a loner, she reckoned.'

Now the flowers made sense.

She was going to ask more, until her PR interrupted. 'A Alpha to Alpha 51.'

'Go ahead.'

'Five One, would you note – DI Cruikshanks requests you call into Cranstonhill before going off duty. He'll be available until 0500 hours.'

'Did he say what it's regarding?'

'That's a negative.'

'Roger, noted.' Anna poked Jamie in the side. 'There you go – the Pieman's realised I'm indispensable.'

'So,' continued Jamie, 'I take it you're not adopting my box theory? I.E.: nothing to do with me, pal.'

'I just want to make sure they cover all the angles.'

She didn't need to justify herself to Jamie.

'So long as you're not taking it home with you.'

'Jamie, I don't make a habit of sobbing on folk's shoulders. Hormones and too much gin, that's my excuse for the other night.'

'Not a problem. I know you don't. I can deal with crying women – when there's a reason, you know? Fuck, you've got to let it out sometimes.'

The air was scented with opportunity. A chance to pare back layers to the shape they'd been. 'That RTA up at Charing Cross – I heard about it,' said Anna. 'Pretty shitty, eh? What age was the kid – three, four?'

'Four.'

'Bet it helps to have someone to talk to.'

She was aware of a gossamer wisp weaving between them. *Don't break it. Don't break it.*

'Not really my style, Anna.'

Weave me a net.

'Oh, God, I don't mean me. I mean Cath. You know, she's been there, seen it. Must make it easier.'

He blew on his hands. 'Och, she's enough on her plate.'

'How?'

'Like I said – the baby . . . stuff. I don't like to upset her. Set her off again, you know.'

'Oh.'

The most effective interview technique she knew was not to fill the gaps. To bite lips, chew pens, nod sagely – do anything other than engage in speech. In this awkward emptiness, fissures would splinter, slowly at first, across surface silences, gaining momentum, uniting tributaries of unease until chasms were wracked and pauses cracked.

His words, when they came, piled out one on top of the other, fighting to be first. 'Anna, I don't know what to do about Cath. I think she's losing the plot. She just cries all the time. Jeez, you thought *you* were bad about old Ezra? You'd think her mum and dad had been massacred when I told her. Went mental I hadn't let on sooner. As if I'd been keeping a secret or something. And when she's not greeting she's screaming at me and the baby. See if it wasn't for Eilidh . . . Anna, I can't even talk to Cath any more. It's like she doesn't want to know. You know, anything about me, about the job?' He sighed. 'Like it's a closed book and I've not to remind her. Then she goes ballistic at the daftest things: she got really pissed off when she heard a lassie she knew as a cop had gone back – as a civvie coms op. Ranted on like, God, I don't know. Like the lassie was a traitor. As if it was my fault. I can't take much more of it.'

'D'you think she's jealous?'

'How d'you mean?'

'Of you, of not being a cop?'

That's how Anna would feel, if she was Cath. Which she wasn't. Oh, God, how much longer were they going to hunker down here? Her leg was all pins and needles. She had to rub it, bumping against him. His jeans felt rough on the back of her knuckles. Don't move your leg . . . don't move your leg. If he didn't move his leg, it meant he still wanted her.

Jamie turned his face towards her. 'Anna.'

His mouth inches from hers. She could taste the memory of the press of it against her, prising open, shaping silent words on skin. Closed her eyes. Felt him touch her lightly in the small of her back, just above the base of her spine. The spine twining all the nerves that snake to the brain; main cable to hotwire your body. She waited.

'Anna, can you budge up a bit – I've cramp in my leg. Cheers.'

Maybe she just needed a pee, that burning sense of a thousand pinpricks between her legs. They crouched in the quiet, a channel of air between them now. So, Cath knew Ezra too. Well enough to come and leave a bunch of chrysanthemums outside his door. Anna had never thought of doing that. But it was such a passive thing, a futile gesture to say it with flowers. And say what exactly? Sorry I forgot about you? Sorry I wasn't there? Sorry the world's a shitehole? Anna could do better than that. She could sit on Cruikshanks's shoulder till he was sick of the sight of her, nudging him to follow what her instincts told her was right. Housebreakers my arse: that graffiti had been a warning. She just had to find some way of convincing Cruikshanks.

Out on the street, a taxi chuntered by, its diesel distinctive and thus ignored. Hoors rarely used taxis during business hours. Crackles burst from her waist, and Anna gladly turned the PR up louder. 'Urgent to all stations: reports of a violent disturbance. Bath at West Campbell.'

Just a street from where they were.

'Roger, Flexi Unit in attendance,' she shouted, clambering to her feet, instantly switching her body back on. 'ETA one minute.'

'Ah, Control to Flexi: believe it's another assault on a prostitute.'

'Shit.'

They thundered towards the locus, Anna in front. Clubbers lumbering in her path, her pushing past them. 'Police! Move! *Move* it.' Scanning left and right, searching for someone running faster than her. As she steamed into the lane, Anna glimpsed a slash of shadow flee from the far end. Saw a female cowering in a doorway, her hands at her cheek, which was spewing blood. Anna kept running. 'Jamie, stay with her,' she shouted. 'Get an ambulance.' Her shoe had worked loose at the heel, slapping against her with every stride. Cold city air slapping her lungs.

Deeper down the lane, towards a maze of broken warehouses. Could be anywhere. Anna stopped running, heart still thumping, bouncing off her ribcage. She tried to breathe softly, thought she heard a scuffling over to her left. Could be rats. Tried to whisper her location in her radio, but reception was crap. Softly as she could, she shifted some corrugated iron, made her way inside a derelict store. Tar black. As she edged along the side of the brick wall, her eyes made out shapes. Neck hairs singing. Someone was there, she could feel it. The dark too quiet, too still. One hand in front, groping out like Blind Man's Buff. The other hand inside her jacket, easing out her baton. Heart hammering still, until she knew that he would hear it.

Girl in the dark. On her own. Adrenaline doused, waiting for a light. A muted noise behind spun her around. Looming from dark, a darker shape, running towards the door. Anna lunging towards him, trying to block his way. Fleeting glance of a thin, pale face as she lashed out with her baton. The shape ducked and darted back from where he'd come.

Rasping in her throat, Anna chasing. Through the depot; a connecting warehouse, pools of grey light from broken windows. Brighter, not bright enough to show a treacherous stairwell. Reaching desperately into air, her foot caught the edge, she over-balanced. Down and down and her head was crashing and she could hear screaming bounce off stone stairs. As she hit the bottom, the screaming stopped, replaced by sounds of blood, swirling in her brain. Everything muffled, except her fear.

She quietened her panting. He was still here, had seen her falling. And she couldn't move, her ankle searing. The absence of light was suffocating. Desperately, Anna felt round, searching for her baton, her radio, something. Her hand made contact with a low curve. Solid, yet pliant. Ridged, rubbery . . . Nausea gripped her soul. It was a shoe. She whimpered even before it struck her, knew it was coming. Second time he kicked, she grabbed his foot, twisting it violently up. Heard him stumble, cursing. Then voices, another voice, shouting her name. 'Anna! Anna! Can you hear me?'

She wanted to sleep, give in to the drowsiness. Not in her body. She was not in her body, it would not move. Forced her voice out with every fibre. 'Down here,' she croaked. 'I'm down here.'

Footsteps, footsteps, then a torch in her face. Jamie. She tried to point where the man had gone.

'It's okay.' Jamie smoothed her hair. 'There's back-up coming. Are you all right?'

He frowned as he wiped some damp from her eyes. Was he angry with her? Then another face – pale, thin, one behind. Scribbled knuckles holding . . . holding . . .

'Jamie!' she yelled, blackness pouring like blood.

8 Nonna

It was Billy's first day out on his own. Unless you counted that sojourn on the door at Ashley Street. They'd insisted he looked at the body too – took him down to the mortuary specially, and it made him sick to his stomach. The old man's face had all swollen up, blueish round his mouth where the lips curled back. Still had his own teeth – thick yellow ones that ridged like tombstones. Snarling or screaming: Billy wasn't sure. Apparently, once the dicing and slicing was done, the mortician would massage the jaw, easing the skin back to something less feral.

Billy wasn't supposed to work alone yet, but there were two off sick with food poisoning, most likely alcohol-induced. Some of the younger guys had been up the dancing – a 999 special where you could get all the beer and nurses you'd ever want. Billy didn't drink, not like that. Why would you want to atrophy your liver so you could vomit and sing in public places? They called his type of face inscrutable, which was just as well. He checked again. Notebook, pencil, aide-mémoires. *If in doubt, son, do them for a breach.* That's what Sam had told him. Radio on. Definitely. He turned the knob, heard the click just to make sure, and switched it back on again. Felt a slither up his vertebrae.

Billy was glad he was on his own. The dour old bugger who'd been neighbouring him rarely spoke anyway, and always made him feel like he was in the way. In fact, the most Sam had ever said was that bit about a breach, when he dumped him here this morning, then: *Just keep the heid, son, and you'll be fine.*

And with that, he'd jumped back into the driver's seat, revved the engine and chugged away, leaving Billy to his destiny. A bit like chucking a kid in the river to see if it can swim. Well, Billy was an excellent swimmer.

'Alpha to 277.'

He jumped. That was his number. Scrabbled for his notebook. 'Eh, go ahead.'

'Anonymous reports of a disturbance at Barrington Drive – the close at number 70. Can you check it out?'

'Roger.' He wrote the number down quickly, in case he forgot.

'Thanks, Billy.'

A ridiculous rush of pleasure that the Controller had called him by his first name.

Barrington Drive was one of many sandstone terraces linking Woodlands Road to the teeming Great Western Road. Billy wasn't from Glasgow, and at first all the tenements had looked the same to him. Buff or grime coloured, four or five storeys high, they lined the city's streets north, south, east and west. He'd learned to look for the subtle differences: Art Nouveau tiles here, plain green wally ones there. Plaster or paint, pot plants or pee. Barrington Drive was a mixture of both. He could hear the shouting from Woodlands Road, quickened his step. An angry wee wumman was throwing tomatoes out a second-floor window, pelting a pure bloater of a man on the pavement below. She was screaming, 'You leave us alone. I no tell you again!'

The man yelled back, 'You owe me, Grandma!' When he saw Billy, he began to walk smartly in the other direction.

'Hi. Hi, you, just a minute.' Billy half ran after him.

For a moment, the man seemed to pick up speed, waddling like fury, then he stopped, turned round. 'What?'

'What's going on?' The vinyl notebook cover was sweaty in Billy's palm.

'Nothing.'

'Look at you – you're covered in tomatoes.' Silky pulp was sliding down the man's temple, glooping on to his shoulder. 'Just – just wait there a minute. Excuse me,' Billy called up at the window. It was shut. He faced the man. 'Eh, right. You'll need to come up with me while I speak to that woman.'

The man's arms curved slightly from his sides, a belligerent bullfrog. 'How? You jailing me or something?'

'No, no, I just need to find out what's been going on, that's all.'

The man eyeballed Billy, too direct. 'What's going on is that some daft old bint should be put in a home. Attacking folk in broad daylight. She should pay for my jacket – look. I've a good mind tae press charges . . .'

'So, she attacked you?' Billy opened his notebook again.

'Aye. Daft old cow. Away with the fairies, know? One of they care in the community ones, most like. Look, pal, I dinny want tae cause a fuss. Just leave it, eh?'

'Em – well, I'd better take your name, in case . . . em. Your name?'

'Aly,' said the man. 'Aly Bain.'

Billy began to scribble. 'Em . . .?'

'That's A . . . L . . . Y, B . . . A . . . I . . . N.'

'Address?'

'Oh, I'm just here for the day. Doing some shopping.'

'I'd better take it anyway.'

'Eh, 12 Simpson Street, Paisley.'

'D'you have any ID, Mr Bain?'

'What? This a polis state or something?'

'No, no. I'm sorry – em, just a minute. I should . . . 277 to Control.'

'Go ahead.'

He wanted to shout for help. Instead, he stalled for time. 'Can I have a wanted missing check please, Lynsey, on an Aly Bain? That's Alpha, Lima, em, Yellow, Bravo, Apple, I mean Alpha, India, November.'

Billy could see the man smirking.

'So, you don't know the lady at all, sir?'

Mr Bain looked pointedly at his watch, sighed and crossed his arms. 'Nope. And I've a train tae catch in ten minutes.'

'Well, I'm sure that's fine. I'll just go and have a word. Eh – I guess you can go. Sorry to have bothered you.'

'Nae bother.' All smiles, now he was on his way.

The close had shining green tiles on the ground floor, banded with cream rope twists. Billy pulled himself up by the banister, iron stud milestones brailling his sticky hands. He climbed to the top floor, scented with busy lizzies and peppery geraniums, and banged on the door with brass fittings and a nameplate for *Iannucci*. 'You have to open up. It's the police.'

Shuffling, clanking, then a garlic breeze escaped. An old, grey man peered from behind the chain.

'Excuse me, sir,' said Billy, 'I need to speak to the lady that was at the window.'

He could see past the old man into the kitchen, where spaghetti draped from a wooden pulley. The woman was standing at the cooker, stirring and muttering.

'Excuse me, madam,' he called. 'Can I have a word?'

She flung her spoon in the sink and stomped towards the door. 'What?'

'Can I come in?'

'Why?'

'It's about the tomatoes.'

'He made a complaint?'

'Well, no.'

'Huh. Didn't think he would.'

'Do you know him?'

Her husband answered. 'No, we don't. I think he was trying to sell us something. My wife, she doesn't like that.'

'Even so, madam, you can't go chucking things out of windows. It's – it's dangerous,' said Billy.

'Rocks, yes. Tomatoes, no. Look, son, my passata's ready – I have to go. Why don't you go and do something useful instead of harassing old ladies? I've enough to be worrying about. If you lot kept your promises . . .' She flapped back to the kitchen.

The old man smiled apologetically, shut the door.

The radio reminded Billy who he was.

'A277, re your wanted/missing: I'm still waiting for his date of birth.'

Billy turned up the volume. 'Ah, roger. Would you just cancel? No police involvement, advice given.'

'Wrong way round.'

'Pardon?'

'Advice given, no further police involvement.'

'Whatever.'

Anna woke on soft pillows, starched linen crackling on her poor, sore face. A strange female peering down at her. Familiar eyes. Green. Viscous. Not the angel of death. It was Catherine Worth.

'Anna. You all right?'

A hallucination. Not enough drugs – it was the husband she wanted, not the wife. Anna blinked. No, still there. 'Whas . . .?'

Cath hushing like a clucking hen. 'Ssh. Your mouth's all swollen where he kicked you. Nothing broken though. Concussion, I think. The doctor'll speak to you in a wee while.'

Anna raised her hand, tried to touch her head. Kidneys on fire, funny smell. Head still there. Bigger.

'The bastard got away, Anna,' sniffed Cath, 'you saved Jamie's life.' She squeezed Anna's throbbing fingers. Anna waited for it to be over. Cath sniffed some more. Sat back up, big arse on Anna's bed.

'Don't you remember? Jamie says you warned him, just before you blacked out. The guy tried to slam a brick or a boulder or something down on his head, but you saw it coming.'

'Aye, more than I did.' Jamie, behind his wife; sporting a bandage round his temple.

Cath took his hand, placed it on her shoulder. 'Look at him, the big numpty. But it's only a graze, because you warned him, and he turned round in time. Oh, Anna, thank you.'

Again with the touchy-feely. Anna's final thought as she closed her eyes was why wasn't it Jamie that was holding her hand? Then the colours drained, and she was left alone.

Pressure on her shoulder, pushing, pecking. Lots of noises, someone perpetually sniffing. *Get a hanky, for fucksake*. God knows what drugs they were giving her as she rushed at a million miles an hour through the ceiling above her bed, through the walls and down, always down to the warehouse, which was white now, with yowling, gurglings everywhere. Gulping, sniffing, padded walls that bulged out and kicked her, shapes of feet stretching through the white like moving shrouds. Sweaty dreams of feet and hands, tearing at her, limbs in pieces. Little bloodied legs, scattered on white, squirming and pulsing like the digits on her hand. An old man, sobbing, searching through the bits of bodies. Then he turned to her, a bundle of limbs drooping in his hands like flowers.

Screaming to get out just brought more medication, injected Lethewards through a drip, until she woke enough to wrench it out. Shaking, she'd begged them – no more drugs. Surely pain was better than this. Anna fixed tired eyes on the pale green walls of the ward, pretending it was home. Her bedroom was bare, like this, but minimal, not sparse. Wooden blinds, laminate floor, off-white walls. *Calico Wash*, the colour was. No family photos, just three pale prints of Japanese geishas, bamboo-framed cherry blossoms blown in from another place. What would they find if they searched her room for clues? If she'd not come back 'cause he'd kept on stamping on her head, this faceless figure that was there still? She could see a hood, some markings on his hand. Glint of eyeballs bulging, nothing more.

A DC had taken her statement this morning; brought in mug shots when she said she didn't know if she could identify her attacker. He and Anna had gone through pictures of all the stick-men down the Drag; little pimping bastards who fed off desperation, charging women for the protection of not being beaten up by other little bastards. The prostitute was no use – saw no one, knew nothing. The DC said she was back on the street almost as soon as they stitched her up, black fibres of thread protruding from her temple. He showed Anna a picture of her too. She took the photo from him, held it at a distance like it might bite.

'Know her? Name's Linda Morrison.'

Anna didn't recognise her. But, then, Linda's mother might not recognise her either. One side of her face, the right cheek, was a mass of crusted scabs, fanning as high as her brow. They swept out in a single butterfly wing, from a single, long gouge by her nose. The girl's right eye had swollen shut, punched purple and puce, and the skin on her left cheekbone was taut and drawn, reaching out helplessly to offer elasticity where there was none.

Anna laid the photo on her bed, to stop it from flapping. Touched her own still-tender cheekbone. They trawled through print-outs from the PNC, listing scars, tattoos, bits missing, pierced or dyed. She would recognise his hands, she was sure, their blue-grey patterns of stars or flags. If she saw them, she would know. But they'd not been in among these print-outs, nor in all the images of short squashed brows and dead-eyed faces the DC had brought.

Anna held her own hand before her face, hiding the vase of pungent lilies Martin had sent. Veins like snakes split over three bony stripes. Even when she rippled her fingers, the bone that led to the pinkie was invisible. One day, these hands would age. She would notice a thickening, then the skin would loosen slightly from the flesh. Darkened pigments would surface and spread in blotched pads. There might be a tremor to signify her hold was weakening. That her body now controlled her mind. That just because she wanted to, didn't mean she could. Her gait would alter, shrivel slightly to assume a more humble status, apologising for taking up too much room. When the plumpness of her skin seeped, so too would the confidence in her voice. She would learn to expect less, accept more. Be grateful for a tiny death in an unknown room. Not crumpled and begging in a body that used to win medals.

Anna's watch and phone were missing, no way of charting the

progress of the day. Mealtimes and toilet trips, ward rounds and visiting times were the hospital compass, and she slept through several of these interludes. The rest of the time, Anna employed the same device she used to avoid folk sitting beside her on the train: a grim set of the jaw jutting into disagreeableness, willing an aura of barbed wire. The inverse flaunting of *if you've got it.* So they left her alone: *she needed to rest*, they whispered gratefully; grapes and Lucozade and barley-sugar votives left on the empty locker. Payment for a good gawp. Bloody Catherine Worth came twice, and once Anna woke to find Jamie stroking her hand, except that was the same time that Patti Smith told her how to escape from the Daleks that were chasing her through a warehouse when they were all inside a giant egg and it might have been better if she'd had people to speak to because when it got dark inside her head the pain boomed like a beatbox, nudging her back down the stairs to where there was only the smell of rubber and urine and total, total fear. Prone in the dirt, having the shit kicked out of her head. Anna didn't jump back up and do her job and stop the bad man from getting away.

Anna wet her pants.

Christ, here came Catherine Worth again. Complete with baby and bags and a bunch of tulips. Why anyone would think that haulking a face like a disappointed lemon into hospital to cheer someone up would work, God only knew. Anna closed her eyes and tried to turn over, but the deadweight of her ankle made it difficult.

'Oh, good – you're awake.' Cath plonked down on the bed, Eilidh dangling like a monkey on her hip.

There was a permanent immense-arse indentation there, Anna was sure. The woman must have put on four stone since she last saw her. Did she not have anything better to do than eat cakes and visit the sick? There was something different about her though. Less frizzy.

'I've been a couple of times,' blabbered Cath, 'but you were out for the count. How you feeling now?'

'Okay.'

'C'mon, let's have a look at you.' Dear God, she was stroking Anna's hair. Then the baby's chubby hand reached out to join her mother's. A pang of milk and powder breezed through antiseptic air.

Anna froze, desperate to move away. Slowly, she rolled on to her back.

'Yeah, that's better. Och, the swelling's gone . . . hey, you sure you're okay?' Cath's voice was wet with concern.

What business was it of hers anyway? Had she just come to rub it in, how low Anna had sunk – being patronised and petted by the curly cow that stole her boyfriend? Fucking Mother Earth, with her fertile haunches and dripping tits, going home to wash the windows and bake a pie for Jamie. Fuck off, fuck off, fuck *off*.

'I'm fine, thanks.'

'You look like you've been crying.'

'I said I'm fine.'

'Okay, don't go all scary woman on me.'

'Pardon?'

'Well, you know.' Cath swallowed. 'I mean . . . well, like that – the way you said "pardon".'

'And how did I say "pardon", exactly?'

'Like you wanted to stick a needle in my eye.'

Not a bad idea. Cath's eyes were like goggles, her mouth clamped in a drooping line. For a minute, she looked like a constipated frog, till she threw her head back and laughed.

'What's so funny?'

'Your face.'

'*My* face?'

'Oh, I'm sorry,' wheezed Cath. 'But you looked like a cat's arse there.' She mimed surprised pursed lips, then started cackling again. 'You'll have to excuse me – it's all part of manic depression, I think. Some days I go a bit hysterical. Still, it all ends in tears.' Cath wiped her eyes. 'Seriously, the things that set me off. On the way in, this guy got out his car, to help an old lady across the road. She was all hunched over, with one of those big frames, and the traffic was building up behind the man's car, but he just took his time, and that was me off – greeting buckets . . . Oh, I'm sorry – really – I just, I can't help it. I didn't mean to be rude . . .' Cath's mouth trembled, ready for another bubble.

What did he see in her? Anna wondered. What was so special about her that made Jamie leave a whole beautiful future with Anna, and stay with Cath, even now, when she was fat and untidy and – shit, the bloody woman was crying again.

'There's tissues in the cabinet.'

'I just wanted to do something, you know,' Cath sniffed, 'to help. If there's anything I can do for you – please phone me. Look, I'll leave you my number. I mean, I know I can't do anything, but . . . I just wanted you to know how grateful I was.'

'Cath, I didn't do anything.'

'But you did – you warned him. Oh, Anna, you've no idea what it's like, depending on someone that . . .' Cath paused, took a deep breath. 'I was so scared when they told me he was in hospital – and then I saw the state of you . . .'

'Cheers. Look, is Jamie back at work yet?'

Cath blew her nose. 'Few days yet.'

'Well, can you ask him to get a message to Mr Rankin.'

'Oh, I think he came in to see you the other day.'

'Yeah, I know he did,' said Anna. 'I just pretended to be asleep. Anyway, can you ask Jamie to tell Rankin I want the twelve-hour patrols to continue down the Drag? He'll just need to substitute two uniforms for Jamie and me – he's got a copy of the detail. Also' – she waited, sighing, as Cath took an old envelope from her bag and started scribbling – 'can Jamie let me know what's happening with the Wajerski case when he gets back? I've phoned DI Cruikshanks a couple of times, but he's never got back to me. Or he maybe has and I've never got the message – my mobile's disappeared.'

'Aha.' Cath reached for her bag. 'It's here. No, Eilidh, no touch. Got your purse and your watch too. I . . . I hope you don't mind. It's just – there was no one else to take them . . .'

Yes, there is, Anna wanted to yell at her. *I've loads of folk, loads of them. They just all have a life; busy, vibrant people who don't have time to skulk round sick beds.* She ignored Cath's chuntering, switched on her mobile to check the call log. Almost instantaneously, an angel swooped from afar. Not so much swooped, as trilled from the confines of her omniscient, panopticoned desk.

'Now, what does this sign say?' The nurse's fingers were jabbing at the notice above her. 'No mobile phones . It's really very irresponsible of you.'

Anna pressed it off, brandished it like a flag. 'Look. All gone. Okay?' She rolled her eyes at Cath. 'This place is driving me insane.'

Cath leaned forward. 'You said the Wajerski case – you mean Ezra? How come you're involved in that?'

'I'm not really involved, just interested. I'd been there a few days before . . .'

'God, it was awful, wasn't it? He was such a lovely man.'

Anna had forgotten the connection. Perhaps Cath could fill in some blanks about Ezra's past. 'That's right, Jamie said you knew him. Has Cruikshanks spoken to you?'

'Me? Nah, why would he speak to me? I've not seen Ezra for yonks, and even then – he kept himself to himself. Talked a wee bit about the war and that, but nothing else really. He was always more keen to find out what I'd been up to – the art of good listening was a "much maligned skill", he said. He had a funny way of talking, didn't he – very courtly.' Cath smiled. 'First time I met him, he came to my aid with his trusty walking stick. There was something about him, even at that age – don't you think?'

'Yeah, a knight in shining armour, eh?' Anna's laugh was hollow. But it was true: even when he was frail and old, Ezra had been "making rescues". He wasn't the kind of man to stand back and watch others in distress. You could see that in the way he'd urged her to follow up the Jarmals' incident rather than his own.

'Nah, I don't mean that. I mean, well, he had a kind of a vibe about him, didn't he?' Cath shuffled to get comfy, making the sheet pull away from its hospital corner.

Anna could feel cold air against her bare, bandaged leg. The gown was riding up past her thighs. What was wrong with using the chair?

'Here, could you take her a wee minute for me?' Without waiting for a response, Cath dumped Eilidh in Anna's lap. 'I'm getting cramp.'

The child was surprisingly solid, tight-packed little limbs all rippling plump like juicy scallops. Immediately, Eilidh stretched out and caught at Anna's watch, pulling it with tiny hands.

'Here.' Anna took it off again, gave it to the baby.

'Ga.'

'Ga yourself.'

'Just watch she doesn't try to eat it,' said Cath, stretching out her legs.

The baby smelled soft. Powdery pink. Definitely her own person, scowling deeply at the watch as she tried to make sense of it all. Anna pressed her spine into the pillows, felt Eilidh's little body relax into hers. It felt good, a living teddy. The hair could be cat fur, and Anna pushed it lightly with her fingers, testing the bounce. She traced a helix on the baby's head, conscious of a harshness in her chest. Began to panic, felt tears nip at her eyes. She couldn't. Stop. Once she was left in peace; if people would just leave her. Stop. She couldn't stop. Willpower seeping everywhere, quiet sobs spilling. At once, she coughed, turned it into a choking fit.

'Oops, sorry – she making you sneeze?' And then the baby was gone, casually reclaimed and swung by her mother, deposited loosely as an extension of her own body. 'Think I over-talced her this morning. Here, have a pear drop, that'll help. Anyway – Ezra. I mean, why is it he's sticking in your mind, even after all this?' Cath touched Anna's bandage.

Because she was outraged, thought Anna, sucking on the sour sweet. Because some little bastard thought he had the right to come and draw filth on an old man's door, then come back and send him cowering to his death. An old soul who'd risked his life to keep the world free, to stand up and be counted, who'd relied on people like her to carry the torch, who'd thought Scotland was a better place than his poor, oppressed homeland—

'Well, he was sexy, wasn't he?' Cath's words were like paint thrown across a pristine wall.

'What?'

'Ezra – I don't mean I'd want to shag him or anything, but, God, you can imagine him being a total charmer when he was younger, can't you? Those eyes . . .'

Anna pulled the sheet back taut beneath her, pushing folds of cloth beneath the thin mattress. Ezra had a kind of magnetism, that was true. She'd felt it like a charge, when he kissed her hand. But – sexy? Maybe Cath's tastes were different. Ezra just reminded her of her grandpa.

'And the way he kissed your hand. Did he kiss your hand too?'

'Yes,' said Anna dully.

'See? He was an old smoothie, so he was.'

Anna considered telling Cath exactly how Ezra died. Nothing smooth about being anointed in jizz as your skull was stoved in from behind. God, she was still prattling on.

'Still, he's with his family now, God rest him. But I'll tell Jamie to keep you posted if he hears anything. I know what it's like, being out of the loop,' Cath added. 'Shite, isn't it?'

'I'm not out of the loop – I'm temporarily inconvenienced.'

'Oooh!' said Cath, waving her hands under her several chins. '*Tempo-rah-rily inconvenienced.*'

Anna didn't respond.

'Lovely flowers,' said Cath eventually, nodding at the bouquet of lilies on the cabinet.

'*All my love, M.*

Hmm – M. Now, is that man, woman, vegetable or mineral? C'mon, spill the beans.'

Anna gave a watery smile. The woman was starting to wear her down. 'Man.'

'M for man. Well, it's a start. Anyone I know?'

Cath was like a dog with a bone. A great big slevery labrador, the kind you saw waddling round the park, panting even on cold days. With damp, malodorous, dark-knotted fur that would never be tamed. Anna closed her eyes, indented her head deeper into the pillows.

'I'm only joking, Anna. I'm just a frustrated housewife who doesn't get out much. Like to have my thrills vicariously. Fine. No names, but lots of juicy detail.'

Vague wisps were the only remnants Anna had of Martin, and those were private. Yet somehow words were forming unbidden, her brain automatically honing off the best bits – anecdotes, shared tastes, embellishing some extras for effect. Acknowledging Martin would give the relationship status, as if she'd had someone special.

'It's just a guy I used to work with. No big deal, really – he wants a bit on the side, I want a bit of fun. No ties, no hassle.' *Now, stop speaking, girl. Don't be pathet—* no, it was out, that little self-indulgent whine she knew she would regret, even as she was saying it. 'But lately . . . it's been more about when it suits him.' One final, sullen child impression. 'Not me.'

'Surely, though,' said Cath slowly, 'when you take up with a married man, you have to accept he's got other commitments too? Wife and kids, for example? Has he got kids?'

'Grown-up ones.' Anna stretched stiff arms. 'Anyway, why should I worry about his family? They're his problem, not mine.'

'Yeah, but d'you never feel guilty?'

'Honestly, no. Why, would you?'

'Well, I'm hardly likely to have an affair with a married man, am I?'

'Why not?'

Cath raised a limp hand from Eilidh's head. 'I'm fat, I'm depressed, I'm a lactating mother – and I love my husband. Anyway, I'd be too scared.'

'That he found out?'

'No, that I'd be tempting fate. You know, *do unto others as you would have them do unto you.*'

The pear drop caught in her throat, making Anna cough. 'Don't talk utter crap. You don't seriously believe there's some celestial Big Brother up there keeping score, do you?'

'Not exactly. But I do believe in God,' she mumbled. 'And I think what goes around comes around.'

'Bollocks. We all make our own luck.'

'In this life, maybe.'

'Ooh, very cryptic. Going to sell me the *Watchtower* now?'

Cath shifted a dozy Eilidh in her arms. 'You asked me what I thought, Anna. There's no need to be a smartarse.'

'Well, you shouldn't shove your morals down a scarlet woman's throat.'

Anna's head throbbed, pulse upon pulse erupting on cells, softer, thicker, denser than the cauliflower they must have replaced her brain with. Cath made her sick, lolling on Anna's bloody bed; all ripe and oozing judgements down from her perfect, wholesome, loved-up plinth, which was really made of clay. Life must be so simple when you have all the answers, lined up smug to take potshots at the great unwashed.

'I'm just saying how I see the world, Anna.'

Well, that's all right then. Screwed shut now, Anna's eyes were smarting in their skull, angry runnels of saline squeezing from corneas, seeping through hollow sinus to coat her throat. She heard her own voice break the silence, low and snide.

'Well, maybe you should see your world from other people's perspective. Your husband's for example.'

'I beg your pardon?'

'Nothing.' Anna felt the bed shake, opened her eyes.

Cath was rocking Eilidh more vigorously than before, her eyebrows twisting knotted rags. 'No, what did you mean? Don't just open your mouth and let your stomach rumble.'

'All right then.' *Hung for a sheep as a lamb, pet:* her grandad used to say that. 'See when the guy comes home at night, after grafting all day, d'you ever ask him how he's doing? Ever stop going on about yourself?'

'How, what's he been saying?'

'He's not said anything. I . . . I can just tell.' Backpedalling, wishing she'd never begun this whole conversation. Watching Cath's face lose colour with every word.

'You two have a lot of meaningful chats, do you?'

'No. Look, this is getting a bit heavy for me. I didn't mean anything by it, Cath. I'm sorry. Let's just leave it, eh?'

'Maybe we should.' Cath stood up, and the mattress rose with her. 'I'd best get this one fed, anyway.'

As Cath's bulk shifted Anna noticed the nurse moving from her station, off to administer a verbal enema to some other poor sod who had more than *two to a bed*. Quickly she switched on her mobile, scrolling through the menu for messages.

'Cheerio then – no, wait. Ssh.' Anna held up her hand, listening. There was a message on the voicemail. 'Listen to that.' She passed the phone to Cath.

'What do I press?'

Anna tutted. 'You not got a mobile?'

'No. Doesn't make me a bad person.'

'Just hold it up, listen. I can hardly make it out.'

A child's voice. Whisper of a distant accent. *Mammy knows about the Fat Man.*

'Something about a fat man?' Cath shrugged.

'That's what I thought,' said Anna.

'It's just a kid. Wouldn't worry about it.'

'But why would they phone me three times? Look, it's on my call log. Number withheld, number withheld, number withheld.'

'Might not be the same person. Secret love child maybe? Toy boy? You tell me. Is Mr Lover-man, em, chunky?'

'What?'

'Could he be the Fat Man? A wee nickname, and someone's caught you out?'

Anna fixed on Cath, trying to ascertain if she was joking. With Cath, it was difficult to tell. Anyway, Martin was very well toned, and his kids were older than . . . shit. Cringing inside, as she remembered how he sometimes named his penis. Idiotic things like the Big Bad Wolf, and how he made her say it, choking as she bit down hard, and harder still as he slapped her arse.

'Well, if it's important, they'll ring back,' said Cath. 'Anyway, we'll away and give you peace.' She scrunched the bag of pear drops as she laid them on the sheet beside Anna. 'And seriously, again – thank you.'

No, but *seriously* – fuck off, mouthed Anna, as Cath made her way from the ward. She felt very tired. Forced herself to reach up and tug the curtain around her bed, then curled up in a wee ball. Two minutes later the zizz of metal on tinny metal told her the fight was on again. 'Excuse me, could you not just leave them shut?'

'Now, have we not discussed this already, Anna? Ward policy,' the angel trilled, skipping off in her little white shoes.

'It's Ms Cameron,' muttered Anna.

The bitch nurse kept peeling back the curtains so they could *keep an eye on her*, exposing her as nothing more than soft tissue and intimate functions. Faces either side – ill, sniffing faces that belched and snored and offered sweeties. Blank antiseptic walls that were a balm through half-shut eyes. In their nothingness, they could be anything, and Anna watched them daily for signs of cracks or peeling. Dinner-time came and went, her salad limper than the one yesterday. Maybe it *was* the one from yester-day. Closed her eyes again, and felt her throat swell. The air was too dry, and her head ached so much she thought sleep would never come.

But it did, and so did morning – six thirty rise so the cleaner could polish the lino. Then cornflakes and UHT, and some luke-warm coffee. Anna had never stayed in hospital before. Never been in hospital before – apart from that one time that didn't exist.

What was the point of keeping her here? She'd had days of this; too many pointless days, merging into fluid nights. Far better to get back home, pull herself together, and get a grip with what was going on down the Drag. Some nutter out there was practising *wycinanki* on women's faces, and those women were entrusted to her. She to them. A mutual fan club of disdain and dependency. She had to get hold of bloody Cruikshanks too, who'd never even made the effort to come and see her, or send a message. Probably writing off Ezra as an epileptic fit gone wrong. Och, that was unfair. Cruikshanks was one of the good guys really, he just didn't set the heather on fire.

She wanted to be doing something useful. Lying around all day just made you feel worse, and Anna had decided she was worse enough to go home. Once she'd got used to it, she told them the ringing had stopped. But the nurse said it wasn't up to them. 'Doctor would decide', when next he deigned to appear. 'Doctor' was very reluctant to let her go. He asked if she'd consider visits from the district nurse. When she knocked that back, he then told her she'd have to return as an outpatient. Insisted that someone's name and phone number be given as an emergency contact. Someone responsible, who would call in on her daily for the next week. *Can't have you not turning up at my clinic, then find you've collapsed in a heap behind the door, dear.*

If she'd had the energy Anna would have told him where to go, but weakness made her meek. They had their own control techniques, these medics, and Anna almost admired their detached concern. Her mother and stepfather were in sunny Spain, from where they'd sent a nice card and phoned twice. She could hardly ask Martin. The doctor was threatening to keep her in if she didn't produce a ministering minder, and Anna couldn't face another bath in someone else's grime. All her friends worked, they couldn't just drop everything to mash her a banana. A fat old woman skunked by, helped by a nurse; the incontinence pad she clutched was a giant nappy for all the world to see.

Then the thought came to Anna – Catherine Worth. She had

said, kept saying, if there was anything she could ever do, she'd only to ask. *Seriously.* And Cath did nothing but mash bananas. Not that Anna would let her within a mile of the house really. The nurse had left the door ajar, and Anna could hear straining from within. Reluctantly, she recited Cath's phone number to her consultant.

9 Aftermath

DI Cruikshanks was knackered. He'd pulled in housebreakers, sex offenders, gay bashers, spoken to more filth than you'd find up the crack of your arse. Had to be civil to them all too, that was the sickening thing. Tapes and videos and Legal Aid. And now they had human rights. What about the human rights of the poor old bastard who gets his head shattered in his own front room?

Cruikshanks had watched fragments of Wajerski's skull picked out from the bloodied mass. Seen the silver matted hair, slicked back with blood instead of the Silvikrin oil half empty on his nightstand. Seen old child's eyelids pulled over empty eyes. Saw his corpse every morning sprawled across the incident boards and every night in the soup of swimming bodies locked inside him. It would pass, he knew. Each one did.

Restorative justice – feeling empathy with the victim – Christ, he did all that crap twenty years ago. Kick the shit out the wee fuckers, and give them a hint of how it felt. But that was a 'knee-jerk reaction'. (And they didn't even mean that to be funny.) He was 'not seeing the full picture'. Everything was in 'inverted commas'. He was a 'dinosaur', an 'old pump'. He'd heard them all before, those witty, insightful put-downs crafted to crystallise the amber that engulfed him. Leaving just enough room to gasp a dying breath. His kind were tolerated – if they did the job and were circumspect. There was no room for black and white any more, for right and wrong and knowing where you stood. Cruikshanks worked within the boundaries that were set. Yes, you could ease these out, tweak and interpret the elastic lines that tied your wrists, but every year they got tighter. What would bluff Jack Regan do? Or sophisticated Poirot? Or the cocaine-snorting hog-cops of contemporary fiction?

Was he, Cruikshanks, the one-off, sharp-as-a-tack 'tec, hero-ically rising above the bigoted dross of his colleagues, seeing things the others, with their collective ignorance, cynicism and prejudices, didn't? Was he the tough-talking maverick that didn't give a stuff for the rules? A corrupter of innocents maybe, doing a line in stolen goods while shagging the DA? Or was he none of these aching stereotypes? Just a middle-aged man with principles and a mortgage, trying to do his best? Toothache. That's what you got after two decades of gritting your teeth.

He'd jumped through the hoops – even done an HNC in Police Studies. Actually quite enjoyed it, the shaping of nebu-lous thought into reasoned argument. He'd tried to explain away the ping-pong of aggression and disdain that crackled between public and police. *There is always tension in policing a democracy*, he wrote. And it was true. It began with a certain brusqueness, some complaints about 'attitude' and culminated in poor sods like Cameron getting the shit kicked out of them. Or worse. From the age weans learned how to say their first emphatic '*no*' it was obvious to anyone with half a brain. Very few individuals, on fewer still occasions, like being told what to do. And the cockier, younger, ruder, angrier, older, blacker, prettier, shorter, whiter, more different or similar the person doing the telling, the harder it was to obey. Still, the public got the police force they wanted. Accountable and constrained. *Public* – he was doing it now. He *was* the public. And his wife and the kids and every other bugger in this station. What did folk think: that they got put in cupboards when their shift fin-ished? Cruikshanks rubbed the crusts in his eyes, flicked on the kettle. The boys would be in soon, and he liked to have a pot of tea on.

He'd need to visit Anna Cameron too, go see if she could give him more details on those medals, 'cause he was fast running out of ideas. No known gerontophiles on his patch, but he'd bloody well worked his arse off to find one. And now the lab was telling him it was the old boy's own spunk. Amazing how the human body reacted in its death-throes. Urine, faeces and even sperm making one last dash for corporeal release. At least they'd found a footprint. Wee it was, size four or five just. Matched the one on the door. Partial, some kind of trainer mark, daubed in Polish blood.

He pinned the photo to the board, stood back. The outline of the print looked like rust.

Anna stretched stiffly on her bed. Her gorgeous, pink-sheeted, king-sized *own bed*. Yet sleep was still sporadic, disturbed by flowerings of pain and the growing quietness of the house that had become an anticipation, louder and louder as the medication they'd pumped her with melted away. Twice, last night, the phone had rung. Not the landline, but her mobile, playing electronic lullabies from the counter in the kitchen. The first jingle had floated into the bedroom, nudged her awake, and she'd gone to investigate, dopey-brave. No message, number withheld.

The second time it rang, she hesitated. She'd brought the phone back to her room, didn't even have to unravel her cocoon of covers, but still she paused. The red blink of the clock told her it was 4 a.m. When she finally answered, the line went dead. Maybe it was work, but they'd have rung the house phone. God, if it was that urgent, they'd have called G Division, had them send a car round.

Anna laughed aloud, a vixen bark. She wasn't so indispensable that her services were required twenty-four hours a day. In fact, Anna was so *not* indispensable that they'd already replaced her on the squad, according to Derek's phone call. Guy called Gus Murray, come from the Traffic. So valued was she that they'd sent Jenny bloody Heath round with a big bunch of flowers. They were tucked behind the storm door when she'd got back from hospital, with a card covered in Jenny's scrawl:

Sorry u weren't in. Get well soon. From all at Flexi.

Anna held her pillow like she was practising a kiss, doubling it over where it touched her aching jaw. Martin would have heard she was home by now. Grapevine gossip virused through police stations. Fair enough he didn't want to be seen in hospital, but he could let himself in here any time he liked. Fucksake, she didn't want him to marry her, she just wanted a hug. Five minutes to check she was okay. Anna pictured Martin cowed at her hospital bed, sneaking in after visiting time to watch over her. Immediately saw the glance at the clock, the distant perching on a chair. Even in her fantasies, he wouldn't have the time. But it hadn't been him there, it had been Jamie Worth.

Her head would stop hurting if Jamie was here. His touch was surprisingly light – ballerina fingers in rugby player's paws. He had this way of scratching, hands spanned across her head, questing tracks with gentle combs that shivered. She shifted the pillow round, her thighs brushing together, tuning, humming. More intense the less she moved. A tiny pressure, feather-soft. At the point her hand slipped down to her groin, a picture of Ezra Wajerski zipped from some recess, two men kneeling, pumping semen on his face. She tore her hand away, threw herself on her back, sickened. Her brain would do that sometimes, hurl some vile image like a spike in her eye, in the place before orgasm, the bit where she settled into the rhythm and the moment. It would strike with mediaeval fervour, smashing the bounds between decency and deep, dank disgust. Anna closed her eyes, clawing for something to take the taste away.

She felt safe with Jamie. On paper she was the powerful one, yet she was comfortable when he chivvied her, dragging her from her desk, telling her to lighten up. With Martin everything was a battle, both of them vying for a supremacy she knew he didn't merit. His rank gave him an arrogance . . . no, that was unfair. It could be him, his nature, but in this job, everyone 'sirred' or 'ma'amed', ordered and acquiescent, it was hard to make a distinction. Perhaps, at home, even Superintendent Rankin made the dinner and rolled on the floor with his grandchildren. Gave them shots in his Sinclair C5.

Children. Anna felt sick when she thought of Eilidh and her father connected. She'd felt the weight of the child on her lap, breathed that head-scent they go on about. When she smiled, Eilidh looked like Jamie, especially round the eyes. Anna had never looked that closely at a baby before, never searched for the whole of two separate parts, sketched on one small face. People did that. Saw each brand-new soul with a lineage of eons. People did that.

The rage that always slevered there was gnawing now at her belly, slapping out its empty, aching tendrils. Cath was just being kind to Anna – she'd seen a wee chink and tried to worm her way in. But Anna didn't think she ever wanted to see Cath again. She loathed her mumsy helpfulness, her possessive touch on Jamie. She despised her sloth, her disapproval, her easy manner in Anna's space – sorting flowers, offering food. Anna could picture her giving suburban dinner parties, beaming round the table as her guests munched on Marks's Coq au Vin, baby gulping at her Venusian breast. No doubt chatting blithely about her pelvic droop, while Jamie died in slow stages of boredom and neglect. Whatever problems Cath and Jamie had, they were not of Anna's making. That world was not her fault. If Jamie made her feel good, then fuck it. That's virtually what he'd said, the night at the pay-off. Compartmentalise your life. Exist in two distinct dimensions. What occurred in one need have absolutely no effect on the other. A whole stash of secret treasures Anna could unwrap in her head, and lay out for slow perusal.

It had been dark and still in the hospital. He'd slipped in, doubtless with a wink and some sweeties for the nurses. Flashing a warrant card was not Jamie's style. He'd leaned over to check her breathing, and she'd been so quiet. Knowing it was him, willing him to stay. Fearful to open her eyes in case he wasn't there. He'd hesitated, then bent his head towards her with a breath-kiss. *I love you.* She knew she hadn't dreamed it.

Someone was ringing her doorbell. Insistent jabs that sounded urgent. She eased herself from the bed, and lifted the stick propped beside her dressing table. Her head was like a hayrick. She tried to flatten down her hair. As her fingers passed her face, she thought of Michelle and his mermaid's apron. Soon she would have Alice.

A long, slow hobble from her room. Part-way in the hall, Anna realised she couldn't answer the door. The sudden sapping made her dizzy, and she rested against the wall, aware of moisture between her shoulder blades. Six hundred thousand people lived in this city and any one of them, at any time, could come to her house and she wouldn't know who it was. Not until she opened the door, when it would be too late. Skin excreting incandescence as she saw them all. Six hundred thousand people could sweep past her in a tirade, toss and ingest her without even meaning to, or there could be one. One that crouched in the crowd and did mean it. Meant every single crunch of her bones like he meant the sawing of those women's poor, torn faces. She couldn't let that in, so she waited, shrinking against her own wall, until they pushed something through her letterbox and shuffled away.

A white card:

Ho, Ho, Ho. Your Countryfair Hamper has been left . . .

Round the back.

How tough was she, hiding in her hall? Feart from a picnic hamper delivery man. In desperation, Anna telephoned her mother.

Caroline Steed was not the type of mum who'd hug you with

floury arms, while sticking on the kettle and kissing it better. Caroline's style was more: ring her front doorbell (never let yourself in, good grief no; well, it wasn't your house, was it?), pop in if she wasn't *just about to go out* (90 per cent chance), and chat about golf or property prices, while never making eye contact. Or it had been until Caroline moved. Living near La Manga, there was absolutely no danger of anyone popping anywhere. But there were plenty of open, sunny fairways, and a new husband who played off seven. A husband who was nothing to do with Anna.

Though it was twenty-eight years ago, the morning the police came to Anna's house had never recessed into a neat memory file. Her dad had been late home off the night shift, but that wasn't unusual. Caroline was getting Anna ready to go to Grandpa's. Bitterly cold that morning – she made Anna wear one of those stupid tank tops over her polo neck. Anna had known one of the cops. They made her go in another room, but she'd listened while they went on telling her mum what had happened, that there'd been an accident, and her mum kept moaning, *No*.

For days, the house had been filled with people and flowers. A few top brass, and some welfare people telling them they'd be all right. What did all right mean? Her mum, doped to the eyeballs, sparks of blame singeing anyone who came too close? Every time she'd climb into her mother's lap, Caroline would shove her off. Anna knew that wasn't right. Her heart was as sore as Mummy's. She could feel it rupture like pockets of tripe, late at night, when memories met shadows. A collection from her dad's station brought extra Christmas presents for Anna that first year. They'd even asked her to the kiddies' party, but Caroline said she couldn't take that. Neither could Anna. Every time she saw a police uniform, for months after, she'd beg Caroline to make it be her daddy coming home. Oh, they managed, she never wanted. Except they were both waiting and wanting for strong arms they'd never feel.

Sometimes, forbye all that, you needed your mum.

'Oh, hello darling. How are you?'

'Not too good actually, Mum.'

'But it's been *ages* now. And they've let you out, haven't they? Has something else happened?' It sounded like an accusation.

'No, no. Just a bit down, that's all.'

Anna could feel her mother tutting. 'But the head's all better, yes?'

'Kind of.' .

'Back at work yet? No, dear, in a minute . . . Sorry. Are you?'

'Eh, no.'

'Anna, it doesn't do to cloister yourself away all day. You need to get back to work, back to where the action is.' Her voice went faint. 'Well, no, I could catch you up . . .'

Anna held the phone like a priest, imagining it poised above the old trout's head. Patterns repeating. That's what patterns did. Changing colour maybe, doubling back, running on to different lines, but the essence was rhythmic. Back to the start and start again. She knew her voice was growing shriller. 'You're a fine one to talk. When did you ever go to work?'

'I did actually. Until the . . . until we moved. Then there was no one close by to watch you. Believe me,' Caroline added, 'it's not a good thing to be stuck at home all day. You need to be with people. Career girl like you.' Her laugh, like lemons.

Anna exhaled. 'I don't suppose you . . .?'

Immediately, the shutters slid. 'Darling, I'm going to have to love you and leave you. Teddy sends kisses, by the way. Look, when you're feeling better, why not pop over for a holiday?'

Fuck Teddy. 'Yeah. Yeah, that would be nice.'

'Great. Well . . .'

'Look, I'll have to go, Mum. Someone at the door. Speak to you soon. Bye.'

Anna rubbed her face in the cushion she was holding, open mouth salty on the fabric. No one was coming to get her, which was good or bad, depending on which way you looked at it. She lived in a conversion, an old stone house in Battlefield. Mary Queen of Scots once stood on the hill above, watching her troops being routed by her own brother. Anna's half of the house was on the ground floor, French windows in the lounge opening on to the garden. Even the back lawn seemed huge and unfamiliar, spiked with stark trees and lurking laurels. There it was – the hamper; wicker, not plastic – just at the corner of the house. Anna limped outside, leaning on the metal stick-thing they'd given her. A small envelope was attached. Typed to:

Ms A. Cameron.
Darling, miss you loads. Hope this helps, you brave girl.
Will be over just as soon as I can. M.

Not just any old hamper. A luxury one, no less. Anna tugged it towards the French windows, unable to lift it and lean on her stick at the same time – multi-tasking dexterity was another thing Cath Worth had that she didn't. As Anna turned to push the French doors wider, a man's gruff voice boomed from the garden behind.

'That you getting supplies parachuted in now, is it?'

Anna screamed, dropped her stick. The patio spun up to meet her, until a solid, hairy hand grabbed her wrist.

'Woah there, cowgirl – you nearly went arse over tit. Maybe baffies aren't the best thing to wear in the garden, eh?' It was DI Cruikshanks, beaming at her over a long soggy parcel of newspaper.

'Jeso – you scared me. What you doing snooping round my back garden?' Anna's heart was bounding off her ribcage. Sweat clagged beneath her breasts, making her breathing shallow.

'As the actress said to the bishop, eh? Well, I got no reply at the front,' he panted, 'so I thought I'd go for a rear attack. Any chance of a seat? I'm peching.'

'You and me both.' Anna ushered him in, levering herself on her stick, trying to stop the spasms flying down her arms from her neck. 'Did you climb the fence to get in here?'

'Ach, don't tell me you're no used to laddies scaling high walls to see you. Here.' Cruikshanks thrust the tattered parcel into Anna's arms.

'Cheers – what is it?' She dunted the door shut with her backside. 'Could you lock it, please?'

'But I'm no stopping long . . .'

'Please.'

'Okay.' He turned the key in the lock. 'It's fish.'

'Pardon?'

'I caught you a nice trout – thought you could have it for your tea.' Cruikshanks frowned. 'It's not gutted, mind; the wife disny let me do it in the kitchen any more.'

The back of Anna's throat smarted. Was this what Cath meant about 'everything setting you off'? God, it had better stop soon. Her breathing was slowing down now, almost normal, but her head still felt woolly and thick. Even her voice was unfamiliar – it sounded like it needed oiled. 'Well, that's really kind of you. Thanks.' She put the fish down on the coffee table, tugged her dressing gown across her waist. 'Eh, can I get you anything – tea, coffee?' If there was anything to offer – she'd hardly been in the kitchen since she'd come home.

'I'll eh . . . I'll maybe take a wee biscuit.' Cruikshanks was eyeing up the hamper. 'It says there's stem ginger shortbread in there.'

'Help yourself.'

'Ooh, lovely, it's Walkers.' He opened the tin eagerly. 'I'm no just here bearing gifts – I need your help too, if you're up to it.'

'About the Wajerski case? I did phone you back, sir, quite a few times.'

'Aye, aye, don't worry about that – and it's Tom, dear, Tom. But how're you feeling in yourself?'

Anna cleared a pile of magazines off the couch. 'Fine, fine. Here, have a seat.'

'Right bastard, eh – doing that to a lassie.' A tiny flinch as he lifted hair from her face. 'Oops, sorry, did I hurt you?'

'No.' Anna sat down, out of inquisitive reach. All the times she'd done that, poked and prodded at a victim like they were just one more production. Professional poking, of course, non-intrusive and essential, not grubby fingering. 'He's done a lot worse than that, anyway.'

'Aye, I know, I've seen the photos.' Cruikshanks plumped down beside her, legs akimbo beneath his jelly belly. 'You know Stewart Street CID are dealing with it now, all five slashings? And yours, of course.'

'Why?'

'You canny exactly investigate your own assault.'

'True. So, have they any other leads?'

'Well, hen, if you canny ID the bastard . . .' He shrugged.

Anna said nothing. What could she say? *He was wee and wiry and I closed my eyes as tight as I could.*

'Anyway, back to Mr Wajerski.'

Grateful, Anna flicked from bruised, stupid victim to incisive, on-the-ball investigator. 'Got anywhere yet?'

'No really. To be honest, we're having a hell of a time. Which is why I want to go over old ground again – starting with these.' Cruikshanks took some paper from inside his Barbour jacket. Four or five sheets, full colour photos of war medals. He slid them towards Anna. 'Take a swatch. Recognise any of them?'

'Where d'you get them?'

'Internet. Just typed in Polish war medals and out they popped.' He sounded very pleased. 'Breggsy's idea.'

They were all very similar, dropped-scone gongs, until Anna flipped the page and saw stars. 'Yep, there was a star-shaped one, like that.' She pointed to a goldish six-pointed medal. 'But the ribbon was different, a brighter blue.'

'Mmm.' Cruikshanks put on his specs. 'That's the France and Germany star. Ring any bells?'

'Nope.' Anna kept looking. 'That one. He had that one.' She jabbed at a pewter-coloured cross. An eagle soared at its heart, four flared arms each bearing letters. She read them clockwise from the top. 'MILI; TUTI; TARI; VIR.'

'Mean anything?' asked Cruikshanks.

'No . . .' Wrote the letters on her phonepad. 'Wait. Yes. Look, rearrange them: VIRTUTI MILITARI. For virtue? He definitely had that one.'

Cruikshanks rubbed his hands. 'Now we're cooking by gas. Least we know one to look for. Any more you recognise?'

'Maybe that one – no, it's an army one. Air Force, Mr Wajerski was in the Air Force. What about his nephew – can he not help?'

Cruikshanks shook his head. 'No such thing. Your Mr W had no living relatives.'

'You sure?'

'Been to the Polish Embassy and everything.'

Anna thought a moment, reluctant to dub Ezra a liar. 'Could it have been a friend – you know, son of a mate, called him uncle, that kind of thing?'

'Possibly. We've asked around the Polish Club, see if there were any weddings they knew of that week. St Stephen's in Partick does all the Polish services. Zilch.'

'Might not have been Polish though,' she said. 'Or Christian.'

'True. He kept himself to himself, your Ezra. Got the impression he didn't have many pals down St George's Cross.'

'Well, he was Jewish. Are most Poles not Catholic?'

Cruikshanks shrugged. 'News to me.'

'So any wedding of his nephew wouldn't be in a church then – it'd be in a synagogue.'

'Aye, but they'd all still be registered at Martha Street. And we've checked. Coincidence, that – us being detectives an all.' There was a harder edge to Cruikshanks's chewing.

'Did you get anywhere on the anti-Semitic front?'

He nudged his specs up his nose. 'Eh, no. Sorry we didn't keep you in the loop. Did someone promote you to ACC Crime? Only I didn't see it in the bulletin.'

'I'm only saying.'

'You think it was a disgruntled Pole then? Didn't like a Jew-boy coming to their club?'

'No, don't be daft. The swastika on his door, I mean – any leads on that?' She tried to keep the impatience out of her voice.

'Well.' Cruikshanks moved closer to the biscuit tin. 'We know the BNP are getting active in the area – my chums in Special Branch are keeping it very close to their chests – but they're no match for our Breggsy. Internet again. Stupid bastards post all their 'publicity' on the web – BNP that is, not SB.'

'And?'

'Let's just say we're exploring every possibility at present.'

'I can read that in the *Evening Times*.'

Cruikshanks gathered up his papers. 'No offence, Anna, but we've all got our own way of working. Let's not have a fall-out the now – specially when you're no yourself.' He stood up, scratched his belly. 'Right, well, cheers. We'll trawl the pawnshops again, now we've a better idea what we're looking for. My gut tells me it's just neds, not dealers. They'll flog the medals for drugs money.'

'So you don't think it was a gay attack any more?'

Cruikshanks zipped up his Barbour. 'No. Wee shites on crack, just – screwing the house, not the old boy. Turns out it was his own semen he was caked in.'

That should have made her feel better.

10 Circle of Sorry

What was he like, lounging about with that stupid bandage on his head, insisting on head massages and back rubs to make it all better, like the big wean he was? Cath squidged another pickle on Jamie's sandwich, pressing it deep into soft white bread. And now that he'd been mothered enough, he was ready for the glory – couldn't wait to get back to work and regale them with tales of embellished heroism. Cath's anger was the anger of relief – the same anger her mother slapped her with when she was five years old and ran across the road without looking, avoiding a van's bonnet by less than a pigtail.

They'd played down what had happened, the cops that came to tell her Jamie was in hospital. She'd always thought vagueness, smiled euphemism helped. Cath had been one of those uniforms plenty of times. On the other side of the door; the shadow with hats you see through the nets before you open up and admit defeat. Making you sit down on your own couch, taking off hats with vicious sloth and ya-a-a-awning mouths distorted and slow. Careful words that Cath knew were nerves, but sounded like insincerities when they bulleted your head. All she'd wanted was to see him for herself, chatting up the nurses with a head like a clootie dumpling. Seen Anna too – out for the count with loose-mouthed dribbles and a filigree of dark roots where her hair fell back. They'd thought there was fluid building up, talked about putting a shunt in. No one had known who Anna's next of kin was until they checked the records at Pitt Street. An address in Spain, but no number. Someone had to get the Spanish police to go to her parents' villa. You'd have thought they'd have flown over. If Eilidh had been lying crushed in a hospital bed, she was damn sure she would. Bloody swim it if need be.

Curiosity, gratitude, a chance for up-close study had led Cath to Anna's bedside. Noticing the stream of flowers and cards, and the dearth of visitors, Cath had watched Anna for ages. Seen past her shapings of flesh and humanity, past black eyelids on bruised cheeks and *knew*. Anna was as lonely as she was.

The other day, when they talked, Cath was sure she could see the beginnings of treacle movements, sense that dullness in Anna's eyes, juxtaposed with vitriol in her voice. Depression was like hypothermia – all you needed was someone to keep you awake, keep treading water with you in a circle of sorry. Poor Anna. Cath had Jamie: Anna had no one. Maybe they could keep each other afloat.

Did you hear that, Anna? *Cath* had Jamie. The bastard.

Right on cue, the bastard breezed into the kitchen, all cheesy bright smiles because he was escaping. Cath thrust his piece box at him as he handed her their daughter.

'I've checked her nappy and she's—'

'Right – all I had was ham and pickle, so don't start, okay? I've been too busy ironing your bloody shirts to go shopping.'

Jamie rubbed under his eye. Why was Cath so quick to turn on him, no matter what he did? Like living with a time bomb. First day back at work was beckoning, and he couldn't be arsed with a fight. She was wiping furiously at the worktop, same small square, over and over again, Eilidh straddling her hip; ignored, hungry and swinging in time. He moved behind Cath, slipped his arms around her waist, reaching for the breasts beneath his daughter.

'You're a star.'

Cath wriggled from his grasp. 'Don't patronise me, Jamie.'

Keep it light, pal. He kissed the top of her head. 'You sounded like Anna Cameron when you said that. Doing her "I'm giving you a row" voice.' He pretended to shudder. 'Scary woman.'

'Yeah, and talking of Anna – anything you'd like to tell me?'

'Can't think of anything. How?'

'Och, just something she said.' Cath turned to face him. 'I was talking to her in the hospital; oh, she wants you to check what's happening with Ezra's case by the way, and get the DI to phone her. And something about keeping up the patrols down the Drag.'

'Fine. Is that it?'

'No.' She picked a hair from the tiny shoulder that nestled into her. 'Sounded like you'd been confiding in her, that's all.'

'What are you on about?'

'*I* don't know. I think I've been very reasonable. Knowing you're working together, not making any fuss. D'you think I didn't suss right away who she was?'

Jamie shook his head. 'And who is she, Cath?'

'The girl you were shagging at Tulliallan.'

'The girl I left for you.'

'Anyway – that's not the point. I know who she is, and that's fine. Feel a bit sorry for her actually. But see if you start mouthing off to her about our relationship – and I mean anything . . .'

'Cath, I have not got a scooby what you're on about.'

'Neither had I. I was just trying to be nice to her in the hospital, and I end up getting a frigging lecture. About *you*.' Cath put Eilidh in her highchair. 'Telling me that I should ask you how you're feeling, pat you on the head for working so hard – stop being a selfish cow basically. Is that what you tell her?' The pulse on her temple was twitching, faster and faster as her voice rose. 'Please don't say you've been trying the *my wife doesn't understand me* line, because I've got news for you: she's already shagging someone else's husband.'

Where the hell had this come from? Jamie was searching his skull, flailing for . . . ach. That was it. Must be. The night they got the doing.

'Cath, for God's sake calm down. She was talking about an RTA.'

'What?'

'A fatality. I'd to attend an RTA that last time I did ovvies – the night Ezra was killed. It was a wee boy. Anna was going on and on about it, asking me how I felt, asking me what you thought. I told her to shove it – in a nice way, mind. Said I didn't like talking about that stuff with anyone.'

Cath folded her arms. 'Why didn't you tell me?'

'Tell you what?'

'About the wee boy?'

'Christ, woman.' He swiped the table with the tea towel. The crack spun off the walls. 'Don't you bloody start. D'you not remember what it's like, coming in off the backshift? You just want to sit and chill. Bottle of beer, crap film on TV. Wipe it all clean till tomorrow. Bloody hell, Cath, if you stored all that stuff up in your head, you'd go mental.'

She moved towards him. 'But that's what you are doing. See if you just talked about these things . . .'

'What?' His hands steepled at his nose, moving, pulling flesh down to his jaw. At his mouth now, opening. 'See if I just told you about lifting him up, feeling him still warm with his wee blue lips? Taking off his clothes in the mortuary. How he had Spiderman pants on, and there was a tiny bit of wee dripping off the end of his willy? Putting him in a fridge. Going three times past his mum's house, wanting to see how she's doing. Not going in. 'Cause you don't go in, do you? If you went back that would be caring. Not helping, not doing your job, just letting a wee sliver of it work its way inside. Then you'd go fucking mental. Christ, Cath, do you not remember anything at all?'

He glared at his wife, her bottom lip a-quiver. Brilliant. Here came the waterworks. Cath's solution for everything. Can't argue with a snotty nose.

'I don't have time for this,' he said. 'I'm going to work.'

'You do that.'

The early part of the shift was reasonably quiet. Jamie had time to give Cruikshanks a phone at first piece break.

'*Ms* Cameron got you doing her errands now? She's no easy satisfied, is she? I was only talking to her yesterday.'

Jamie knew it was a mistake to phone Cruikshanks. Getting involved in a case that had nothing to do with him. Made him look like some bloody do-gooder, or, worse still, a CID groupie. So, he blamed Cath. 'Aye, well, for my wife too actually. She used to know Ezra quite well.'

'Ach, it must be hard tae keep track, son. Well, you can tell both the lovely ladies in your life that there's nothing doing with Mr Wajerski. All my leads are as dead as him. So, if your missus has got any gen on old Ezra, I'd be delighted to hear it. What, Breggsy? Aye – with a pickled egg, mind.' Cruikshanks hung up, his fish supper calling to him.

Jamie could feel his cheeks hot. Too bloody warm in this room, all the windows steamed up. These sandwiches were rank and all. Bread curling at the edges, ham rubber-pink and slimy. Jamie chucked the lot in the bin, picked up the *Daily Record* for the football scores. He'd get a curry later on.

Rankin had continued the twelve-hour shifts in Anna's absence, even though there'd been no more prostitute assaults. The Drag seemed quieter to Jamie, muffled almost. Girls not looking you in the eye, some of their brass neck tarnished. Air thick, like it was brewing. He'd felt it like this once before, years ago, when a young prostitute had been murdered. A pall had hung above the streets, a palpable fear usually hidden underground. But the murder had released it, billowing into a blitz-spirit of paranoia. Girls as jerky and cautious as startled does, swift-talking and tearful and scurrying from sight. They never caught the killer, so closure never came, just seeped and dwindled as the woman's peers died off and new ones took their places, girls that had never heard of Margo, or was it Margaret, and did it matter, since she was gone?

Even with this sense of impending explosion now, even with the increasing violence, the studied cruelty of the attacks, nobody was talking to the police. They'd tried, all the Flexi cops had, each with their touts, their favoured lassies, but there was a bitter stoicism in the women's silence, comments like: *Yous are all the same;* or: *Don't pretend you give a shit.* And one barbed tut, slipped out from garrulous Lily: *It's their own stupid faults, they junkies.* Everything the Flexi Unit heard or saw or suspected about the slashings was collated and passed to CID, but, without Anna there to keep tabs and keep pushing, little was passed back. Gus Murray, the AP sergeant brought in to replace her, was a tosser. Rocking no boat but his own in his haste to make the next promotion, and lick the next arse. He'd decided Jamie and Alex had to work the second half in uniform, though it was completely contrary to Anna's plan.

'Ach, these girlies can take care of themselves,' he'd said. 'A wee anti-violence patrol up the town will be far more productive. Tell you, performance-related pay is a wonderful idea – an extra tenner for every ned you bring in, eh, boys?'

Boys. Gorgeous Gus was at least five years younger than Jamie. But he didn't bother arguing. Do what you're told, get paid, go home, be a drone. He found he no longer cared. Only by its absence was he aware of that missing spark, the fuel that fired his working day, made him twist and leap to impress. It felt empty without Anna there.

When he'd seen her in hospital, sleeping, fist clenched against her face the way Eilidh's did when she was teething, Jamie's world had moved slightly. Not spun or transformed, just tipped a little on its axis. Touching her, remembering a long-distant softness he'd derided as neediness. And what was wrong with neediness anyway? With someone needing you? He could barely remember how that felt. Without meaning to, he had kissed her face. Just a whisper, tasting her skin, wanting more. Only a kiss, deposited, not reciprocated, a fleeting nonsense, that glancing of mouth on flesh that we do all the time, a nothing in the scheme of things, but somehow, somehow, that single cathandjamie skin had shifted, peeled back to Him and Her. A thin wedge of Anna prising her way between.

'Alpha to Alpha 523.' He jerked as his radio intruded.

'Two three. Go ahead.'

'Aye, Jumbo, sorry about this. Place is going like a fair and I've nobody in One Section. You've got wheels, haven't you?'

'Aye.'

'Would you attend a report of a Code Two Six at 120 Kennedy Street? Flat 8/3.'

Jamie's guts flickered. Not again, please.

Alex took off his hat, checking the list of codes he kept tucked in the lining. 'Code two six, code two six.' He ran his finger down the list. 'Fucksake, man. It's a sudden pudden.'

'I know. Put your hat on, you arse.'

'A Alpha to Alpha 523.'

'Five two three.'

'Ah, Jamie, would you note this report is from ambulance control. Appears to be a cot death.'

'Roger, noted.'

'Sorry, pal. Update me on arrival, yeah?'

'Aye, roger, Paul.'

Kennedy Street was up in the Townhead, the furthest reaches of A Division. At that time of night they got there in five minutes, slipping through empty roads and scattered litter, away from bright hard city lights to softer, dull yellows and sombre grey walls.

'Jamie?' Alex spoke quietly.

'What?'

'I've never done a cot death before.'

Working in the city centre, that wasn't unusual. Places like Ashley Street, places with houses and communities, were covered by Cranstonhill and Partick, but Alex had never worked from either of these stations. He'd always been based at Stewart Street, with its scattering of flats up at Townhead, and its warehouses in the Merchant City that were gradually being colonised by trendy twenty–thirty-somethings. In the main, though, the subdivision was shops and offices, pubs and clubs. You could be an expert in shoplifting by your second day in the job, could spot a breach merchant after doing a single backshift and would have learned the French for 'Don't leave your suitcases on view when you park the car' as soon as the lighter nights came in. But. But. Dealing with folk who actually lived there, who weren't just passing through, that was rare.

'It's okay, Alex. Just focus on doing your job. Can you mind all the questions you need to ask?'

'I think so.' Back in the hat for a blank sudden death form.

'Well, just be direct.'

'Have I to do it then?'

'Best way to learn,' said Jamie.

'I don't know, Jumbo.'

Jamie relented. 'See how bad they are, okay? Shock does funny things to folk. They're not thinking straight – they'll answer anything. See tomorrow, when it all sinks in, or they've been doped up by the doctor, you don't want to go back then. Okay, this is it.'

An ambulance was parked outside the concierge station of the high flats.

'Right, lads, this way.' The wee man was dancing in his eagerness to take them up the stairs. 'Lift's out,' he said as they passed the pock-marked metal. 'And it's the *eighth* floor.'

Jamie was out of breath when they got to the door. 'Okay, Alex, take your hat off.'

He knocked, pushed it open when there was no reply. No commotion either, no flurry of medics barking orders. The hall was filled with pram. Green and blue squares with a wee chick toy suspended from the hood. They squeezed past. 'Cheers, mate. We'll shout you if we need you.' Jamie closed the front door on the concierge, forcing him to step back.

A man in a green overall came into the hall. 'Hi, folks. We're in here.'

He directed them to the living room. A young woman sat on the edge of a couch, elbows on knees, hands twisting hair. Rocking back and forth. Back and forth. Another woman at the window, her velour top stained, arms crossed tight hiding her breasts.

It was Angela from the Drag.

Jamie sensed Alex about to say something; nipped his elbow. 'Hi, Angela.'

She looked past him. 'Hi.'

'I'm very sorry for your loss.'

She stared at him, puzzled.

'Angela, it's Jamie. You know, from . . .' Fuck oh fuck oh fuck. God give me strength, give me words here, please. How did he say this? 'From work?'

She nodded. 'Fuck, aye. So it is.' Almost smiled at the irony.

Awkward, stupid, he wafted his hat across his fluorescent jacket. 'I know, didn't recognise me with my clothes on.'

Immediately, the other woman flew from the couch, pummelling him on the chest. Scarlet eyes scummed yellow, shaking her head like there was water in her ears. It was Francine, Angela's wee sister, thick words splattering. 'Shut your hole, ya fucking cunt. Don't you fucking . . . fucking . . .' Lost in her fingers as she crumpled again, head back to her knees.

'Oh, God, I'm sorry.' Jamie knelt down in front of her, trying to catch the hands that were pushing him away. 'Francine, I'm sorry.' Looking up at Angela. 'I'm so sorry – I didn't mean that.'

Angela shrugged, impassive. Immune.

'Francine, please.'

Francine pushed Jamie hard, knocking him off balance. He wobbled, steadied himself on the arm of the couch. Stood up. 'Look, I'm really sorry about this, Angela, but we're going to have to ask you a few questions. You know, for the records.'

She nodded.

'See while Alex does that, would it be all right if I went through to see . . .' Jesus Christ. He didn't know its name.

'Gemma,' said the ambulance man.

'Angela, would it be all right if I went through to see Gemma?'

Silence.

'Right, I'll be back in a wee minute,' said Jamie. 'Alex.'

Alex was feeding his hat through his fingers, backwards and forwards like a steering wheel, mirroring the rhythm of Francine on the couch.

'Alex, maybe Angela and Francine would like a cup of tea first.'

Alex followed him into the hall.

'Remember, when did they put her down, who checked her? When did she last have a feed?'

Alex reached for the form inside his hat. 'Fucksake, man. This is shite. The wean can only be a few days old. I seen Angela down the Drag—'

'Do not refer to a form when you're speaking to them. Now, put your frigging hat down,' Jamie whispered, 'and go and make some tea.'

Two doors off the sparse, white hall were open: kitchen; bathroom. A third slightly ajar, the fourth shut tight. He tapped gently.

'Come in.'

The room was dark, a nightlight splaying fans of soft yellow up one wall. It was a neat, small room, space enough for a chest of drawers and a slim, cheap wardrobe unit, built over a single bed. Purple duvet cover, purple teddy; half a dozen brooches studded through a silk scarf across the mirror. Francine's room. The cot sat under the window. Beside it stood the second ambulance crew.

'All right, pal?' he whispered.

'How you doing?' Jamie replied.

The man pulled the coverlet back a little. 'Girl. Six days old. Gemma Margaret. Mum put her down about nine-thirty, same as usual. I canny get that much sense from either of them, but I think they'd moved the cot in here today, so the mum could get a wee sleep. The sister came in an hour ago and the wee soul was away. No coughs or colds to speak of. They'd obviously tried to resuscitate her – the mum was holding her when we arrived, so I don't know what position the body was in. No evidence of any injuries that I can see.'

She was lying on her back, face turned towards the window. Long and sturdy, tufty blonde hair like a wee Mohican and her mouth with that half-parted pout Eilidh did. Eilidh's lips were never grey-flushed blue. One little fist grasped at nothing.

'Okay.' Jamie moved the blanket up. 'A523 to Alpha.' He'd turned his PR back up, and the response was too loud. It ripped the stillness, made them both jump. 'Aye, Control. At the locus. Confirm one female child. Would you oblige and contact the casualty surgeon, and have CID in attendance? And someone from the FACU if there's anyone on. We'll also require the shell.' He clipped the mouthpiece back on to his jumper. 'What about the two lassies?' he asked the ambulance man. 'Did they seem out of it at all?'

'On something, you mean?' A long slow shake of his head, a changed perception of Jamie. He could trace it by the slight widening of the man's pupils. 'How could you tell – state they're both in?'

'Fair enough. If you could just give me your name, pal, and your neighbour's, you guys may as well head.'

'Bill Atkins, and in there's Gerry O'Hagan. Both Maitland Street.'

'Cheers.' Jamie put his notebook away.

The ambulance man tapped the side of the cot, the long bit where the rails joined. 'Aye. See you then.'

Jamie heard him in the hall, talking quietly to his mate, then the click of the latch as they let themselves out. He should check on Alex, but he didn't want to leave the wee one on her own. And the boy had to learn, same as Jenny. Jamie shivered. Poor old bastard. It was the first time he'd thought of the pale sprawled shape in Ashley Street as the man he knew as Ezra. At least the old sod had had a life, however crappy.

Jamie moved the cover again, off the baby's nose. Eilidh hated anything tickling her face. You'd see her at night, squirming and rubbing at Godknows what – even the silk bindings of her cot bumper. If one brushed against her face, she'd make these squidges with her mouth.

The door opened.

'Jamie, I've spoke to Angela. Francine's not up for it though . . .'

Angela was at his back, craning over his shoulder. 'How is she?'

'She's fine, really. I've tucked her in – she's fine.'

'Thank you.'

He ushered them out, shut the door. Back to the living room. Francine hadn't moved, hadn't changed her pace.

'Is it okay if we sit down, Angela?' Jamie asked.

'Aye.'

He sat beside Francine. 'You okay, pal?' Forcing her hands gently from her face.

'It's my fault,' she sobbed. 'If I hadny moved her . . .' Again, she pushed him away. 'No even a fucking week. We couldny even keep her safe a fucking week.'

He let her go, folding back into her crumpled cower. Knowing it was pointless; words were pointless.

Angela turned to Jamie. He saw the same apprehensive expectancy weighted in her eyes that he saw in Alex. A roving desperation, seeking guidance, seeking reassurance. 'What are we waiting for?'

'The doctor.'

'The doctor?' She sounded surprised. Hopeful.

'It's a police doctor – he's got to check things.'

'Oh.'

'Angela,' said Jamie. 'You understand that the doctor will have to take Gemma with him?'

First sign of anything on her face. 'Why?'

'It's okay. It's just for a wee while. They need to check, to examine her.'

Francine jumped up, moved towards the door. 'They won't cut her, will they? They canny cut her, they canny hurt her.'

Alex had his hands on her shoulders. 'Ssh. It's okay, Francine. It'll be fine. The doctor won't hurt her.'

'Angela.' Fuck. Jamie hated this fucking fuckpig job. 'We'll need to take Gemma's blankets with us too. Okay?'

The doorbell rang. It was the casualty surgeon. 'Evening.'

'Hello, Doctor.'

'How are things?'

They did it right, these doctors, not whispering, not brisk. Jamie passing the information on like a baton. All this repetition surely helped. The doctor spoke to the sisters, told them what he'd do. He offered Angela some sedative. Gave one to Francine.

'In here?' the doctor asked.

Jamie took him in, lifted the covers. 'Do you want her out, Doctor? Big light on?'

'No, no, that's fine. Um, yes, the light please.'

He got his stethoscope, opened the poppers. Listened at her chest for nothing. Felt her neck, touched her legs. Turned her over with care. Darkening vein trace below her spine. Put her back, closed the poppers.

Raised the eyelids, let them drop. Navy blue.

'I'll wait outside,' said Jamie.

Before he left for work, he always checked his own baby; a talisman, to ensure his safe return. Did it today, Eilidh rattling the bars of her cot, squatting like a monkey.

'Hello, you.' He'd swung her out. 'How's my girl, sweetness?'

Little pliant body curling round his neck, sucking at his ear. Jamie had felt his daughter's nappy, before he took her down to her mother. Bone dry. And Cath going on about fucking sandwiches. Did she not see, did she never see now, this beautiful miracle that they had made? Always wiping and sighing and scolding and sighing, because their life was full of Eilidh.

'No need, no need. I'm declaring life extinct at' – the doctor checked his watch – '12.17 a.m. Can't issue a death certificate, obviously. There'll need to be a post-mortem – does the mother know?'

'I've told her.'

'Well, hopefully it'll be tomorrow or the next day at the latest.' He closed up his bag, put his specs away. 'Have you contacted the mortuary?'

'I've asked for the shell.'

The doctor picked up his bag. 'I'll just check on the mother before I go.'

Doorbell again. Liz Maguire, a DC from Stewart Street. 'All right, Jamie? Shit, division's going mental, eh? Murders, hoor-slashings – I'll be able to buy a wee place abroad at this rate. In here?'

'Yes. Oh, bye, Doctor. Liz, gonny not say—'

'Mr and Mrs – what's their name?' Liz asked Jamie, as she went towards the living room.

'There's no Mr. And it's Cairns.'

'Angela Cairns? Is that no one of your hoors? Ah, Mrs Cairns. We've a special room over at the police office. Would you like to come down there with me?'

'Why?'

'Well, I'm afraid I need to ask you some questions.'

Francine leapt up, pointing at Alex. Screaming. 'He's already asked us a load of fucking questions, ya stupid cow. Get the fuck out our house. Get fucking everyone the fuck out our house and leave us alone.'

Doorbell again. It was like bloody Sauchiehall Street. The undertakers. 'In here?'

Jamie opened the bedroom door. The man went to lift the baby. 'No, wait. Wait the now.'

Back to the living room. Liz Maguire was still talking at the girls. Jamie spoke over the top of her. 'Angela, Francine. That's the gentlemen here to take Gemma. Would you like to see her?'

Angela nodded. She helped her sister into the hall, through to the room. 'C'mon. C'mon, Francine, that's it.'

Jamie motioned for the undertakers to come out. Francine held back, grabbed at Jamie's arm. 'Don't leave me.'

Angela was at the cot. She unwrapped the blanket, lifted her baby. The legs didn't drape themselves over her arm, the fist didn't open. Walked to the wardrobe, cradling her daughter. Took out a little cardigan. Jamie had to say something.

'I'm sorry, Angela. You can't . . . we have to take her dressed. The way she was, like.'

She nodded. Picked up the blanket that had been in the cot. 'This okay?'

'Yes.'

She folded the blanket around the baby's body, gently bending down the fist to swaddle it too. Stroking Gemma's face, covering her with little kisses. 'Francine.' Held the baby out to her sister.

'Jesus fuck.' Francine pushed past Jamie, past the mob in the hall.

'Here, dear, let me,' said the undertaker. 'We'll look after her, I promise.'

He carried her out in his arms, thank God. Jamie didn't want to know if they had wee white shells for tiny corpses.

A detective sergeant arrived as the undertakers were leaving. 'Right, boys, you can leave it with us now. Oh, I brought some bags for the property. Just get it all labelled and leave it in the room, okay? Cheers.'

Jamie and Alex went through to the empty bedroom. 'Right, Alex, we need to strip the bed. Put each sheet in a different bag. Check for any evidence of drug use – watch out for sharps. Fuck, don't look at me like that – just do it.' He spread the bags out on the dressing table. 'We'd better label the mattress too. And we'll need to get her clothes.'

Alex had snot running out his nose. 'Her clothes?'

'Yes, her bloody clothes.'

'Who gets them?'

'We do.'

Jamie squeezed past the dressing table to strip the cot. A tiny tug pulled him back, his jumper caught on one of Francine's brooches. A childish collection of shiny happy baubles: a crude

Pierrot mask, that freaky spider, a spiky enamel flower-shape, beribboned like a medal. And a horseshoe, pinned upside down. Automatically, he unclipped it, turned it round. All the luck ran out if you hung a horseshoe upside down.

There were only two blankets. Two thin blankets, one sheet and a mattress with airholes like the books tell you. Didn't take long to bag and seal them. He always kept property labels in his pocket. You never knew the minute.

Alex wiped his eyes, rough and angry. 'Can we go now?'

'Aye. Let's go.'

'Are we going to say cheerio?'

'Nah. C'mon. Let's get this over and done with.'

Going down the first flight of stairs, Jamie paused on the landing. Heard the beginnings of a long low wail, like a siren or stretching on a rack.

11 May the Force be with You

One long sharp fang. Piercing.

Metal-whetted, slevered bloody mucus.

It was here again. Running, running, rancid breath at her neck. Heaving her breasts, cupping them naked in her hands as they ripped from her lungs. Beside her, in front of her, the black mass grew and it whipped and it turned and it *tore*.

Stinking great teeth in its endless maw.

Awake, asleep, Anna saw the phantom face in every bottle. At first, it was a shadow, growing sharper each time she tried to ignore it. Part taut, scared human, part crusted demon, its tracery of scabs fanned scales across her brow, an urgent, evil, frowning wing, scored in single black nib, blotted all across her face. This face that would not go away, behind her eye when she blinked, superimposed on the body that kicked her nightly. Kicking and crunching her into oblivion, razors for hands, razors for feet, each salty blade a vicious kiss.

She could see it, but she couldn't feel it. Observing postmortems, with their quiet clinicians and their sterilised steel, you could see the cold press of tension as scalpel met skin, could hear the pucker, and the tiny, tearing slice. But you couldn't feel what that girl Linda had felt. Couldn't feel the amazing air-sharp pain on open epidermis as flesh unfolds, turns inside out, sinew severing in thick, stringed lumps from anguished flesh.

Anna's pain was duller. It was the ache of knitting bone and dispersed, bruising blood that had stayed inside, not gushed out. Pocketed, trapped cushions that congealed then healed. And

Ezra's pain – that must have been a mixture of the two – the blunt thud of blows, then the acute crack of bone ripped out through ragged tissue. Did one cancel out the other, in a kind of startled numbness? Was that what her body was doing now, bubble-wrapping itself?

She roared, slammed her head hard, twice against the cushions, desperate to break these plates of lethargy. Stiffened on the second spasm, suddenly aware of another face watching her, a real one, pearly-sketched at the living-room window, mouthing words through glass.

It was Cath Worth, waving like a demented granny. How long had she been standing there? Anna closed her eyes as firmly as she should have closed her curtains.

Then a shout, through the letterbox. 'Anna, it's me, Cath. You had a relapse?'

Could the woman shout with any more resonance? Now the neighbours would know all her business. Anna shuffled into the hall.

'No. Just didn't feel like getting dressed.' She peered round the door, the gap only shoulder wide.

'Well, can I come in?'

'It's a bit of a mess . . .'

Cath pushed past, straight through to the living room. 'You're not joking.'

Anna knew the place was a tip. Newspapers and magazines littered the carpet, dirty dishes and cup rings scarred the blond wood of the coffee table.

'Why don't you get someone in to clean if you're not feeling up to it?'

'It's fine.'

'Well, yeah, compared to my house it is, but . . . Look, do you want me to wash the dishes? It'll only take a wee minute.'

'No. I don't. Why are you here, Cath?'

'Nice to see you too. The hospital phoned me, said you'd not been turning up for Outpatients. Oh, here, they're beautiful.'

Cath raised her hand to a string of delicate baubles that hung above the door. Each one a different pastel shade, sugar plums varnished with lustre.

'What are they?'

'Eggshells.'

'Did you make them?'

'Mmm-hmm.'

'D'you make this too?'

'Make what?' Anna followed Cath's gaze.

'This tapestry thingy – it's fab.'

On the wall behind Anna was a beautiful crochet-like wall hanging, hearts and diamonds and little curlicues, each quarter a perfect mirror of the rest. All the gaps and loops were scalpel-precise. It had taken Anna ages to get it so exact, and she'd used all different colours in the design too. Flat and precise, ironed to an inch of its life before she cased it in the frame. Cath leaned closer, trying to see past the sunlight bouncing off the glass.

'It's not a tapestry,' sighed Anna, 'it's *wycinanki*.'

'What's *wycinanki* when it's at home?

Anna sighed even louder. 'Polish paper cuts. Mr Wajerski had some in his house.'

'Well, it's very nice anyway.' Cath took off her jacket, floated into Anna's kitchen. 'Will we have some tea?'

Mutely, Anna followed her. More than anything she wanted to be left alone, to unpick and lick and not have some stranger bustling through her kitchen. Then this drumming in her heart would stop.

Cath ran hot water into the kettle, to make it boil quicker. 'So, anyway, I was asking Jamie about Ezra, but he says it's all gone quiet. Well, he grunted it from under the duvet this morning – he's in a bastard of a mood. But, from what I gathered, I don't think they can find a single person to fill in the blanks. I'm pretty sure Ezra had no family at all. That was why he didn't go home after the war.' She opened Anna's tea caddy, took out two teabags. 'He missed it though, don't you think?'

'Suppose.' Anna licked her paper-lips. She hadn't realised how dry she was. 'Cruikshanks has been to see me already.'

'And?'

'Same thing. No witnesses, no pals, nobody cares.' She slumped against the worktop, trying to ease the weight on her throbbing leg. 'Story of my bloody life.'

'I'm surprised Cruikshanks didn't get any joy at the Polish Club. Ezra was a regular there. Are you sure they went to the right one?'

'How could you get a Polish Club mixed up? With what – a pole-dancing club?'

'Ha, ha. There's two, you know – one at St George's Cross, and one in Kelvingrove.'

The water shrieked into steam, and Cath poured it into two big spotty cups. Coffee cups.

'I'm sure Cruikshanks checked them both.'

'Well, I've been thinking – there must be something we can do. My sister's a student at the Art School. Now, I'm sure Ezra went there – decades ago, obviously – but . . . I just wondered if it would be worth asking if they knew him. I think it was silver-smithing he taught, or jewellery-making maybe?'

'That's right, that's what he did before the war – in Poland.'

'Okay then, how about a trip to the Art School?'

'I don't know, Cath . . .'

Those white china mugs, right by Cath's hand – *they* were her tea mugs.

Cath reached for the milk carton on the worktop. 'D'you take milk? Urgh.' Shook it, sound of double cream slopping inside. She poured the yellow globules into the sink, coating dry-dock dishes. 'Anna, I don't think you're going to get any better holed up here, do you? What does your doctor say about going back to work?'

'I just tell him I'm having dizzy turns, and he writes me another line. And I've these to take.' Anna rattled a bottle of pills. 'Uppers or downers or something.'

'Let's see: oh, these – give you a hell of a migraine . . .'

'Haven't tried them, whatever they are. Plus my ankle's still buggered.'

'Look' – Cath wiped her hands on her skirt – 'I don't know you that well, and I'm sure you'll tell me to mind my own business, but that's nearly two weeks you've been off.'

Mutinous Medusa glare. Anna could see herself reflected in the kitchen cupboard. If only her snaking hair could turn Cath's tongue to stone.

'D'you not think you'd feel a lot better finding the bastard that did it, instead of moping round feeling sorry for yourself?' She handed Anna a brimful cup. 'And what about those poor lassies down the Drag? You're not much help to them here, are you?'

Anna's face was crumpling. She watched it, horrified. Scaffolding bone dissolving in saline, and she could feel her lip go. Hot tea dripping from its saucer puddle, splashing on to Anna's bare feet. Cath was the only person she'd seen since Cruikshanks.

'I'm frightened.'

'Don't be daft. You'll be ready for him this time.'

'No. I mean . . . I'm frightened to go out.'

Only whispered, but the sound resonated from every wall, seeping its yellow stain across her home. Laughing at her with cancer-teeth, clicking its tongue and shaking its head.

Then Cath was taking her cup away, leading her back into the living room. 'Right. Go get washed and dressed. You can come home with me for lunch, then I'll get Jamie to contact Welfare. I'm sure they've got counsellors or therapists you could talk to.'

'No. Thanks, but no.' Anna shook her head, pendulum brain striking painful fluid. 'Look, I know you're right. But I can't . . I know Jamie's your husband, but how could I face him – any of them – at work?' Her sinuses ached.

'Will you at least phone the Welfare Section? Lots of folk must go through things like this – they're not going to judge you.'

More snivelly words, all oozing pulpy-mushy from Anna's face, like the skin had been stripped. 'I feel so . . . pathetic. It wasn't like he did anything to me. You know. Compared to what he did to that poor Linda . . .'

Sobbing again, proper heaves, huddled on the couch.

'But he could have. He would have killed me. In that stinking dunny – I keep seeing his face at night. Only it's not his.'

Cath took her hand. 'So he's a vicious wee bastard. So get him. Bloody hell, if you can't fight back, Anna, and do something about it what hope is there for the rest of us? Did the hoor know him?'

'No. Said he was just a punter.'

'There you go. A pathetic wee wanker like all the rest, who can't get a shag unless he pays for it.'

Anna tried to smile, but the nerves in her cheek were still quivering. Off on their own wee jaunt to sad-land.

'I do know how you feel, Anna. There's days I don't want to set foot outside, and other days I can't bear to be alone in the house.'

Anna pushed hair from her eyes. 'But you've got Eilidh.'

'Exactly. Speaking of which, I have to get home. I just wanted—' Cath stopped, waited as Anna's mobile played some Bach. 'You want to get that?'

Anna rummaged through magazines, knocking them to the carpet.

'No, it's there.' Cath pointed to the coffee table.

'Oh. Right. Hello? Yes. Yes. Sorry – who is this?' Anna frowned. 'Uh-huh. That's right. Is that you that's . . . Say again.' She clicked her fingers at Cath. 'Pen, *pen*. Can your mummy not . . .?' A pause. She scribbled something on a scrap of paper. 'Okay. Okay then. That's fine. Ten minutes.'

Anna dropped the phone. Leapt up, bashing her shin on a wooden corner. 'Shite, shite, shite.' One leg cradled while the other hand pulled off her pyjama top. Beneath the seersucker fabric, ribs like pressed leaves.

'Anna, what are you doing?' asked Cath.

'I've got to go. That was – ach, it's too complicated. Remember the Fat Man call?' The top was round her neck.

'Here. Put your arms up.' Cath helped her untangle herself. 'Was that him?'

'Yeah. Wee boy. Says his mum knows something. But she can't speak. Says if I meet her now, before Ama comes back – whoever Ama is . . . Shit, this is bleeding.'

Anna dabbed her shin with newspaper. Her ears fizzed with the incline of her head, painful bubbles, and she had to sit down. Had ten minutes passed yet? She couldn't find her watch. Eased her pyjama bottoms off, something sticky stretching off her fingers.

'When did you last have something to eat?'

'I had some toffee . . .'

Ah, that's what it was.

'Shit, what's the time? Cath, grab me a pair of jeans from the washing basket, would you? And a top, any top. Quickly.' She tried to stand again, wobbled on disjointed knees.

Cath pushed her gently to the couch. 'You're not going anywhere. Get your arse in that chair.'

'Cath, I have to. Help me up, please.'

'Tell me what it is.'

'It's to do with Ezra – I think. I left a note for his neighbours – the Jarmals – did you know them?'

'Nope.'

'Anyway – they've disappeared, the neighbours. Could be a witness. That was her wee boy saying she's too scared to speak. But if I go now, he says she'll be on her own.'

'Where?'

'I don't know. Some café – Capaldi's?'

'Yeah, I know it,' said Cath. 'London Road, just past the Tolbooth. Used to be on my beat.'

Anna was up again, making for the door. 'Shite, that's bloody miles away. Oh, Christ, c'mon – we're going to miss her.'

Cath grabbed her car keys. 'Anna, you're stark bloody naked. And you're not fit to get out of bed, let alone the house. You stay here and I'll go.'

'Don't be daft.' Anna pulled a coat from the hallstand. 'It's me she wants to speak to.'

'Has she met you?'

'No.'

'Well, I'll just say I'm you. What's her name again?'

'Eh – Jarmal. Mrs Jarmal. Cruikshanks still thinks it's an HB gone wrong, but someone had painted a swastika on his door – did I tell you that before?'

Cath was running down the path, Anna calling after. 'He said she'd dogshit through her letterbox – I need to know if it's connected, if she knows who it was . . .'

'Okay. Got that,' shouted Cath through the driver's window. 'Wee boy, Asian lady. Dog poo. Death.' She started the engine, Anna's voice competing with Radio Clyde.

'You sure you'll be all right? Do you want me to try and phone Jamie?'

Cath turned down the radio. 'For God's sake, Anna, I know the score. I'll be fine. Take some details, give you the statement.' She nodded at Anna's groin. 'Full frontal now. Bye-bye.'

Anna double-locked the door against imagined wind. She should pace a while, like an expectant father, but her knees were too stiff, head too sore. Cath would never make it in ten minutes. She considered phoning E Division, getting them to send a car. That might scare the woman even more. Did dialling 1471 work on mobiles? Number withbloodyheld. Capaldi's. Had she written the name down right? Should she ring them, tell them? What? Cruikshanks. What would he say? Anna wasn't used to this panic. It felt like some wiring had come loose. She played impatiently with the bit of paper. Folding it into submission. The sheet was a fan now, concertina bellows in a quivering sheaf. Flapping numbers on one side, letters on another. Christ. *Letters.* She smoothed out the paper.

Bambina,
Glad you're home. Poppa not well. Asking for you. We need to get
the money back. What have you done that the police want you?
Please be a good girl for Nonna. I'll wait up for you. xxx

The note she should have given to that hoor, the one with the
scabby legs. Shit, she'd promised the old lady.

Had ten minutes passed yet? Anna went to phone Cath, then
remembered the stupid bint didn't have a mobile. She should
have taken Anna's. Capaldi's was a café, not the sort of place
you'd arrange for a secret meeting. Miles from the West End too.
God, she should never have let Cath go on her own. No, Cath
would be fine – she'd phone when she'd some news. Half an hour
max would be all it took to get a quick statement. Once Anna had
read it, she'd decide whether to get CID involved. Might be a kid
at the wind-up, but her instinct told her it wasn't. Bollocks. Cath
was right. Her mother was right. She needed to get back to work.
Maybe there was a dog-walking service for people like her –
Action Against Agoraphobia. Anna dug out the phone number
for the police Welfare Section. They were very friendly.
Appointment made, she took another bottle of wine and hunched
up beside the phone.

Cath checked her watch, then herself in the mirrored splendour
that was Capaldi's. A museum piece of wooden booths and
marble counters, the café served the best ice cream in the city.
Mr Capaldi (junior), a thin, greying little man, dapper in his
white coat, served boilings and fudge from the towering glass
jars behind him, while his stout curly wife scooshed the
espresso machine with practised style. The ornate booth she sat
in had an illustrated mirror on the wall, and the puckered glass
gave a soft reflection of her neat new head. Thank God for
magic serum. Red and blue patterns on the mirror ghosted
across her face.

Of course. *Wycinanki.* Wee papery pictures, usually cut in

newsprint. Cath remembered it now, framed in pine on the walls of the Polish Club. They had hens and stuff up in the dining room – nothing so delicate as Anna's creation. And she'd seen it somewhere else. A bit cruder, done with scissors rather than a craft knife, but careful cuts all the same – lily shapes and doves, all tinted faint reds and blues. Cath had seen it on the morning of Eilidh's christening, in the envelope Jamie had been asked to give her. It was stuffed in a drawer somewhere, getting crushed. A work of art Ezra had laboured over in his dark, dank room, so delighted for a baby he'd never met.

For the first time in ages, Cath wondered what right she had to feel so sad. All those days she wasted snivelling and sighing, when she had a husband and a baby and a home and love. This heaviness had to stop one day, and she was so fed up waiting. You could wait for a lifetime and still not have moved one inch. What had Ezra been waiting for, all those years in his damp single-end? To be alone, to cultivate no one but strangers and loose connections: that must be the worst thing in the world.

The clock on the café wall ticked on and on, walnut burr round a copper face. Forty minutes after Anna had taken the call, and there was still no sign of Mrs Jarmal. Cath got here in twenty, it was unlikely she'd missed the woman. She'd need to be going soon, though. Jamie was out early tonight, some football thing with the school again, and she was meant to be bringing his tea home. Though why he couldn't go to Morrisons . . . that was her. Had to be. Pretty face swathed in dark fabric, holding the hand of a little boy. Cath half stood, waved her hand, then turned it into a tucking-back of her hair when the woman froze. The boy propelled his mother forward.

'You the polis-lady?'

'Uh-huh.'

'One what put that card in the temple?'

Cath had no idea what he was talking about. 'That's right. And what's your name?'

'Doesny matter. We've only got a wee minute.' He sat down,

spoke rapidly to his mother, who covered her face with her hand, nodding. He moved along to let her in the bench beside him.

Cath pointed at her cup. 'D'you want some juice? Ice cream? What about your mum?'

'Naw. Listen. You want to know about Mr Whiski?'

'Did you know him?'

'Wee bit.'

Their edginess was beginning to affect Cath. She found herself looking round, checking they weren't being overheard. 'Well, Mr, em, Whiski thought some bad men might have been annoying your mum.' Right away, a leading question. Had she not listened on her Female and Child Course? This was not the time for careful probing.

The boy spoke again to his mother, Mrs Jarmal replying before he'd finished.

'Yes, she says she was very angry with the man.'

'*The* man. Just one man?'

'Uh-huh. I told you on the phone – the Fat Man.'

'Yes, that's right. So, what did the Fat Man do?'

'He pretends he's nice. Gives you stuff.'

'What kind of stuff?'

'Money, sweeties.'

'You or your mum?'

The boy scrunched up his nose. 'My mum doesny like your sweeties. Says they taste like bloody crap.'

Cath nodded, smiling over at Mrs Jarmal, who was still whispering at her son. 'Okay, but tell me about the Fat Man.'

Mrs Jarmal was increasingly agitated, talking constantly as her son spoke. Cath couldn't tell if she was angry at the boy, or the Fat Man, or Cath. The boy shouted something that cut across all her outpourings, and the woman became silent once more.

'So, he gives you stuff, but then he wants it back. And he started being horrible, shouting at us in the street – Paki bastards and that. Said he'd get the troops on to us.'

'Who're the troops?'

'*I* don't know.'

'Did the Fat Man put dog's dirt in your letterbox?'

The boy's eyes darted up. 'How d'you know that?'

'Mr Wajerski told me.'

'Oh, right. Aye. An he done that paint-thing on Mr Whiski's door – I seen him. He's a big bully, so he is – wanted Mr Whiski to take a loan of more stuff.'

Cath scribbled this down on the napkin in front of her. A witness who could place the Fat Man at Mr Wajerski's door. The pen caught on the soft tissue, and she had to hold the paper taut with her other hand. There was a jingle of beading as Mrs Jarmal leaned over and snatched the napkin from her. Cath looked up, their eyes locking. She put her pen away. 'What d'you mean, more stuff?'

'The sweeties and that. He kids on he's nice at first.'

'So why didn't you tell anyone?'

'My mum was feart. I'm no feart of him, but. Big fat pig.' His little chin was jutting out, below the same scared eyes as his mother.

'I can see that.' Cath smiled. 'Now' – she paused for the regulation beat – 'you know Mr Wajerski's dead, don't you?'

'*Aye.*' The single word emphasising her stupidity.

'Well, does your mummy know anything about what happened that night? The night he was killed?'

The quick-fire question, the even quicker response. The woman was clearly distressed, shaking her head, tapping her fingers on the side of her skull.

'Ssh.' The boy placed his hands on top of his mother's. 'We heard someone shouting . . .' He halted. Mrs Jarmal had sprung from her seat, and was pulling at his arm. Two men were approaching their table, shouting at her in the same unfamiliar tongue. Mrs Jarmal hurried towards them, raising palms like scales of justice.

The boy followed his mother. 'We got to go, missus. Sorry. We got to go.'

One man took Mrs Jarmal under the arm, led her from the café. The other turned to Cath. 'You have no business with us. We have done nothing wrong.'

They were gone before Cath even thought to move. The table was fixed to the floor, the bench solid against the booth. Difficult enough to squeeze into, it was harder still to get out. Cath wriggled along to the edge, unfurled her legs and dived to the door. 'Wait. Please wait. Where can I get hold of you?' she shouted after the boy. 'The Fat Man – what did he look like? Just wait a minute, please.'

By the time she'd reached the door, they had disappeared round the corner, towards the Barras Market. Cath started to run. Black bin-bags and sandwich boards littered the pavement, and she weaved to avoid them, gulping market smells in panting breaths. Hot stink of brine from the oyster bar, a spatter of crusty vomit, the fresh green leaves of a fruit stall. There was shouting behind, but they'd gone in front. They must have doubled back. An arm like gammon hooked over her, and a woman shrieked in Cath's ear. 'Theeve!'

Cath could barely breathe, the weight of the battle-scarred forearm pressing on her larynx.

'You don't pay, you theeve! *Theeve!*' The grip loosened sufficiently for Cath to be flung around. A bristling Mrs Capaldi was screeching. 'I sick of you junkies. I know your face. The polis are coming. I no a charity. I sick of you all.'

Cath tried to shake her off, but the woman was a big hairy clamp. She could see folk in the street beginning to form a circle. 'No, you don't understand. You've got to let me go. Here, here, take my purse.' Cath jerked her head towards her shoulder. The strap of her bag was cutting into the flesh where Mrs Capaldi was tugging at her.

'Is full of stolen credit cards. Theeve-bitch. I *know* you.'

'You know me because I used to work here, you stupid cow!' Cath bawled back. 'You're hurting me. Bloody let me go.'

'I take you back for the polis.'

She'd got Cath by the hair now. Scalp and skull straining like they were Velcroed with barbed wire. Cath could see only feet and pavement as the woman wrenched her along the street. She jerked her head back sharply, striking Mrs Capaldi on the nose.

'*Puttana la Madonna!*' Mrs Capaldi released Cath, her hands flying to her face. '*Non vedo!*'

Blood pumping between her interlocked fingers. Cath mirrored this action by clasping at her own malevolent mouth. She searched for help, some channel of escape, appealing to the passers-by who were melting one by one as her panicked gaze met theirs. 'I didn't mean it. Oh, Jesus. I'm so sorry. Oh, God, I didn't mean to hurt you . . . Oh, God, are you okay?'

Mrs Capaldi was staggering backwards, lowing like a heifer. '*Lurida vacca!* She try to kill me!' She weaved off the kerb and stumbled into the road.

'Here, it's all right, I've got you.' Cath put her arm against her jailer's back, steered a sobbing Mrs Capaldi through the hingers-on that remained, and led her round the corner to the café. She had to find Mrs Jarmal. If she got Mrs Capaldi to the door, she could leg it. The husband could look after her . . . The café was empty. And still, Mrs Capaldi's hands were cradling her face, shrouding the mess Cath had made. She must have broken the woman's nose. Cath backed her into a chair in the passageway that led to the café toilets.

'Right, you sit here and I'll get a cloth.'

Cath went behind the café counter, soaked a dishtowel under the tap. She had to get to a phone. Tell Anna there was a terrified woman who had seen it all, out there, somewhere in the Barras among the pirate CDs and the woodwormed furniture. There was a freezer in the back kitchen, and she grabbed some ice cubes in another towel, wrapped the whole lot in the damp one, and took it out to Mrs Capaldi. Shit, maybe she should call an ambulance while she was at it.

'I am so, so sorry. Look – is there a phone I can use?' As Cath reached down to apply the ice-pack, a tall blonde policewoman strutted through the door.

'There a Mrs Capaldi here?' she called to no one in particular.

Cath raised her head. 'Yeah, we're over here,' she shouted through the open doorway.

Just a young lassie. Her long ponytail swung down her back and she was chewing away at gum. 'Believe you'd a wee bit of hassle, Mrs Capaldi,' said Blondie, not bothering to introduce herself. 'Lucky for you I was just down the road. Fail to pay, is it?'

'I'm not Mrs Capaldi,' said Cath. 'That's Mrs Capaldi. I'm the fail-to-pay.'

'What?'

'Only I'm not. Bit of confusion there.' Cath had gone that simpery way. She could feel herself standing like a little teapot, hand out ever-so-casual to explain it all with perfect clarity, and how they'd all laugh and laugh and ignore the fact she'd broken some old woman's nose. 'I was actually taking a statement from a witness – a possible murder witness. In fact, it's really vital we track her down. Could you give your Controller a shout, see if . . .'

Blondie stopped chewing her cud for a minute. God, she hated the backshift. The longest shift they did, and the most frustrating. Neither a beginning nor an end, just an eternity of afternoon, stretching bleak into evening and eating up your life. You always had plans to get things done on the backshift. All that blank, fluid time, waiting to be filled with outstanding enquiries, phone calls, tying up of loose ends. But pishy crap continually got in the way – call to a shoplifter – sorry, no one else free to attend. RTA – push the car over to the other side of the street, so it's not on your beat. Backshift was being ordered from the office to stand mind-numbing guard over a dangerous building. A sentient sentry to point out to gormless pedestrians that yes, the sign and the big barrier really did mean the road was closed, yes, even for them, no, it didn't matter that they'd be quick. All your plans up in the air, till at the end of the week you'd achieved nothing but missed opportunities, projects half done and a vague sense of disorientation. She was supposed to be report-writing this afternoon, had it planned for days. Instead, here she was interviewing some dizzy bitch who thought she was Nancy Drew.

'Right, so – you were taking a statement? From her?' She nodded at Mrs Capaldi, whose fleshy jowls dripped backwards as she tipped up her head and clamped her nostrils.

'No. You see, I was—'

'Rosa! Rosa!' Mr Capaldi appeared in the doorway. Mrs Capaldi rose majestically at her husband's voice, and a torrent of Italian slapped Cath in stereo. The Capaldis began to push her, gesticulating at the policewoman, poking Cath in the chest. The policewoman yelled louder than them all.

'Right, folks, that's enough. Ee-nough. Now – you.' She pointed at Cath. 'You said you were taking a statement. You a cop?'

'No, no, I—'

'She a bloody nutter. She no pay for her order, then she do a runner.' Mrs Capaldi's voice was muffled and snotty. 'She break my nose.'

'*Si, si.* She theeve from us, know?' Mr Capaldi was jumping on the spot, filling the space as if in compensation for his diminutive stature.

'So you did this?' the cop asked Cath.

Mrs Capaldi had whipped the towel from her head. Her nose had doubled in size, the damp cloth smearing blood and bogeys across the wide contours of her face. It was true. Red and green should never be seen.

Blondie raised her PR to her lips. 'Right. I'm taking you up the road so we can sort this out.'

Cath laid her hand on the policewoman's arm. 'Can you just listen to me?'

'Get your hand off my arm.'

'For Christ's sake, will you let me explain?'

Slow, slow, quick, quick, slow, heart and voice in an uneven dance.

The cop smiled sweetly. 'Ho, *doll*. Speak to me like that again, and you'll be spending the whole night in the pokey. Now sit in that chair and shut up.'

Like they'd squeezed all the air out, Cath drooped into the seat. Then she started yelling. 'One o one, three one seven.'

'What?'

'That was my reggie number. One o one, three one seven.'

The cop recognised the rhythm of the numbers allocated to each officer on joining the force, and paused long enough to give Cath the chance.

'I used to work in Stewart Street, then London Road. Metal Mickey still in the bar? I was with him when he got the doing that gave him the steel plate in his head.'

Blondie put her radio down. 'Who are you?'

'My name's Cath Worth. I was a cop in E Division. You can check it out. I am *not* a junkie thief.'

Blondie cop was tapping her teeth with her pen. She had to believe her.

'Mrs Capaldi probably recognises me because this used to be my beat when I first started. Look, it's a long story, but I was helping out a friend. Anyway, this witness did a runner and I tried to run after her. I would've come back and paid, honestly. What was it – a coffee and a fly cemetery? Jeez.' She turned to Mr Capaldi. 'You remember me, eh? I used to come in here with Casper, years ago. You know, Casper – loved your lasagne – used to take a load of it to his pals at the mortuary? Mind?' She nodded encouragingly.

A nasal whine to her right. 'And what about my nose?'

'Mrs Capaldi, I am truly sorry if you got hurt, but you were tearing chunks out my head. Look.' Cath ran her fingers through her hair, collecting clumps of frizz for examination. She was sure she could feel a bald patch, bent her head to show Blondie. 'Please, you have to believe me.'

Blondie sighed, got out her notebook and tried again. 'Right, you want to tell me exactly what happened?'

'It's really important that you speak to a Sergeant Anna Cameron. She's in the Flexi at A Division. A murder there, a Polish man called Ezra Wajerski. I don't know who's in charge. What I do know is that a potential witness and her wee boy have just been grabbed by two men and huckled into the Barras. An Asian woman, about five three, five four, in a dark blue robe and headscarf. Wee boy's eight to ten, wearing a red jumper and school trousers. The two men were both in their early thirties, Asian, but in Western dress. One had a brown short coat on – like a storeman's overall.'

Cath thought she would weep as the cop finally shouted her Controller. 'Ah, E Echo, would you put me on talkthrough? Obliged. Echo 119 to all stations. Report of a possible abduction. Potential witness to a serious crime last seen in the vicinity of the Barras. One Asian female . . .'

12 Sirens

Anna was wakened by a thump, thump, thump in her head. She'd expected a hangover, but nothing as violent as this. The noise was detached somehow from her brain and it thumped and it thumped and it wouldn't go away no matter how she pressed her ears into the pillow and she worked out the noise was coming from outside her body. From outside the house. Bleary-eyed, she clambered out of bed, knocking over a bottle on the bedside table. Draped her dressing gown round her naked shoulders. All the doors leading to the hall were closed, and she could only make out a silhouette against the frosted glass. Her heart curled in on itself, like burning paper. She didn't know if it was night or morning. Cath had never phoned, though Anna had sat for ages waiting, just her and some wine and some G&T and then just gin. The figure was too broad for a woman, too tall. If she could see him, whoever he was . . . her ribs were doing that xylophone drill, a hollow wooden frenzy – no, it would be black in here – he had the light behind him. He wouldn't know she was there.

The man was thudding again, more vicious this time, not pausing but rattling and banging and was that a kick a fucking kick and this was *her* house. No bastard was coming into her house, because once they did, that was it. There'd be nowhere to creep into except the potholes of her head, and then she'd never get back out, so fuck no way, no way and she was thinking all this, kind of, as she grabbed the spear from the wall and unlocked the door.

Jamie rushed at her, grabbed her arms.

'About bloody time too. Where the hell have you been? And what the fuck do you think you were playing at, getting Cath embroiled in some half-arsed . . . The Tank's going to crucify you by the way. He is off his bloody head, slavering, the works. Jesus, Anna.'

Jamie must have seen fear-glazed eyes, for he slowed a little. 'Sorry. But what the hell did you think you were doing? Cruikshanks is near to tears – the only decent lead they've had and you send Cath. Cath – God, she's no even a polis. She didn't even have a bloody mobile phone. Anything could have happened to her.'

'Is she all right? Did she speak to Mrs Jarmal?'

He swept his hand from eye to temple. 'Aye, just enough to scare the shit out of her and send her into hiding by the sound of it. We're just back from London Road – never had to bail my bloody wife out before.' A slow grin spread.

'What? What's so bloody funny? What happened?'

'She did a runner out the café after your Mrs Jalliwally.'

'Jarmal.'

'Aye – ended up fighting in the street with the café owner. Not paying for her tea and buns! Meanwhile the star witness disappears into the ether with two strange men, never to be seen again.'

'Shite. But did she say anything? Jarmal, I mean.'

'Load of crap by the sound of it – some fat man vandalising the old boy's door. Anyway, you can read all about it at the office. The Tank wants you in there now.' He sniffed the air. 'You been drinking?'

'No.'

He lifted up her wrist. 'Nice spear you've got.'

She was still gripping the ornamental javelin, little fur tassels quivering with indignation. 'It's an assegai.'

'Whatever. Looks the part. But how the hell d'you not answer your phone?'

' 'Cause no one's bloody phoned me.'

'Aye they have – been ringing for bloody hours.' Jamie was on one knee, behind the hallstand. He held up a white wire, tiny plug tip attached to nothing. 'That's why. Your phone's unplugged.'

'I never did that. Anyway, there's one in the bedroom. I'd have heard it.' Anna opened the bedroom door, pointed to the phone by her bed. It was unplugged too.

'You losing the plot completely?' said Jamie, shaking his head.

She was plaintive. 'I didn't unplug it.'

'God, Anna. Don't start. Just admit you were too pished to remember.'

His nostrils were widening, mouth turning cruel. 'I mean, you stink like a bloody jakey, and your head's obviously fucked. Nice of you to fire Cath off into the unknown, then go and get your head down.'

'I didn't—'

'Why in God's name did you not ring Cruikshanks, tell him that the woman had phoned and leave it to someone who knew what they were bloody doing?' He was up close against her face.

'There wasn't time.'

'Bollocks.'

'I don't know,' she shouted at him. 'I thought I was doing the right thing. How did I know your stupid wife would balls it up?'

'She's not stupid. You put her in a terrible position. What did you think you were doing?'

'She wanted to bloody go.'

'So fuck, you stupid cow! You should have stopped her.'

'You said you loved me,' she yelled.

He dropped his arms. 'What?'

'In the hospital. You said you loved me. I heard you.'

'Oh, Anna.' He spoke softly. 'Please don't.'

'Do you?'

'I was upset.'

She laid her head on his shoulder. 'So am I.'

'Anna, I can't do this.' His voice vibrating on her skin.

She had to. Had to take his hands inside her dressing gown, pass them over her waist. 'Do you love me?'

'Fuck, don't do this,' he whispered.

'You used to love me. You said you did, then you pissed off and left me. Why did you say you loved me? Which bit of me do you love?' She shifted one hand up to grip her breast. 'Do you love these?'

His voice fragmented, kaleidoscope words. 'I love my wife.'

She licked the side of his face, not caring any more. 'What about my arse? Do you love it?' He let his hand be placed there, in the cleft of her buttocks. She moved his fingers back and forth, deeper between her legs.

'Go on. Check out the pussy. You like nice pussies, don't you?'

'Please, stop it.'

'It's soo lovable, Jamie. Go on, love it. Just love a bit of me, I don't mind.'

'*Stop it.*' He gripped both her wrists, high above her head. Slammed her against the wall, hard brick solid behind her. His eyes black, searching. Slow lowering eyelids, a movement of heads. His mouth finding hers, tongue forcing lips apart, stubble grating face. Kissing her, gouging with tongues and fingers, Anna spinning, hands moving past her face, opening and closing like a cat yearning to claw, but still he held her fast, bodies pressed hard; she could feel him moving beneath his clothes, and she moved her hips towards him. Hands hurting against the wall. He was forcing her flesh into the wall. When she thought she could no longer bear the pressure, it stopped.

Slowly, still kissing her, never stopping, never. She could smell herself on him, head filled with everything and nothing. Hands traced up her naked skin. She parted her legs with his fingers there. Sucked at his bottom lip, whimpering like a child. Inside her now, nudging, pushing.

'Please,' she moaned.

The word woke him, made him fall away like she had bitten him.

'Jesus.' His face a mockery of lust turned to dust. 'Jesus.' He backed away, zipping himself, wiping his hands on his trousers. 'I'm sorry. I can't . . . I need to go.' He pulled the door open, twisted his neck. Not looking at her. 'You'd better get dressed. Get yourself down to Stewart Street. Rankin wants to see you.'

'Jamie.'

'No, Anna. No.' He closed the door, a quiet whumph.

She was shaking, tiny tremors on all her limbs. Drips like albumen between her thighs. Her smell would be under his nails.

The belt on her dressing gown trailed on the floor. Anna seized it, tying it roughly round her waist, bundling up the exhilaration that was riding her despair. Her tongue rasped over her mouth, one more silent, delicious time. Sticky, tepid saliva, too thick to slake. She needed a drink. Hauled herself to her feet, leaning stiffly on her good side. Tea. A warm glow in a cup that was good for shock.

She limped to the kitchen, whole body barbed alive, her ankle aching. Rankin couldn't touch her – she was officially off sick. By God, she rubbed her eye with the heel of her hand, that wasn't wrong. They couldn't make her go into work. Rankin could go fuck himself. Or have the cleaner do it.

She fumbled for the light switch, silver spotlights snapping on fingers of halogen. On the worktop, two spotty cups pooled in too-bright light; one branded with lipstick that wasn't hers.

Cath.

A rush of slicing cut where the name passed through. Anna hadn't been expecting that, had carefully not thought of Cath.

More than a pound of flesh spilled, tearing open quicker than Linda's face. Then Anna gave a deliberate, *so-what* shrug. That shrug that pops up like toast, when you know you are more deserving, have higher motives than the mundane world would understand, and are not some sad, lonely, past-your-sell-by cow. She went to the fridge to get some milk. None left. Plenty of wine, mind. Hampers of the stuff. She picked up a bottle of Chateau-something, weighed it in her hand, then flung it with as much brute force as she could muster across the room. It struck off the edge of a cupboard and shattered into heavy clunking chunks, wine raining down on beech lino.

'You could have got me some fucking milk!' she screamed. 'You could have got me some milk.'

Looming dark arms and bulks of buildings, jostling, jeering, clapping him on. Waving him off. Out of town, leaving hulks of grey and red stone behind. Eventually, the air opened a little and moonlit clouds began to puff above the smog. Suburbs dwindled to villages, people to sheep. The road narrowed and soared black, up and twisting over the Campsie Fells that flanked the city to the north. Jamie drove three miles before he started crying. A solid block of emotion hammering at him, and he couldn't distinguish its components. He only knew it hurt beyond pain, that moment of anticipation when you strike your funny bone. It hurts so much, for an instant you can't feel it. He pulled over, and slumped his head on the steering wheel, gripping like it was the only tangible thing left. His tears terrified him.

Jamie was not a man of emotion. He didn't cry at funerals, nor when his daughter was born. Didn't cry when he stripped dead infants. He didn't. Saw himself as a man of quiet principles. Och, he might flirt a wee bit, might take the piss. Might speak to things in court that he'd not strictly seen – but these were oiled currencies in a rusty world. Whatever else, he was honest. At its basic level, where it mattered, he knew the value of the truth.

He should go home, say nothing, clear this up. Tell Cath the truth. They always told the truth. It was a mistake, no reason, a mistake. *Fucksake, man. Stop snivelling.* He thought if they'd just gone on as normal, him and Cath, then things would sort themselves out. She wouldn't. He wouldn't. Never. They had a pact. They would have been all right. He wasn't a bad person. Cared about Anna, yes, but he loved his wife.

Put it down to experience, and forget it. He could hear Derek's calm voice of reason. *Fucksake, man, it was just a shag.* Alex's tone would be slightly incredulous. *Well, son, if you're truly sorry . . .* his mother's sorrowful shake. *You want to fuck her again, don't you?* Ah, that would be Lucifer himself. Kind of belly-bumping confusion you'd want to talk over with your best friend.

Cath.

Only that wasn't true. His Cath had gone months ago. Eilidh's birth had killed her. It wasn't the baby's fault, it was his. He couldn't keep Cath safe; she'd been replaced by a woman he didn't know. Anna was just the mercury flare that made him see that. Poor Anna, who didn't know what day of the week it was.

Anna's fear, her vulnerability – that was the reason Cath gave, when Jamie went to retrieve her from the police station. Not in answer to Rankin's screeching, but said quietly, in the car, on the way home. When he was yelling at her. Apart from that, Jamie and his wife had hardly spoken. He'd been furious with her, at the embarrassment she'd caused, the potential risk to his career. The snide comments and wanted posters and whistled tunes from *Porridge* and *The Great Escape* he'd have to endure. And the fact she'd become so stupid to think all this was a game. Cath didn't want to know, no longer cared that children died and life went on and women's faces were slashed as they sold their bodies.

It was late when Jamie had arrived home. Cath on her back, diagonal across the bed. He'd slept on the couch, so he didn't disturb her. In the morning, in the moment when consciousness flows too thickly, his first thought had been Anna. He got dressed in the dark and returned to her.

Red flashes, angry noise. The clock flashed 8.30 a.m., but the noise that roused Anna wasn't her alarm. Shriller, twangy – her mobile phone. It was Jamie. 'I'm at your front door.'

'Why?'

'I didn't want to scare you. Can I come in?'

'Fuck off.'

'Anna, you need to go see Rankin. He'll have your bloody stripes if you don't.'

'I don't care.'

'Yes you do.'

'Well, it's too late now, so who gives a shit?'

'Look, it's not. I told him there was no reply last night. Said you must have been out for the count with all the painkillers you were taking.'

'Great. So now he thinks I'm a bloody junkie.'

'Anna, going to let me in? I'll take you to the station.'

'I don't need your help.'

'Anna, please. I haven't slept. We need to talk, sort this out.'

'I'm not a bloody *this*.'

'Cath told me how scared you are.'

'Fucksake – comparing notes, were you?'

'Anna . . . last night. It was my fault, totally.'

He was offering her a way out.

'Anna. C'mon, I don't want to have this conversation in the street. Will you bloody let me in?'

She walked to the door, still talking on the phone. 'Come on then.'

He held two paper cups of coffee. 'Anna, can we—'

'I don't want to talk about it.'

Did he regret the feel of her? Hands and tongue and breath and body in octopus oblivion? Did she? His face was sallow-white, hair black. Mouth beautiful.

'Go and get ready and I'll drive you in,' he said.

'I thought you wanted to talk?'

'Jeez – you just said you didn't.'

'I know. I . . .'

He put the coffee down on the hallstand. 'D'you want to know what way I'm dealing with it?'

'Uh-huh.'

'Okay.' He coughed. 'Well. I figured that we've, you know, we've been together before. So last night doesn't count. It was nothing new, just a different time from when it should have been – out of sync if you like. Like Narnia.'

The inside of her lip was ragged. 'Right. And do you find that's helping?'

'Not really.'

'Great.'

There, in that moment, she had two choices. To fling herself, begging, at his feet, and give in to every weakness circling overhead. Or to be Anna. She watched his face, all tight and held-in. Fought the sigh that was shuddering through her body.

'Okay. I'll . . . look, just sit there and I'll go and get some clothes on.'

It was hanging there, ripe for the picking. *No, I prefer them off. No, let me come with you.* Any one of a hundred innuendoes, dripping with fruitfulness, begging to be plucked.

'Sure.'

Anna ran a shower, where her needy tears could mingle undistinguished from the suds. The water dashed her face, stung her eyes. She worked methodically down her shoulders and her arms, waiting for the knock. By the time she'd reached her feet, she was starting to wrinkle. She turned off the water and stepped out. Still no Jamie. Big gloopy strands of hair dripping, so she swathed a towel turban round her head, cosied up inside her bathrobe. It felt a little better. Lots of big soft things round an empty middle. Doughnut woman. Some of the clothes on her bedroom floor were still cleanish. She mixed them round with her bare foot until she found a jumper and jeans.

'Okay, that's me.'

Jamie put down the newspaper he was reading. 'Sure you're going to be okay?'

'Yup.'

He took her hand.

'Jamie . . .'

'We've got to get you through that door. C'mon now. Deep breath, then jump.'

'What?' He couldn't be serious.

'Swing your arms and jump. We'll jump together, into the great unknown.'

'You are bloody mental.'

'I'll look after you, I promise. Trust me.'

So she did.

Rankin was as she'd expected. Patronising, fierce and a touch pathetic in his posturing. 'And do we have any more of our little friends on a retainer? Perhaps your milkman would like a wee hurl in the Drugs Squad? Or maybe you have a neighbour who'd like to book some speeders? I'm sure we could arrange it.' All the time he was ranting, the bastard made her stand.

'As I explained, sir, the circumstances were extreme. Mrs Worth is an ex-police officer, and I thought for expediency's sake—'

'You thought for *expediency's* sake, did you? Can you spell that, Sergeant Cameron?'

T. H. A. T., you big tosser. 'Yes, sir, I can.'

'Mmm. Mmm. I'm sure you could. Frankly, Sergeant, I think you are a disgrace. You've showed extreme lack of judgement . . .'

Oh, you're so not wrong there, Physic Super.

'You've put a civilian in grave danger, and you've lost us the strongest lead we had in the Wajerski murder. I don't need to emphasise how damaging this is to your prospects, do I?'

'No, sir.'

'Ever been disciplined before, Sergeant?'

'No, sir.'

Although if you spoke to Martin, he might disagree.

'And as for the debacle with these hoor slashings. I mean, I told you to jail the bastard, not offer yourself up as a bloody sacrifice.'

'Sir, I can assure you that will be my main priority.' Her ankle was throbbing.

'Oh, did I mention? In your absence, I've appointed a new sergeant to lead the Flexi Unit.'

'I heard. But now I'm coming back, sir—'

'Shut your fucking face,' he shouted.

He was doing the good cop, bad cop thing all on his own.

'Now, as I was saying, Sergeant Murray comes with very high recommendations from Traffic North. My original intention was to have him oversee the transition of traffic wardens to local authority control, but I now feel—'

'Sir, you can't move me to traffic wardens.'

'Sergeant, I can do whatever the buggering bollocks I like with you.'

His smile slid beneath her ribs.

'You've proved ineffective both as a leader and a police officer. Traffic wardens is probably aiming too high, but we'll give it a whirl while I decide what to do with you. May as well squeeze some use out of you while we can, eh? When you can be bothered to come back to work, that is. Now get your arse out my office and out my station.'

It was her station as much as Rankin's. He couldn't stop her going up to check on . . . for fucksake. She pulled the handwritten sign off the door. They'd called it *Operation Bad Blade*. Liz Maguire looked up from a newspaper.

'Morning, Sergeant. How's the head?'

'Surviving.'

Anna winced as she clocked her own photo on the wall. So used to recording corpses, IB's photographers had developed the skill of positioning and lighting every face they encountered as if it were a death mask. Yet some cops still chose IB to do their wedding photos on the cheap. Bloody and bruised, but still with all her own teeth – that would be Anna's epitaph. She was last in an illustrious line – six little maids, all in a row.

Pamela Macklin, twenty-eight: the first. A haggard waif of a girl who had no teeth, several abscesses and four kids to four different men. Her cut was small and deep, more of a gouge. Perhaps he'd practised on her, unsure of how much pressure to apply, and the blade had stuck instead of skimmed?

Simone Carruthers, eighteen. Thick dark curls, heart-shaped, torn-open face. Too young, too pretty. Was she one of the ones who thought being a call girl would be glamorous fun? A sugar-daddy-coated way to coast through college? Stupid wee cow.

Carole Guthrie, twenty-one. A skinny blonde, some freckles still visible beneath stitched flesh and the thick slick of foundation she'd plastered on. One jagged flick down her left cheekbone. Anna was sure she'd seen Carole somewhere before.

Rebecca Bytheway, nineteen. Yes, Anna remembered her from the Drag. Not only the name, but the fact they'd lifted her in a public toilet – sharing a picnic of red wine and French bread in a cubicle with a speccy bald guy. Only distasteful aspect being that he'd paid Rebecca extra to dip the bread into the toilet bowl first, then wipe it under the rim before tucking in. She was the girl who'd been slashed with the broken bottle.

Linda Morrison, thirty-three. Same age, same night. Two cuts for the price of one. The long slash down like all the rest, then the sweeping curve out that arced like fireworks when Anna closed her eyes.

Each face more scarred than the last, swelling to a silent, slash-free crescendo:

Anna Cameron, thirty-three (related police assault).

Anna took a pen from Liz's desk, scribbled *Sergeant* in front of her name.

'So, apart from them all being hoors – any connections?'

'Well, we're working on the files you guys have given us, but nothing obvious. It doesny help that none of them want to talk to us – won't even tell us how much cash they had stolen.'

'Ah, that'll be for tax purposes.'

Liz frowned. 'Thought you'd be taking this a bit more seriously, Sergeant. You know, it could be one of your traffic wardens next.'

'Don't be a smartarse, Liz – it doesn't suit you.'

Jamie had waited for her, drove her down to Cranstonhill. 'D'you not think you should just go home now?' he asked.

'I want to speak to Cruikshanks.'

He shrugged. 'On your head be it.'

'I'll phone you, okay?'

'When?' he urged.

'Soon.'

Surrounded by familiar lockers and bodies and sirens and smells, Anna's confidence was growing. Even Rankin's spittled diatribe and Liz Maguire's nonchalant cheek had made her feel better. She belonged in this world of uniforms and order and strength. The DI was in the incident room, stuffing himself with a bridie and beans, all squidged inside a buttered roll.

'Inspector . . .' she began.

He raised his hand, pointed at his mouth. Chewed and swallowed, waved at a chair. 'Anna, how you doing?'

'Fine. Look, about Mrs Jarmal.'

'Ach, it's done now. End of the day – it was your postcard to thon temple that made her get in touch in the first place. One of our liaison chappies is working on tracing her, though it's like getting blood out a stone.'

'Yeah, I know, but—'

'Anna, just leave it, eh? I've done my greeting over this one. What's more important is that you tell me everything you do know.' He took another bite.

'That's all. I put my number on the card, copied down the lettering on the Jarmals' door and asked anyone that knew them to get in touch.'

'And the wee boy?' His words were fluffed with pastry.

'*Mammy knows about the Fat Man.* That was it. What about the number he phoned from; can you trace it?'

'Aye, to a phone box in the Calton.' He burped. 'Pardon. My guess is the family have done a runner, staying with relatives maybe. Your pal Cath said the woman was shitting herself. Haw, Breggsy.'

A thin young man with ginger sideburns sidled over.

'Fetch me those profiles would you, son? I'm going to try cross-referencing—'

'Hey, boss.' DC Graeme Hamilton leapt in the room. 'Got a match back on they teeny trainers. Nikes.'

'Shite.' Cruikshanks scowled. 'I was wanting them to be some obscure foreign crap; no bloody bouncy moonboots for bandy neds. Well,' he sighed, 'you'd better do the usual anyway. Check with stockists, manufacturers, blah-di-bloody-blah.'

'Your heart's just no in this one, is it, boss?' Hamilton grinned.

Cruikshanks chucked back a couple of pills. 'My heart's no in, full stop.'

'Eh – were the trainers important?' asked Anna. 'Is that them on the board?' She pointed at the footprint.

Cruikshanks smiled. 'Like I said, no harm done. You away and get yourself better, hen, and leave the clean-up tae us.'

The world was whirling all around her, scrutinies and decisions and hunches and fact, all filtering through this sieve that was Cruikshanks. How could he be sure nothing fell through the mesh? He'd never met Ezra, never seen him as anything other than a corpse. That was how it worked, though, how you warded off those tiny wounds that lingered. Poised like darts, here in this room now, Anna could feel them, feel Ezra, feel Linda working their way in. Too much. Too many splinters, all honed with the knowledge they were nothing to do with her. Anna had no right to feel their rawness. She was just a jailer of hoors.

13 Tiny Links

Hoary ice still laced the pavements, though it was near lunchtime when Anna emerged from the Welfare offices. Wrapping her camel coat round her, she walked down the concrete steps, out into the pedestrian precinct. A row of young saplings, skeletal arms wind-stripped, wore individual skirts of wrought iron to guard them from dogs and boys. Tiny strings of lights were threaded in lieu of leaves. Bigger, more lurid bulbs swung between the lampposts, each post crowned with a coronet of grinning snowmen. Despite the cold, a wintry sunlight bathed the whole, and Anna felt good. The counsellor she'd seen had been lovely – a middle-aged lady who didn't offer any advice, just gathered Anna's thoughts with tiny nods, like a shepherd with his dog. They'd talked about her work, what she did, and before she knew it Anna found herself speaking of things she'd rather not. Like how, although her bruising was going, she wanted to keep shielding her head, keep her body safe by staying inside. Like how, at night, she slept with her light on. Briefly, fitfully, until a noise or clammy dread woke her. Like how when she'd been lying in the dark, waiting for him to kick in her skull, she'd pissed herself.

None of these things fazed the counsellor. She just nodded, and with each nod Anna felt a little lighter. What she was saying seemed to be okay. When the hour was up, Anna wanted to continue. But the woman was not her pal, she was a counsellor, and so another appointment was made. That was okay too. Don't mix business and pleasure.

No, really. Don't. Not quite shriven then. That was one thing she hadn't mentioned.

Anna was going back to work after Christmas. One of the few things the counsellor had told her. Confront each fear when you feel strong enough to do so. Anna wasn't sure how to define this 'strength' but, buoyed up by her hour's sympathetic hearing, she phoned the office on her mobile before she'd reached the end of the precinct. Resuming work, even if it was bloody traffic wardens, was official. Decision made, Anna had a free afternoon. What to do with the last slice of the sick cake? Not meet Jamie for lunch, that was number one priority. Not think about Jamie or Cath and her several phone messages, urging her to get in touch.

Shopping. Generous Christmas shopping. Not that Anna had a surfeit of giftees to gift to. Her mother and stepfather, an aunt in England, two or three friends. She wandered into a department store, the old-fashioned kind, galleries looping a huge inner courtyard, each balcony adorned with plastic swags of green and realistic gold pine cones. An overpowering deluge of perfumes cloyed in the cosmetics hall, as she dodged the bullets fired by panstick-orange soldiers. Upstairs to gifts, gents and cookware. Her stepfather loved cooking, and Anna knew he didn't rate the cast-iron pots and pans in the local markets. Her mother loved food. So a set of Prestige saucepans with a lifetime guarantee would be appreciated as a thoughtful choice. She hoped. She could've gone for Christmas, she was sure. But Anna preferred to go in the summer, when the sun was hot and Martin went off on his boat.

He'd love this jacket. It was navy, beautifully cut in heavy fabric, with gold buttons. Discreet ones. It might be an idea to get it, in case he made one of his extravagant gestures. To make up for not being able to visit her. They'd had a long phone conversation. Obviously, he couldn't come to the hospital, and then he'd been away on a course down at Bramshill. But he'd seemed really upset, and he had sent the lilies, and that hamper. And she had shagged Jamie, so maybe they were square. Yes, she'd buy it. There was only one left in his size, and, as far as she knew, Harriet wasn't the kind of wife who kept tabs on his clothes.

Anna passed the children's department. A glittering tableau of mirror pond and children skating preceded the entrance to Santa's grotto. All the frozen figures were clad in the finest Christmas fashion the store had to offer. A dumpy little girl doll, fingers questing in polythene snow, reminded Anna of baby Eilidh. The dummy was wearing a plum-coloured velvet bolero and dress. The dress had a jabot of cream lace at the neck. Anna saw the same outfit hanging on a rack nearby. But all the sizes were in ages. What age was Eilidh?

'Excuse me,' she asked an antler-wearing assistant. 'I want to buy this outfit, but I'm not sure what size to get.'

'Well, what age is she?'

'I don't really know. She's about this size' – Anna gesticulated hopefully – 'and I don't think she can walk yet. But she sits up straight and she eats. Apart from milk, I mean.'

The girl thrust a dress and jacket at her. 'Probably about a year. Go for twelve to eighteen months, then she can grow into it if need be.'

'Right. Thanks.'

The assistant was gone, scurrying towards scuffle sounds emanating from Santa's den. Voices raised as she pulled the curtain open. 'Haw, missus. That Santa's reeking of bevvy. Called my wean a wee shite, so he did.'

Anna fingered purple folds, enjoying the softness. The colour would be rich against Eilidh's curls. Not that the baby would get excited, but Cath would like it. It was the kind of thing she seemed to like. A bit like curtains actually. God, what if it was hideous? You don't go round dressing babies in household furnishings. And why did it matter if Cath approved? Velvet was not reparation. *Dear Cath. You know how you said if there was anything you could do to help?*

Would Jamie think it kind, this gesture, or would he recoil at the intrusion? God, she liked the kid. She just wanted to give it a present. As Anna was swithering over sizes, her mobile rang.

'Hi, Anna. It's me, Cath. Please don't hang up.'

Anna's tongue thickened. What could she say, what could she say? What did Cath *know*? She dumped the dress back on the rack and made for the stairs.

'Hello, Anna,' persisted Cath, 'are you there?'

'Yes.' Did her voice sound normal?

'Where are you?'

'Eh – in town.'

'Good. Meet me outside the Art School in twenty minutes, okay? It's important.'

'No, wait . . .' stuttered Anna over the silence of an empty line.

All Cath had done since Capaldi's was worry about how she could make it up to Anna. Tried ringing her several times, but got no reply. It was the debacle in the café that tipped it. Must have been. Cath felt so stupid. She wanted to hide away whenever she thought of it, which was several times every day. Anna hadn't been in touch since – no wonder. Trusting her to do a simple interview. God, that poor woman: Cath had sent Mrs Capaldi flowers, in gratitude for her dropping the charges. A counter-threat of assault charges from Cath had also helped – that had been Jamie's idea, not Cath's. Hence the flowers were a secret, which Jamie would see as an admission of guilt.

Cath missed Anna. Tentative, chary, like two cats circling perhaps, but there'd been the beginnings of a friendship there, Cath was sure. And she desperately needed friends just now. Without Anna, Cath might have lost Jamie. Whatever turgid torpor their lives had slipped into, she couldn't bear him not being there.

According to Jamie's monotone replies to Cath's questions, Anna's number was up. Rankin was ready to have her disciplined, and no one in the Flexi Unit wanted her back. Well, part of that was down to Cath. She'd buggered up big-time, but maybe she could make it right. So Cath had got her sister to ask around. Delving into Ezra's history might help Anna score some points with CID – and help Ezra too. Someone had to. There was an elderly professor at the Art School who said she remembered Ezra, and Cath had arranged to meet her, wrapping it up like a present that Anna could not refuse.

Anna was waiting outside when she got there.

'Hiya.' Seemed nervous, shy almost. Poor soul was still scared to be outside. On impulse, Cath kissed her on the cheek. 'Hello, you. How you doing?'

'Cath, what's this about?'

There was no need to be so narky. She smiled broadly at Anna. 'You're looking well. Can we . . . look, can I just say how sorry I am about Mrs Jarmal. I know you trusted me, and—'

'Cath, please. Forget it. Look, I don't have much time. Is that it?'

God, woman, cut me some slack. Cath's laugh would have put a hyena to shame. 'No, no, I could've put that in a wee card. I've something much more practical for you. Come on in.'

The Art School hallway was very dark, blackened wood beams arching in sinuous leaps above them. Oblong white panels stretched down in languid droops, tiny panels of coloured glass shimmering purple and blue, and the air was heavy with scents of spirit and paint. Thick dark spindles, bathed in red light, edged long narrow flights of stairs.

'Up here,' said Cath. 'How's your leg, by the way?'

'It's fine.' Anna looked away.

Was she embarrassing Anna? Cath had tried her best: slapped on some lippy, even done her hair with that serum stuff again. Put on a new top – ethnicy, very 'in', the woman in the shop had said. Covered several layers of flab too – bonus. Through gritted grin, Cath tried again. 'Like I said, I reckoned Ezra used to work here, so I asked around. Professor Arlington – here, that's her office here – she remembers Ezra. I thought you might want to speak to her, do a bit of digging. I'll – I'll wait outside if you like,' she added, aware of Anna's increasing discomfort. The woman looked like she was being marched to her execution.

'Don't be daft.' Anna chapped the door. 'Professor . . .?'

'Arlington.'

Professor Arlington was designed for an age even older than herself. Though unlikely to have been born at the time, her ear-sharp bob and elongated elegance showed a yearning for the twenties. Her accent was warm. 'Sergeant Cameron, yes? And – Catherine – you're Suzie's sister, I believe. Please, come in.'

Over to you now, pal. Cath determined to play the silent side-kick. She'd done enough damage as it was. The professor offered them tea from a pewter jug, steely grey as her hair. 'So – Ezra . . . hmm? You ladies under his spell too?'

'Hardly – this is a murder investigation, Professor.' Anna helped herself to some paper lying on the desk. 'May I?'

'I jest, my dear, I jest. You wanted to know more about him? Oh, a pen too – are times so hard for our girls in blue?'

'My apologies' – Anna scowled at Cath – 'I seem to have left my notebook in the car.'

'You help yourself, dear. Well, it's been many years since I last clapped eyes on old Ezra. Many years.' Her eyes squeezed like a purring cat. 'What a gent, don't you think? Charming. He taught here when I was a student – so good with his hands, that man. In fact, if you like, I could show you some of his work; it's just down here.'

They left the little office, down ebony corridors to a vast white studio. Ranked round the walls were oak and glass cabinets, tall as bureaux, and full of delicate jewellery and silverwork. Salvers and beaten jugs, little goblets and massive chargers. At the front, painted white twigs lit with fairy lights held strings of beads and silver rings. 'See, that little bangle there, the one with the tiny links. That was the kind of work Ezra did.'

Professor Arlington opened the cabinet and hooked the bracelet with her pinkie. 'Such gentle fingers, so patient. And with the students too – well, he was quite a one.' She dropped the bracelet into Cath's outstretched palm.

'How do you mean?'

'Put it this way, my dear. Several young ladies shed tears when Ezra upped and left this establishment.'

The bracelet was finer than chainmail, the clasp a single slim lily that dripped in the light. Its shape was similar to the flowers on the *wycinanki* Ezra cut for Eilidh's christening.

'Where did Ezra go when he left here, Professor?'

Anna didn't seem interested in the bracelet. Crisp and businesslike, she was eager to move on. Cath knew that was the right way to be. A cop couldn't be sentimental – what use was that? Or, at least, they couldn't show it. See, she'd gone wrong there too. The slagging she got when her neighbour caught her with a packet of ham in her raincoat pocket, surrounded by stray cats in West Princes Street. Pan the mewling wee bastards' heads in, aye – but feed them?

'Off to find his fortune,' said the professor. 'He got friendly with the Flax family. Wonderful jewellers, you know. The mother was a part-time student here. She'd married *in*, you understand – didn't have the family touch – so they sent her here for some refining. Now, wait . . .' She led them out of the studio and into a smaller gallery. Facing them on all sides were portraits and photographs. 'We call this the Rogues' Gallery. Former students and staff – we keep them just for fun. Now, where, where . . . ah, here we are. Allegra Flax.'

A slim, dark-haired woman with pale green eyes looked down from a gilt-edged frame. It was a hand-tinted photograph, so nothing looked quite real. Cath had seen pictures in the same style illustrating the old books her mother collected: gripping reads like *The Girls' Book of Heroines*, and *Angela Saves Saint Ursula's*. The woman was wearing a light blue sprigged dress, and the apples of her cheeks and her lips were stained ruby-peach. Round her neck was a fine silver chain, a tiny lily pendant caught in the dip of her thorax.

'You know, I don't think we have any pictures of Ezra. Anyway,' continued the professor, 'Allegra here was so impressed with Ezra's skills that she offered him a job. Her husband was quite a bit older, and they needed someone with fresh new ideas. Particularly *European* – Ezra could even recreate Fabergé, you know.'

The woman in the picture didn't smile. Her gaze was distant, distracted as if there were something going on just off camera, something that she'd much rather be involved in. Cath had the sense that she'd only just sat for an instant, to be captured in a flash, then gone, while some other, more patient, mortal had filled in the blanks later, with coloured chalks.

They followed the professor back into the corridor. 'I'm not really sure what happened after Ezra left; that would have been around 1950, and I went back to Kirkcudbright not long after. I would've thought he'd set up his own business eventually. Never seemed the kind of man to take favours or charity. Working for someone else wouldn't have been his style for long. Maybe you should talk with the Flaxes – I think they've still got a shop somewhere in town.'

'We'll certainly do that, Professor Arlington.' Anna shook her hand. 'Thank you very much for your time.'

'My pleasure, ladies. I hope you find the creatures that killed poor Ezra. I swear, I felt sick to my stomach when I heard he'd passed on.'

She left them at the foot of the stairs. There was a public payphone in the foyer, with a Yellow Pages on the shelf beneath. Anna began flicking through the thin sheets.

'Well?'

'Well what?'

'Was that useful?'

'Hmm – we won't know until we find the Flaxes, will we?'

We. That sounded good. Cath would just stay schtum, offer to drive. Anna's long, thin nose poked towards her chest as she searched for any likely entries. No bumps, no hooks, just a clean, sheer line of cartilage, drawn like a sketch, above two thin slashes for lips, which were chewing at themselves as she scanned the pages. Anna wasn't really a harpy. More like one of those cool girls at school: the prefect who was also captain of the netball team and had her much older boyfriend pick her up at school. The kind who clearly didn't need the approval of the disco dollies and who made your heart flip if she favoured you with a smile.

'Here.' Anna tapped the page in front of her. 'Flax and Flax – Jewellers of Distinction. Wellgate Wynd – where the hell's that?'

'It's off the Trongate, up at the back of the Amusement Arcade; you know, the one by Burger King. Want me to show you?'

Chauffeuse and native guide – Anna would have to take her along for the ride now. Cath tried not to get excited, tried not to notice the pathetic-ness of both feeling, and ignoring, this rising sap.

They walked towards Cath's car. 'She was very *theatrical,* the professor, wasn't she?'

'Hmm.'

Anna moved so quickly. Only a trace of a limp in her loping, swooping strides. How would she know when to stop, marching in front of Cath like that? Renfrew Street, where the Art School sat, was a long, narrow road, bridging the crest of a steep hill, which dropped away down various side streets. Cath's car was parked down one of these perpendicular streets. She just hoped the handbrake had been ratcheted on firmly enough.

'Think she was a frustrated actress? That's what I wanted to be, you know.'

'What?'

'An actress – down here – it's the—'

'Maroon hatchback.'

'Yeah . . . anyway, that was my thing. Wanted to be famous, have loads of people adoring me.' Cath was aware she was prattling on, but, maybe, if she kept talking, Anna would forget to say that she'd jump a taxi and go to Flax's on her own.

'Why would you want to be famous?' Anna made it sound dirty.

'Dunno. So I could be remembered for something, I guess. You know, leave my mark. In you get. So,' Cath started the engine, 'what did you want to be?'

'A cop.'

'Aye, but before that, when you were little.'

'A cop.'

Tucked away in a dingy back lane, Flax and Flax – Jewellers of Distinction – struck Cath as just the sort of place Professor Arlington would frequent. It also belonged to a different age, when ladies in furs would take tea and have their maidservants accompany them to take the silver for replating. Like all cities, Glasgow grew in spurts and ripples. First the pioneers, the settlers in search of water and space. Then the partitioners and controllers, parcelling land and altering the sweep and seep of rivers, allowing the traders to sail up deltas, to let the merchants pay the builders to build grander homes to house their growing wealth. Wealth fuelled by industry that was encroaching on the very same merchants' land which was now teeming with the bodies they'd lured in from the country, to man the industry that now spoiled their views, its stink encroaching on their grassy arbours.

So they moved out, these rich folk, created suburbs on virgin land, having drained the inner city dry and left the mighty heart of the place they'd created to rot with neglect and hunger and the souls of the serfs left trapped in bursting slums who'd dreamed of hope and space of their own. Only the poor and the slow and the desperate remained in Glasgow's scrag-end. Half of Wellgate Wynd had been boarded up or pulled down, ugly gapes across the cobbles. Two tenements remained. . . one bestriding the Wild Pig pub, the other housing a bygone jeweller's. A discreet brass plate and bell quietly coughed the entrance to Flax and Flax. They rang, were scrutinised through netted surveillance (nothing

so crude as cameras here), and then silently granted admission.
A corpulent, black-haired man waited to receive them.

'Good afternoon, ladies.'

Flax and Flax was an ebony jewel-womb; crimson satin back-cloth in the window, smudged, flaw-swirled glass and wrought-iron shuttering. No hint of what lay within. A treasure cave with smooth, rich rosewood walls burnished by reflected glory. Bright, fine glitters everywhere, in glass cases, under counters, on bracketed shelves. Flax and Flax were purveyors of all good things, it seemed: heavy gold chains, platinum rings, antique rubies and emerald lozenges, but its true raison d'être was diamonds. Hundreds of them, ranged by carat, colour and cut.

'And how may I help you today?' The jeweller smiled with gold-tipped teeth, dabbing his upper lip with a yellow duster.

Anna proffered her warrant card. 'Sergeant Cameron, Strathclyde Police. I'm sorry to trouble you, sir, but I need to ask you a few questions.'

'And I'm her colleague – Cath Worth.' Cath stretched past Anna to shake hands with the man. Felt fingers with the texture of damp sponge. She noticed a thick square pinkie ring, squidged beneath a knuckle like knotted bratwurst. The letters H and A were intertwined on the surface of the ring.

'Police, eh? I thought you didn't work here any more.' Again, he dabbed the duster on his fleshy jowls. 'Each time I ring, it seems you're not at home.'

'I'm sorry, Mr – Flax?'

He nodded. 'Lionel Flax. Last of the line, I'm afraid. Once, this was a thriving family concern. First my grandfather, then my father – Harold—'

Cath could see Anna, poised to speak, and she knew whatever it was would ride over the top of Lionel Flax's mournful mean der. Her interruption would be kinder.

'Your shop is wonderful. I never knew there was a jeweller's down here.'

'Sadly, not many do any more. We survive on trade of course –

wholesaling these little lovelies.' He stroked the glass beneath him, where some of the larger diamonds were kept. These stones were rougher, unfinished. They didn't sparkle with the luminosity of their sharp-sliced cousins, snug in rings and pendants elsewhere in the shop.

Cath had never agreed with the parachute style of policing, but she just knew it would be Anna's bible. Barge in, do what you had to, then bugger off. Cath had been taught differently. Her tutor cop, a wily old whippet called Frank, had been grudging with his words, but generous with his sentiment. One of his favourite sayings was: *Take time to smell the roses, lass, 'cause that's usually what's masking the shite.* But she couldn't hold Anna off for ever.

'Sir, if you could just give me a minute of your time, I'm here about a gentleman I believe you or your family may have known. His name is Ezra Wajerski.'

The man's face darkened. 'Why are you here?'

'I've just said.'

'No. What has he done? Stolen from someone else? Even now, when his flesh must flake from the bone? Is he not ancient?'

Anna's lips were pinched, white. 'Sir, I don't know what you mean.'

'So old, and yet so evil still. How can they admire that?'

'They? Who're they?'

Cath cut in, 'Mr Flax, Mr Wajerski hasn't done anything – he's dead.'

At once, Lionel Flax's smile returned. 'Dead, you say? Ha. May God be praised.'

'Why do you say that, Mr Flax?'

He ignored Anna, turned back to Cath. 'Did he die badly?'

'Well, yes. He died alone, in—'

'Mr Flax, we're not at liberty to say how he died. But what we do need is help piecing together why someone may have wanted him dead. I take it you did know Ezra, then?'

'I knew Wajerski, yes.' Mr Flax spat on the wine-patterned carpet. 'Did I wish to know him? No.'

'I believe he was a friend of the family?'

'He was no friend of the Flaxes.'

'But he worked here, yes?'

'For a time, when I was a child.' Great, fat arms shuddered on the counter. 'I do not wish to speak of him.' Flax stared, bug-eyed, at Cath. 'Can she make me?'

'Not unless you're being detained, sir.'

'And am I?' he asked Anna.

'Of course not. I just need—'

'Then all I have to say on the subject is this: that old bastard deserved everything he got. I hope he suffered for hours before they dragged him down to the bowels of the furnace, where I pray he shall be consumed for eternity. Now, if that is all, I want you ladies to please leave my shop.' His duster was at his face again, furious dabs around his mouth and eyes.

Cath pulled the door-latch down. 'We're sorry to have upset you, Mr Flax.'

'Please – just go.'

Anna barged past Cath and out on to the street. Everything was a competition with her, even leaving a bloody shop. 'Hey – wait up, Anna.'

'What the fuck did you think you were doing in there?' she spat. 'Why didn't you let me do the talking?'

' 'Cause you were making an arse of it. He's the sort of guy you sook up to, flatter a wee bit, then sympathise with his story – not demand a Q&A session two seconds after meeting him.'

'And you're always right about people, aren't you, Cath?'

They were power-walking across King Street car park, cars and people dodging to avoid the fiery angel that was streaking through their midst. Anna swirled the same, invisible distance around her as the woman in the photo. When she was simmering with anger, like now, with all her attention focused on a point that was not Cath, her eyes slid away behind a third eyelid, like a cat or a lizard looking to another reality that wasn't shared.

Cath would carry on blithely, be a trouper, and see if this veil would lift. 'Not always, no. But what d'you reckon to Lionel? Could he be your Fat Man? Bit of a bloater, and rich with it. And, now, I may be wrong about people here, Anna, but I got the impression he didn't like Ezra much.' She smiled wide, telling her brain they were having some banter.

'Yeah, tell you what: why don't we trot off to Cruikshanks just now? Tell him we were playing at Cagney and Lacey and there's an angry diamond merchant who's the answer to all his prayers. Hmm, apart from the fact I doubt Flax could make it up Ezra's stairs without having a heart attack, and he was left-handed, while the post-mortem shows Ezra was struck across the face by a small, right-handed person; oh, and his feet are about a size fifteen, and the footprint recovered at the scene was a four or a five. Apart from that – yeah, you go for it, girl.'

They stopped beside Cath's car. She clicked the central locking open. 'Why are you so angry with me, Anna?'

'I take it there was shag-all on daytime TV today, and that's why you thought you'd pick on me?'

Cath drew back, like from a slap. 'I'm only trying to help.'

'No, you're not. You're sick. What you're doing is getting your kicks, Cath, and wasting my time. Why not go on one of those Murder Mystery weekends if you're that desperate? Or join Neighbourhood Watch. I mean, I get paid to do this. What's your excuse?'

The back of Cath's eyes were smarting. Words punching her on all sides, bitchy, furious, cruel, cruel words, spouting like a gargoyle. This tirade was undeserved, no matter what traumas Anna was going through. 'Same as yours, I imagine. That you wish you'd done more to help Ezra. Because Anna, let's get one thing clear – this isn't your investigation either.'

Anna slammed the half-open car door shut. 'You know your problem? You're a nothing person. You've got nothing in your empty life, so you're trying to sniff round mine. Well, you meant nothing to Ezra, and you mean nothing to me. We're not friends,

Cath, so stop panting round me like a collie dog. Away and get back to your nappies or iron your dishtowels or whatever it is you do all day. Just fuck off and leave me alone, because I can't take any more of your well-meaning whines.'

Anna marched away from the car, her words still buzzing and biting in swarms round a bloated corpse.

14 Mistletoe and Wine

Christmas Eve and all's well. Anna took the dress out again, held it in front of the window. It *was* pretty. Eilidh would look like a Victorian cherub. She'd gone back to buy it that morning, pretending she'd take it round to Cath's later. But she knew she wouldn't. Guilt had tasted like anger at first, then reduced to dull acceptance. Anna was a dirty cow. Anna had no scruples. Anna had no shame.

Anna ached for fingertips to smooth her brow and tell her she was loved. Her heart was empty, appalled at what it found there: no humanity, just the desire to save herself at all costs. A picture of cells came into her mind. Cells spooked her, with their thick steel doors and echoing darkness, their little hatches for foetid air. She'd felt their claustrophobia right at the start, in her probation, doing her stint as female turnkey. An old asylum seeker – illegal immigrants they were called then – was choking with fear.

'Put your arm back through.'

'No, darlin', no. I got to breathe.'

Thin-haired arm, persistent in its defiance.

'You have to do what I say.' You have to obey me.

'I don' want it shut, man.'

You draw out your stick, bang it hard against the door. 'I'm in charge. Put your arm back through.'

'But baby, I got to breathe.'

And it won't go back, this wizened spider limb that can't reach you. So you hit it and you hit it to protect yourself.

When put to the test, Anna was not good. From the first time she put on her uniform, from the first time she could choose what she would be, Anna was a coward and a fraud who shielded herself with ignorance and denial. After all the things she'd done and said to her, Anna would never see Cath again. She'd wash away her image, till it was never there. Christ, she'd used that tactic for worse things than Cath Worth, with her face like a puppy's being tied up to drown.

If Cath hated Anna, then she'd leave her alone. Toughen her up for the killer blow that one of them would receive. Like a curse or a mythical quest, one must die so the other might live. And why the hell should it be Cath that was the victor? She'd had her chance with Jamie, and look how happy that had made her.

Anna stowed her booty in the hall cupboard, turning the heating on while she was there. It was icy, colder than outside. Should have put it on 'timed' before she left the house. Leaning over to touch the radiator in the living room, desperate to soak up some embryonic warmth, she saw her answer machine was flashing. Martin. He'd said he'd phone tonight. He knew she was out today. The machine had recorded every word exactly. Didn't even have the decency to chew the message up a bit, or cut it off before the, most certainly final, end.

'Darling, hi, it's me. Look, it's really awkward, this. Harriet and I have been asked away skiing. Its actually Simon's girlfriend. Well, fiancée now – did I tell you? Anyway, her parents have asked us all to Chamonix for Boxing Day. So, we're off tomorrow – amazing we could get flights. Anyway, I know you'll be terribly busy, and I'll see you when I get back. With a *big* present, I promise. Bye, darling. Bye.'

Amazing, how succinctly he'd crammed all that vital information into the slot of time before the beep. Precise and polished, rather like his lovemaking. Well, she could take back the blazer when she returned the dress. She'd better phone Cruikshanks too. Offload on to the professionals and get back to her hooring. Although even the slashing investigation was no longer strictly hers.

'Can I speak to DI Cruikshanks?'

'Who's calling?'

'Anna Cameron.'

'Oh, hello. It's Brian Welsh here. Em, he's not available right now, Sergeant. He's preparing for the Queen's speech. Well, no really – he's just about to do a telly appeal.'

'For Mr Wajerski?'

A pause. 'That's right. How?'

'I just had a couple of things to tell him about Ezra, that's all.'

'Like what?'

She didn't like the DC's tone. 'Like, can you get Mr Cruikshanks to call me?'

'Look, Sergeant, with all due respect, DI Cruikshanks is a very busy man. I'm sure I can pass on a message.'

'Look, *Breggsy*, just get him to phone me. Tell him it's in relation to a man called Lionel Flax, all right? Can you remember to do that, in your busy, busy office?'

'Certainly, Sar-junt. And a very Merry Christmas to you too.'

'Up yours.'

Carol concerts or cartoons on the telly, Slade and Wizzard on every wavelength she tuned in to. She switched everything off, made a coffee. Her blank, safe home was closing in on her, its silence an indictment. She'd return the clothes today, get them and her out of the house. No car though – it would be impossible to park. She'd take the train, maybe grab a bit of dinner. Surely there'd be no office parties on tonight.

Town was frenetic, so many people all with desperate intent. Immersion therapy, her counsellor called it. Sink into your fears, and touch the bottom. Then push off hard and float through the pressure. Her attacker might be ploughing through the crowds right now, searching for a cardi to give his nan. She pictured him at home, wrapping presents or eating beans on toast. Doing the *Record* crossword, ink-patterned fingers smudged with newsprint, pressing on the pen. Just a normal wee guy, not a monster. Nothing to be scared of. Anna went into the department store.

There was Customer Services. All she had to do was hand the clothes over, get her money back. Gone without a trace, simple as that.

'Is that all, dear?' asked the assistant. 'Just the blazer?'

'Yes,' said Anna, stuffing the tiny dress back in its bag.

She drifted along Buchanan Street, down towards the river. Christmas shoppers surged and heaved, and every way she turned was against the tide. A burrowed worm had been niggling her, the instinct she relied on biting back. Cruikshanks had mentioned St George's Cross. But there was that other Polish Club Cath had spoken of, near Kelvingrove Park. What if they hadn't checked there? She found herself at the edge of Jamaica Street – a favoured corner for generations of Glaswegian sweethearts to meet. There was a bus due that would take her right along Argyle Street, out towards the West End. It would do no harm to pop into the place. Might put her in Cruikshanks's good books. Aye, right.

The journey was quick, pushing out from the bustling city centre, past multi-storey flats and seedy grocers. No frantic rushing shoppers here. The club was near the park gates, up a melancholy side street that opened into a grassed grey square. Dark tenements lined three sides, the fourth capped by black iron railings and the park beyond. It was shaded here, very cold. Only a small card by the bell distinguished the Club Sikorski from other closes. Anna pressed the buzzer, and the door clicked without response. Like entering an old aunt's flat. Mad swirly carpets in green and red, potted palms in brass containers. A marble bust of General Sikorski glowered in greeting. There was nobody there. To the left of the entrance was a door marked *Bibliotek*. Anna tried it. Locked. She noticed a stairwell beside the door leading down. The lintel was low, making her duck to get by. Ezra had been the same height as her, when he stood to bid her good evening. Taller, with his hat on. Voices coming from the left, and Anna found herself in a bar with Formica tables and maroon plush banquettes.

A solid young man with a baby's grin was wiping glasses behind a red laminate counter. 'Hi there. Can I help you?'

She took out her warrant card. 'Sergeant Cameron, Strathclyde Police. It's just some routine questions, sir, about a gentleman who may have been a member. Mr Wajerski?'

'Aye, Ezra. My dad spoke to someone about him last week. Quiet old soul, didn't come in much.'

So they had come here. Just as well she hadn't scurried to Cruikshanks with her latest theory.

A woman playing the fruit machines called over to the barman. He answered her in Polish. 'Sorry. She gets the jitters if I don't keep feeding her pound coins. Anyway, Ezra. What did you want to know?'

She was here now. She had to make it sound convincing. 'Em – was anyone at the club a particular friend of his?'

'Not really.' The barman lined up shot glasses on the shelf behind. 'They've each got their own, you know – tumblers, I mean – for the vodka. Over fifteen types we have,' he beamed, 'and that's before you start on the flavoured ones.'

A deep voice boomed from the corridor. 'Anthony!'

The barman hung up his cloth. 'Well, there's always him, Simon. He's also *Zydzi*.'

'*Zydzi*?'

'Jewish. C'mon, I'll take you through.'

The restaurant lay on the other side of the stairs. It had a Tyrolean air, with carved dark wood chairs and checked cloths. Rows of plates and round paper cut-outs brightened Artex walls, spiced wafts of cloves and cinnamon fought with beer and fag-smoke.

The barman nodded at a rotund gentleman, red of face and cravat, who was scooping food with a chunk of dark rye bread. 'You could ask Simon. Two of them used to sit together sometimes.'

The old man glanced up, staccato-ed something Polish. The barman frisbeed his response straight back. It was met with a shrug and a slurp.

'Good luck.' He grinned at Anna as she walked towards the florid diner. The man continued eating.

'Excuse me – Simon? My name's Anna.' She smiled. 'I was . . . a friend of Ezra's. I believe you knew him?'

The man wiped his mouth with a napkin. 'Darling. You think I'm a fat old putz? If Ezra had a classy goy-girl like you, I would know. Tell your Uncle Simon the truth now. Did he owe you money?'

She was too quick. 'No, why? Did he owe many people money?'

Simon took a cigar from the packet in front of him, rolled it across his palm. He tapped it once, placed it in his mouth and lit it, puffing till brown seared red. 'Ha. Then it is the other.' He exhaled into his thin comb of hair. 'You're the pretty one they use for undercover work. Now me, I think that is a nonsense. You want to use the plain ones. Pretty ones always catch the eye – and the heart. Buy me a beer with your expenses, pretty-pie.' His eyes beseeching dark.

Anna laughed. 'You're good, Simon. What're you having?'

'Hoi, Anthony.'

The barman popped his head round the door. 'Yessir!'

'Two Zywiec, and another plate of *golabki*. You will like that,' said Simon, scraping back the seat beside him.

'What is it?'

'*Golabki* – you never had it? Cabbage leaves, stuffed with mince and rice, potatoes. Is very good.'

She wrinkled her nose. 'No, really, I'm fine.'

'You're paying.'

The beers and food were with them at once. The *golabki* came in an earthenware bowl. 'Eat, girl, eat.' Simon nodded as she cut into the tomato coating with her fork. The food was thick and unctuous, sliding like lumpy oysters. He smoked all the while.

'Mmm – kind of lasagne-moussaka. Very nice.'

He patted his stomach, sat back. 'So, what you want to know about Ezra?'

A slither of cabbage leaf had worked between her teeth. She played it with her tongue as she spoke. 'Were you two friends?'

'I suppose you could say. Of necessity, yes. All bloody *Katolici* here. The priest lives up the stair, you know? Ezra and I wouldn't go to their masses, of course, but we met for the tea and cakes after. And the festivals. Catholics are always having festivals, don't you find? Next week, for example' – he stubbed one cigar, lit another – 'we have the breaking of the bread. That is good – is for all of us, you see. We each take a piece to welcome in the New Year. Nice, you know? Makes us all feel Polish.'

Anna swallowed a lump of potato. 'Did Ezra have any family? He mentioned a nephew.'

'There was a sister – Vanda, I think – but she died at Auschwitz. Part of the reason why Ezra never went back . . .' He stared into the ashtray.

'Because there was no one left?'

'No, my lovely.' Simon lifted his head. 'Because his country had soaked up so much blood.'

She ate a little more of the *golabki*, pushed the plate away. 'That was very nice, Simon. Well chosen. Could there have been a son though? His sister's, I mean.'

'No, I think the girl was very little – ten or twelve perhaps.'

Anna had no prepared strategy, no clever sequence of words to divine a source. She scrabbled a little more, noticing for the first time how fat Simon was. 'Okay. What about women? Did Ezra have any lady friends?'

Simon tore another hunk of bread. 'Ha. There was no one permanent. In his day, though, Ezra was a fine man. Biggest *schlong* in Glasgow!' He sniggered through his food, pelleting her with breadcrumbs.

Ezra had a fine, straight nose, she remembered, the kind that would cleave its way through a crowd. She imagined the sacs beneath his eyes ironed flat, the hoods thrown off to show deep roan.

'I saw Ezra a few days before he died,' she said. 'He'd a wad of notes on him.'

'Darling, we are Jews. One roll only?'

'But he lived in squalor.'

Again, the shrug. 'Maybe Ezra liked to treat himself in other ways. Nice food, the gee-gees. Cinema, perhaps – the GFT does a marvellous Polish season.'

'How well did you know Ezra, Simon?'

He laid down his spoon. 'How well did *you* know him?'

There was no natural light in the little restaurant. Mock Victorian lamps cut small, dust-coloured circles on each of the tables. When it was full of chomping, chattering revellers, swigging tankards and singing folk songs, perhaps the room would be a happy place. 'I only met him the once.'

'Ha. See. Still he makes me jealous. Even in death, he is *bawidamek*.'

'He's what?'

'You know – ladykiller.' His cheeks puffed over his eyes.

His frog-face annoyed her. 'Look, Simon, I'm not even on this case. I just want to find whoever did this. Make sure they pay.'

'But they will, my love. *Adonai yikom damo*.'

'Adoni what?'

'God will avenge his blood. So the Torah tells us.' Simon rolled up his napkin, dropped it in the empty bowl. 'Listen, all I know about Ezra's money is that it came and it went. There was a man he talked about – Milligan. Said he would help him sort it out.'

'Who's Milligan?'

Simon pouted. 'Phff. Bank manager maybe. Who knows. Now, you like puddings?'

Any longer and she'd be walking him home. 'No, thank you. I need to go. Oh – one more thing. Did Ezra ever mention a man called Lionel Flax?'

'Don't think so.'

'Or his parents – Harold and Allegra?'

'Allegra, you say?' Simon chuckled. 'Oh yes, there was an Allegra. Beautiful woman, by all accounts.'

'Yes, she was.'

'Darling, you could not have known her.'

'No, I saw a picture of her, at the Art School.'

'Of course – that is where they met, you know. A tragic tale of love and death.' His smile was weak. 'Truly, Ezra was *bawidamek*.'

'What happened?'

'Well, I did not know Ezra then. But he talked of her, a little. He truly loved her, I believe. I think she was the other reason he did not go home.'

'You're sure this is Allegra *Flax* we're talking about?'

'Allegra was the only name he said. Alas, the woman was married. Is that not always the way? The ones we desire are outwith our grasp? Perhaps that's what makes them so wonderful, heh?'

'Simon, please. What happened to Allegra?'

'Well, great shame on them all, of course. How else does a tragedy end? Allegra fell pregnant, left her husband and little boy, and went to live with Ezra.'

'So, he *did* have a family.'

Simon rubbed the cigar between his thumb and index finger. 'No, sweet girl. He did not. Allegra died after a long, painful labour – and the child was stillborn.'

A harshness in her chest. Belly dragging like toothache. Lionel Flax had lost his mother, so that Ezra could lose his child.

'And Ezra?'

'Ezra kept breathing, I suppose. That is all we can do.' Simon smoked the rest of his cigar in silence, blue wafts curling to thicken the air. A screech of laughter broke through from the other room, and someone put Wizzard on the tape player.

She pushed her chair back. 'Thanks for your help, Simon.'

'A pleasure, pretty-pie.' He smacked his lips. 'I will see you again.'

The shock of sharp air after soupy fug raked Anna's throat. Dusk had descended; soft light dissolving over diamond cold, and she was glad of her coat. Window twinkles from the sparse dotted Christmas trees failed to herald anything but the darkness outside. Most students went home for the holidays, and the street was empty. Everything bleak and still, until a troublesome wind came stoating, hassling the leaves and clamouring unseen branches like hollow bones against the railings. Sounds of sharpening, whetting of teeth and smacking of lips. Sky blown black, hard grits of gold staring blankly from their place in the heavens, and a chill like ghosts passed across her neck. She quickened her pace, not looking back.

On Christmas morning, in two different houses, two people awoke with the same thought: I wonder what you're doing? One had the thought instantaneously erased, with toast and an excited voice squealing, 'Doddy! Da, bid doddy!'

The other rose, did yoga stretches, had coffee and a bagel. Donned moleskin chinos and drove to the cemetery. The graveyard wasn't far – about fifteen minutes' drive from where Anna lived and close enough that she should visit more often. It served nearly all of the city's south side, and stretched over several acres. There were as many bodies above as below today; families everywhere loving their dead before they could enjoy the rest of Christmas. From her father's grave she could see the children's section. Bad enough with windmills and toys, it was unbearable with baby trees and Christmas cards. Anna didn't want to see any of the mums there. She didn't want to see they were real, that their babies had been real. Wee ones they'd had to leave alone and cold in the mud, not able to stroke their hair and make it better.

Beside Anna's dad there was a German man, a husband, wife and two of their daughters and three other policemen. Each policeman's stone had the *Semper Vigilo* crest carved proudly above the name. Whether he'd been killed in a bank robbery or died in an accident, he was still a cop. *Always vigilant.* Except he'd not been, her dad. He'd not bothered to see the lorry swinging past his car. She laid her flowers on the chilled earth.

'Merry Christmas, Dad.' Anna patted the top of the marble. She glanced round, bent over again. Briefly touched the stone with her lips. 'Love you.'

This afternoon, she'd go for a jog. Crisp empty air to flee through, chasing her breath, she'd run across Queen's Park and down to the boating pond where they'd sailed a blue wooden boat with white sails he'd bought for her in Woolworths. One of Anna's earliest memories was dangling on her daddy's shoulders, swaying above crowds of shoppers on her way to the highlight of the week – Woolworths sweetie counter. Each Saturday he'd take her, unless he was working. Spread before her eyes was every kind of sweet imaginable: rhubarb-and-custards, penny dainties, pear drops and, their favourite, fondant mint creams. Crisp white on the outside, with a soft bite like toothpaste. They'd take a wee poke and spend as long as she liked considering and examining, selecting her spoils. There was always a limit to what she was allowed to stuff in the bag, though. *That's enough, Annie-kin,* he'd say. *Know when to stop, darling. You'll make yourself ill. And what a mess you'd be in then, eh?*

Ezra's funeral would be soon, but she wouldn't go. She wanted to imagine it full of friends and thanksgiving: his pals from the Polish Club, friends from the synagogue. Professor Arlington perhaps, and Simon. Even Lionel Flax, saddened at his outburst and forgiving in death. His anger was that of an abandoned child, not a sadistic murderer. Old girlfriends would come for the eyes and hands that touched them. And Ezra's nephew, doing the oration, telling how his uncle lived like a pauper, yet was really a king. And, after her jog, she'd have a glass of champagne and a turkey crown.

Cath shouted up the stairs after Jamie. 'See if Eilidh's woken up yet, will you?'

'I doubt it,' he shouted back. 'She's knacked. Been rocking on that thing since six, remember.'

Without doubt, it had been the star present of the morning. A sturdy plastic see-saw, with a special seat for one in the middle, so no siblings were required. You just clambered on and rocked yourself sick. Eilidh insisted it was a dog.

'Dod,' she kept patting it. 'Nie doddy.'

Jamie had cleared all the paper away from the lounge. He'd left the dressing gown on the floor by the tree. It was grey and blue, chosen to match the slippers she got for his birthday. 'More grey. Great.'

'What's wrong with grey?'

'No, no, it's fine. Really.' He'd got her underwear, two sizes too big.

'Size 20?' she'd blurted. 'God, most guys get stuff too small.'

'How? Who else buys you underwear?' As quick as that, deflecting her hurt and making her defensive.

'Don't be stupid. But look.' She'd held it up, half-laughing at the elephant cups. Encouraging him to join in.

'The receipt's upstairs. I'll get it.'

Briefly, on the horizon, Cath thought she'd seen a glow, a space that she could climb through. She'd even planned how she would get there, building a tentative ladder to a different path. But Anna Cameron had torn that away, made it permanent night again, and Jamie was now finishing the job, sealing her in, brick by sneer, by disdain by disinterest. Cath was too tired to fight it any more.

It was Jamie's mum's turn to have them. Tinned soup and frozen turkey breasts, with Asda's luxury Christmas pud. They went and they ate, and everybody was very jolly. Eilidh got a teddy and a doll, Cath an umbrella and scented drawer liners. As always, Jamie had a jumper and he put it on at once, kissing his mum and effusing over the colour. Grey. They left at eight, Cath driving, Jamie pished. In the red tinge of traffic light, his head lolled in the seat beside her, and she dabbed a dribble from the corner of his mouth. She was bursting for a pee. On the main road now, and she put her foot down. Too late, the flickering blue signalled her to stop.

Shit.

She smiled, then tried contrition. Desperately sighed that the baby needed a feed. Finally told them her husband was a cop. But the Traffic were hewn from inhuman stock.

'Is that right? Blow.'

Green light for go. Thank God she was breastfeeding – Diet Coke all night. Jamie woke as the cop was writing her a HORT1.

'Oh, for fuck's sake, man.' He yawned. Sat up straight when the luminous sleeve reached in with the piece of paper. 'What's going on? You hit something?'

'Sir, your wife was doing fifty in a thirty-mile zone.'

'Jesus Christ. You dozy cow.' Nice how he stuck up for her. Then he tried the charm. 'C'mon, pal. I'm a cop and all – gie's a break, eh? It's Christmas bloody Day.'

'Indeed it is, sir. And a very merry one at that.'

Jamie fumbled to unbuckle his seatbelt. 'You being a smartarse, pal?'

'Jamie,' she shushed. 'Would you just shut up. Right, is that us now? Can I go?'

'Now, if you'd just like to step out of the car and open your boot.'

'You taking the piss?' Jamie had got the seatbelt off, and was halfway out the door. 'I'm in the bloody job, ya dick.'

Cath tugged him back. 'Jamie, for God's sake will you just sit still and shut up.'

The Traffic cop's neighbour had come round the other side of the car. 'We're well aware of that, *pal*. Which is the only reason I'm not doing you for a breach.'

He reached across Jamie to Cath. 'Give us the keys, hen – we've to check all the cars we stop this week. Part of Operation Christmas Cracker.' He shook his head. 'Don't ask.' After a cursory glance inside, he returned the keys. 'Right, that's us. C'mon, Pete.' Pete and Jamie were eyeballing one another through the windscreen – Pete with a piercing challenge, Jamie with a skewwhiff squint.

Cath waited until the Traffic car had disappeared. Her chest was thumping with the shock of being stopped. 'You're a bloody tube, Jamie. You—'

'*I'm* a tube? Who got done for speeding? Who got lifted for bloody assault?'

She turned the ignition. 'That was all sorted out.'

'You think? You have *no idea*. Do you? *Do you?*' The aggression in his voice woke Eilidh. 'Are you determined to fuck me up at every turn?'

She wouldn't speak to him when he was like that. There was no point. He was in the mood to pick a fight. His dad had been winding him up, asking him about promotion, and if he'd been at midnight mass. Only the promise of his mother's custard had kept the peace. Jamie adjusted his position, muttered a few more syllables, another couple of 'fucks', then lapsed back to wherever he'd been. Eilidh chewed a plastic star. 'Tinka.' She waved it in the mirror.

'Clever girl. Twinkle.'

Their street was an avenue of light. Some houses had an outdoor *and* an indoor tree. Others had sparkling sleds. Mrs McGinty had a bloody Santa that played 'Jingle Bells' every time the door opened. Cath had left their tree lights on, so it would be cosy when they came home. But there was only a black space where their glow should be. Jamie must have gone right in behind her and turned the lights back off.

'Right. That's us.' Cath shook him awake.

He licked his lips with a blue-grey tongue. Stared at her a minute, as if trying to place her. 'You know something, Cath? I used to love you.'

Her heart dropped through the core of the earth. She carried Eilidh, still strapped in her booster seat, into the house, and shut the door in his face.

15 Whip It

Everything was back to normal. The tree had been recycled into garden mulch, the baubles boxed. Anna liked things down as soon as Christmas was past – it felt less melancholy that way. Her flat had reverted to its usual pristine condition and Anna had gone back to work as she said she would. Going down the Drag, interviewing the poor sods who dealt with threats of violence every day, and jailing, whenever she could find a reason, the pathetic excuses for manhood who loitered there, was excellent therapy. She could reassert her authority and exorcise her anger all in one.

But business was slow. Punters were strapped for cash after Christmas, and there was no equivalent of a January sale down the Drag. It was piece break, and she'd sent Alex back up the road. It was none of his business what her business was. He was the best kind of neighbour to ease her in – eager, obliging and obedient. Her reception had been as expected: a handshake from Derek, a slap on the back from Alex and a grunt from Rankin. Jenny was due in later and Jamie . . . Jamie was on sick leave. Again. Anna kicked a can into the gutter. She knew what he was doing. A few days at home, immersing himself in familial responsibilities, leading him on to the path of righteousness, now the initial tug of his groin had slackened. That's why he hadn't come to work. For that way lay temptation and tremors and beating hearts. And broken homes and damaged children. Beautiful children. With deep dark eyes and splendid noses and what was she on? Good. So. Leave it up to him. She was a free agent; one who didn't have to wheedle and cajole. He would come to her again if he wanted to. Nothing to do with her.

As was Mr Wajerski's murder. CID had made that clear when she stuck her head round the door. That prick Breggsy, strutting like he owned the place. DI Cruikshanks was *in a meeting, and could he help?* She'd felt embarrassed, mumbled that she'd come back later. No point in mentioning Simon and the Flaxes to that wee ginger mutant.

Anna circled the block a few times, saw no one. Knocked on a peeling door in one of the side streets. A friendly woman answered. 'Hello, pet. Come away in. Don't think I know you.'

Anna shuffled her feet on the step of the Den. 'Sergeant Cameron, Strathclyde Police.'

The woman's face closed a little, slightly as the door. 'What d'you want?'

'I just need to ask a couple of questions about the assaults that have been taking place on the girls.'

'We already told you all we know.'

'Please.'

The woman stepped back, allowed her in. Carefully, Anna wiped her feet on the *Welcome* mat in the shabby hall and followed her through the back.

Tonight, only a handful of women were in. Two ducked and preened in front of a mirror, sharing jokes and lipstick, while a third lay feet up on a couch. Anna recognised her as Derek's tout, Angela, her stomach now as concave as her eyes.

'Hi, Angela.'

Angela looked up, scowled. 'Who the fuck let you in?'

'What did you have then?' Anna smiled, nodding at her tummy.

'Fuck off,' was the gruff reply.

Anna could do blunt. What she was best at. 'Look, Angela, I need your help. It's about that bastard that assaulted Linda.'

Angela blew some smoke rings. 'I thought yous had the cunt banged up?'

'No. We don't know who it was. Linda said she never saw his face.'

'Aye, no this time, maybe.'

'What d'you mean?'

'Nothing. So, she got a tanking again. So what?'

'So, this guy seems to be a real sadist – gets off on hurting women.'

Angela lit a new cigarette from the embers of her stub, then crushed the dowt in the ashtray balanced on her chest. 'They all do, hen.'

This was pointless. 'Angela, please. He used a blade – well, have you seen Linda's face? Or Rebecca's? Or Carole's?'

'Aye.'

'You have? Well, you'll know—'

'No, I haven't. But it's an "I". That's what the lassies say he's carving on their coupons.'

An 'I' could be someone's initial. All the photos had been taken straight after the assaults, but the scars hadn't scabbed over at that point. 'Are any of them about, d'you know? Linda maybe? I'd really like to speak to her. If we can find a pattern, some kind of link . . . it would really help.' She knew it sounded weak, even as she said it.

Angela looked at Anna, pupils black and piercing. 'What's with the big concern?'

The other two women slipped from the room. 'Eh – we're off tae the Doctor's now, Angie.'

'Aye – nae bother. Hope you pish all over his car.'

The Doctor was a regular, a GP who paid a tenner each for girls to take a black bin-bag from the supply he kept in the boot, squat in the headlights of his car, and urinate into the bag. He paid an extra fiver if they worked in pairs. The bags were then knotted, handed over and the transaction complete. Easy money, unless you splashed your scants and had to work the rest of the night with a soggy arse.

Angela finished her second cigarette and swung her legs to the floor, sitting upright. 'Did you know Linda was a nurse? Before she got on the junk, I mean?'

'I didn't realise—'

'No, didn't think you would,' she sneered. *She* sneered. At Anna. Mocking her accent, her careful concern. 'Tha-at *ba-astard* what scored Linda. Tell me, Mrs Polis-wumman, what do you see when you look at us? Us pros-ti-tyoots.' It was a sensual word, the way she dragged it across her tongue, letting it flow through browning teeth.

Anna searched her pocket for a pen.

'Ho, I'm talking to you. You actually think I wanted this?' Angela pulled at the lank strands behind her ears. 'I was going to be a hairdresser, me.'

'Could you not try and get off the drugs?' *Useless, Anna, useless.*

Angela gurgled. Horrible, hopeless sound. 'Christ, do you not think I've tried? Do you honestly think I'd be down here, punting my hole tae creepy bastards two weeks after my wean died, if I didny have tae? I have tried and tried till there's nothing left. I'm injecting intae my feet and I've more fucking pus and abscesses than I've skin.'

She kicked off a stiletto and brought her bare foot up on her other knee, to rub at purple, mottled toes. A greying nail was hanging off her big toe. Angela swore as she tried to push it back into its bed.

'Did you say your baby died?'

'Fuck, do yous lot no talk at all? I take it communication skills isny a requirement for being a polis?'

'Oh, Angela – I'm so sorry.'

'No you're no,' she sighed, 'and I'm no interested, hen, anyway. Look, what is it you want?'

If nothing else, Anna respected Angela's honesty. What good would conjured platitudes make, a winsome, tragic smile, a careful patting of her shoulder? In another day, in another place, Anna would be seizing that very same baby, taking her from her mother's drug-addled breast and placing her in care. Angela was right; honesty was all she could give her back.

'He hit me too, you know. That guy – at least I think it was. Stoved my head in with his feet.'

'So how comes the cavalry's no charging down and kickin some butt?' Angela shoved her swollen foot back in its PVC. 'Because I canny say I've noticed a pure massive polis presence on your behalf either.'

'Dunno. I'm not very popular at work right now.'

'No kidding?' Angela reached for her handbag and put her cigarettes and lighter inside. She put the bag on the floor, lay down and turned on her side with her back facing out, hugging a cushion into her belly. 'See if you come back after midnight, Linda'll be at Bothwell Street. I'll tell her you want tae see her.'

'Thanks, Angela.' Anna went to leave the room. 'I *am* sorry for you.'

Angela's voice was muffled by the couch. 'Ho. Turn the bloody light out.'

Anna's shift finished at eleven, when Jenny and Sergeant Gus Murray, the Traffic wallah threatened as her replacement, took over. Rankin had been bullshitting her – Murray was some Accelerated Promotion guy. He'd jetted in from Traffic, would spend a few more weeks with the Flexi, then sweep off to do a review of Licensing. Four years service – made you sick. But it meant she was staying put. Flexi was a poisoned chalice no other bugger wanted to do. Who'd want to do it on days like tomorrow, when she'd to escort the twelfth loyal Orange coven or whatever the hell they were. The Lodge members wished to exercise their democratic right to see the Old Year out by whistling their way to Glasgow Green, and everyone else was tied up with the Hogmanay party in the Square. Orange Walks in winter – was nothing sacred?

'Sarge.'

'Jenny.'

Brief nods.

'This is Sergeant Murray, gaffer.'

Long black coat, elegant smile. His hands stayed in his pockets. 'Hi there. How you doing?' His inflection was Glasgow-lite, the reelly nice south-side lilt of a 'totally-bonkers' disc jockey. 'Great to have you back. Heard *all* about you.'

What? What have you heard? 'Hi. So, what's been happening?'

He ran slim fingers through expensive hair. 'Och, don't you worry about that the now. DBR's in my – on the desk, if you want a read. Just you ease yourself in gently and we'll keep the place ticking over till you're up to full speed, yeah? All quiet so far then? Never mind, we'll liven the place up a bit. Now, Jenny – you fit?' Winked at Alex. 'Daft question, eh?' He swept his crombie like a cloak.

'See you later, gaffer.' Jenny dipped her head at Anna, a gesture for which she felt ridiculously grateful.

'Right, bye Jenny.' Anna had only asked as a courtesy. Of course she'd checked the daily briefing register – did it before she came on duty. Noticed the thoroughness of the minute, earnestly-looped script, neat underlinings and alternate colours of black and green. They must issue all AP guys with their own set of felt-tipped pens.

'Night then, Sarge.'

'Off somewhere nice, Alex?'

He grinned, flexed his hands in a cat's cradle. 'You know me, boss. Like to keep my hand in.'

'So I've heard. Be good.'

Anna drove back down to the Drag, parked up outside an all-night burger bar. She waited inside the greasy joint, playing with the sugar sachets. Less conspicuous than standing on the street or sitting in her car, and if Jenny or Gorgeous Gus spotted her, she could say – yeah, well, best they didn't spot her. About five to, Anna made her way to Bothwell Street. There was a huge, ornate clock protruding from the building at the corner, a popular gathering place for some of the women who covered that beat. Linda was already there, talking to another girl, who disappeared to darkness as Anna approached.

'How you doing, miss?' said Linda.

Under thick make-up, her skin puckered round embossed flesh. Triangles of blusher blurred the bumps. Anna's fingers ached to rub across, feel the ridges that might have been hers. She couldn't afford to be anything other than brisk and businesslike.

'Hi, Linda. How you doing? Let's see you, then.' Anna moved her under the streetlamp, sick yellow turning the girl's face to wax. 'Shit, that looks sore.' One straight sharp line, and a second, curved score, no, two interlocking bevels, in the shape of an African shield. In amongst the swelling and shading of the photograph, she'd never noticed this third slice. 'What *is* that?'

Linda was silent.

'Is it a number? Looks like a 10 to me.'

'Haven't a clue.' She assumed a casual lilt. 'I know one lassie had them play noughts and crosses on her face. Suppose this isn't *that* bad. Ten out of ten, eh? I'll need to make that my trademark.'

'Did Angela say I wanted to speak to you?'

'Aye, miss. She's a smack-heid though. Doesn't know her arse from her elbow.'

An hour in a strip-lit pit serving thick boiled coffee for this.

'Angela seemed to think you knew the guy that did this.'

Eyes darting anywhere but Anna. 'Naw. No way.'

'So, you'd never seen him before?'

Linda jigged from one foot to the other. 'Nope.'

'Linda, d'you remember *anything* about the man that scarred you?'

The girl touched her cheek, the part that was still soft. She swallowed. 'No.'

'What about his hands – was there anything distinguishing about them?'

'They held a blade?'

'Very funny.'

'No actually, it's not. It's no fucking funny at all.'

Anna scuffed her boots along the kerb. 'I'm sorry, Linda. That was a stupid thing to say.' She looked up again. 'Okay, you didn't see who did this. But, it's happened before? Someone's cut you before?'

'Aye, well, aye, no cut exactly. Hurt me, yes. But that wasn't him.'

Anna was cold and tired and near to tears. Did these women speak a different language from her? Had she missed something subtle in translation? 'Why would Angela think I should speak to you then, Linda?'

The girl rubbed her nose on the back of her hand. 'Shit, brass monkeys, in't it, miss?'

Anna didn't answer. She stared. A stare that went on and on, finally bullying the girl into speech.

'I never got his name. One of your lot. Wanted a freebie.'

'You mean a cop?' Didn't matter how long you did it – the cess-pit stench still kicked in when you agitated it with your big polis stick.

Linda nodded. 'Aye. I did it the first time, but then he started pure taking the pish.'

'What did he do?'

'Och, you know, every other night. Warrant card in my face, prick down my throat. It was scaring off my clients. Bad enough with the cosmetic surgery, you know?' Fingers at her cheek again. 'I told him I wasn't for it any more, so he belted me one. Well, quite a few times. Then he got . . . right, put it this way – it's just as well it's like throwing it up the Clyde Tunnel, know what I mean?'

Anna leaned against the wall, felt the sandstone behind her back, sharp corner worn smooth by rubbing shoulders. Glasgow's backbone was tight-packed twinkling mica that shone beneath the grime, crumbling when it was stone-cleaned, because it was only the decades of pollution now that held the stone together. Pollution made the world go round. You saw its gourd-hollow face in war zones, when the liberators became the new regime. When little girls became the spoils of war. You saw it in children's homes, in boys' schools, in women's ruined flesh. In a war hero's tiny tenement, brave head crushed like scabrous lace. You saw it in your friends, yourself.

Anna switched to automatic pilot. 'Would you be able to identify this man if you saw him again, Linda?'

'Och, aye. Never forget a punter, me. Or a face, for that matter.'

16 White Feathers

The Orange Walk would wend its way from Overnewton Street to Blythswood Square. From there, they'd join the rest of their cronies and snake down to the Green. Socialist heart of Glasgow, Glasgow Green was used to marches and rallies. Popular place for hangings too. And laundry, sheep grazing and prostitution at various times in its history. The van stopped at the corner, where Billy Wong was waiting. His face brightened at Anna's approach. 'Hiya, Sarge. Glad to see you back.'

She jumped down. 'Cheers for the lift. Hi, Billy. Have a good Chr—'

'Maddy!' shrieked a high-pitched voice. 'How you doing! Here, look – it's me!' One of the flute band was jumping up and down. Oversized plumes on his cap masked his face. The silver flute he waved was wrapped in seed pearls, and matched his silver boots.

The sergeant seemed to know this little pixie man. She walked over, brushed one of the feathers aside. 'Shelly, is that you?'

'Annie Oakley, as I live an breathe.' The man tweaked her cheeks with excited hands. 'How the hell *are* you, doll-face? D'you get the card I sent? Made it myself – Christmas and Get Well card in one.' He winked at Billy. 'Big glittery centrespread of a male nurse dressed as Santa. Signed by yours truly – and smudged by Alice.'

Sergeant Cameron actually hugged the man. 'Oh, yes – it was a masterpiece. I've had it framed. Anyway, Shelly, what the hell are you doing here?'

'Highlight of my year, so it is. Not.' Shelly unrolled his tongue and stuck two fingers in his mouth. 'We've aye done it since I was a wean, but I canny be annoyed. It's my big brother really – pure loves it. Only chance *some* folk have tae get dressed up and go for a dauner, I suppose. Anyway, show me the scars. Are they minging?'

Billy thought he'd better walk away. He crossed the road to join Sam.

'Would you look at that – the gaffer's a fag hag,' said Sam, leaning out the van window. 'Mind, that one's no the worst of them. Aye, right team of dolls you've got this morning, eh Billy-boy?'

The Master cockerel was gathering his chicks around him, strutting and puffing, bowler hat incongruous among the anoraks and shell suits. Except for the women. Middle-aged to a man, they were all neat in navy blue. Maybe some black – you couldn't be sure. Sober, like a funeral. And unlike many of their men. The oddest thing was their heads. Billy had been here long enough to know hats were rarely worn, even in this cold city. He'd seen some headscarves, and baseball caps of course. But most of these women were wearing hats. Wee fancy ones, like you'd get at a wedding. Perched at jaunty angles, pinned with kirbies and tucked with hairnets. Some even had feathers in them. White ones, a bit stubby. Not plumes, more like pigeon feathers.

'What's with the hats?'

'Haven't a scooby, son. Take your mind off their faces? That one's got a coupon like a half-chewed caramel.' Sam nodded at a well-built dame pushing ripples of thick grey stocking into a white stiletto shoe. 'Jesus, wouldny mess with thon, I'll tell you.'

Billy wondered if he should be doing something. Twice, the man with the bowler had smiled over at Sam, nodding his approval. Twice, Sam had belched. He maybe didn't speak much, but Sam seemed to know what folk were up to before they knew themselves. He caught Billy's arm.

'Ho, you. Don't you be going over there and fraternising.

They'll sort themselves into their wee rows, then they'll go when the gaffer tells them, no before.'

'Aye, but what do I do?'

Sam spat out the window. 'Escort them. One at the front, one halfway along at the side. Make sure they don't obstruct the pavement, or go over to the wrong side of the road. Watch the hingers-on. Watch for any trouble. Stop the traffic to get them all across in a oner. Be a fucking polis. But' – he put his face close to Billy's – 'see, whatever you do, son, do *not* march in time to their drumbeat.'

'How not?'

Sam tipped his hat far back from his forehead and rubbed his baldy bit. 'Cause I'll rip the arse off you if you do. Christ, do they no have the Orange Walk where you come frae?'

'Eh, no really.'

'Officer. Excuse me, officer.' The bowler hat man adjusted his sash. 'That's us ready.'

'Is that right? Well, you'll have to wait a minute yet.'

'Why?'

' 'Cause it's no me that's in charge, pal. It's the lady.' Sam pointed at Anna.

The man scurried off to speak to her.

'Look, Billy, son, I don't know if you're a Tim or a Proddy, and I don't really care. Pakis, Chinkies, doesn't matter to me. But these bastards make me sick. So, if you're gonny be my neighbour, you don't march in time – got it?'

'Aye.'

'All right, Sam?' Anna called over.

'Aye, Sergeant.'

'That's them ready to roll, so we'll get on. Thanks again for the lift. Right.' Anna turned to Billy. 'I'll lead them – you get them telt.'

There were a few sniggers as Billy raised his voice. 'Okay, folks. If you'd just like to get in line, then we'll be off.'

A female voice called out from the ranks. 'Speak the Queen's English, son. We canny understand you.'

Anna walked to where the voice had come from. 'You'll under-stand what the Cornton Vale means, won't you? Rhymes with jail?'

Billy stood as erect as his five feet six would let him. Wondered if the sergeant was just chucking him to the lions for a bit of sport. He could handle it. He nodded at the stewards, but before the band had even tuned up, Anna Cameron was off. 'Right, move it folks.' She had a beautiful face, thought Billy; but carved in stone. Nobody would argue with such set precision. In her own way, she was inscrutable too.

Billy fell into step at the side of the marchers. There were about forty or so, and it was his job to make sure they didn't weave on to the wrong side of the road. With it being a Sunday, the roads were quiet, and keeping one lane clear meant they could wave the traffic past instead of it building up behind them. Less disruption these buggers cause the better, Sam had said.

'Does your mammy know you're out, son?'

He ignored it.

'Och, the wee soul hasny started shaving yet. Leave him alone.'

The music stirred them on. A rhythmic drumbeat held it steady, while the flutes and whistles caused their hips to sway. Just a tiny sway, a jaunty swagger, so they could maximise the space allowed them. Billy found it near impossible not to march in time. Whenever his mind wandered, he'd find his feet paying close attention. Then, literally, with a start, he'd do the wee skip thing they'd taught them at Tulliallan. It was supposed to get you back on the right track, so your right, right, left, right, left was the same as everyone else on the drill square, but it worked just as well in reverse.

A tourist was taking pictures of them all. 'Hey, honey, it's some kinda parade. Look.'

Now they were going past a church. Sam had told him the music must be cut at churches. Only the big bass drum was allowed to keep thumping. Tradition, you see. It kept them in step.

'So, what made you want tae be a polis?'

That woman again. He could see her hat out the corner of his eye. White net, it was, with a single feather pointing backwards. Billy concentrated on his feet. It was a good question. One his own mother had asked. Left, right, left, shit, skip. No one they knew was in the police. Thought it odd; uncomfortable. Not the family way. His father had insisted on university. So, he went. Studied politics and law. He'd kept his side, now they had to keep theirs. But they weren't happy. People looked at him differently. He'd noticed that already. Yes, there was a distance, but there was also a respect.

'Gonny give us a wee smile, son?'

'You're awfy wee for a polis, son. Is he no awfy wee, Iris?'

Aye, well, sometimes. Billy was looking forward to the famous camaraderie they all talked about. Part of a team. Belonging. So far, no one had looked up from their card school when he came in for his piece. He'd read all the leaflets and crap lying about the office. Today, he'd buy a paper. Maybe they were like this with everyone.

Up ahead, he could see the sergeant had moved from the front of the march. The music hadn't stopped like it should have. There seemed to be some kind of scuffle, but Billy didn't know if he should leave his place and go up. There were only the two of them. Then he saw Anna's hat go flying off. He ran up past the marchers, and found she had the Lodge Master in an arm-lock.

'Where the hell were you?'

'I'm . . . I'm sorry, Sergeant. I wasn't sure . . .'

'Aye, well, lucky for you I'm still in one piece.' She shouted in her radio. 'Alpha 51 to Alpha.'

'Roger. Go ahead, Sergeant.'

'Aye. Request a van St Vincent at Holland. One for the office.'

The radio crackled back. 'Eh, be advised. No vans currently available. All tied up on escort.'

'A51 to Control. Would you note: I've just jailed the Master of the Lodge.'

Pause. 'Ah, roger, noted. Van en route.'

'Ho, c'mon now. That's a pure liberty. Let him go.' The aborted marchers were revolting. At least ten of them had encircled Anna and Billy. One had the drooping face of a crew-cut Samurai, and looked strangely familiar.

'You canny jail the Master.'

Still holding her prisoner, Anna rounded on the youth who was noising her up. 'You wanting the jail and all, son?'

'Aye, you and whose army?'

Billy was fascinated. They weren't lions. They were hyenas. 'Will I keep them marching, Sergeant?'

'No, just wait. The van won't be long.'

The marchers had all gathered round now. Blessed were the peacemakers, the wee men in their bibs and sashes, who were trying to restore some order. It was the women who screeched the most. Them and the onlookers, the raggle and the straggle that pushed their buggies and drank their cans in stalwart support.

'Fuck it, there's only the two. A Chinky and a wumman.'

'Aye, fucking intae them.'

'We'll save you, Mr Tait.'

Billy couldn't feel his tongue. He drew his baton from his belt, and flicked his wrist. Quick as a whip, the baton shot out to its full length.

'Hai-ya!' shouted one of the crowd.

'Everybody was kung-fu fighting!' yelled another.

He could hear all these voices, but couldn't see the mouths.

'Pick one, Billy,' hissed Anna. 'Anyone'll do.'

Billy walked towards the group the fat guy was in. His baton rested across his chest, jerking in time with his heart. 'Right, fucking hard men. I suggest you move away quietly. Now.'

Nothing. He couldn't see. Couldn't see Anna.

'Okay then. Which one of you is wanting the jail?' A voice that was not his, deep with menace. He'd practised it so often. Ever since he came to this place, ever since the jibes and the bullying began and he realised it wasn't fair. They'd stopped sniggering, but weren't backing off. Grey and red buildings were swaying, rising high above Billy's head, dipping edges and wheeling to meet one another in the pale sky, where the air was thin.

'Right, enough!' screamed a woman. She ran in between the sergeant and the mob. 'Fuck off now, the lot of yous. You and all, Andrew.'

Up close, it wasn't a female. It was the guy with the silver boots, shoving the fat man backwards.

'Shelly, don't,' panted Anna. 'It's okay. Don't you get involved.'

A Mexican stand-off. Then klaxons sliced the morning calm, and the crowd began to scatter, some back to their ranks, others into alleys and beyond.

'Howzitgaun there, Sergeant?' Sam leaned out his window, one elbow resting on the sill. 'Tut, tut. Very bad form that. Jailing such a respected member of the community. Good morning to you, sir.' He doffed his cap at the Master. 'If you'd just like to step inside, we'll continue the parade from the comfort of my van.'

'Just take him up the road, Sam,' said Anna.

The driver shook his head. 'No can do, Sarge. Inspector says we've to head up the parade in case there's any more trouble. So Mason Boyne here shall go to the ball. Well, as far as the church anyway, then it's off for Sunday lunch at Stewart Street for you, you lucky man. Get your own wee plastic tray an everything.'

Another cop jumped out the passenger door, and opened up the back. 'In we get.'

The Master realised they weren't joking. 'This is preposterous. Do you know who I am? I have every right to walk the Queen's highway unimpeded. I know your superintendent . . . I'll be speakin tae ma cooncillor . . . Mr Milligan'll have somethin tae say about this.' His voice was muffled as the door shut behind him.

'So, how come you're the one with no hat, Sarge, and not the boy?' asked Sam, climbing down to stretch his legs.

'Och, I know,' said his colleague, twisting the lock shut. 'It's because he's yellow!'

'Haw, fuck face.' Sam blocked the cop's path to the front of the van. 'Apologise.'

'What?' The cop started laughing.

'I said, fucking apologise.'

Anna spoke quietly. 'You heard the man. You can do it now, or I can put you on paper.'

'It's fine,' said Billy. 'Really. It was just a joke.'

The remainder of the marchers were watching with interest. Better than *Wildlife on One*. 'Sam,' said Anna. 'Get this lot moving. Now.'

Sam shouted at them. 'Right, get yourselves in order. One of you stewards come up the front. Any bloody one of yous. I don't care. Yous lot, start your whistles and that. C'mon. Do yous want to march or no?' He turned back to face the cop. 'Well?'

The cop eyeballed Billy. 'I'm terribly sorry if I offended you, Constable Wong.' He nudged past Sam and opened the passenger door. 'That is your name, isn't it, Billy? Wong, I mean? Am I right, or am I Wong?'

Anna laid her hand on Sam's arm. 'Sam, how do you and your pal fancy finishing off the escort? I think me and Billy deserve a wee seat.'

'Absolutely, Sarge.' Sam dropped the keys into Anna's hand. 'Right, you – shank's pony. Shift your arse.' The other cop grumbled, got out.

'Billy, you go in the back with Mr Tait. Whoa, whoa – and your name is?' Anna touched her hand against the cop's chest.

'Craig.'

'Craig what?'

'Craig Armstrong.'

'Armstrong what?'

'Eh, Sergeant?'

'Clever boy. You've not been on your cultural awareness course yet, have you, Craig? I'll be having a wee chat with your inspector when we get back. Now, fuck off to the end of the march and don't noise up anyone else. Sam is under strict instructions to leave you where you fall.' She grinned. 'That right, Sam?'

'I'll bloody trip the wee shite up myself if he starts.'

'Language, Samuel,' said Anna, hauling herself up by the door.

She drove off slowly, allowing the marchers time to reassemble in a flaccid crocodile. Even her gear changes were languid, the steering wheel pushed through clawed fingers in tight, deliberate movements. Little gasps to blow out frenzied air and calm her down.

Billy copied her, in through the nose, out through the mouth until the pistons stopped pummelling his chest. 'That was nearly a riot, eh, Sergeant?'

'Yup,' she replied. 'Best medicine ever.'

'Sergeant, please,' said Billy, leaning up close to the grille. 'Can I talk to you? That man. I recognise him.'

'Who?' She was concentrating on avoiding the weaving, unsteady legs that flitted like bluebottles beside the body of the parade.

'The one the ladyboy pushed away.' His voice was fighting against flutes and the engine, but he didn't want Tait to overhear.

'You mean Shelly?' They were crawling past the marchers, on the wrong side of the road, so they could get to the head. Both Shelly and his brother had vanished.

'Yes, the big guy with him – I've seen him before.'

'That's Shelly's brother. You've probably seen him round Woodlands.'

'No, he said he was from Paisley. Only here on a visit.'

'You sure it was the same guy?' Sam had stopped the traffic, to wave them through a junction. She put the blue light on, just in case.

'Yes. An old lady had been throwing tomatoes at him from her window.'

Anna laughed. 'Why?'

'They wouldn't say. But, Sergeant – she was Italian.'

She blasted the horn at a doddery old git in a Metro. 'So? I don't get it.'

His eagerness for her to see became impatience. 'Italian – probably Catholic. Different. Not a Protestant Orangeman. Neither's Polish, Jewish, Asian – and, Sergeant, the guy's really fat.'

The Master was beating time through the metal side of the van. 'Gonny shut him up in there?' Anna shouted. 'Look, Billy, we'll talk about it back at the station, okay?'

When you separate the weft from the warp, initially it will stick. Fibres, long used to clinging, will spiral and split themselves before they tug apart. Once a reasonable channel is made and there is purchase on both sides, the cloth will rend in one satisfying rip. But that essential weakness must be worked on first. And, if agitated from either end, so much the better for a clean tear. It's worth noting that patches rarely mend the underlying weakness, however pretty they may appear.

The presenter was a kind of Delia Smith for sewing. She was determined to confuse the viewer with long words and complex patterns, thereby lending her subject (how to rip a bit of cloth) some gravitas. That home channel was a sump for every failed home economics teacher who could convince a producer they were less boring than the one before. Cath didn't know why she watched it.

'How's your steak?'

'Tough.'

'Would you like sauce?'

'No.'

'How was work?'

'Fine.'

'They glad to see you back?'

Silence.

Jamie had been off with 'stomach ache', though it hadn't

stopped him stuffing his face with Eilidh's selection boxes. Cath had nagged him about his sick record, being off again so soon after the assault, and, next thing she knew, he'd signed up for a double shift – out on early, then back out tonight for the bells.

'Anna back yet?'

'Dunno.' He picked up the newspaper.

She dropped her cutlery on the plate. 'Jamie, have I done something to annoy you?'

He sniffed. 'What makes you say that?'

He'd been drunk. She kept clinging to that thought. If he'd even remembered what he'd said, it would have been with relief that he'd not really said it. Just imagined that he had in the anger of the moment. Perhaps that's why he was quiet. He wasn't sure and he was waiting for a sign, a smile to show she knew he didn't mean it.

'I love you.'

'Good.' He turned on the news.

Cath could feel herself like ivy, crawling and clinging even as he withdrew. Being humble was alien, but she felt she must tiptoe round this hole. She imagined there was a blanket over it, so you couldn't tell where it began. One step too far and oblivion grinned. There was a party on later across the road, but now he was working they couldn't go. It wasn't even double-time for Hogmanay, though it buggered up everything. The neighbours had said she could bring Eilidh, but loud music and smoke and no husband were three pointed reasons not to bother.

'So, when d'you think you'll be home?' she asked.

'God, Cath, I don't know. Am I on a curfew or something?'

'I only asked.' She'd meant to snap, but the blubbing erupted instead. It would only make it worse, and she fought the distorting of her face. She tensed, waiting for some snide quip that would make her feel more ugly, some acid rain to erode the soul, and was astonished when he came over and crushed her towards his chest. The bumphling of his jumper blocked her nostrils, but she didn't care, hot face pressing deep as it could into the hard ridges of his body. Desperately tasting his scent. He kissed the top of her head.

'I do love you.'

There. It had passed. She could breathe again.

Cruikshanks was interested in the theory. As the days passed and Mr Wajerski atrophied, he had fewer facts to trade with. He prised thumbs in an imaginary waistcoat, puffed out his gut. 'Of course, being in the Orange Lodge isn't a prerequisite for being a racist murderer, you know. I mean, some of my best friends—'

'No, but it does suggest a degree of intolerance, wouldn't you say?' Anna sat on the edge of her seat.

He shrugged. 'They'd argue they're defending their faith. Isn't that what Muslims do when they set up separate schools, or—'

'Och, give it a rest. It's something: the guy lied to Billy, was fighting with an old woman, lives nearby, comes on very aggressive, is a keen "defender of the faith" as you put it and part-time Orange bandsman – and I have it on record that he's cruel to animals. It's worth pulling him in, eh?'

Cruikshanks peeled a banana. 'What about the gay boy?'

'Shelly? He's a wee soul. I can't see him—'

'Gay – pervert – tossing the old boy off for kicks.'

'Christ, now who's making assumptions?'

'Anna, in this job I have to look at every disgusting, absurd, improbable and depraved notion that a human mind can envisage. If I've thought it, so has someone else.' He bit a large chunk of banana. 'God, I hope they have. So,' he munched, 'we'll bring them both in. This Billy – d'you think he'd fancy a stint as CID aide when he's out his probation?'

'If he lasts that long. Anyway, if you *are* bringing Shelly in – can I come with you? He's kind of a pal.'

Cruikshanks whirled the banana skin into the bin. 'Oooh, bad idea then, don't you think?'

'I'll not get in your road – just soften the blow a wee bit. He did help us out at the parade, you know.'

She kept her tone very light. Stupid not to think they'd speak to Shelly too. They'd bring him in on a voluntary certainly, unless his brother started playing up. Shelly's brother was a bully – did he bully Michelle? Anna had never lifted a friend before, wasn't clear what purpose she would serve by being there. Make sure they gave him a cup of tea? Make sure they didn't make him cry? Her first thought was to keep in Shelly's good books so she could get her cat. To stand there and say, look, this wasn't my fault, I'm not like them, like she tried to the time they'd broken up an animal rights demo outside some lab. A desperate signalling of eyes above the gag. United you must stand, even when you're kicked in the bollocks by your picketing brother, because if the thin blue line slips into an ellipsis, anarchy ensues. Was that true? Anna wondered. Would the sky crash down if you did? If you flopped on the road with the peace protesters and asked for a draw on their spliff?

She only knew the shop, not where Shelly stayed.

'Thought he was a bud of yours, Sarge?' said DC Hamilton.

'I said I knew him.'

'Shop's fine,' said the detective inspector accompanying them. Cruikshanks had stayed behind to 'manage things'. This one was a torn-faced cadaverman, who plainly did not want her there. 'After you, Sergeant.'

Tropics Ya Dancer had gone festive fiesta-fabulous. Spicy chilli lights sparkled on four sides of the glass. Two inflatable mermaids with winking, blinking, flashing breasts framed a quartet of dancing fish, each wearing a Santa hat. Shelly must have rigged up a wind machine or a fan or something, because the mermaids both had wigs that fluttered behind them. Paper flowers rustled on papier-mâché rocks, and a huge treasure chest full of rum and sweetie coins gaped open; Santa's red felt bottom just visible. Silver letters on the chest said: *Come on in to my box of delights.*

No familiar bell tinkling. Instead, a tinny baritone: *We wish you a merry Christmas* – the open door activating a singing Billy Bass.

'Coming, I'm coming – I wish,' chortled Shelly's voice. 'Oh, hiya doll. You come for that wee puss tat? She's pure pining away in here.'

'Hi, pal.' Anna smiled at him. 'Yeah, I'll pick her up next week, if that's okay. Look, Shelly, this is a wee bit awkward. We need to have a word with you – and your brother, if he's in.'

Shelly shook his head. 'Aye, ah know. He was bang out of order the day. I pure telt him you were my buddy—'

The DI coughed. 'Excuse me. Is your brother here?'

'Naw, he's at the hoose. How?'

'Where is that, sir?'

'Hairy Mill.' Shelly sighed. 'That's Maryhill to yous, occifer.'

'Fine, we'll swing by your house on the way to the station. Don't worry, sir, it's just routine.'

Shelly's face had more lines than Anna remembered. 'Maddy, what the hell's all this about?'

'They want to talk to you about—'

The DI broke in. 'Thank you, Sergeant, we can take it from here.'

'I can't say, Shelly, it's up to them. It's not about the march, though – forget that. They just want to ask you a few questions, then they'll bring you straight back, won't you?' she demanded.

'But I havny done nothing. Yous are fitting me up for shag all. Oh God. My face.' He slapped his cheeks, drew the hands down to his neck. 'They'll scar my face with acid in the jail.'

'For God's sake, Michael,' Anna snapped, 'stop being so melodramatic. You're not going to jail, you're going to the police station. Purely on a voluntary undertaking.'

He started to cry. 'Don't shout at me. And don't call me Michael.'

The detectives stifled laughter.

'You don't have to go if you don't want to, you've done nothing wrong.' Anna put her arm round Shelly's shoulder. 'These men want to ask you and your brother a few questions about an inquiry, and once they've done that, they'll take you home. All right?'

'How can I no answer your stupid questions here, then?'

The DI took his arm. 'Sir, it would be better for everyone if you came along to the station. It's more comfortable there.'

'Will I be long?' Shelly sniffed. ' 'Cause all they fishes'll be needing their dinner.'

'Shouldn't think so.'

'I'm a volunteer, did you say?' Shelly asked Anna.

'That's right.'

'So, *you* don't need tae pure ruin my image by hanging on like my boyfriend.' He pulled away from the DI. 'Hold on till I get my jacket. Maddie' – he jutted his head back through the beaded curtain – 'you'd better take Alice the now – just in case. M'on through a minute.'

She followed him into the surprisingly drab back shop. 'Aye.' Shelly kicked past some boxes and a torn *Radio Times* calendar. 'All fur coat and nae knickers, me. Whatthefucksthisaboot?' he whispered urgently.

'The old Polish man – but don't say I told you,' she whispered back. She scooped up a mewling Alice from the shelf she was lolling on. 'Hello, baby. Oooh, look at you. Aren't you a big tiger now?'

'Eh – everything okay in there, Anna?' called the DI.

'Aye, just scratching her pussy, so she is.'

Anna shoved Shelly. 'Quit it, you.'

He took a brown duffle coat from the peg. A yellow and green poster curled on the plaster beside it, listing a series of dates below a head and shoulders photo of a dark-haired man. The image had been defaced with acne and an arrow through the head. Two drawing pins pierced where the eyes should be.

Anna twisted one of the pins. 'That your voodoo doll?'

'Nah. Local councillor. Total toley.' He secured the last of the toggles. 'Right – how dae I look?'

'That is *so* not you.'

'Aye, well, I'm best no drawing attention tae myself in the pokey.'

'Shelly, you're not going to the bloody pokey. Unless – is there something you're not telling me?'

He patted her cheek. 'Would I lie to you, doll face? Okay, Mr DeMille,' he shrilled. 'I'm ready for my close-up.'

17 Unsteady Legs

There should have been a video camera to record it. Some bunting, a fanfare, delighted applause. A clever-kiss for a clever-clogs. Eilidh had taken her first steps. It began with a casualness that belied its significance. They were sitting on the carpet, Eilidh had taken off her socks, and was trying to get a toe in her mouth. Decided it would help if she heaved herself aloft to drape elbows on the sofa. She'd been using the sofa as a pier from which to cruise for weeks, spanning podgy fingers, shuffling balustrade legs. This time, one foot was raised to join the hands. Cath watched her baby stumble, flailing paws catching unanchored cushions as the foot didn't reach, stomped down. Wobbling like a rocking horse, the partner foot slid along the carpet, catching up, taking over. Momentum drove her on, once, twice, till she fell at the third. Eilidh gasped. Lowered brows already dark, checking with her mother to see if she should cry.

Strings snapped inside Cath, twanging cat-gut tickling her chest. 'Clever girl. You walked! You are *so* a clever girl.' She held her hand towards her daughter. 'Your bot-bot sore? Mummy kiss it better?'

Eilidh raised her bum in reply, scrabbling her own hands up to grasp the table leg.

Jamie was sleeping. Cath wanted to dash up, shake him into this moment, but hesitated. It would keep. Elements had shifted somehow, and it was her appeasing him. For what, she didn't know. Had she pushed him too far with tears and tantrums? He'd always been her safety net, an ever-elastic swathe from which she could jump so high, or curl up and be rocked to sleep; which made this sense of slippage more acute. Especially now.

Her breasts ached above her hammering heart, working twice as hard as usual. Soon these deflated sacs would spill over and milking would begin again. It would be a pearl, one day, but the nacre in her belly was mean and thin at this moment, like her joy; which was really terror. Coming up for air one final time before the perpetual drop with lead-lined stomach, and she didn't know if she could do it again. She'd not even stopped breastfeeding. Nature's contra-bloody-ceptive. It was supposed to stop the burrowing cells from digging in, halt the flaring skin, the dislocating bones.

Knowing what was coming was worse, and so was knowing what she would lose if she didn't. The final assassin stab. *Et tu,* body? Still, that too would keep until he woke. So would the note pushed through their letterbox that morning. Unstamped, unsigned, just three little words printed in schoolboy-neat script.

'*Watch your husband.*'

Why? Did he do tricks?

The bar's faux-French frontage opened off a faux-Italianate courtyard that was really just a paved street. A scattering of tables sat hopeful outside, surrounding a statue of a naked winged god. In true Glaswegian style, someone had stuck a traffic cone on his head. This could have been forgiven as ironic urban éclat, if they hadn't also squidged the remains of a pizza round his naked, bronzed buttocks. Unfamiliar high heels caught on uneven slabs as Anna tripped past. Rankin had told her to wear something half-decent – *not those bloody bovver boots.*

She was too early, but she had to get out of the office. Jamie was due in, and she wasn't ready. She needed time to think about many things, not just him. What Linda had told her, for one thing. Stewart Street CID for another. They were showing their usual rigour when it came to investigating assaults on hoors. Liz Maguire had even suggested that the slashings might not be connected with Anna's attack at all. *I mean, you canny say for certain if it was the same guy you were chasing from the locus. Could've just been some mad jakie you disturbed in the warehouse, couldn't it? Different person, different MO?*

True, Liz, true. And that would mean you can detach the police assault, the important one, from all the rest. Let them fester in the apathy they were used to. In a way, Anna would prefer that. She didn't have 'victim' stamped all through her like rock. Not like those other girls. It was a random, anonymous anyone that had given her a kicking. A perk of the job. He was a no one, no motive, no chance, who'd crossed her path briefly and left a vicious, bright slime trail. She could deal with that. What she couldn't deal with was this maggoting in her mind. That Ezra Wajerski was waiting for something, somewhere in an empty room.

Shelly's brother had an alibi – Shelly. They'd been together all evening apparently, a fine night of drinks and kebabs. According to Cruikshanks, the brother, Andrew, had no motive either. Without Mrs Jarmal, there was no one to ever connect him with Ezra. Cruikshanks said he'd interview the old bird Billy had dealt with, see if there was a link there, but what would that prove? That Andrew had a quarrel with an old lady, and neither wished to make a complaint. Shelly's brother did have pre-cons though. Minor assaults, breaches, some petty theft. Nothing damning, except a lapsed membership of the British National Party, dismissed as youthful folly. Still, Anna had no doubt that he'd vandalised Ezra's door. But murder? No proof. Yet.

Rankin had dispatched her on some PR mission. The council were setting up a 'working group' on prostitution, and he'd volunteered Anna to represent the police. *It'll be all bleeding hearts and women's issues anyway, so it's right up your street, Cameron.* He didn't bother with 'sergeant' any more. She crossed the road to the City Chambers, which hulked across the east side of George Square – or Red Square as it had been renamed by locals, thanks to a generous slap of pink tarmacadam between the flower beds. A plush black limo was parked at the double yellow lines outside the front portico of the Chambers. Anna spun the revolving door in a heavy half-turn, walked over the mosaiced bird, bell, fish and tree of the city crest, past blank-eyed Victorian Graces supporting the weight of the world and seventy-nine toon cooncillors, and up a marble staircase to a corridor tiled in chartreuse green. Painted blue and yellow curlicues spanned the glazed plaster ceiling and the whole effect was that of a long, and very vulgar, public toilet. The smells wafting from the councillors' buffet suggested curry was on the menu.

Anna found Councillor Dalgleish in the panelled library. Large and thick-lipped, he was puffing on a cigarette and chatting to a journalist. Anna recognised him as John Burrows, local government correspondent, sometime crime reporter and total personality bypass.

'It's all to do with improving the city's health, John. Have you got that down right? Aye? Though, between you and me . . .' The councillor stopped as Anna came in. 'Oh, hullo, dear, what can I do you for?'

'Councillor Dalgleish?'

'That's right, hen.'

'Anna Cameron. I'm here for the meeting? I believe you're chairing this new working group on prostitution?'

'I am? Oh, that's right. More of them, that's what I say, eh, John?' He nudged the correspondent, who joined him in a macho chuckle. 'Have a wee seat, hen.'

Councillor Dalgleish gave the document before him a cursory glance, then stood up. 'Aye, seems fine. Well, John, I'd better get on. Be seeing you at Charlie's do, no doubt.'

The reporter put his notes in his pocket and followed the councillor. At the door, Dalgleish stopped, dropped his cigarette butt on the marble border, carefully avoiding the fine wool carpet that stretched almost to the edges of the room. He ground out the embers with his foot, kicked the butt back into the corridor.

Brushed the ash from his lapels and smiled at Anna. 'Right, dear. Let's get this show on the road. You from the Exec?'

'Strathclyde Police, actually.'

'Away. You're far too pretty for a polis. Coffee?'

The meeting was interminable, an unholy stew of the earnest, the strident and the cynical. The council's policy officer was a woman of indeterminate age, with piles of brown hair and a fluffy black cardigan. She banged on about commercial sexual exploitation, and providing 'routes out' and 'exit strategies'. A woman from some collective talked about the oppression of the patriarchal society and a woman's right to choose viable options. Councillor Dalgleish rose in Anna's estimation when he snorted, 'Aye, and would you chose it as a job for one of your daughters, *Ms* Donnachie?'

Anna explained the role of the police in relation to the punters. No amount of advertising or censures or policy statements would alter the legal position. These men had committed no crime. 'I understand that the Scottish Executive is looking at changing legislation, but, at the moment, our hands are tied.'

'Well, what about the violence that's a daily occupational hazard for the women? Why do you ignore that?' snipped a girl wearing red tights and a Rape Crisis badge.

'If incidents are reported to us, we deal with them.'

'Now, Sergeant, that is arrant nonsense. Look at the string of recent slashings on sex workers. Five young women – five, Sergeant, who've been scarred for life, traumatised, degraded. Have there been any arrests? No.'

'With respect, we've had virtually nothing in the way of eye-witness accounts. We're working on what little forensic—'

'Oh yes Forensic evidence?' The woman's blazing eyes swept round the table, mustering them all to collude in her outrage. 'You'd think that would make a difference? I know of a client who reported a violent, anal rape to one of your officers. You know the response?'

Anna could guess it. 'No.'

'She was told that the police weren't there to act as a debt recovery agency. They suggested she should make sure "they pay her first next time". That woman is *still* receiving medical treatment for her injuries, Sergeant.'

'I can't comment on individual cases, but what I can say is—'

'You can't hide behind that trite—'

'Now, ladies, ladies.' Another councillor tapped his cup with a spoon. He was a thin man, young, with oily hair and orange skin. 'Chair, may I make a comment?

'Certainly, Councillor Milligan. Fire away.'

He waited, secure in the knowledge that so would they. 'It seems to me that we're all talking at cross-purposes here. The position is that we, as a council, have agreed a policy of total eradication. We accept that prostitution is harmful to all concerned, and has no place in a city like Glasgow.' He raised his hand at the clamour of voices. 'Having said that, words are cheap. We need action – action from ourselves, action from the police, action from all the agencies seated round here. Why don't each one of us put our proposals on the table. Personally, I believe the root is poverty. The drugs, the loan-sharking, the exploitation that traps these women – it's all to do with poverty. Eradicate that, and you eradicate prostitution. Chair, if I might remind you of my suggestion for credit unions . . .'

A groan from Dalgleish. 'Gordon, we're no hear to talk about your moneylenders . . .'

Milligan. *Milligan.* The man Ezra was going to see. Who would be his councillor and therefore Shelly's councillor and thus the face with the drawing pins on Shelly's wall. Anna's mind skipping like hopscotch, stitching one notion to the next as she dipped to seize the peever stone. The padded leather squeaked beneath her as she shuffled to keep up, one ear on the meeting, whole brain back at Ashley Street. When they'd all put in their tuppence worth, and she'd agreed to extra patrols and – shit, Rankin wasn't going to like that, but, anyway, she had without realising it and she kept smiling over at Milligan and when they'd

all stopped talking and folk were shuffling their papers, she
darted to the door, just in front before he slipped out.

'Excuse me, Councillor Milligan. Can I have a quick word?'

He flashed a startling grin. 'It'll need to be mega quick – I'm
just off to catch a train to Edinburgh.'

She moved briskly down the stairs with him, heels tip-tapping
like a damsel in distress. The bloody things were giving her a blis-
ter. 'You mentioned moneylending?'

'No, I mentioned credit unions.' He sounded exasperated.
'Exactly the opposite. Credit unions are a way for the community
to be their own bankers – not have to suffer with twenty per cent
interest that gallops to forty after a week, then your door gets
panned in, then your head.'

He walked even faster than her, this man.

'I know what credit unions are, Councillor. But the moneylending – I'm interested. Do you have experience of that yourself?'

He snapped the cuffs on his bright blue shirt. 'Sergeant, I may
dress a bit jazzy, but I can assure you it's all legit.'

'No, I don't mean you.' she smiled. 'I meant your constituents.
One in particular. A gentleman called Ezra?'

Milligan shook his head.

'Ezra Wajerski?'

'Means nothing, I'm afraid.'

'He lived in Ashley Street – that is in your ward, isn't it?'

'Yes – oh, God. Was that the old man that was killed? Polish
guy?'

'Yes. Did you know him?'

'No, no, I just read about it. Terrible thing, though. He mentioned *me*, did you say?'

She felt her brilliant inspiration sputter. 'Not him. A friend of
his. Said he was going to see you – well, someone called
Milligan – to help him sort out his money.'

Milligan stopped walking. 'Well, I run a debt advice surgery in
Willowbank Primary – he'd maybe heard of that. I put posters up
in all the shops. It gets really bad around Christmas, you see.'

'Really?' Anna stopped too. 'That's very interesting. Tell me, what do you know about moneylenders in the area, Councillor? You must hear things, if folk are coming to you for help.'

'Not very much. Only that they exist. Bit like prostitution – a necessary evil. To be honest, I try not to get involved in all that. Less I know the better. But if I can offer folk an alternative, stop them going to these people in the first place—'

He threatened to begin proselytising again. Anna cut in. 'Have you ever heard of someone called the Fat Man?'

Milligan screwed up his mouth. 'Yeah, yeah, I have, come to think of it. Well, Fat Bastard's what I've heard. Why?'

'Do you know who he is? How many folk have you heard talk about him?'

'A few. Sergeant, I'm sorry, but I really do have to run now.' He rummaged in his breast pocket, disturbing the three-point hanky. 'Look, here's my card.'

'Councillor . . .'

'Gordon.' He grinned. 'Call me Gordon.' Those teeth had to be capped.

'Gordon, would you have any objections to speaking to one of my bosses about this?'

'Not at all. Give me a bell tomorrow, yeah?' He twirled the revolving door, and was gone in a flash of glass.

Back at Cranstonhill Anna cornered Billy, on his own in the muster room, eating from a carton. 'That woman, the one fighting with Andrew Semple. What exactly were they shouting at each other?'

'Em – it was all Italian really. Lots of Latin sweary words, I guess. Eh, hang on' – he took out his notebook – 'I wrote it down right after. Yeah, something about passata, and he said, *You owe me*. But she'd shut the window . . .'

'You owe me – you sure?'

'Yeah. His shirt was ruined . . .'

'Billy. You're a genius. Seriously – Mr Cruikshanks is very

impressed with you. Speak to you later, all right?' She walked backwards as she spoke, in a hurry to get to the Incident Room.

Cruikshanks was pulling on his anorak. It was quilted, navy, and smelled of the sea. One square of the fabric had torn – on a fish-hook, Anna guessed – exposing the white puffy padding.

'Anna, sorry, can't stop.' He zipped himself up. 'They've just—'

'No, you've got to listen to me. Andrew Semple – you said there was no motive.'

He grabbed her hand, shaking it with a double fist. 'Anna, that's just it – they've traced Mrs Jarmal. Bloody Bradford, would you believe? So, well done, you. I've just booked the boys a flight the now.'

'Okay, brilliant. But listen. Semple's a loan shark.'

'Whoa. Way off beam.' If it wasn't Cruikshanks, that smile could have been patronising. 'We've found out he's still involved with the BNP. Possibly the National Front too – Special Branch are checking.'

'Yeah, maybe, but he's not so selective when he opens his tally book. I reckon he'll arrange business with anyone. Maybe even gets more of a buzz out of signing up the ethnics, who knows? I've spoken to Councillor Milligan – he does money advice sessions out the West End. When I mentioned the Fat Man, he'd heard of him.'

'You did what?' Cruikshanks had one glove on, one glove off. His smile had stiffened like egg whites.

'Well, it was Fat Bastard he said, but—'

A black wash passed over Cruikshanks's face. The smiley baker's boy had vanished. 'Sergeant, that is privileged information. That is a direct quote from the only possible witness we have to this murder, not something to be casually passed in conversation. Who gave you the authority to start questioning people on my behalf?'

The warning signs had come too late. But she could recover this. Cruikshanks was a mate. 'No, it wasn't like that. I was at a meeting, and when he said his name, I remembered what Ezra's pal had said—'

'His what?'

Such a cold room. You'd think they'd get the heating fixed. 'His pal . . . Simon.' Her words were tiny, wishing themselves back in the warmth of her mouth.

'Who the fuck is Simon?'

The bustling office had quietened to a hum.

'Well, I was at the Polish Club, and I got talking to him.' She withstood the urge to curl up on the ground.

'Why were you at the Polish Club?'

'I just thought, well, you said you'd not had much joy there, so . . .'

'So you disregarded direct orders, not to mention protocol and courtesy, and just called in, did you? When was this?'

Anna wondered, when she blew the eggs, did the yolk feel anything as its yellow split and spilt? The little ovum that would have grown up to be a chicken, had it not slopped down the sink. She imagined the furore if people used other kinds of foetus for self-indulgent expression. Or was it foeti? *Yes, here's an unborn lamb in formaldehyde. No, darling, it's art. Of course its mother didn't miss it.* No, wait, that's been done. Okay, how about painting a picture with the umbilical blood of a newborn – whoops, no, been done too. Or dissecting living flesh, fresh from the womb, and hiving bits off to graft on to other bits. Just to see if you can, because it's there and you think you could, so you test yourself and push boundaries until there's no going back, 'cause there's nothing real left. Imagine that.

She should have stayed off sick for ever.

'Em – just before Christmas.'

'Just before Christmas.' Cruikshanks nodded, taking the piss now. Nasty, nasty. 'I see. And this Simon, what did he tell you?

Phlegm tickled in her chest. 'He said Ezra's money came and went. He said he'd mentioned someone called Milligan, who was going to help him.'

'Sergeant, has all this unauthorised, potentially vital information been placed in HOLMES?' Cruikshanks was bending as he spoke, shoulders crouching. Perhaps his temple would come to rest on his chest. It would if he kept drooping like that. And whispering too. She knew that trick, and deserved it. 'Has it been examined and evaluated by my trained detectives and used to augment this inquiry? Has it? Has it?' Banging on the desk, wishing it was her head. 'Has it fuck!'

'I know, I should have. It was when I was off—'

'So you're no a cop when you're on the sick, is that it? You know your trouble, don't you?' He was losing it now. 'You're no a bloody cop at all. You're just a stupid wee lassie who's shagging a super. Think I'm buttoned up the fucking back? Christ – Graeme, get her out of here. Take a fucking statement and get her hunted. Breggsy, get me a bridie. And a fucking Bovril. Move it.'

The storm passed over her head, just one bolt penetrating. The vicious kind, that kept exploding in little clusters inside. They'd found her out at last. It would be the easiest thing to give her statement, hand in her warrant card and go home. It was what she wanted to do, at that moment. To do the Vicky at them all and run away. Who would care if she went? And who'd care if she stayed?

The DC followed her out. 'I, eh, I need to take a statement, Sarge. He says you're not to write it. Sorry.'

All she did was put dates and times to what she'd already told Cruikshanks. Added in the bit about Lionel Flax. Of course it looked bad on paper. But it hadn't seemed like an investigation when she was talking to folk about Ezra. It had felt like getting to know him. So where was over a decade of police service now? She was still a naïve sprog who hadn't toughened up. Like that lassie Sylvia and the dog.

Anna left Cranstonhill and returned to Stewart Street. Rankin had urgently requested her presence. A clipped call across the airwaves. *Sergeant Cameron to report to Superintendent Rankin immediately.*

Rankin couldn't even be bothered toying with her. 'Unorthodox? No. Incompetent? Supremely. Do not speak. A run down, if I may. Day-to-day performance – lacklustre. Relationships with colleagues – interesting. Flawed, certainly. Judgement – appalling. Sick record – poor. You lack fibre, make rash decisions. But now your integrity has been called into account. It seems you have deliberately withheld information from an ongoing murder investigation, one in which a friend of yours, I believe, has been implicated.'

'Sir, Shelly isn't a friend exactly—'

'I said, do not speak.'

There was a song playing in her head. 'I'm Going Down'. It alarmed her slightly, how she was detaching herself from this whole mess. On an out-of-body self-destruct, because there was no one to hold her down. That's what they say makes you come back, isn't it – the earthly voice of a loved one, calling you? Well, bloody Alice couldn't speak. But she could, Anna. She could open her mouth and tell him to *get tae*.

'Why not, sir? What bloody difference is it going to make now? I've given Detective Inspector Cruikshanks several significant leads during this inquiry. Granted, I was remiss in not fully apprising him of every aspect, but the individual facts I *had* gleaned didn't amount to much until I made the connection with Councillor Milligan. As soon as I did that, I went straight to CID, *sir*. I'm being penalised for nothing more than doing my job. For being honest and diligent and going above and beyond my remit to catch a bad guy. Because that's the bottom line, sir. It's maybe one you've forgotten, stuck in your office with Seve and the *Herald* crossword, but that's what the polis do. They jail bad guys, and that's all I'm trying to do.'

Rankin fanned himself with the newspaper. 'Phew. That was some speech, Sergeant. While we're on the subject – twelve across: makes heavy weather of light work.'

She fixed her eyes on his framed certificates, biting a quivery tongue.

'Actually, I'm surprised you didn't pull the female card. That one's always difficult for us to brush aside.'

'I never have done, sir.'

'No, that's true. Well, let's see. Remind me – Flexi Squad. Cars, jakies, shoplifters and hoors. Hoors: now there's your chance to shine. Councillor Dalgleish – terrible man, isn't he? – informs me we'll be stepping up patrols in the area. To catch the Mad Slasher Man?'

She glanced at Rankin, trying to gauge his expression. 'Yes, I was kind of put on the spot . . .'

'No, no, that's fine. He seems to think it was some kind of undercover operation too.'

'Now, I never suggested that, sir.'

He laughed at her. 'I think it's a great idea, Sergeant. Shows flair and initiative. Start it after the holidays – you can keep Sergeant Murray for another couple of weeks to keep up the numbers. Take a couple of girls off the shifts too, if you need.'

'Sorry, sir, I—'

'That's okay. Don't have to apologise. It's out of my hands now anyway. The Divisional Commander will be making a report. Do yourself a favour and just get me some results, Sergeant.' He folded the newspaper into a smaller square, picked up his pen.

Presumably, she was dismissed. She waited, unsure.

'Do you know why I'm such a nasty bastard, Sergeant?'

'No, sir.' The guy was a bunkernut. Was he sacking her, chatting her up or patting her on the back?

'Arthritis.' Rankin pushed his chair to the side of his desk, rolled up his trouser leg. ' 'Cause of this. Total bugger.'

A livid scar ran across his shin and round his kneecap. 'They used a crowbar. That's why I drive the Sinclair – comfiest way to travel. And why I'm stuck in this office. Still' – he pushed the black cloth back down to meet his sock – 'I'm sure you'll look better in stockings than I do, Sergeant.'

Anna made a point of looking for Jamie. Couldn't put it off any longer. He was mooching in the squad room. She wanted to stroke his forehead, cover it in kisses. 'Hi, Jamie. Have a good Christmas?'

'Not really. You?'

'Quiet.'

'Anna, I'm not sure what's happening here.'

She tucked her hair behind her ears. 'Me neither. It was *you* who came to see me. All: *trust me, trust me,* then you go off sick.'

'Yeah, I . . . Trying to get my head straight, you know? But, you said you'd phone me.'

'I could hardly phone you at home, could I?'

'Right, sorry,' he sniffed. 'I forgot you'd had practice at this.'

'Och, Jamie, if you're going to start being snidey, you can just piss off. I don't need this, you know.'

He reached up his hand to trace her cheekbone. 'I'm sorry. I'm just . . . I mean, what d'*you* want to happen?'

'Christ, I don't know . . .'

Did she have to decide *everything*? 'I want someone to—'

'Whoops – sorry, folks.' Gus Murray swung on the door, like a big lanky monkey. He raised one finger to his lips. 'Private confab. Ssh, ssh. Backing off now.'

'No, you're all right, Gus. Room's all yours.' She smiled brightly at them both. 'Nothing private in this office.'

18 Mental Maw Scissorhands

Anna pulled the fishnet gusset from between her buttocks. Be obvious, Rankin told her, so she'd raided petty cash and bought her and Jenny *PVC punk skirts!!* at the joke shop in Queen Street. One black, one scarlet, both with fetching studs. Dusted off her crimpers specially too. Anna breathed deeply as she squeezed, tasting frazzled hair and singed hairspray. You had to spray it first, to make sure the crimps went rigid. Of course, the hair melted if the clamps were held for too long, so she just did the top layer, to rough it up a bit. Anna roughed up well. Lashings of black eye liner, grey shadow, a gouge of red lips and her face was done. Finally, on with the gear. Leather-look vest, the black mini, not the red, and a pair of studded ankle boots.

Jenny was up for it too, after a bit of stage-managed posturing. Pneumatic breasts and long black legs were perverse and liberating all at once, and they both walked up and down the corridors and offices more times than they needed, feigning impatience at the catcalls and whistles. 'This is bloody ridiculous. We shouldn't have to do this,' muttered Jenny.

'Shut it, you.' Anna gave a leery cop the finger, then pulled her skirt down over her thighs. 'I know. Piece of nonsense. I think Rankin's disciplining me in his own wee way.'

'We could go to the Federation about this, you know,' said Jenny.

The Federation was not a *Star Wars* fan club, but the police equivalent of a union, or the nearest thing they were allowed. Forbidden by law to strike or work to rule, the police relied on goodwill, lobbying and fear of crime to make their voices heard. As well as promoting their members' interests, the Federation provided welfare support and did a nice sideline in arranging legal advice and representation for officers under investigation or on trial. They could keep costs down by buying in bulk.

Anna had already paid a visit to the Federation. Gone straight after the meeting with Rankin; not to raise a grievance, just to see what her options were, if Cruikshanks or the Divvy Com or whoever took it further. A balding man in a striped polyester shirt had shown her in.

'Right, dear. Anna, is it? Sit down, sit down. I've read your files and I think we've quite a good defence. How do you feel about ill health?'

Anna hadn't understood. 'Ill health? I go the gym three times a week, swim – there's nothing wrong with me.'

'Eh, no, dear. I mean *mental* health.' He managed to both emphasise and whisper the word. 'It's just . . . seems to me you might've gone back to work too early. After that unfortunate business down the Drag. Quite traumatised by that, weren't you?'

Realisation dawned. 'No way. I've not worked my arse off for ten years to have them say I'm a nutter and shuffle me off with a pension.'

The man had stretched back in his chair, exposing sweat-stained armpits as he clasped his hands behind his neck. 'You might find it's the most prudent option – financially, if nothing else. If, as you say, you withheld vital evidence from a murder inquiry, and your superior officer wants to take it further, well. I mean, I doubt they will, these things are usually internal, but if they did, then we can certainly put you in touch with a solicitor – John James and Partners are very good. And of course, we can offer you representation at any disciplinary proceedings. Have you had papers served? No? Well, that's promising. So. That's what I'd suggest really. But, other than that . . .' He wafted his hands in the air, then laid them on the desk before him. With finality.

Anna had gathered up her coat and bag. 'Well, thanks for your time. It's a pity I wasted mine.'

He'd showed her out, anxious to get back to his menu planning. The Federation Conference was only two weeks away, and the Hydro needed numbers confirmed. He'd to work out the seating plan too. 'Think about ill health, if the worst comes to the worst. At least you'd have some income. I shouldn't say this, but you could maybe even sue the Chief. After all, you self-referred for counselling, didn't you? No one came chapping at your door.'

'No, I don't think so.' She wanted to salvage her career intact, not make plans for her retirement. 'But you're right about saving money. Tell me, who is it I contact about cancelling my Federation subscription?' she'd asked as he opened the door.

No, she wouldn't be bothering the Federation again.

'Hey, Sarge,' whooped a voice, 'you always wear fishies under your uniform?'

'Fuck off, Walrus Face,' Jenny shouted, at the same time as Anna replied, 'Well, that's something you'll just have to dream about, Samuel, cos, let's face it, you ain't never gonna find out.'

Anna's jeans and tailored shirts had never got this reaction.

The walk down to the Drag convinced Anna they should definitely get a lift back up the road. Mind, the wee lassie who called her 'Mental Maw Scissorhands' had been quite witty. Before the team split up, Anna went over everything one more time. She'd drawn up the plans so that she would be observed by Gus Murray, who would step in if required to defuse any problem situations without blowing her cover. Jamie would do the same for Jenny, who was positioned round in Cadogan Street. None of the girls on the street knew they were being infiltrated by polis, though the sluggiest druggie would catch on pretty quick when two new parrots squawked into town. They had to stand out enough to attract attention, but not ridicule, and Anna wasn't sure she'd got the balance right. She'd chosen not to use any PWs from the shifts either. At least she and Jenny knew the area, knew the women and many of the punters.

Anna's breath formed clouds in crystalline air. The nutter with the knife was not the man who'd attacked her. That man was just a jakey, disturbed from sleep as she clattered down the warehouse steps, lashing out in meths-soaked fear. Whoever the slasher was, it wasn't the man who hurt her and even if it was, she didn't want him in the shadows, watching her now, as she pulled at the heel of her boot, loosening the tightness round her ankle.

'So, you'll stay in the security room in the insurance building?' she asked Gus. 'Manager's ex-polis. He's agreed to keep the CCTV camera trained on the corner of West Campbell and the lane. I don't intend to move from there unless something happens, and obviously I won't have my radio switched on. I'll guard you with my life, Anna. Don't you worry.' Gus winked at Jamie.

'I'm not worried. I'm confirming you understand the arrangements. And Jamie, you stay in the bin store behind the Land Services building. A lot of girls take the punters down to the underground garage, so mind you don't get embroiled with anything else. Your job's just to be Jenny's lifeline, and pull her out at the first sign of *anything* that looks dodgy.'

Jenny rubbed lipstick off her teeth. 'So what's my job then, if I need a big strong man to rescue me?' She dropped the compact in her bag.

'Same as mine, Jenny. Bait. Attractive new bait that might flush out our serial slicer.'

'Gaffer, you know these things never work.'

'You know that and I know that. But it's political. They watch too much telly at the City Chambers. Rankin gets bonus points with the cooncil for putting his money where his mouth is, and you and I get to keep these lovely skirts.'

Jenny patted her scarlet butt. 'Och, well then. Fair enough. That's worth freezing my arse off for.'

'And a lovely arse it is too, Jennifer,' said Gus.

Jenny yawned.

'Why have you got *him* watching your back?' muttered Jamie.

Anna shrugged. 'Rankin's plan, not mine.'

'Bollocks.' He dunted her with his shoulder. Stayed close.

'Bollocks yourself.' Their mouths were inches apart.

'You look like you're going out guising.'

'Cheers.'

'You want my jacket?'

'It's just not sexy enough.'

'*Are* they sussies?'

'All right, guys?' Gus slapped his gloved hands together. 'Shall we rock and roll?'

They let Jamie and Jenny walk on ahead. Anna would stay further up the hill, nearer to where the last attack had been. The uniformed security guard was waiting for them at the door of the insurance offices. Gus tapped his nose as he slipped inside the soft-lit foyer.

Anna's head was itching. She tried to scratch beneath the helmet of hairspray, but it was impenetrable. It was around ten o'clock and folk were heading out, to the pub, up the dancing, for a lumber. There were a couple of clubs in Sauchiehall Street, popular with footballers and white-blonde women, who stared at her as they clittered by. Their skirts as short as hers, yet they peered down peaky noses like she was clad in puke. Anna adopted the distant vigilance of the professional streetwalker, fuzzing faces into so many blobs. She exhaled slowly, blowing circles into air. A few cars circled. It wasn't a car she wanted. This man didn't drive. All five women had been clear that he'd approached them on foot, from behind. She'd picked this spot because of the lanes. There were two, one directly at her back, the other running parallel with the street across the road. If she turned around and stamped her feet, he had a 360-degree opportunity of approach. Another woman shuffled alongside.

'Howzitgaun?'

'Hi.'

'Like your hair, pal.'

'Cheers.'

'Got any smokes?'

'No, sorry.'

'S'okay. Bloody Baltic, eh?'

'Yeah.' Anna walked slowly to the edge of the kerb, feeling the woman's eyes on her back.

'You new?'

'Mmm.'

'First time?' The woman's pointed boots were alongside her own.

Anna didn't answer.

'S'okay. We've all been there.' She blew her nose.

They stood a while, Anna conscious of the woman's gaze resting on her profile. She must look like a cartoon, all that kohl and lip liner. The worst kind of prostitute parody. This girl would know her boots were wrong, the fishies only tights. She'd be able to tell her hair was a joke: too stiff, too false like her face.

'Look, hen, nae offence like, but you sure you're doing the right thing?'

Anna shrugged.

'I mean, we all need the money and that, doll. But we don't need the grief.'

She was younger than Anna, a pretty brunette with cold sores round her nose. She lit a fag, offered Anna the packet. They stood together a while, sharing the silence. Couple of times, the woman houghed gunk up from the back of her throat – but never spat it out. Just sniffed at it, then swallowed. It must have been going round and round like recirculating air – up nostril, down throat. The thought made Anna want to puke. Eventually, the woman spoke again.

'Can I say something, by the way?'

'Mmm?'

'See, if you can, piss off home the now. Go back and take a kicking, knock some gear, go down the dole. Whatever you need to survive. But don't do this, hen.'

A black Primera pulled up. The driver fiftyish, neat and bespectacled. 'Evening, ladies.'

The woman drew on her fag. '£10 for a hand-job, £25 oral either way, £50 for the full bhoona. Cash upfront.'

He opened the passenger door.

'Away home, pal, eh?' She dropped her cigarette at Anna's feet. 'This place'll fucking rip you.'

It was getting busier now. Twice, cars stopped, and Anna shook her head. 'I'm waiting for someone.' The first one drove off with a *fuck you*. The second car was red, with go-faster flame marks and a giant spoiler. Three boys in it, one white, two Asian. 'How much?'

'I'm waiting for someone.'

'Tough. We're waiting for you, dream girl. C'mon. What d'you say? Three on one.'

'Naw, three-*in*-one, ya dobber,' snorted his companion.

'Not interested.' She wished she'd brought some cigarettes. It would give her something to do.

'Here, whore. Look at this.' The white boy was dangling his dick out the window. 'Get your gums roon my plums.'

'Gie's a gobble,' sang his buddies.

'I told you. Not interested. Now piss off.'

The white boy's nostrils widened. 'Ho. You watch your mouth, you cow. Or I'll come and shove it so full you'll no be able tae speak.'

She could hear them whispering. The back passenger door began to open. There was no one else on the street. Gus should be appearing just about now. Where was he? Where the hell was he? The white boy got out the back, cock still dangling.

'You ready for me, bitch?' He wiggled his hips. The front passenger was getting out.

'Make it quick,' called the driver.

Where in Jesus' name was Gus? Anna fumbled in her bag, trying to locate her PR.

'Ho, you'll no be needing your purse, gorgeous.' The white boy grabbed her arm, tugging the strap from her shoulder. 'We'll no be paying, know what I mean?'

No one else on the street. She made her voice hard and low. 'Piss off, sonny. I'm no the real thing, trust me. You don't know what you're dealing with.'

He brushed his hand across her left breast. 'Boom, boom. Boom, boom.' Tweaked the nipple. 'Naw. All seems pretty real tae me.'

She seized his wrist. 'Right, that's it. Strathclyde Police. You're under arrest.'

The boy stopped, looked at his mate, who burst out laughing. 'Is that right, doll?'

'Yes, that's right. Now, stand against the wall. You, out the car.'

The driver tapped his temple. 'Trust you tae pick a loony. C'mon, just leave it.'

The white boy pushed her against a lamppost. She could feel his penis stiff against her thigh. 'So, where's your handcuffs, doll? Do we get that later?' His breath stank of garlic and beer. Tongue poking at her mouth, probing her lips as his knee prised her thighs and she was back in the dunny, her bladder singing a shrill, high note that paralysed the pain from his feet on her head. Legs going, voice gone.

'Shite, Bonners. She is and all.' His friend had been rifling through her bag. Her warrant card lying loose among the tissues. 'Fucking move it.'

The car screeched off, leaving her kneeling in the street to gather up the contents of her bag. Heart banging *bastards. Bastards. Bloody little bastards.*

'Hey Anna, Anna – you okay?' Gus smarmed out the lane behind the insurance office.

'Where the fuck were you?' She pushed herself up from the pavement, knees through her tights.

'Hey, now wait a minute.' Gus raised his hands, palms up. 'You were handling the situation fine. Everything was under control.'

'Everything was not under control, you stupid bastard,' she yelled. 'Anything could've happened.'

'Nonsense. I think you're overreacting a wee bit, don't you? You were perfectly safe.'

'Get your jollies, did you? Watching him rub his dick up my leg?'

'Now look, Anna, I'd heard you were a wee bit irrational, but, come on . . .'

'Did you get their number?'

'You were closer, Anna. Surely you . . .'

She found her PR, switched it on. They were on a different frequency, so they could use talkthrough without interfering with the rest of the division. 'Alpha 51 to Alpha 523. Jamie. Just call the whole thing off. Tell Jenny to—'

The Controller cut across all radio traffic: 'A Alpha to all stations. Report of a disturbance in Waterloo Street. Sounds of female screaming. Stations to attend.'

Waterloo Street lay at the bottom of the Drag. Gus's heels, though stacked, were not as precarious as Anna's.

'Keep going over the hill, then turn right at the bottom,' Anna shouted to him. 'It's where that gay pub is. Move! Alpha 51 to 523: Jamie, did you get that? Switch back to the divisional channel. Control, keep us on talkthrough.'

She heard Jamie's voice. 'En route, Control. ETA one minute, max.'

'Alpha 51 to 523. Jamie, where's Jenny? Repeat. Where is Constable Heath?'

There was a babble of voices, her message drowned out.

Bloody stilettos. She ran downhill, the tights working themselves lower with each lope, until they hung like a fishing net below her skirt. Tried again. 'Five one to Control. Has anyone located the whereabouts of Constable Heath?'

Her radio spluttered, she placed it at her ear. Jamie's voice again, panting. 'Anna. She's with me. She's fine.'

'Sergeant Murray to Control.'

'Roger, go ahead.'

'Ah, would you note, one male apprehended at the scene. Ambulance required Waterloo at Wellington. Female with severe facial injuries.'

'Roger. En route from Maitland Street. Any officers hurt?'

'That's a negative.'

'Well done, Gus,' said Control.

Oh, well done, Gus. Anna waited, then added her own thanks. 'We still on talkthrough, Control? Brilliant. Good work, guys. I'll meet you in a minute. Wellington at Waterloo, yeah? See you. Out.'

She hobbled down the remainder of the hill. The crackling conversations continued. Ambulance had arrived. *Stations requested to keep the posse back.* Which end of the lane should the van go to? *You should know, ya big poof. You're down there every other night.* They'd got a body. They were on a high.

A speeding hatchback hailed her. 'Get it up you, ya dog.' She didn't bother to acknowledge them. It was universal then, that feeling; when what you wore overtly invited contempt. Women in uniform, pretending they didn't care.

A blue light pulsing on the opposite side of the road jabbed her eyes. She limped to the van. Door gaping, running engine sending warm fumes curling into iced air. Lots of people gathered, and a dread weight pushing her forward.

It was him.

Two ice-burning eyes stared impassively. Anna pulled back, though she knew there was mesh between them. She recognised the face, of course she did. It belonged to the feet that had hammered her skull. Every day since she'd returned to work, she'd been searching for and dreading this. He scratched his nose with cuffed hands. Two asterisks, pinkie and thumb. A twisted letter on each finger in between. Indigo ink spelling F-T-P. Then she noticed Jamie, her Jamie, sitting, flushed, beside him. *You okay?* he mouthed.

Kept her voice calm. 'Take him up the road. CID will want to interview him anyway. I'll go along to the Royal to see how the hoor's doing.'

'Eh, Sergeant.' Jenny touched her arm. 'Uniform's already got someone with her. Should we not go back to the office, get cleaned up?'

'Don't tell me how to do my job, Constable Heath. You go with Jamie, do what you like.'

Quick and curt, only she'd meant to say *thanks*, ask her how she was.

Rankin wound down the window of his car, parked directly behind the van. At that moment, she hated him too. Normal supers would be at home with a whisky at this time of night, not prowling after his men with a dustpan and brush. Why in God's name would you want to be here if you didn't have to?

'Good work, my Flexi-ble friends,' he drawled. 'Jump in and I'll give you a lift, Sergeant. You too, Gus. We'll need to get a statement from you all.'

Gus was in the front passenger seat before Rankin had closed his mouth.

Anna saw the prisoner wink at Jenny as she got in the van beside him. 'Or-right, darlin'?' Grating Irish Paisley-pattern that surprised her.

Jenny sat on the wooden bench facing. Raised her foot and kicked him in the balls. 'You don't fucking speak.'

'You tell 'im, Tonka,' said Jamie.

By the time Anna and Rankin reached Stewart Street, the prisoner was standing at the back bar, flanked by Jenny and a uniformed cop. The turnkey had finished searching him, and his property was being put in an envelope. Some loose change, couple of tenners, house keys. On a sheet of paper lay one opened Stanley knife, sharp as a canine tooth.

Jamie hurried up to the bar. 'Sorry, sir,' he said to the OD. 'Nature calling. Cold night air.'

As Jamie was the other arresting officer, the cop moved back, let Jamie take his place.

'Right, Jamie,' said the Duty Officer. 'Let's have it.'

'You are charged that you did, on today's day and date, within Waterloo Street, Glasgow, assault a female currently unknown, to her severe injury. Do you understand the charge?'

The male nodded.

'Do you have any reply you wish to make to the charge?'

The male shook his head.

'Inspector, we also wish to interview him with regard to five previous serious assaults with similar MOs.'

'CID have already advised me of that. I believe they're dealing.'

'But, sir . . .' Jamie looked at Anna, who remained silent.

'Now, children, don't let's start fighting over who gets to chat to our mystery man.' The Duty Officer motioned to the turnkey. 'Put him in number two, it's empty at the moment.' He turned to Rankin as the male was led away. 'Wee Paddy bastard won't give us his details, sir. Doesn't want a brief, either.'

As the two men consulted, Anna slipped into the lift behind the turnkey. 'Here, I'll come up with you.'

'Oh, cheers, Sarge.'

First floor. Menswear and bedding. The turnkey unlocked the passageway gate. 'Numero two. In you get, and I'll get you a mattress.'

Anna watched the prisoner circle the cell, casual as a dog would sniff a lamppost.

The turnkey slid a thin plastic mattress across the floor. 'Here you go. Short of blankets, I'm afraid.'

She stopped the turnkey from removing the handcuffs. 'I'll do that. Just want to see if I can get his name out of him. Give me a minute, would you?' She smiled widely. 'I'll catch you up.'

'Aye, fine, Sarge. Nae bother. I'll catch you back downstairs – gie's the keys when you're done.' He dropped his keys into Anna's hand, moseyed back up the cell passageway.

The man was wee and thin when you saw him close up. Weedy almost, and that made it worse. He spread himself out on his mattress.

'Remember me?' Anna's tongue was swollen. 'No, you probably don't. I'm just another burd, and I guess we look all the same to you.'

'Not at all.' He lifted his head. 'Sure, pig burds smell different.'

It was enough.

'Well, maybe you'll remember the smell as you made me pish myself down in that warehouse. It kind of went like this.'

Anna seized his collar, dragging him from the thin ledge to the stone floor. He was too surprised to do much about it. She slammed his head several times on the concrete: single, rapid movements. Howling like a wean, and she knew someone would come.

'Fuck you, you bastard!' she screamed, raining kicks and blows into his foetal form. 'Fuck you, fuck you, fuck you!'

Jenny came running at the noise, closely followed by Jamie and the turnkey. It took all three of them to yank her away. Then the Duty Officer and Rankin arrived.

'What in Christ's name is going on in here?' bellowed Rankin. Anna was being held by Jenny, with the turnkey and Jamie dragging the bleeding suspect to his feet.

'Dat bloody cow tried ta kill me,' he screamed, pointing at Anna.

Anna saw all the people in the cell; saw it was the superintendent that had spoken. Her mouth was tired, slower even than her brain. 'He jus . . . went mental, sir.'

'Is that right?' demanded Rankin of the turnkey.

'I . . . I don't know, sir. I wasn't there . . . I—'

Jenny broke in. 'Yes, sir. I came in just as Sergeant Cameron was attempting to undo his cuffs. He lunged at her, then he slipped, striking his head on the floor.'

Rankin stared at Jenny. Jenny stared back.

'Right, get the casualty surgeon out to have a look at him. And you' – he stuck his finger hard in Anna's collarbone – 'I want you in my office, right away.'

Anna went to follow, but Jenny caught her arm. 'It's him, isn't it? The one that beat you up?'

'Leave me alone.'

'Don't tell them, Sarge,' she whispered urgently. 'Don't tell them anything. You've never seen him before, and he just went mental. We both saw that. All right?'

Anna followed the men.

Jenny leaned back against the wall. What possessed her to stick up for that boot? The stupid bitch was going to confess all, and end up firing Jenny in. Right away, Jenny had known. Soon as she saw Anna looking at him in the van; the dull terror you couldn't mask. That's what gave them the kick. *No man has the right . . .* What all the posters at the front desk said. Maybe not, but they did it anyway.

Anna watched herself walk down the corridor, knock on the super's door. Could hear him speaking through the ringing in her head. She was steadfast. Say nothing. They can do nothing. Bawling at her now.

'If your actions have ballsed this case up, I'll have you. And, if he makes a complaint . . .'

'He won't,' said Anna. 'He'd never admit to getting a doing off a woman.' Woosh. The truth, just like that, spilling over itself.

'I'll pretend I never heard that, Sergeant Cameron. Let's hope for your sake he doesn't. Now get the fuck out of my sight. I really can't take any more of you.'

'Yes, sir.'

She saw Jenny on the way out.

'Okay?'

'Yeah.'

'Good.' Jenny raised her voice. 'I'm just going up the Royal to see how the girl's doing, Sarge. We're still not sure who she is – her face is really mangled. You coming?'

Anna found herself sitting beside Jenny, as they drove through hospital gates. The girl was in Intensive Care, hooked to a series of drips and machines. Her face was pulp; the padding wisped over with matted red hair. She'd already lost an eye. Anna scrutinised her, lifted the unconscious woman's swollen hand, and recognised her. It was the girl from the cells. The one the old lady had asked Anna to give a note to.

'Antonia.'

'What?'

'I know her. Her name's Antonia. Nuccini or something like that.'

Jenny frowned, shook her head. 'No, Sarge, it's not. I know her too. Her name's Sandra Tamburrini.' She moved closer to the other side of the bed, touched the undamaged hand. 'Look at her hand. Sandra's always had a crooked pinkie. Can't straighten it.'

Anna kept a grip on her side. 'It's not. It's Antonia. I met her a few weeks ago – had to do a strip search.'

'I'm telling you – it's Sandra Tamburrini. She's been down south for a couple of years, but it's her all right.'

'Are you sure?' Loosened her hold. 'I don't understand. She told me her name was Antonia.'

'Yeah, I'm sure. I got to know her quite well before she left. We were both pregnant at the same time. She's got a wee boy – Josh. Must be about three now. She'd to leave him behind when she scarpered.'

Anna dropped her pen. It rolled across the floor, tutting at her. 'You've got a kid? she asked sharply.

'Yup.'

'You . . . what age?'

'Catriona. Like I said: three.' Jenny took a deep breath. 'I'm on my own and my mum watches her. I also have two brothers, a sister in Canada and an ex-husband who likes beer and punching. Any problems with that?'

'I . . . I'm sorry. I never knew.'

'Yeah, well, I'm not. Anyway, it's not an issue. This is.' Jenny took Sandra's flaccid hand. 'Look, I know Sandra's mum. Will I go and tell her?'

Anna flinched as she inclined her head. Aching so much that any movement hurt. 'Yeah, if you're sure. On you go, Jenny. Thanks.'

Anna told the policewoman outside to go for a coffee. Sat on the chair by the bed, watching the green blips and squiggles tracing fingertip life. The girl still had ulcers on her leg. The one Anna had burst was crusted over now, others wept on skin that was somebody's daughter, who'd been born and fed and had smiled in school photos. Who had dreamed of growing into something wonderful.

If this girl wasn't Antonia, did the grandmother know? The grandmother who thought her baby had come home. And where was the real Antonia, and why had Sandra been using her name? She looked again at the face, saw shapes this time in the blood. The *I* again. And a circle, just as on Linda. Then another curve, like a smile or a tongue. *I O U.* He'd had time to carve his claim in full.

Anna screwed up her eyes, trying to concentrate, make connections, but the adrenaline was scouring her innards and nothing was being clear. Her hands and feet felt separate, like some electrode was making them dance and shimmy. Then a light kiss glanced the top of her head, and Jamie was there, beside her. And she could relax.

'All right, you?'

'Hiya.'

Jamie moved his arms across her collarbone, easing the flesh. 'Jenny says our redhead isn't Antonia then?'

'No. Says she's called Sandra. Tamburrini. Ever heard of her?'

'Nope.' Said it like he didn't care.

'You'd've thought the female turnkey would've known. I thought they knew everyone.'

'Betty's only been doing the job a year or so. She was a cleaner before. *The* cleaner.'

'*The* cleaner?'

'Aye. *Rankin's* cleaner.'

'You're bloody joking.'

'No. Got herself a promotion. Why d'you think Rankin works so many weird hours? Fits in with Betty's shifts.'

'That is disgusting.'

'Och, I don't know. Fine pair of legs on her, has Betty. She'd do for your work anyway.'

She put one of his fingers in her mouth. 'That what you say about me?'

Finger easing across her tongue. Holding the pressure, for just one heartbeat, then slipping back out. 'Way you're going you won't even be at my bloody work.' He came round the front, crouched down beside her. 'Anna. What happened in the cells?'

The hole in her tights was getting bigger. 'I lost it.'

'Big-time. You've got to be careful . . .'

'Please kiss me.'

He laced his fingers in her hair. She pushed against his lips, shoving her tongue deep inside, raking nails through scalp. Tried to put her hand inside his shirt, till he broke away.

'Eh, that's Sandra's mum here, Sergeant.' Jenny stood in the doorway, shielding a dumpy grey woman. She wore a turquoise raincoat, black eyebrows contrasting with drained, sparse hair. Hesitant, she waited for admission to her daughter.

'Eh, I'll leave you to it.' Jamie shuffled by Jenny, ''Scuse me.' Gave what passed for a sympathetic grimace at the woman.

Anna offered Mrs Tamburrini the chair. 'Here, please. I'll . . . I'll go and get a nurse.'

Anna edged past Jenny, who came after her, into the corridor. 'What the hell are you playing at?'

'Just leave it, Jenny.'

'I told you to leave him alone. Are you stupid?'

Fight or flee, fight or flee. 'Don't you dare speak to me like that.'

Jenny crossed her arms. 'Why – 'cause you deserve my respect? He's a mate. His wife's a mate. They *need* each other right now.'

'And what about me, Jenny?' Haggard laugh. 'We all need someone.'

'Yeah? So get your bloody own. D'you never wonder, Sergeant, why you only pick men who're spoken for?'

'What're you talking about?'

'God, you really think we're that thick? *Everyone* knows about you and that super at Policy Support.'

'My life is none of your business.'

'You make it my business when you start humping in public on top of a dying hoor. Jee-sus wept. Why don't you just go home? Leave me to deal with this, right?'

Anna's head, her neck were on fire. If she hurried, she might catch up with Jamie.

'Anna,' Jenny called after her. 'Cath's pregnant.'

19 Hatching

'Here, boss. Take a look at this. It's a body the Flexi brought in last night.'

DI Cruikshanks picked up the crime report. 'Serious assault. Caught red-hand . . . ugh – took her eye out. Bleggh. So?' He dropped the sheet on his desk. 'Hardly need the professionals for that one. Your point, caller?'

'Stewart Street CID are interviewing him re five other slashings,' said Breggsy.

'Good for them. All on their beat?'

'This last one was right on the boundary.'

'And I care because . . .?'

'Check out the note attached,' said Breggsy.

Cruikshanks turned the paper over. Stapled on the back was a compliments slip. 'Body brought in . . . blah, blah. Carving IOUs blah, blah – ach, shit, it's from Suzie Breadknife.' He grabbed his throat with one hand, mimed a manic stabbing action with the other, curling the paper into a dagger. 'Can that bint not leave me alone?'

'Anna Cameron? Thought you liked her, boss?'

'I did. Until she became a liability. Och, I canny be annoyed reading it. Tell me what gems the daft cow's turned up for us this time. Her star witness was a waste of bloody time.'

He was still smarting from the wasted trip the guys had to Bradford. The detective super had not been amused. Flights, hotel – and the meals. God, the meals. One DC had been stupid enough to claim back for swordfish steak, crêpes suzettes and two pints of lager. Mrs Jarmal had insisted, through a translator, that she knew nothing about any moneylending, any visitors to Wajerski's house, or, indeed, much about Wajerski himself. Even when threatened with Immigration, she'd been adamant. Either she was shit-scared or she was telling the truth, and it made little difference. 'I saw and heard nothing.' That is what she would say – in the interview room, in a statement, in the witness box. So he was back to square one. The fiscal had released Wajerski's body. The old boy's property was bagged and boxed downstairs. And Cruikshanks had nothing but a nasty taste in his mouth.

'Cameron's saying this ned's been carving IOUs on hoors' faces, and he might be worth an interview. Moneylending theory again, boss. Also says his distinguishing marks include the initials FTP on his right hand . . .'

Cruikshanks sat up straighter. 'Fuck the Pope, eh? Go on.'

'Appears to be Northern Irish, refuses to give a name. She's requesting we get on to the RUC—'

'It's no the RUC any more, Breggsy. Poor bastards have all been sanitised, mind? It's the' – he paused to make inverted commas in the air – '"Police Service of Northern Ireland", if you don't mind. You know they made them hand back their long service medals and everything? Leave no trace – except the bloody amputees and the widows and . . .'

His daughter had applied to join the police. Told him that morning over Coco Pops. Twenty years old and she still liked her Coco Pops. Calmly announced she was quitting uni – would chuck her Honours course, just do an Ordinary degree and be finished and raring to go by the summer. His wife told him to tell her. *Tell her, Thomas,* she said. He knew it was bad when he was no longer Tommy. *Bloody tell her. No way.* And his head said, 'You stupid girl.' And his heart swelled to splitting like an overblown plum.

'Anyway . . .'

'Sorry, son. You were saying.'

'So, I did. Put in a request.'

Cruikshanks wasn't sure if this was a good thing. Should the lad not have waited until he was told?

'Didn't want to waste your time, sir. Not till I knew if it was worth it.'

'And? Is it?'

Breggsy picked up a sheaf of waxy paper. 'They faxed over about forty possible mug shots. Based on age, colouring and that. I tried to narrow down the fields: went with the moneylending, sexual offences and serious assaults. Thought the tattoo might clinch it, but it's not that unique over there . . .'

'I can imagine.'

'Anyway. I'm just going to Stewart Street the now, boss. Fancy a hurl?'

'I do indeed, Breggsy, my man. Can we go via the Bakers Oven? I feel a celebratory pie coming on.'

Cath smoothed the skin around her belly. She was lying on a desert island, had built the fire up really high. And a ship, the same ship each time, seemed to be altering course. She raised her hand weakly against the sun and watched through spanned skin as it never reached her, turning once more for open sea. All around her, sand. Golden delicious, to be crammed in her mouth and eaten, filling and silting its course till it spilled from her nose and ears and never, never, not even bloody once, killed her.

'Mama.'

'Whatwhat?' She opened her eyes.

Imagine a tropical beach, that's what the woman had told her, when she went to ante-natal classes. Och, not this time, the time before Eilidh was born. The instructor would walk lightly among the lumbering mums-to-be as they lay in awkward recovery positions. She'd twitter about 'lights in their stomachs', imploring them to find a 'special place'; to envisage sky through trees, feeling the leaves rubbing as you pushed through to your secret beach. She would lull with soft promises that this place was always there, hidden deep within you. Draw the curtains, put your feet up and bob's your uncle.

Pish.

Eilidh squatted beside her mother's head. 'Dahr-ya!' She was walking properly, chunkily, everything new pleasure.

'Yes. There I am! Where's Eilidh?' Cath hid her eyes behind her hands. Eilidh tugged at her arm. 'Pee-pee *boo!*'

'Aaagh! There's Eilidh.'

Eilidh clapped her hands. 'Aes A-ee! Way dodamama? Way doda?'

'Where's Daddy?' Cath sat up. 'Daddy's at his work.'

Eilidh nodded. 'Go tawok.'

Cath still hadn't told him. She wondered if she waited, and waited until the purple flares crawled from her groin and her breasts inflated and spilled above her gestating belly, when he would notice. To notice would involve looking at her, something his eyes seemed programmed to avoid. Jenny Heath had come round last week, and Cath had ended up bursting to her. Poor Jenny was only dropping off some clothes her Catriona had grown out of. They sprouted so quick, they hardly wore them at that age, and Jenny always dressed her daughter in Next and Gap. They'd got talking about how big Eilidh was getting, and she'd been so nice and Cath hadn't spoken to another grown-up in ages.

Then Jenny had squealed, and Cath had set her teeth in a rictus smile and said, yeah, it was a shock, but she was really chuffed. And not to say to Jamie because she hadn't told him yet.

Weird thing was, she wanted to talk to Anna too. Unattainable Anna, who wanted nothing to do with Mrs Fuckwit Forbes; *vacuous vache extraordinaire, appearing bi-annually at a labour ward near you*. A conversation with Anna was like a douse in cold water – not pleasant, but good for you. Cath needed someone to tell her that she was right to be terrified. She needed someone to *know* that she was terrified. Not having kids – Anna had made that choice. A healthy, healthy choice that Cath wanted to hear justified.

It was not a debate to be aired at Mums and Toddlers; yes, they moaned, but none of them meant it. Cath knew when she looked at Eilidh that she loved her, loved her more with each new person she became – and *that* was it. If they came as shrink-wrapped people, she could cope, but this was coming as a baby, a gaping maw that would rip its way forth to consume and resume the status quo. And Cath had nothing left to give.

Did any other woman in the world feel the desperation she did? For always, ever, one unalienable fact. Women are wombs. You might ignore that open sore at your centre, but it was there all the same. Monthly pain and lifetime wonders flitting in and out and round about like a pesky fly. And, if you do succumb to that tug in your gut, then nothing is ever the same again. Patted, congratulated, shunned. Prodded, talked at, squirming. Taught, advised, persuaded. Labelled, stamped, tagged. Frightened, crying, begging. *Sore.*

Finally, emitting dirt and life. And nothing is ever the same again.

Having survived this ordeal, do they give you treatment for post-traumatic shock? A critical incident debrief? Wee hand-book maybe? Nope. Tea, toast and a good old suturing to redefine your fanny from your arse. Torn, battered, your girl-hood truly gone, you emerge blinking into the light of motherhood. How dare you think you were invincible? Your body has cracked and multiplied and will never be the same again. And neither will your mind. Will you morph into some-one's shadow, living only to serve? Will you paper over the cracks and hit the dance floor, puff the fags, or bang on the boardroom table like you've never been away? Or will you twist and turn in a flagellation of guilt and doubt, wondering where the balance lies? Me? Or it? Or them?

Nobody had told Cath that. It was her mind she missed the most. So. How do you scoop those unthinkable thoughts from your foul-smelling head and square it with being a good mother? Cath didn't think she could. She needed to talk to Anna.

Eilidh plonked down beside her, snuggled in. 'Ta.' She took the ball of paper clenched in her mother's hand and began to chew.

'No, Eilidh. Dirty.'

'Duh-teee,' she giggled, tongue pinkly glistening.

Cath prised the soggy paper away, smoothed it out. She wanted to ask Anna about these notes too. Another one arrived yesterday. Pushed through her letter box, addressed to Mrs Worth. It just said: '*Well, are you? His boss certainly is.*' Cath had thought nothing of it, at first. Some smart-assed advertising campaign. But when she looked closely she saw the note was handwritten, very neatly, tiny letters, and not printed at all. If she held the paper up to the light, there was a faint watermark. A crowned thistle that announced it was the property of Strathclyde Police.

Anna would know what they were on about. Yesterday, Cath had found Jamie in Eilidh's room, crouched at the side of the cot. But the cot was empty – Eilidh had been in the bath with Cath. He looked like he was stroking the sheet. Mumbled something about making the bed when Cath came in. If Jamie was in some kind of trouble, Cath had a right to be told. Anna would know. She'd been surprised at her urge to see Anna. If someone had told her a few months ago she'd be seeking Camel Features as a confidante, she'd have cackled maniacally. Like you do. Because she *was* manic, she'd decided. Definitely; all this incoherent paranoia spooling like vultures in her brain.

The letterbox clanged. Morning post of bills and junk and another pale envelope, same as the other two. A fluttering plummet as she slit paper with nail. Unfolded the white sheet, read the black words underlined in green: '*He's a gaffer's tout – and she's loving every minute.*' Cath sat on Eilidh's brick box, rested her head against the plastered wall. The words formed instant meaning. *But she'd always known.* She struggled to hold them at bay. Could mean anything. He could be getting extra overtime, longer piece breaks, cushy jobs, and someone was taking exception. *But she'd always known.* He could be working secretly for Discipline and hadn't told her. He could be doing some undercover work he couldn't explain, and needed secret meetings. *But she'd always known*. She knew how cops gossiped. How they saw everything with jaundiced, practised, beady eyes. The paper scrunched in her fist. Gaffer's tout, teacher's pet. All one. Might not be Anna – gaffer was an interchangeable handle for any boss. There was a handle, up there. Cath reached over to pull herself up by the door. An ache like cold custard, seeping from scalp and chilling her toes, and she wondered what she would do.

Anna pressed *save*, pushed her chair away from the desk. At last, she had something decent to put in Rankin's report. The Irish ned was a body for one serious assault, and a suspect for at least five more. Of a sixth, there was no mention. Jenny had been right. To identify Paddy as Anna's attacker would have left Rankin no option but to dig deeper into the 'lunging' in the cells. Some bloody lunge to bash your head four, or was it five, times in quick succession? She liked the name Paddy. Made her think of a cat. Wee scrawny Alice pit-patting her way round the flat with paws too big for her. The ned still wouldn't give them a name.

CID were stealing the Flexi's body anyway. Cruikshanks had finally listened to her. He was on his way over and she'd prepared as much as she could. A mate in the Met had done some late-night checking on Antonia Iannucci. She'd died in London two months ago. No next of kin listed and no suspicious circumstances – it was an HIV-related illness. Sandra Tamburrini was not known to the Met, but Anna had e-mailed her SCRO photo just in case. Ally said he'd get back to her as soon as he could.

It was just a feeling she had. The IOUs, Mr Wajerski's missing money, the money troubles Simon had mentioned. If they could identify who Paddy was, find out if he'd links to moneylending . . . but what was his link to Mr Wajerski? None of the crappy, sparse witnesses they'd dredged up had ever mentioned an Irishman in the close. She was wishing too hard. Paddy slashed prostitutes. Maybe he thought he should get it for nothing, and the IOU was a tasteful joke.

Anna's door swung open. 'Good morrow, fair maid.' Cruikshanks gave a courtly bow. Evidently, she was flavour of the month again.

'Hello, Inspector. You got my note?'

'Did, did, did. And look, look, look.' He waved a fax before her. 'Your man. Just had a peek at him in person. We'll get his prints matched for sure, but, unless he has a clone, ugly wee bastard that he is, the gentleman I'm about to interview is one Mark John Galletly.'

Anna read Galletly's notes:

> *Warning signals: Knives, concealed blades.*
> *Distinguishing marks: Tattoo on right hand, FTP; tattoo on left hand, five asterisks; tattoo on upper right arm, Red Hand of Ulster; tattoo on left shoulder, Rangers FC crest. Tiny penis –*
> no, she made that one up.
> *Known associates: Arnold Simpson; Peter Mallen; Ian Campbell; James Tait.*
> *Background intelligence: Bodyguard to Arnold Simpson, BNP candidate for Burnley 1992; member of Grand Orange Lodge of Ulster; member of British National Party 1985 to current; Possible links with Combat 18.*
> *Additional notes: Special Branch require to be alerted regarding any known involvement with this male.*

A whole screed of previous convictions: serious assaults, robberies, racist attacks, distribution of racist material, public order offences; some in Ireland, mostly in England. None in Scotland, though. Two counts of extortion and one of 'causing or procuring involvement in usury'.

Anna nudged the phone across her desk. 'Would you like to phone Special Branch from here, Inspector?'

'Indeed I would. And did you notice how wee his feet were?'
She thought for a moment Cruikshanks was taking the piss.
'No bigger than a five, I reckon. Here, have a fly cemetery.'

The boys from Special Branch buzzed in within the hour. Not quite wearing shades, but there was a brusqueness and strut to their every movement that radiated like Ready Brek and demanded a respectful distance.

'Well, what they saying?' Jenny whispered to Anna.

'Don't know. Cruikshanks has been in there for ages. He's not been allowed to interview Galletly yet. 'Scuse me.'

Anna went to the bog. She'd been avoiding Jenny since the hospital. Couldn't avoid Jamie, though. He was coming round tonight. These hushed rushed glares and stuttered smoulderings were getting to her. They were going to *talk*, nothing more.

Thump on the cubicle door. 'Anna. I know you don't want to talk about this, but it's really important.'

'Would you like to come and sit on my knee, Jenny?'

'Jamie doesn't know. About Cath being pregnant, I mean. Please don't say anything. Don't say I told you. That's all. I'm going now.'

'Good.'

Ah, now, she wasn't going to say anything, not even to herself. Had rinsed that part of the conversation clean. Because she had a chance here, to start something new and fresh. It happened all the time. Feelings ebbed and flowed, and Anna had no obligation to any but her own. She couldn't change the way she felt and she owed the world nothing. Her bowels opened and she relaxed into the push, flushing quick before the stink hit.

'Anna, Anna, sorry, I'm – Jeez – somebody die in here?'

Anna disliked the familiarity of her first name being used. Yes, she'd told them to call her it, but Jenny never had till now. 'Bloody hell, Jenny, would you piss off?'

'Cruikshanks wants to see you now. Quick.'

Anna came out slowly. Washed her hands, patted her hair. 'Did he say why?'

'No, just that it was urgent. He's in your room.'

One wide-o had his feet up on her desk. Cruikshanks smiled at him. 'Ah, Anna, this is Stevie from SB.'

'And I'm Phil,' said the other, shaking her hand. 'Good to meet you. Your bud here's a chap we've been keeping an eye on for a while. Thought he was still in London. Glasgow's new turf for him – well, for his extra-curricular activities anyway.'

'Not with you. Do you mind?' She edged past his colleague, who reluctantly swung his feet round.

'He's a regular at Ibrox for the football, and he likes nothing better than to partake of a nice Orange Walk. But we've never had him flex his muscles up here before. Suggests to us that the Handy Andies are extending their kingdom.'

'The who?'

His neighbour leaned forward. 'The Red Hand Commando – proscribed under the Terrorism Act. They use Galletly as muscle. I know, you'd hardly think it to look at him. But he's an evil wee bastard, takes no prisoners, and has no qualms. Modern terrorism uses all means at its disposal to defend the cause: moneylending, prostitution, robbery. We reckon there's been a half-hearted attempt to get a foothold up here in Scotland, maybe hooking up with football casuals, local thugs with loyalist leanings, that kind of thing. But whoever was put in charge here's botched it up and Galletly's been sent to collect what's due.' Sat back, smug as a bug in a rug.

Cruikshanks asked before Anna could. 'And is Galletly capable of murder, d'you think?'

'That's what we're here to find out,' Phil answered. 'Firstly, I'd like to run cross-checks on all his known associates. Particularly any he has in Scotland. Then we'll move out to all your local neds with sectarian or racist-type convictions, or links with loyalist organisations and that. Then I'd like to—'

'Excuse me,' Anna interrupted. 'Can I see his pre-cons again?'

'Sure.' He passed her the print-out.

'Ta.' She ran her finger down the list. 'Tait. Thought so. Tait was the name of the Lodge Master we jailed for a breach at New Year. This could be a relative. And we've already spoken to someone else involved in the incident, remember, boss?' She turned to Cruikshanks. 'Andrew Semple. The one I thought was the Fat Man?'

Phil winked at her. 'You're my kind of girl. What you doing later this evening?'

She winked back. 'Plucking my nasal hairs.'

'Now there's a picture I'll take back home with me.'

Cruikshanks frowned. 'You want me to bring Semple in again?'

'Yes, I think we'll talk to Tait and Semple, and anyone else that was there. I want to find out how much they know about Galletly before we interview him.'

That would mean Shelly. Someone else she'd been avoiding. Anna followed the men out of the room. 'Phil, can I ask you a favour?'

He hung back. 'You want me to hold your tweezers?'

'Ha, ha. Look, Semple has a brother – Michael. Goes by the name Michelle.'

'I see.'

'Yeah, well, exactly. He's not a bad lad. Stepped in to rescue us when things went pear-shaped at an Orange Walk. He's a wee bit sensitive – I think his brother intimidates him. I'm not trying to influence you in any way' – she shifted her weight on her hip – 'but could you go easy on him?'

'For you? Anything.'

'Och, I knew you were a star.'

They'd been at the zoo, Jamie and Eilidh. He hated them. All those vacant faces, yearning through the perspex. They made him sick. Cath knew that, but it was a party, some woman called Philippa's kid, and she said they had to go. Eilidh wanted to see the ingie-phants, and Cath was too sick to take her. Sod all wrong with her if you asked him. If anything, she was getting fatter again, yet she kept refusing food. Just lay in bed and gawped at the ceiling. Each day he hammered on a smile, willing her back to life.

Aye, there's the rub. Trained to tell convincing porkies, he'd almost fooled himself. One minute you're praying, next you realise you no longer care. Especially with half-forgotten stepping stones glinting through the swamp. Anna had asked him to drop round that evening. Said they needed to sort things out. He'd calculated a trip to the zoo with mammies and nannies would put him in credit for a 'night with the boys'. Jesus. Just as well he no longer went to confession. No mirrors for the soul required, thank you. And if he asked his mates? *Your hole's your hole. Get in there.* No. So. The only thing to do was not think.

'Hi, babes. Had a good afternoon?' Jamie saw his wife's face, and the words dried like sick at the corners of his mouth. Eilidh struggled to get down. 'Look. There's Mummy.'

'Mamamama. Big jaffs. Seen big jaffs.'

'Did you?' She bent to kiss her daughter. 'Where's your giraffe? Where's Gerry?'

Eilidh chortled. 'Aa-ee get Jelly.' Her toys were in the other room.

Jamie moved towards Cath. 'What's up?'

She sat like an old woman, tucked in her favourite chair. 'Jamie. I've been doing some thinking.'

'Sounds ominous.'

'We're not getting on very well at the moment, are we?'

'Meaning?'

'You know what I mean.' Cath tried to remember all those things they said in magazines. *I feel*, not 'you did'. 'It's . . . it's as if you'd rather not be here, you know? That's how I feel. And you won't talk to me about it. So, maybe you'd talk to someone else.'

He hung his jacket on the back of a chair. 'Uh-huh?'

'Jamie, I'd like us to go for counselling.'

'What? Ah, very funny.'

'I'm serious. I need to know what's wrong.'

'Nothing's wrong.'

'Jamie, I feel you drifting away from me.' That was the best way she could describe it. Everything felt fluid in her life now; it all kept slipping through the fist she'd made. Each morning, cupping water in her hands. By the time it reached her mouth, only dribbles. Some days, nothing. Whirling clockwise down and down, and her desperate to halt this sucking rush.

'What psycho-babble bollocks did you get that from? *Marie Claire* or *Trisha*?'

'So, you're not unhappy?'

'I'm fine.'

'Well, I'm not.' Cath stood to face him. 'I can't take any more of these silences, of you brushing me off and—'

'Fuck, that's rich. It's okay when it's me, though? I've had a year of dancing attendance round you, putting up with your moans and your moods. Soon as you get a taste of your own medicine you start whining like the bloody wean.'

'So that's what this is? Revenge?'

'That's what *what* is?' His lip arced. 'Christ, maybe you should go for counselling, right enough. Treat your paranoid delusions the same time they do you for bloody manic depression.'

A prim pursed cheap-shot, stunning her to tears.

'You bastard.' Her hand flying across his face.

Jamie rubbed his cheek. 'Least I can still trigger some emotion in that frigging corpse of a body. Would it suit you if I hit you back?'

Cath walked away. Counted to a million. 'I'm going to go to my sister's for a few days, okay?'

Brittle, brittle air. She waited for it to settle, to crackle and split, then his arms would feed her body back its strength. And he'd tell her not to be so stupid and they'd tell each other everything and it would be okay.

'Fine. You do that.'

Eilidh tottered through the door. 'Jelly!' She hugged her mother's knees. Cath lifted her. 'I'm taking Eilidh with me.'

'Nah, I'll save you both the bother. I'll go. I was going out anyway.' He picked up his jacket.

'I mean it, Jamie. I'll not be here when you get back.' She ran after him, watched as he got in the car.

He wound down the window. 'Neither will I.'

20 Tongues

They'd got a warrant to turn the Semples' place. Phil had asked Anna along. She was meant to be meeting Jamie, but he'd understand. Her persistence had pushed this inquiry forward, and there was no way she was missing out on the kill. If that's what this was. The Special Branch car was slick and unobtrusive, Breggsy's saloon trundling behind them.

'How come you're not bringing Andrew Semple too?'

Phil was sitting beside her in the back seat, Cruikshanks riding shotgun with Stevie. If a ned was in custody, it was standard practice he witness any search of his premises. 'Scared he'll do a runner?'

'He's too feart to crawl out from under his stone,' replied Phil. 'We *did* ask, but it's bad for business if he's seen in public with us – that way lies a knee-capping.'

'Seriously? You think his house is being watched, then?'

Phil shrugged.

'So, did you get Drew Semple to burst to knowing Galletly?'

'Sergeant Cameron. Why do you think they call us *special*? Not only that, but I got him to burst to putting the guy up in his spare room. Told him forensics would prove it anyway.'

'You're joking!' It took a moment. 'But – doesn't Shelly live with his brother?'

'Mmm. Yes. I'm afraid so. Think your golden boy may have feet of clay.'

Anna leaned her head against the car door. Shelly knew

Galletly. Shelly knew his brother knew a loyalist fixer that slashed instead of spoke. 'And what's he saying to it?'

'Michelle?' Phil stretched his arms above his head. 'Oh. We've got him all excited about what might happen to him in the jail. Still, I think he's more crapping it from his brother's pal than he is from us.'

'How?'

'Near shat himself when we mentioned Galletly. Gibbered like a baboon. But he's sticking to the hymn sheet. They're smooth, these guys. Always have a secondary story rehearsed just in case. He and his brother were out on the razz the night your Mr Wajerski was killed. Showing Galletly the sights. Michelle swears blind Galletly's just a pal of his brother's, up here for a visit. That's what the brother's saying, and no doubt Galletly too, when we speak to him. A three-way alibi. But that's before we trash this place. Out you get.'

The flat was damp and poky. A huge aquarium on a built-in shelf took the place of a hearth. Shelly's room was lush with quilted satin, tented above the bed. Pale curtains spawned black mould where they skirted the windowsill, and a poster of Brad Pitt gazed manfully down from the wardrobe. The other two rooms were basic – grey carpet, floral curtains. One had a camp-bed and a pile of Tennent's cans, the other six boxed TVs, two single beds, a broken fridge and a melamine cupboard. Phil split the cops into teams. They worked methodically through the piles of junk. For a wee flat, it was full of crap. They were looking for two lots of evidence. One, the most likely, was proof of money-lending: tally books or ledgers, other people's bank books, dole, Giros, family credit stuff. But, in among that, Anna hoped for a bloodstained Polish medal. She was so sure now. She could feel Mr Wajerski cowering as Galletly pushed him to the ground. He was screaming at the old man for money, then when shouting didn't work, breaking his head instead of his spirit. Raising Wajerski up again by his trembling, puckered neck, then pound-ing the back of his skull with a single, violent blow, striking sharp on the chest of drawers. That was where the impact had been; on the pointed corner. That's why there were splinters in his scalp.

They searched everywhere, upending couches, emptying cupboards. Found no blood, no money. In the second bedroom, a small rucksack contained nothing more than a crumple of clothes.

'Travels light.' Stevie nodded, coming in with Cruikshanks. 'Typical bog-boy. We're all done, Phil. Bugger all through-by.'

'Reckon these are knocked off then?' DI Cruikshanks opened one of the boxes.

'Hmm – what do you think, Stevie?' said Phil.

'Nah. Reckon he runs a crêche for orphan tellies.'

Cruikshanks ignored them, began tugging at the TV inside.

'Here, sir, let me, my hands are smaller.' Anna reached in, slipped her hands down either side of the tight-packed plastic, the TV sliding squealing from its box. Cruikshanks took the weight from her, freeing Anna to lift the polystyrene casing left behind. The space beneath was crammed with small bundles: rent books, bank books, family allowance passbooks.

'Yuss,' said Phil, slapping hands with Stevie. 'Whole box of witnesses here.' He unravelled a skein of production bags from his pocket.

Anna carefully held the edge of a British passport, flicked it open. The pages stuck to her plastic gloves. It was a woman's passport. Name of Jarmal. She held it up to Phil, who tossed it in a bag. 'Most valuable thing she had to lodge with them, I guess.'

The other boxes held similar treasures. One contained a single ledger, like a bookkeeper's. Inside was a series of letters and numbers. There was a page each for A to W. Some had many numbered entries, others were empty.

'Wonder what happened to X,Y and Z?' said Cruikshanks.

'Maybe they'd not got round to them yet.' Phil supervised the bagging and labelling of each individual piece of evidence. Breggsy was sent to get more production bags. Each bag sealed with a metal clip, tags like brown luggage labels signed and counter-signed. Phil made sure everyone would get a speaky, even Breggsy who'd only been guarding the door. 'Okay, pal, you're speaking to finding this, these books and they passports. All right?'

A speaky meant court, and court meant overtime. Breggsy eagerly scribbled his name on the label. When everything was loaded in the boots of the two cars, Phil made one last sweep of the flat. 'What about middens?' Anna heard him ask.

'Done,' came Stevie's reply.

'Fuck. Fuckety-fuck-fuck.' Then Phil called out, 'Right, troops. Let's call it a day.'

'What else were you hoping to find?' Anna asked as he got in the car.

Phil's eyes were always on the move. 'We can't even prove Galletly touched that stuff, far less there's a connection with the Handy Andys.'

'Oh.' She thought a minute. 'What about forensic?'

Phil put on a girly voice. 'Och aye, gaffer, can you sanction Scenes of Crime to dust a flat to prove a guy was staying with a pal who said the guy was staying with him?' His laugh was curt. 'You can guarantee he's no had a finger near they rent books.'

'What now, then?'

'We wait,' said Phil. 'We watch and we wait and we see what happens now.'

Anna didn't like the way he said it.

Jamie was waiting back in Anna's office at Stewart Street. 'Where the hell were you?' His cheeks mottled.

'Whoa, cowboy. I'm sorry. Duty called.'

Anna could afford to be glib. She'd just turned a house with Special Branch. In the Support Unit, she'd got to hang around at major events, sure, but never taken centre stage. The Support Unit slid through the background like so many shape-shifters, moving smooth as oil. It had been suggested when she qualified as a firearms officer that she might like to 'develop her experience'. Anna knew what this meant. An attractive female who could hold the Queen's posy and handle a Hechler and Koch was always special. But she didn't fancy life as a royal bodyguard and it was a bit like the Masons. Join, and *then* we'll tell you what we do. Now, she wondered what she'd been missing. Phil and Stevie were wide as the Clyde, but they were skilled, professional and single-minded. Neither of them had given their rank, they were both roughly ages with her, yet they'd clicked their fingers and the whole of A Division had jumped.

'So, where were you?' Jamie's voice tugged at her.

'Jamie, something came up.' She lowered her head. 'Special Branch – had no choice. Look, they've finished with me for now. Let's get out of here.'

Humphing boxes was one thing; sitting in on interviews was another. Phil had made it plain he and Stevie would be doing all the talking. Even Cruikshanks was having to sit this one out. As they were leaving, her phone rang.

'Don't answer it.'

'Just give me two ticks.' Anna picked up the phone. 'Hello? Ally, how you doing? You're joking. Och, that's brilliant.' She grabbed a pen, scribbled on a pad. 'Definitely her, yeah? You're pure dead magic, so you are.' She laughed. 'I know, it's like Tunnock's tea cakes and square sausage: you don't miss them till they're gone.'

She saw Jamie's fingers tighten as she laughed again. 'I don't know – set up a Hamesick Scots Society. Organise a haggis hunt.' There was a pause. 'Now you're just boasting, you big perv. I know. You take care too. Cheers.'

'Love the pseudo-Glasgow,' said Jamie.

'Meaning?'

'Nothing. Can we go now?' He opened the door wide.

'That was my mate in the Met – you might remember him . . .' Anna started. 'No, it was on a sergeants' course down south. Anyway, mind that girl Nooch, well, the one we thought was

Nooch? Ally told me she'd croaked it down in London a month or so ago. So, I was wondering how Sandra Tamburrini was calling herself Iannucci. I sent Ally a mug shot of Sandra, and he checked with various vice folk. That's him just got back to me. Says she didn't work much down south, but they did recognise her. The couple of times she did get arrested, she passed herself off as Nooch there too – they both had red hair, you see. Worked the same patch, same Scottish accent. She even knew where Nooch's granny lived. Now, I seem to remember Jenny saying something about Sandra having to leave her kid behind and run away. Is Jenny on tonight?'

Anna didn't wait for his reply. She picked up the phone again, dialled the Controller. 'Yeah – hi, Lynsey. Could you give Jenny Heath a shout, ask her to come in . . . oh, is she? Great. Put her on, would you?' Anna covered the mouthpiece with her hand and carried on talking to Jamie. 'Maybe Tamburrini wasn't even safe using her own name in London. When she heard Nooch was dead, she thought it would be safe to come home and pretend she was Nooch here too . . . hi, Jenny – look, I know you're knocking off, but have you got a minute to come through? It's about Sandra Tamburrini. Yeah? Sure? I won't keep you a minute, promise.'

Jamie raised his eyebrows. 'You two best pals now?'

Anna was still thinking out loud. 'She was keeping a low profile anyway – no one down the Drag seemed to know her, and she'd never been lifted by any of us, had she? Apart from that one time.'

'Who?'

'Sandra Tamburrini,' she tutted. 'She'd obviously run out of money and gone to the Drag for a quick fix. Only, second time she did it, her past caught up with her. Unless . . .' She stood up. 'Unless Galletly wasn't after her at all. Maybe he thought she was Nooch too. Give me that file there, would you?'

Jamie chucked it across the desk.

'Ta. I just want to see what the mum said again.'

Anna had been so caught up binding Galletly tight to Andrew Semple and to his moneylending and therefore to Ezra Wajerski's murder that she'd thought little of the girl in hospital. Tamburrini was still in a coma, unlikely to recover.

'Sarge.' Jenny tapped on the open door, frowned when she saw Jamie.

Anna smiled like it was all official. 'Jenny, tell me again what you know of Sandra Tamburrini. Why did she run away to the Big Smoke?'

'The usual – fleeing a violent partner.'

'She wasn't in any debt?'

'None that I was aware of. That bastard took every penny she ever earned anyway. And her kiddie. Total gangster he was – is. One James Spence, currently residing in the Bar-L.'

'So, why did she come back?'

'According to her mum, well, it's all in that statement I did for CID.' Jenny nodded at the file Anna held. Was there a hint of reproach in her tone? Anna had been guilty of ignoring her squad's workload. Ach well, she could add it to the big bag of guilt she was already lugging around.

'Okay, okay.' Anna scanned the page. 'Here's the one from Sandra's mother: My daughter . . . blah-di-blah . . . never seen the wean in years. Staying with his Granny Spence . . . Jenny, that's it! Sandra came up for the chance to see her wean again. She took Nooch's name when she heard James Spence was in jail, figuring it would still be safer to return as someone else. So, she comes up here, calls herself Nooch so Spence doesn't hear on the grapevine she's come back, and yes . . .' Anna glanced back at the statement, 'the mum's saying the two grannies came to an arrangement. So' – she looked triumphantly at Jamie – 'Sandra was nothing to do with Galletly. It was a prostitute called Nooch he wanted, not Sandra, and poor Sandra was just in the wrong place with the wrong name. Jenny, what are CID saying to this?'

'To be honest, Sarge, the reason why Sandra's in hospital isn't sky-high on their priorities, I don't think. She's just one in a series of worked-over hoors that they're hoping to wrap up asap. Look – I really need to go . . .'

'Sure, on you go.'

Jamie waited for the sarky quip.

'Thanks for your help,' said Anna.

'Eh, right. Cheerio, Jamie.'

Anna didn't look up, kept reading through her notes. 'They're wasting their time investigating why he chibbed Sandra—'

Jamie sighed. 'Anna, I'm sorry, my head's mince the now.'

'No, look, it's simple. Galletly must be unaware Nooch was dead. He's sent up here to call in various debts, act the hard man on defaulters. This is a big business, you know, and the Glasgow arm's not been performing well. They're not raking in enough for the cause.'

'How d'you know all this?'

'Special Branch – top secret, okay? You never heard it from me. So, some of the non-payers are prostitutes, and he's working his way through the list, when he hears the name Nooch. Or maybe he's heard that she's working up here now, I don't know. Anyway, bingo, he thinks, that's a bonus, and poor Sandra gets chibbed. If CID asked him why he attacked Nooch – not Sandra Tamburrini. I don't think it had anything to do with her. I bet if they spoke to the granny—'

'Whose bloody granny?'

'Nooch's granny – that old bird who came up to Stewart Street for her that night.'

'But that wasn't Nooch.'

'I know, but she didn't know that . . .'

Jamie slammed his fist against the door, two, three times. Hard. 'Anna. Cath's left me. She's gone to her sister's.'

'Oh. Does she know . . .?'

'Christ, I don't know. It all came out of nowhere. Anna, I really need to talk to someone.'

The moment hung, ripe as an apple. It would be so easy to reach out, pull him towards her and bite. Feel it dripping down her chin – just a little juice, enough to make her skin glisten. Luscious liquid velvet dripping. Do it again. *Feed me.*

Jamie sat back in his chair, rubbing his eyes. The shirt tugged away from his belt, the lowest button undone. A dark line of hairs beckoning down to his groin, where her tongue could ease down, she could taste him . . . Feel him in her belly, feel the life he gave her burning back again, calling to her, begging her to stay. He could have chosen to share her life and she could have chosen to keep it, keep their baby safe and warm inside the womb it was planted. All those years ago, she could have chosen to feel what Cath must be feeling now – alone and scared and brave and resolute. They say your blood pumps twice as fast round your body when it's working two hearts; better than any empty excitement Anna had clutched and clawed at since. She'd never let herself feel that rush, only panic, terror and then ice. Ice embalming cells that were nothing and could be vacuumed away like so much dirt. Did cells have hearts? By Christ, they had ghosts, though; caged inside her, fluttering always like a pigeon behind a hearth. If she'd told him then, at Tulliallan – would he have stayed? If she'd said she was pregnant, would he still have chosen Cath over her? If she said she loved him now, would it rub away all their pasts?

Do unto others . . . Anna's benchmarks were raw and tangible and admirable, not supernatural nonsense.

Do unto others . . .

'So call the Samaritans.'

Jamie jerked upright. 'What?'

'Look pal, I'm sorry, but I'm up to my eyes here. Phone a friend, right?'

'What the fuck are you saying?' He loomed, a triangular mass, above her.

'Duh – I think I'm saying, "Thank you – and Goodnight." A bit of fun's one thing, but I'm not getting embroiled in a domestic.'

'Well, fuck you.' Venom splatters on her face.

She licked a fragment of his saliva from the edge of her mouth. 'So you have. And for your next trick?'

He smashed the Anglepoise lamp from her desk, turned and left.

Cath didn't know what to do with herself. Her sister had gone out, and the solitude was clinging. Just her and Eilidh and the bump in her gut. She tried the word on for size. *Singlemum.*

Not Catherine Forbes, because she'd died. Not Mrs Cath Worth, because *he* wished she'd died. Singlemum with empty time, when horrid thoughts came creeping. She'd always thought she'd just walk away. If Jamie ever cheated she would sever all contact, and possibly his balls. Then go after the woman and slit her throat. Not so easy when it was real and you wanted to know, had to know and kept imagining this whispering painful wish-hope: that you were wrong, but if you weren't you didn't need to know.

Was Jamie worth fighting for? If he had really done it, that is. Why was Cath so ready to believe, to see her husband entwined and open in another woman's embrace? See Anna's hands on flesh that belonged to Cath, kissing limbs, spreading legs. The nausea swelled again, and Cath took a bottle from the kitchen. Fancy stuff, not your usual Asda plonk. She poured and she drank. First she tasted new life, tart and bursting on her tongue like sherbet lemon, then she savoured the spice that came after, heavier and filling. If anyone had been watching, they might have thought it a little sordid, seeing this woman slugging like it was breath, tears and wine splashing on her face. They might have grown concerned as they saw her take another bottle and kiss the sleeping baby. They might even have phoned for help when they saw her run a bath and plunge right in, seaweed hair floating atop her immersed skull, toe tapping out a rhythm on the tap. Tappy tappy tap. Tappy tappy tap. Tappy. Tappy. For ages. Then still. Underneath the water, Cath was humming, very loud. Words skittered round her head, snatches of a pop song. *What I am is what I need, is what I want – WHOA-WHOA! What I need is –* Is it what you need?

Over and over, till she began to feel dizzy. Then another refrain joined in the confusion. *Whoa-whoa. What I am is . . . Who am I? Who am I? Who am I? Whoa-whoa.* It was getting hard to concentrate. Who was she? Submerged, her lungs were bursting, and another song was intruding, getting in her road. *In out in out in out. Breathing, my beloved . . . Breathing . . .* She supposed she'd better. But it was so warm in the water, and she was nearly there. In a soapy bubble. *Who am . . . out.* She stopped tapping. Little floaty bull's-eyes and orange ripples, like an aboriginal sky inside her eyelids. *Please, God, help me. Make this stop.* Feeling faint and on the brink. A darker sky. Then she lost it completely as a bouncing baby sun took shape behind her eyeballs, laughing over all with a big Eilidh-face. Instantly, her eyes opened, stinging with bubbles.

Dark in the green abyss. Through water, Cath could make out the bathroom window. High and wide, no need for a curtain. Outside, the opal light of dusk, milky cloudlets wisping into navy. Bright poke of a star right up in the corner.

Whoosh!

A trajectory of gold shot past the window. The star had burst. Then another, and another. A confection of burning jewels, silver and purple, green and pink, zinging and pinging in graceful arcs. Noiseless fireworks, dancing at her window. Cath sat up, gasping. Breath kicked at her chest and she could hear the sea in her ears, awash and echoing. She shook her head vigorously, climbed up on the ledge at the end of the bath and stretched to tug the window catch. Even on tiptoe, her nose barely reached over the sill. Gulping in the evening air, Cath searched for a rocket or a Catherine wheel, but they'd finished as suddenly as they'd begun. She breathed deep, and all the black softness came rushing in to meet her. All the wide world, from her bathroom window to the city lights beyond. No more fireworks. But there was a smell. Cordite or burning, not coming from outside. From below.

Her ear began hurting in the cold. Cath drew her head inside. Dizzy. It was slippy on the ledge. The smell was getting stronger and her ears were still roaring. There were clouds of steam coming up through the floor. Thick grey, like smoke and the heat was getting stronger. She started to cough – had to reach for the window again. Had to reach for the baby, still inside the other room.

'Eilidh!' she screamed and turned, and slipped. Her head struck the floor and her body followed, sprawled beside the rising smoke.

They were still interviewing Andrew Semple. Shelly had been released, and Anna had refused to see him. She'd left a note for Special Branch, one for Cruikshanks, who was long gone, in a huff, and another for the DC dealing with Sandra/Nooch's attempted murder, which was still being treated as a separate investigation but linked with the prostitute slashings. So, in that case . . . She left a note for Liz Maguire too, just for good measure.

Anna stuck her head round the bar on her way out. The backshift Controller was on his piece break, and young Billy Wong had been stuck in as relief.

She raised her hand. 'Night, Billy.' Once she'd got home, she would let her mouth uncrumple. Let it spill the noise that was grating on her innards.

Billy seemed agitated. 'Any station to attend. Please. Fire service en route from an incident in the south.'

'What's up?' she asked.

'We've a fire in Cranstonhill, Sergeant, but the fire brigade are at some big inferno in Govan and the Tunnel's closed. Their ETA's ten minutes.' The boy looked scared.

'Where's your sergeant, Billy?'

'Em . . . he's taken a flyer, ma'am, eh, Sergeant.'

'Is the building occupied?'

'I – I don't know, I didn't ask. Probably. It's in Woodlands Road, so there'll be flats above.'

'Right, Billy, keep shouting for someone to attend. And phone the refreshment room at Cranstonhill. Where's the OD?'

'In the loo, I think.'

'Okay. You're doing fine.' She took the squad's car keys from the hook. 'Tell the OD I've gone down. What number is it?'

'It's a shop, Sergeant,' he shouted after her. 'Near the top of Woodlands Road. A fish shop, I think.'

It was only as Anna was cursing the tossers who'd left the car with no petrol that his words impacted. She dropped the nozzle with the tank half full and ran to the gates, wrenching them open. The quickest way was up and on to the motorway, coming off at Charing Cross. With the Clyde Tunnel closed, there was more traffic than usual. No klaxons, no blue light, only her horn to blast her way through. Shit, she should've taken a marked car. Vehicles were hardly shifting, and she dipped on to the hard shoulder to rumble her way past. The queues started at the approach to the off-ramp. Traffic was building, and nothing was moving. No hard shoulder left, but she was nearly at Charing Cross. She could see an ember-glow in the sky, to the right, behind St George's Road. Exactly where Shelly's shop would be. With the flats above where Jamie said his sister-in-law lives, and that's where Cath had gone. With the baby.

'Fuck it.' Anna jumped out the car and ran the length of the slip road, ignoring horns and screeches. There was a footbridge across the twisted layers of Charing Cross, but the stairs coiled away from where she was running, so she kept going, across the snarled traffic. She could see the reason for the gridlock: a lorry and a taxi, used to sparser evening traffic, had collided, but she couldn't stop. She wedged between bumpers, climbed on to someone's bonnet.

A small crowd was gathered outside the blazing shop. The fire had taken hold completely, licking upwards two or three storeys high. Her heart soared as she saw the Cranstonhill van roll up across the road.

'Sergeant Cameron, Stewart Street,' she gasped at the lone

cop. 'I want you to get these people back. Take them across the road to the park.'

He hurried away, waving arms at human traffic. She grabbed at a woman in her dressing gown. 'Excuse me, is there anyone still in there?'

'I don't know, I don't know,' the woman sobbed. 'We just heard glass breaking, then screaming.'

'Okay, on you go with the policeman.'

Anna scanned the crowds for any sign of Cath. 'Alpha 51 to Alpha. Billy, what's the Fire Service ETA now?'

'Three minutes.'

In three minutes the wooden struts inside would crisp to charcoal. Other closes' occupants were spilling into the street for a better view. She ran to a Sikh man, ushering his children from the ground-floor flat. 'Sir, sir. Police. I need your help. Get me a couple of blankets, soak them in water first.'

He hesitated.

'Sir, I think there's a baby in there.'

The man told his children to cross over the road, darted back inside. Anna looked at the mouth of the shop. Howling red through shattered glass, clawing further and further up the height of the building. Upwards, not sideways. The wind seemed to be blowing straight, and the door to the close – just a few metres to the side – was not yet fully ablaze.

'Here, miss, here.' The man thrust a sodden blanket at her, kept one for himself.

'No, I need them both.'

'I will come with you.' He pushed her forwards. 'The baby's mother?'

Anna shouted above the clamour of the flames. 'In there too, I think.'

'Then you will need me.' His brown skin amber in the glare. She noticed his turban was saturated like the blankets.

Anna nodded. Pointed to the close, so the cop across the street knew where she was going.

'Hold the back of my trousers,' she told the man. Slowly, they edged their way inside the building. Grey, acrid smoke slashed at her throat, cauterising the insides of her lungs. 'Keep low,' she shouted. 'More oxygen.' The blanket weighted on her back, the heat coming in solid thick waves. Her breath curdling outside, within her – air too choked to inhale. Dense like molten polythene.

Cath's sister lived above the shop. One floor, two? Anna tugged her companion's hand towards the stair. Each step invisible unless brushed by fingers or nose. She made them both kneel down, crawl up with heavy blankets to the next landing. There was a darker hole in the darkness. Anna lay on her back, kicked the first door. 'Fire!'

Her companion hammered on the second. 'Get out.' He yelled at Anna, 'Is it this one?'

'I don't know,' she screeched, coughing as non-air drove deep into her lungs. 'Kick it!'

The man kicked and kicked until the lock gave way.

'Now this one!'

He crouched and stumbled towards her, using his feet against the wood until it too cracked and separated from its frame.

'I'll go in here,' she mouthed. 'You take that one.' She motioned for him to keep down.

He nodded.

The heat was searing through the floor now, burning her palms as she felt her way across the hall. A crash from somewhere below made her halt, checking the floor was still intact in front of her. Her hands fanned out, touching a right angle, where skirting board became opening. Charcoal candyfloss air, scalding her cheeks. Stink of burned flesh inside her nostrils. Inches inside the room, she felt thin metal, then soft mesh like webbing, bulging inwards to let her hands rest on something small and warm. Her hands crept up the webbing, pulling her up to the top. A smooth rim, then over and she fumbled inside the travel cot. Found blanket, face, Eilidh, with desperate fingers and hauled her out. The cot toppled, striking Anna's temple as she crawled out on one arm, the toddler cradled in the other. The man on the landing, choking.

'Take her down. Get your arse down those stairs and get out,' Anna shouted. She placed the lolling child in his lap and a spark of fire flared up the stairwell. It seemed to jerk his consciousness. Anna saw him place Eilidh across his chest, wrapping her in the blanket. Shuffling on all fours to the stairs, then lost in the enveloping smoke.

Soft pockets on her palms, rasping pain. Only aware her skin was blistered when she stopped moving. Another spew of vicious flame and the smell of burning hair was everywhere. She patted at her head, feeling raw heat. Back into the flat, but it was getting harder now to move. The floor was smoother here, rubbery almost. Bathroom or kitchen. A shrieking tear of timber thrust her forward and pure fire spurted like screams. Anna slammed the door of the room behind her, trying to keep the flames out. Felt cracking porcelain, then some hair. 'Cath. Cath,' she croaked. 'Can you hear me?' She dragged the head into her lap, sobbing with relief. 'Stay with me, Cath. Stay with me.'

The noise outside was unbearable, but Anna felt strangely calm. She couldn't fight fire. She had gone as far as she could go. The window was a small irregularity, high up the wall. Even if she could drag Cath up to reach it, they wouldn't both fit through. The dampness of her mouth had evaporated, roasted meat instead of tongue, licking at leather lips.

Sitting, rocking, listening to crackles and snaps. Cath's head somewhere on her knee and all around groans and crashes. Brittle smashes cascading down her spine and Anna at the centre. It felt fine. She waited in the dark, hot dryness, eyelids heavy, drifting into sleep. *Close your eyes and hang on tight.* Would it be quick? If Cath was right, then she'd be saved, while Anna burned to a crisp hereafter. Not if she hung on tight, though . . . tight as leeches on to Cath.

21 And Give You Peace

A disembodied voice. 'Sarge, there's some nutter screaming to see you. Says its name's Michelle.'

Then another, just a bit disembodied, bustling at the rim of her vision. Green bulk, mouth opening in a freckly face. 'Not now, pal, okay?'

Anna was concentrating on the white tin ceiling. The air smelled polish-clean, then she realised it was pumping through the transparent mask that circled her mouth and nose. The paramedic moved from her line of vision. She was conscious of a dull metallic thumping. Reminded her of that Orange Walk.

A falsetto chant now. 'Maddy. Maddy. I know who done it.'

The mask was just on elastic. No pipes up her nose she could feel. She pushed it off, coughing as a gravel pit shifted in her throat. 'Let me . . . speak to him.'

'What's that?' The paramedic's head above her.

'Let him in.'

Shelly's purple mohair was torn, tears coursing through the smuts on his face. He grabbed Anna's wrists. 'Look what they bastards have done tae my shop. My fucking fish. Jesus. Deep fried in their frigging tanks. Maddy, Maddy. You've got tae help us.'

Anna pulled her hands away, pushed up on to her side. The paramedic handed her a bottle of water. A long, clear draught that stung and soothed and gave her back her voice. 'Help you?' she croaked. 'Like you've been straight with me?' Choked on the speed of speaking, and a kidney-shaped paper bowl appeared under her mouth. She watched saliva drip down to stain its grey-ness, feeling cold ropes on her chin. 'Aye, right.'

'Straight. You want straight? See what they've bloody done tae me? They think I grassed them up when I bloody didny. Well, fuck them all. I've had it.' Shelly tugged her arm. 'C'mon.'

'Shelly, I need to get to the hospital. There's a wee baby near died—' Anna stopped, glanced at the stretcher opposite. Apart from her, the ambulance was empty. 'She's not . . .?'

'She's hanging on, pet,' the paramedic said. 'The mammy's still with us, too.'

Oh, Jesus, yes. The mammy. Anna took another swig.

'None of this is my fault.' Shelly wiped his eyes with his sleeve. 'Want tae know how yous found fuck-all at my place? Cos your search was shite, that's why.'

'How?' she coughed.

'Take me home and I'll show you.'

'Shelly, is this about the moneylending? We did find stuff – loads of it.'

'Are you a total fuckwit?' She'd never heard his voice so harsh before.

'Right, bugger that, pal. You're getting the jail.' The cop she'd heard talking moved back into shot, reaching in to grab Shelly's arm.

Anna stopped him. 'No, wait. You on foot or in a panda?'

'Panda.'

'Will you give us a lift to Maryhill? Please?' As Anna moved upright, her stomach heaved. She retched into the bowl still in her hand.

'Sarge, you need to go to hospital.'

'I will, I will.'

She was scared Shelly would change his mind. At least, that's what she would say, after, when they were berating her for ignoring procedures and jeopardising an investigation and risk-ing her health and any other crap they would doubtless throw at her. And if she didn't stop to think then she would never know if it was to avoid Cath or to purge her soul a little deeper because she could have, should have, stopped it sooner; and the *it* – well, it could have been Jamie, or it could have been Ezra, because his death was always on her hands if she'd just stayed a little while or asked about the money, because she didn't believe him even then, or if she'd asked the beatman to check in on him, or if he'd lived in a decent house in safe streets and didn't need to barter his life away, or if she'd found his killer quicker and if she'd made her daddy stay at home *or* if she'd not had her womb sloughed raw that was not happening *that thought* was never, never there *or* it could have been the thrill of the hunt closing in for the kill and shooting high on the self-gratifying rush of knowing you were right and that right, *your* right has prevailed.

Near death – *what* a tonic.

The journey was made in silence, Shelly staring straight ahead. Anna needed noise. '*Is* this about Mr Wajerski, Shelly? Speak to me.'

'Naw,' he sniffed. 'Just leave it.'

Shelly's house was dark and empty. The cop followed them inside.

'Just you.'

'Shelly, if you're going to show me something, I need corroboration.' Thin air was sweeping across the shallow pans of her lungs, making her head spin. Everything was so light. Shelly flicked on the hall lamp, carried on walking. He led them straight to the bathroom. Kicked the pale avocado panel along the bath. 'Did yous look in there?'

She knew, she knew, she knew she was right. Anna nodded at the cop, her heart quickening. He squatted, tried to prise his fingernails between the rim and the side.

'I'll get yous a knife.' Shelly's voice was flat. He went to the kitchen, came back with a vegetable knife. 'Just stick it in the corner and give it a twist.'

The panel came away easily. The cop took a torch from his

belt, shone it round the metal bowl of the bath. There was a box of soap powder wedged at the side. Anna used the knife to pull it towards her. Inside was an old dishtowel, wrapped round some jewellery. She rolled it open. Not jewellery. Medals. Three metal flowers pushing through cloth.

Then Shelly's words flowed, in a familiar torrent. 'I didny know, I swear. They just telt me they were hot, and tae hide them for a bit.' He was on his knees, rummaging behind the bath. 'Telt me tae get rid of these and all, but I didnae. Pure my size and everything.' He dragged on a pair of laces. 'Nikes. *Purple*. I mean, you don't get many of them.'

Anna put her hand on top of his. Resisted the urge to squeeze. 'Try and keep them off the ground, Shelly. That's it. Okay, I've got them.' She held the trainers by their laces. 'Have you worn these at all?'

He shook his head. 'Naw. Gilly telt me tae burn them. He'd already got me tae stick them in the machine, but. Will that matter?'

'Dunno. It's amazing what they can do at Forensics, just with tiny traces. Okay, Shelly, I'm going to have to get CID down here, and they'll be wanting a statement, right?'

Keep him talking keep him talking keep him talking. She shook her head at the puzzled cop. 'I've not got a radio. Away and shout DI Cruikshanks, will you? Tell him it's in connection with the Wajerski murder. He needs to get down here.'

The cop moved into the hall.

'You want to tell me about it first, Shelly?'

'Aye.' Shelly plunked his bum down on the edge of the bath. 'It wasny Drew, man. Cross my heart. We'd all been on the bevvy – a pure bender. We'd ran out of cash, but Drew kent where there was a lock-in. Bastards wouldny open up for us though, without flashing some cash, and Drew didny want tae lose face. Telt Gilly he knew where he could make a withdrawal. I guess it was the old boy, right enough – they never said, I swear. Drew said he'd gied someone a payout just that day. The plan was Drew would wait ootside, so the old boy didny know, like. He'd just think he was getting done over, but he'd still have tae pay Drew back, see? So Gilly went up hisself.'

'And?'

'On my mother's life, I don't know. Drew said Gilly was gone five, maybe ten minutes, then he comes back oot with the moolah and they medals. Said the old dosser—'

'He wasn't a dosser.'

'Sorr-y.' Shelly flapped his hand. 'Well, whatever. Gilly said he was all pure gurgling and that, and there was blood all over the place. *Afore* he got there, mind. Like, aye right, says I. So, the old boy pure flung his heid on the floor hissel, while shouting, "Haw Gilly, pal. Gonny just scoop up that cash and they medals? Help yourself, son, eh? I'll no be needing it." Aye, *right*.'

'And Drew saw nothing?'

'Fuck, it wasny Drew but, I swear. Drew can turn up the volume, know, but he wouldny beat someone's brains out – Yid or no.'

'You know, Shelly, I warm to you more and more each day.' Anna's fingers were itching for her notebook, desperate to record each inflection and expletive that would forge a chain.

'Well, you know what I mean.'

'So how long did Drew say Galletly was in Ezra's house?'

Shelly shrugged. 'Ten minutes, tops.'

'Long enough to trash the place, anyway.'

'I guess.'

'And the hoors? How did the lassies Gilly slashed fit in?'

'Ach, they were on the racket sure. One of the lassies used tae live round here, and she got a few of them signed up – joy tae work with, know? You always knew they'd pay it back with inter-est. Except the one what started it – Nooch. Fucked off tae the Big Smoke owing us about ten grand. There was only her granny left and she didny have that kind of dosh. Once she done it, and word got round that fuck-all had happened tae her, the other hoors thought they could ease up on the payments too. Stuff like that – it was all getting pure out of hand. That's when they sent up Gilly.'

'But why, Shelly? Why you? Your shop was doing okay.'

'Once you get started, it's kind of hard tae knock them back. Drew said – och, you know – for the cause and that. We skim aff a bit, the rest goes across the water. We'd went tae Belfast for a Walk . . .' His eyes were wild. 'Maddy, he's my big brother.'

'What about the ledger? How can we work out who's who?'

Shelly tutted. 'It's no exactly rocket science. Each page is for a street – A is for Ashley, Arlington, blah-di-blah, and the number's just the house number.'

'So A 12 – that would be Mr Wajerski's?'

'If you say so.'

Guts spilled, his face had taken on a surly pout. They waited, the three of them, in Shelly's living room, perched on a thread-bare couch. Shelly's fingers worked through a hole in the arm, twisting the knobbled tweed yarn until his flesh turned purple and bulging.

As Anna expected, Phil and Stevie arrived before Cruikshanks. She took them into the kitchen and explained. Bit her tongue near in two to halt the *So, I was right all along* ending she so wanted.

Phil shook his head. 'Brave guy. He's probably signed his own death warrant.'

'Ah, well, you know what they say,' said Stevie. 'Hell hath no fury . . .'

The familiar smell of Dettol, cabbage and human piss slicked Anna's nostrils as she pushed the swing door. The floor was tiled, a mosaic crest dead centre – serpent looping cross. A Victorian arrogance – those guys knew their buildings were here to stay. Ward Six, Respiratory, was on the second floor. She could hear steady, rasped panting. Two rows of beds, curtain width apart, each with tanks and tubes. Jamie was stooped by Cath's bed, his cheekbones darting angles off the light. Holding his wife's hand. Though her mouth was concealed by a misted mask, Anna saw Cath's eyes crinkle and soar, laughing at something he'd said.

Anna shoved the door open, into the cosy ward.

Cath wriggled the mask down to her chin. 'Anna.'

'Right.' Jamie stood up. 'I'm going to get a coffee, then I'll give Yorkhill a ring, okay? See you in a bit. Anna.' He nodded at his feet. She nodded back.

'Hi, Cath. Got you some grapes.'

'Thanks. Stick them on the table.'

Anna rustled her bag, took out the fruit. There was another parcel, wrapped in tissue. 'Em, I brought you this too.'

Cath peeled back the paper casing, smoothed her hand over rich cream lace. Velvet sleeves soft as sorrow.

'It's for Eilidh. I meant to give it to her at Christmas.'

Cath slipped her mask back on. Shudder in, sigh it out.

'You okay? Will I get a nurse?'

'Nmfine.' She shook her head. 'Sit.'

'God, I'm sorry. Is the baby . . .?'

'Baby's fine,' she wheezed. 'S'a determined wee bugger. How d'you know?'

'Jenny told me.'

'Thought she would.'

Two other patients in the ward. One had a canopy of plastic above her head. She wore it well, the giant rainmate pinning her down; looked the type to wear one. The other sat in a chair by her bed, doing a crossword, feet perched on top of an oxygen tank.

'So, this is a bit of role reversal, eh? Me visiting you, I mean.'

Cath dropped the mask again. 'Yeah, only I'm still not the hero.'

'Don't be daft.'

A nurse came in to check Cath's wiring. 'And how are we today, Mrs Worth?' Smile switched to serious as it landed on Anna. 'Not too long, eh? It's really only close family allowed at the moment.' A crisp swivel to the left. 'And it'll soon be bath time for you, my lady.'

Cath wrinkled her nose as the nurse departed. 'Used to love baths.'

'I noticed. Many folk d'you think could soak through an inferno?'

'Well, I had my music on. And I was thinking. Best place to clear your head.'

'You do that too?' asked Anna, helping herself to the grapes.

'What?'

'Meditate in the bath? I love it – like a sorbet for the mind.' Anna put the bag on the bedside table.

Cath pulled her weight stiffly upwards. They were almost eye to eye. 'Hey, did you see the fireworks? They were fantastic, weren't they?'

'What fireworks?' said Anna.

'Just before I conked out. You must have seen them. They were beautiful.'

'Nope.'

'They were definitely there.'

'Was that before or after you bashed your head?'

Anna was surprised at the easy chat. Did she *not* know, truly? 'Maybe they were your lucky stars,' Anna said, mouth full. 'Anyway, did Jamie tell you we got the guy? You know, the one for Ezra's murder. Same mob that torched your place, we think – and slashed all those girls.'

'No. Jamie tells me nothing.'

A silvery silence.

'C'mon then, give me the gen,' said Cath. 'I'm all ears. Pin-drop clean from wax and water.'

What an odd thing to say. Anna checked for signs of a smile, but there was nothing. She carried on. 'They found Galletly's shoes, which matched the footprint at the locus, *and* had traces of Ezra's blood. He also had some of the medals, and details of all the folk they'd been loan sharking to. It's all in code, so it'll take them a while to get round them all. But we can even cite that Mrs Jarmal as a reluctant witness, since she was one of their customers. Though I guess with our Irish nutter locked up, she might be brave enough to come forward of her own volition.'

'But why did they kill Ezra?' asked Cath.

'As a warning? They knew he was alone, had no family. Perfect example to set the rest of the defaulters. Shelly's brother was too soft, you see. Galletly had been sent up by the big boys to sort Andrew out, show no mercy in teaching him how it's done.'

Cath sucked some more from her mask. Her eyes were watery. 'Poor Ezra. He didn't deserve that.'

Anna traced grapeskin with her tongue. 'No, he didn't. He was a nice old man. But hey – we did it, we jailed the bastards.'

'*You* did it.'

'No way – we were a team, Cath; you made me keep going.'

'No, Anna, let's be honest. You're a one-man band – always have been.'

Anna sensed a growing nastiness that she didn't want to unleash. Keep it casual; everything light and uninvolved. 'But, enough of that. How's Eilidh?'

'Fine. They're keeping her at the Sick Kids at Yorkhill for a few days, just for observation. Jamie's mum's with her just now, then my mum'll take over at night-time. Means Jamie can get over to see me, then get a sleep tonight. They've all been really good.'

'And what about you and Jamie? I, eh . . . I heard you'd moved out.'

This was it. Hit me. Hit me. Hit meeee.

'Ha. Well, we're talking, as you can see.' Cath leaned back on her pillows. 'Kind of. To be honest, I don't know what I want to say to him yet. To anyone really.'

Anna ate some more grapes. She didn't understand what she was doing here, picking and probing until it bled. Perhaps she wanted it, wanted the pus to erupt.

'Anna . . .' said Cath.

Anna bowed her head and waited.

'D'you ever feel like your head's going to explode? You know, 'cause it's so full of whirrings and clankings – like you can hear the machinery of your brain, and it makes it hard to think of anything at all? Does that make sense?'

Anna nodded gratefully. She was throwing her a line, surely. 'Kind of. Sometimes, if I notice I'm breathing, I start to panic. Because, once I've noticed, it doesn't come naturally and I have to concentrate on every breath.'

'Y'know.' Cath dipped back on her bed, rubbed at the nape of her neck. 'This isn't the life I meant to have.'

'But it's a good one, eh?'

'Yep, I suppose it is.' Cath picked up the outfit lying in her lap and gave it to Anna. 'I don't want this.'

Anna tried to push it back into her hands. 'But it's for—'

Cath wheezed once more into her mask. Beaded breath glittered inside the plastic, and her lips were moist when she pulled it away. 'Anna, you were right. I'm not your friend. I'm Jamie's wife. *That's* what I want.'

Her eyes direct in Anna's. An intense flicker of gold, tiny, tiny wee against the green. Beyond all reasonable doubt. That was the rule of law cops worked to – and why there were so few convictions.

Anna lowered her gaze first. 'Well, I'm going to head now. You take care of yourself, Cath.'

'You too.'

Anna collected her things, buttoned up her jacket. Beige, of course, with a simple collar.

'Anna.'

'Yes?'

Cath closed her eyes. 'Thank you.'

At the stairs, Anna met Jamie.

'Oh, hi.' The paper cups he held became fragile Dresden, desirous of the utmost care. He licked his teeth.

'Jamie,' said Anna, 'whatever you're going to say, don't. Please.'

'We can't just leave it like this.'

'Yes, we can. We should have left it a long time ago.' She put her arms around him, conscious there was coffee on either side of the gap. Kissed his cheek and breathed in the boy he'd been.

'You stink of smoke.' His voice was soft.

'Yeah. I should give it up.' She touched his shoulder. 'Go see your wife.'

'She's expecting, you know.'

'Yeah? Congratulations.' Anna checked her watch. 'Look, I need to go. I'm doing a ten to six, and I need to see a man about a dog before I start.'

Holm Street was just a lane. A manky, scrawny stink of a lane, smeared with saunas and derelict buildings. It was very narrow; taller buildings in adjoining streets hanging over like voyeurs. Anna watched Martin arrive. She didn't want to keep him any more, not even the scrapings she'd been allowed. But the residue of the sleekit wee bastard had to be good for something. She stepped forward to meet him, yellow under pallid neon.

'Anna, why in God's name have you dragged me out here? Leaving frenzied whisperings on my answering machine?'

'It's private. I wanted to talk.'

'Yes, you're right there. Now look . . .'

His collar was grubby. A pompous grub.

'Martin. Chill. I'm not after your body any more. Just your help. You see, I get the feeling there's some kind of posse after me at work. I've been told to be at Professional Standards tomorrow at three. You know – Discipline – right up your street.'

Martin opened his mouth, but she carried on speaking.

'Don't pretend you don't know what I'm on about. I may have been hot-headed – and hey, you always liked my head – but I get the job done. I don't deserve a medal, but neither should I be crucified. So I didn't follow procedure. So I was a little hasty with my fists . . .'

'And your boots too, so I heard.'

Anna shrugged. 'Who hasn't been? At the end of the day, my

little indiscretion could dissolve into the ether, don't you think? I mean, it's quite unfair one indiscretion could wreck your career.'

'Anna, is that what you brought me out here for?' He laughed. 'Don't even try and blackmail me. It's not as if I have any influence. Even if I did, I've no intention of getting embroiled in your difficulties.'

'Darling, you've got no choice. I thought you'd *want* to help me.' Her mouth, her hands were quivering.

Sweaty grub, dancing on a line.

'I doubt revealing our little fling would damage me professionally, and, quite frankly, Harriet and I have weathered those kinds of storms before. You didn't think you were *special*, did you?' His eyes opened wide in a parody of shock.

Anna paused. 'Darling, I *know* there's been others. In fact, that's kind of the issue.'

'What are you wittering on about now? Christ, I always preferred you when your mouth was full.'

Martin moved back to his car, pulled the driver's door open.

'I rest my case. Unfortunately, Martin my sweet, the act of love I'm alluding to doesn't involve me. It's one of your other friends. A young lady by the name of . . . em, Linda, I think it was. She works around here. Shall I call her over to say hello?'

Martin's hand was still at the door handle.

'Look how taut your fist is, darling. Funny word, that. *Fist*. Can sound quite violent if you force it. Best not to say anything just now, Martin. Just you have a wee think about it.'

'What is it that you want?'

'There's a job coming up at Tulliallan. In charge of a social justice unit – looking at training in relation to human rights, social inclusion, that kind of thing.'

Martin was dismissive. 'That not a bit social-worky for you?'

'It's an inspector's post.'

'Now, come on. How can I possibly have any influence on that?'

'Oh, you know. Friends in all the right places.' Anna's laugh was grim. 'Did you not tell me you play squash with the Director of Training? And the super at Professional Standards – your son's godfather, right?' She tried to keep her tone steady. 'You know me, Martin. This is all I want – I promise. Sort it and I'll go away. But do it soon.'

'You're talking unadulterated bollocks,' he spluttered. 'Away with the fairies – they all know that.'

Anna knew he wouldn't burst so easy. 'Maybe they do, maybe they don't. Mud sticks, so why not wallow in it together? I'm game if you are.'

'What about . . . the woman?' He didn't meet her eyes.

'Doesn't know your name. She'd know you again, mind. I promised her you'll not be back down here, and she seemed okay with that. Easily pleased, you see. Well, you'd know that.'

Martin got into the driver's seat, slammed the door. Then he wound down his window. 'If she doesn't know my name, how did you know it was me?'

'Let's just say us girls compare notes. See you, Martin.'

Cruikshanks was Anna's new best friend. Promises of single malts, kisses all round. Andrew Semple had been only too keen to save his own skin when it came to a murder charge. Vouched he'd waited outside, saw Galletly emerge with a wad of cash, a bag of junk and blood on his shirt. The shirt was long gone but Cruikshanks could *smell* the blood on the trainer, even before Forensics made the match. Andrew was also singing sweetly for Special Branch, too thick to realise that the three tiers of names he could supply to the police would never reach the top – they were only footsoldiers like him. But also never realising that the top of this murky, Hydra-headed organisation, some day or night, would most certainly reach him. Semple had implicated Galletly in all the hoor-slashings too, which Forensics would stamp indelibly on him, once all those lovely little swabs were matched up. Cruikshanks begged Anna to come down the Station Bar with them.

'Sorry, sir – duty calls in ten minutes.'

'Listen, serious now, hen. About what I said – please accept my apologies. You've way tholed your assize. We're all square now. You were the backbone of this investigation, and I'll make sure they tossers up at Discipline know tha. I mean, I told the Tank not to—'

'Sir, what'll happen to Ezra Wajerski's stuff now?'

The sum total of Ezra's wordly goods lay in four bags inside a wire cage. 'Fiscal'll release it. Anything worthwhile'll get auctioned off, rest probably binned. How?'

'Can I see it?'

'Sure. On our way out anyway. C'mon, troops – I'm buying.'

Cruikshanks left her in the store.

'Just chuck the keys on my desk when you're done, okay? And listen – we'll probably just be on our second wind when you knock off tomorrow. So, I'll have them lined up for you, okay?'

'Would that be pints or firm young detective constables, sir?'

'What are you like?' His words echoed back through the tiled corridor.

The transparent bags were sealed, in case of temptation. And what temptation. Some bundles of letters, old clothes. A pipe, two lighters. Books. Sheet music for – she squinted in the dull yellow light – violin. Photographs. Through thick plastic, two figures visible – a tall, handsome boy with peat eyes and a little girl in a pinafore, gazing up in adoration as the boy ruffled her neat hair. Another, tattered one, of a dark-haired woman smiling softly out beyond the camera: Allegra, puffy hands round a swelling belly. Behind the bundle of snapshots, a cardboard file. The bag was tied loosely, and Anna shook the air inside, catching one edge of the folder so it could fall away from its sibling. A round paper cut-out nestled inside. Intricate snipped pictures of hens and flowers and little hearts, all carefully coloured in faded blues and greens. *Wycinanki* – like the pictures she and Ezra had on their walls. His big fingers couldn't have cut it so carefully. A girl had made this, not a man. A little lost sister, or a nesting wife.

Anna bowed her head and wept, painful silent sobs so no one would come.

Only Jenny in the squad room when Anna arrived.

'Evening all.' Jenny smiled. 'You sure you should be back at work?'

That had been Anna's mistake last time, letting four walls box her off and amplify everything. Last time she'd been a victim – this time she was a star. Saved the day on every count, so bring it on, the basking, the back-slapping and the coy *och, you knows*.

'I'm fine. Where's the guys?'

'Watching some vital Scotland match in the southern hemisphere. Well, in the refreshment room, but, you know what I mean.' Jenny lit up a fag. 'So, what's the drill for tonight? I brought my sussies.'

'Better not let Gus hear you say that. I think he's got the hots for you.'

'Dirty wee bastard's got the hots for anything with a pulse. You know, I was out with him last week, and I swear he was giving it the old heavy breathing any time we saw a car parked up.'

'The job's in safe hands, then.'

Jenny flicked her ash on the floor. 'Yeah, look, I heard you're up at Discipline tomorrow, gaffer. I've never said a word, I promise – about the cells, I mean.'

'No, no, God, I never thought you had. I think you'll find that's just one of many "conducts unbecoming" they'll raise.'

'But surely after last night . . .? I mean, that way balances the scales surely. You saved two lives.'

'You really think it works that way? They could argue that's another indication of my instability. Still, you never know *Adonai yikom damo*, as they say.'

'What?'

'"You'll get your revenge in heaven" – something like that.' Anna was suddenly eager for approval. 'I went to see Cath tonight.'

'And?'

'She's good. They're both good.'

'They?'

'Yeah, they.' Anna checked her watch. 'When does this match finish?'

'Not even half time.'

'Right, stuff the alpha males. Alpha males – get it?'

'Hmm.'

'You and me, down the Drag – whaddya say?'

In silent accord, they walked rather than drove. 'Fancy a crisp?' said Jenny, offering a pack of salt and vinegar.

'Cheers.'

'You know, that was a really brave thing you did, going in for Cath and the wee one.'

Anna shoved a handful of crisps in her mouth. 'What any of us are paid to do.'

'Bollocks. You going to tell them Galletly was the one who gave you a doing?'

'Absolutely not. And give them enough rope to hang me? He's going down for murder anyway.'

Jenny poured the remainder of the crumbs from the packet into her hand. 'What makes you tick, Anna?'

'Being wound up.'

'Funny.'

Anna was so tired. The night stretched on like over-chewed gum, the hoors came and went, just like their punters. They warned a few, jailed a few, tapped one a couple of smokes. By rights she should take a flier, seeing as they were calling her up to head-quarters tomorrow. What difference did this circular pantomime they were performing in make anyway – her and Jenny and the hundreds of jaded souls that looped round and round in grim, misshapen wheels? The match had finished – Scotland glorious once more in defeat – and Derek and Alex took over while she and Jenny ate. Lukewarm chips and a kebab, standard night-shift fare, just the job to solidify your guts. In perfect equilibrium, she munched, Jenny smoked and they watched the tail end of a black and white Western.

'Take the car out in the second half?' Jenny asked.

'Absolutely.'

As Anna was picking up the keys, Derek came in with a young hoor. She was hopping from foot to foot. 'Mr Waugh, I'm gonny pish myself. Please.'

'You'll need to wait till I get the turnkey, hen. Oh, Sarge, can you keep an eye on her till I get the turnkey to take her to the bogs – she's no been searched yet.'

Anna recognised the pinched pale face. It was Francine, her features now sheened with the same hard lacquer as her sister's.

'Evening, miss.' The girl was shivering in tight denim.

'Evening, Fra—'

Pinned to Francine's lapel was a tiny brooch, shaped like a star on a blue striped ribbon. Six points of gold, with a heart of enamel. Anna gripped the girl by the sleeve, whispered urgently. 'Come here, you.'

The nearby detention room was empty, and she shoved Francine inside.

'Where did you get that?'

'What?' Brazen, brazen hussy.

'Don't fuck me about, Francine. Where did you get this medal?'

She stuffed her hands in her pockets. 'Found it.'

'Where?'

'Canny mind.'

'Now, what night's this?' said Anna, stopping her tongue from skittering like her heartbeat. 'Thursd— no wait, that's us into Friday morning now, isn't it. So, if I ask the OD to keep you in custody, that'll be tonight, tomorrow night and Sunday; jeez – will you manage that long without your, what is it – jellies?'

Francine rolled her eyes, her hands jittering at her side. 'Someone gied me it.'

Anna forced her face against the younger girl's, whittled her voice to steel. 'Francine, can I suggest you stop playing games? The man who had those medals has some very dangerous friends. And I mean mental. Heard of Nooch at all?'

She blanched.

'If I was to let it slip that you'd got hold of one . . .'

'The old man gied me it, I promise,' she whimpered. 'Said I was his special girl.' Francine cradled her face with purple nails, and began to sob.

Anna stared and stared at the greeting girl, at the medal dancing on her sobbing breast. Pictured pale, curved fingers fumbling with the ribbon, patting it fondly and stepping back, hoping she would realise this was worth more than money, than all the money he could ever find. An electric epiphany rippled through Anna's skin, air boiling into all manner of bubbling, charged particles while the girl snivelled on beside her.

'Right, Francine. Time you started telling me the whole story, eh?'

'How – what's my sister said? Miss, you canny listen tae her. She's fucking flipped since the wean died.'

Anna's brain worked quickly, grasping at entrails of thought. 'She felt it would be better for you in the long run, Francine. You can't run away from something like this.'

Again, the wait: what Cath had done to her in the hospital, what she was doing to Francine now. The slow formation of the cautious void that will be filled by whoever is weakest. And Anna could feel her surety swell with each heartbeat that passed unchecked.

The girl's lip trembled.

'Francine, d'you hear me? This is too big to keep inside you.'

'Christ, I didny mean it.' Tear-stained begging-face. 'I swear on my mammy's grave. Honest tae God – he kept slobbering on me, trying tae push his tongue in my gub. He wouldnae stop, and I just freaked, miss.'

Anna had to be sure. 'Who wouldn't stop, Francine?'

'The old boy,' she wept. 'That Polish punter. He was one of my regulars – just a wank, mind. He never usually touched me. Fuck – I didny mean tae hurt him. But he started pure grating my cheek with his bristles and licking at me; it was like my grampa all over again.' Francine bit at the side of her hand. 'It was like my grampa was doing it, miss,' she whispered.

She closed her eyes. 'It was just a wee dunt I gied him, miss, and then he fell . . .'

Anna left her car at the station. It had been a long night and she wanted to clear her head. She followed the line of the underground down the hill from Cowcaddens to Buchanan Street. Saw a slow play of light rise on sandstone. Too early for the trains to be running in their clockwork circle; she wanted to walk, in any case. Feel the cool promise of morning about her face as the dark slipped off and shapes became solidity.

St George's in the Tron church waved its banner in the breeze. *Open to All* – but the door was locked. Anna kept walking down to St Enoch Square, named for St Thenew, mother of Glasgow's patron saint. Her boy, St Mungo, was everywhere – in crests, museums, schools. It was he who, led by two white bulls, founded the city by the Molendinar Burn. Up where the Royal Infirmary and the cathedral were – that was where Glasgow had been born. No one remembered Thenew; raped as a child, thrown from a cliff in her father's shame and left to drift to Culross in a coracle. But it was from her that Mungo had sprung.

An elegant suspension bridge linked the south and north edges of the River Clyde. Georgian mansions with leafy prospects hinted at the greening suburbs beyond. Once across the river, Anna could be home in twenty minutes if she kept a brisk pace. Heavy oak door and slatted blinds. Bare feet on polished boards crisping into clean white sheets and a soft mewing at her ankles. She leaned on the thin iron balustrade. The Clyde was empty brown. They said you could get salmon in it again, and someone had spied a seal up at the weir on Glasgow Green. But it was still a frightening river, full of unknown currents and silted, shifting depths. The wind was thickening, bridge quivering and pinging beneath her soles. She put her hand in her jacket pocket. Tiny points like cats' claws raked her fingers. Drew the medal out. In the fish-hued light it seemed mottled. She rubbed it with the sleeve of her jumper, smudging whorls into whispers.

And dropped it in the river.

Sally is watching the news with her husband when name she ought not to recognise: Mark Bretherick.

Last year, a work trip Sally had planned was cancelled at the last minute. Desperate for a break from her busy life juggling her career and a young family, Sally didn't tell her husband that the trip had fallen through. Instead, she booked a week off and treated herself to a secret holiday. All she wanted was a bit of peace – some time to herself – but it didn't work out that way. Because Sally met a man – Mark Bretherick.

All the details are the same: where he lives, his job, his wife Geraldine and daughter Lucy. Except that the man on the news is someone Sally has never seen before. And Geraldine and Lucy Bretherick are both dead . . .

'For those who demand emotional intelligence and literary verve from their thrillers, Sophie Hannah is the writer of choice. *The Point of Rescue*, her third, combines a creepily irresistible page-turner with an exploration of motherhood's taboos.'
GUARDIAN

'The tension is screwed ever tighter until the final shocking outcome'
DAILY EXPRESS

'Hannah doesn't allow the tension to slacken for a second in this addictive, brilliantly chilling thriller.'
MARIE CLAIRE (Book of the Month)